Wrath of the Ruined

Wrath of the Ruined

The Bloodrune Saga

Book Two

Elsa Frey

Contents

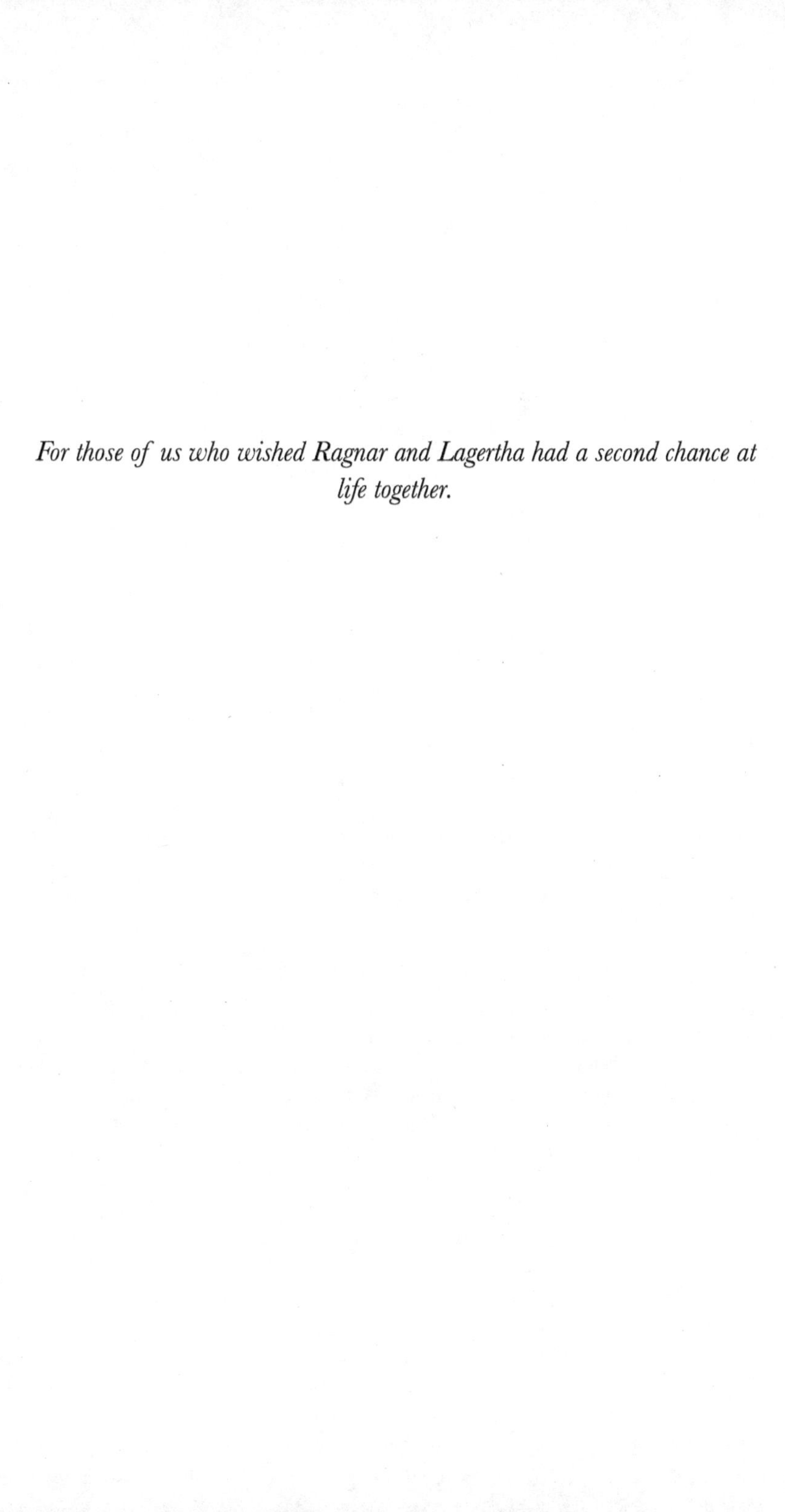

For those of us who wished Ragnar and Lagertha had a second chance at life together.

Content Warning

This work contains explicit sexual content as well as death, violence, blood, forms of suicide/sacrifice, stalking, mental health references - especially anxiety and panic attacks, and mentions of physical and mental abuse.

Vylheim
Skaldir
Stormdal
Torsholt
Mara
The Wasteland
Daganfold
Torstad
Mara's Keep
Ravensund
Myrr
Einnland
The Hall of the Gods

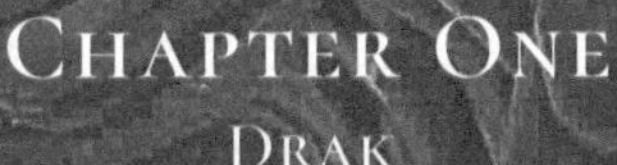

Chapter One

Drak

It was rather convenient that one of the stupid fucking vampires hunting my wife came after her in the throne room, where I could settle into my seat as king and watch the show. All I needed was someone to bring me a goblet of wine—or preferably, blood.

I leaned forward with my elbows on my knees and my fingers clasped, absorbing every second of the fight. From the throne, I had a perfect view of each blow. I smirked as Lux slashed at the vampire with a silver pendant.

The show was getting good, though I didn't love that it had interrupted our conversation. After four weeks of curating a plan, Lux had agreed to come to the throne room and discuss it with me. *Four fucking weeks* after she came back to Mara's Keep, and she was finally ready to talk. Then this creep stalked out of the shadows and attacked her, ruining my chance.

The vampire's speed outmatched Lux's movements every time, but she was smarter.

Ever the clever little killer, Lux drew his attention to the silver pendant by slashing at him with it. He misinterpreted the pendant to be the primary threat and lunged for it. What he didn't know—what only I knew about Lux—was that she always kept the wooden stake strapped to her thigh beneath her skirts. Even when she was nearly naked and sprawled across her bed in the room beside mine. My cock stiffened at the thought of it.

I scooted closer to the edge of the throne, my gaze following their every movement.

When the vampire bolted for the pendant, Lux let him knock it from her hand. It fell between their feet, the chain a pile of glinting metal. Then she allowed him to pin her to the cold stone with her thick autumn braid sprawled out on the floor beside her. All of this was to make him believe he had the upper hand.

I chuckled and shook my head. One of these days, those who betrayed me would realize that their strongest vampires were powerless to take down the huntress. Lux had already destroyed eighteen of them since she came back to me. They'd have to bring the whole damn army to reach me or my wife, and Mara's Keep was built to be impenetrable against such a siege.

"Good luck," I muttered, as if Lux's sister—the leader of the damn vampire army—was somewhere nearby and could hear me. She wasn't. I knew that much. They were trying to remove us the easy way first. Lux wasn't a trained huntress yet, and she didn't have experience, so I could see Silver's logic in trying to attack her now. But what she failed to realize was that Lux had already spent a lifetime defending herself, even if it wasn't against vampires.

Lux grunted under the weight of the vampire pressing his knee on her chest. I shot to my feet. There was no way he would win, but I didn't like the sound she'd made. My wife would never suffer. I'd see to that, although she didn't want my help.

"Do you want me to tear him apart?" I asked.

Lux twisted her neck, straining to see me from her spot on

the floor. The look she gave me was one of pure frustration. "Fuck you, Drak!" she said. "You're distracting me."

The enemy ignored our bickering as he moved in a blur. Candlelight flashed along his fangs as he seethed and struggled to keep her in place. Beneath him, she wriggled free; her face tinted red, the white scar from another vampire's fang stark against her cheek. His hands closed around her throat, and every muscle in my body twitched to go help her.

But if I did, she'd only chew me out afterward, and when you're trying to convince someone to marry you, pissing them off would be a terrible setback. I shouldn't call her my wife, yet I couldn't help myself. Something within me drew me to her, and it had nothing to do with her fate as a vampire huntress.

Lux gasped, breathless, but she wasn't done. She twisted and reached through the high slit in her skirt, ripping the stake from where it was strapped to her thigh and angling it toward the weak spot in his ribcage.

I sat, wishing again that I had a drink in hand while I watched this bastard get destroyed.

Since becoming the huntress, Lux never failed to win a fight, but the little tricks and allowances she used to throw off her prey's focus worried me. Sometimes, I forgot I could sit back and watch the idiot who defied me and my crown die a miserable death, and I didn't have to lift a finger. The moment he or any of the other vampires or humans followed Silver, they threw away their loyalties and became my enemies.

Lux stabbed the stake at the vampire's chest, but he retaliated with lightning speed, smashing the heel of his palm against the stake and knocking it from her hand the way he had with the silver pendant. It clattered to the floor only a few inches away from them.

"Can I offer my lady a hand?" I said, amusement curving my voice.

Lux released a string of curses, my name mixed in. She

bucked her hips, throwing the vampire's weight off balance. My lips curled. She flipped to her side and reached for the stake, but as always, the vampire was faster.

It didn't matter that he beat her to it because it was all a ruse. She was free now. She smashed the silver pendant into the side of his face, drawing a pathetic cry as he dropped the weapon. Tendrils of steam rose from his burning skin. Lux swiped the stake from the ground and shoved it halfway up into his ribcage. He gripped it to stop her from pushing deeper, but her abilities as a huntress gave her the strength to overpower him.

With one final huff, Lux plunged the stake deeper, and his heart exploded with his entire body turning to ash. She stood over her kill, panting. Damn if I didn't want to make her pant like that.

Aware of my stare, she turned to me and marched away from the dust shuddering on the floor. The storm outside raged hard enough to blow a draft through the castle's hall and make goosebumps pebble over Lux's skin.

"Never do that again," she snapped. She pointed the tip of the silver tree pendant at me as if it were a switch or a rod she'd use to punish me. "What if he'd gotten away and Silver heard the king is fighting alongside the huntress?"

"So what?" I smirked. "Can't a king protect his lady in his own damn castle? All it'll tell her is that you have me and all of my loyal subjects on your side."

A low vibration of thunder rippled through the stone, as if the gods were reminding me that this fortress wasn't as invincible as I believed. But Silver was no god, and one of these days she'd realize the scouts they sent to lure us out into the open were sacrifices.

"It only makes me look weak." Lux huffed as she spread the slit in her skirt. My gaze dropped to her bare leg. The only thing covering her thigh was the leather straps of the holster I'd made for her to carry the stake against her leg. Only inches from my reach, I had to squeeze my hands into fists, resisting the urge to touch her exposed leg.

This pull between us wasn't why she came to me four weeks ago. She'd wanted me, briefly, and more than that, she wanted the help I could give her. Apparently, she didn't feel the same draw that I did.

I relaxed my hands as if I could release this inexplicable obsession I had with her.

After securing the stake and dropping her skirts to fall back over her leg, she pinned me with her gaze. "Silver and her army need to know that *I* can stop them. Your loyal subjects won't exactly be with us on the way to the tree of Yggdrasil." That much was true. Surviving the wasteland would be a feat only a vampire and a huntress with god powers would attempt. The remaining vampires loyal to me would stay behind and guard Mara's Keep. She tucked a loose hair behind her ear as she continued. "Even if we beat her there, she'll be at our heels and we'll have to fight to stop her from burning the tree."

"So let it burn." I shrugged. Fury tinted her all-black witch eyes. That was obviously the wrong thing to say. I waved my hand and leaned my back against the throne. "Yes, sure…" My voice dripped with sarcasm that was sure to piss her off, but I couldn't help it. Ridding the gods' access to this world was a victory in my humble opinion. "Let's *not* free your mind from a bunch of asshole gods. Great idea."

She bared her teeth and stepped closer. With her hands splayed on the arms of the throne, she caged me in, and I lapped up every second.

"That tree gives me access to my powers," she said, "and you know this. Besides, without it, you can't become a god."

"The tree itself won't make me a god." Though I needed to do as Odin did, hanging from the tree for nine days to gain the wisdom of how to kill a god. Once I killed a god, I'd become one, replacing Odin or Freya or Loki's roles in the ether. That was what my mother had learned when she was a seer. That gods bled. They died. And their killer felt a surge of power and pain all at once as they absorbed powers from the dead divine.

She scoffed, a grim smile twisting her face as her gaze flicked to the tattoos peeking out of the collar of my tunic. "My point is, you have to stop them from burning it as much as I do."

"And that's where my plan comes in." I straightened. "As I was saying before that idiot interrupted us, we make your sister and her army believe you're weak."

"What the Hel is wrong with you?" Her mouth dropped open. "That's the exact opposite of what I want."

"Then allow me to explain," I said. "We lure her here instead of meeting her at Yggdrasil. *Her*, not her little minions. She will come for this throne with a few of her vampires in tow. We know this is all she wants." I laid my hand over hers where she gripped the throne's arms. "She'll come to take it from you herself if she thinks she's the only one left with the power to control vampires. You're the only thing standing in her way. Binding yourself to a vampire will convince the entire kingdom of your powerlessness. News of our royal wedding will spread, and the second you're bound to me, she'll be here. I guarantee it."

"Are you really suggesting I marry you?" she scoffed. "Did you forget you already tried this?"

"Except I'm not suggesting a real marriage this time. We'll do the ceremony, but you'll never vow yourself to me, which means your precious powers will remain untouched. No binding, no risk. We can be careful with the sealing and make everyone believe it. Trust me, if Vylheim believes it, so will Silver."

Lux tilted her head, not intending to show me the long curve of her neck that I couldn't stop staring at. If only fighting fired her up the same way it did for me, then I'd know what the Hel she was thinking. It drove me wild that I could only hear her thoughts when she desired me.

She scanned me like an opponent in a fight, yet the spark of interest in her eyes betrayed the fury beneath. Curiosity suited her. "You're saying we fake a marriage?" she asked.

"Exactly." With her this close, I memorized every inch of her face. "The ceremony, the rings, the—" I stopped myself before suggesting the consummation. "Because Silver knows, as well as we do, that if we marry, all your powers as one of the gods' witches and their chosen will strip away. You won't be the huntress. You'll be my wife."

"And the queen of Vylheim," she said.

"That too. That'll bait her more than anything else because this throne has that kind of power. It makes you want to take a seat here more than anything else." I ran my hand along the armrest, but Lux wasn't listening to me drone on about this stupid hunk of bronze.

She slumped slightly, and I wanted to pull her into my lap and let her rest after the fight had taken it out of her. Even with the strength of the huntress, her heart was weak, and I hated that I couldn't fix it for her.

I kept silent, still. One wrong word and she'd get spooked. I knew this plan was already on the edge of something she'd ever accept because of how dangerously close it was to giving up her powers. If everyone believed she was helpless, they'd come at her with full speed.

But I'd be there for her, and I'd never let her get hurt.

The servant's door groaned and then fell shut, but I didn't break eye contact with Lux. The only person who'd dare come into the throne room at this time was my advisor, Axel.

With the soft approach of his footsteps, Lux pushed off the arms of the throne and straightened, giving Axel a taut smile before looking down at me. "I can't wrap my head around this right now." With a wince, she palmed her face, and blood suddenly drained from her features. A sure sign that the gods were yelling inside her mind.

I leaped to my feet, but when I reached for her, she yanked away. Her hands shot to her temples as she paled to a ghostly white. "Lux," I said.

Shaking her head, she squeezed her eyes shut and put more pressure on her temples. I couldn't help glancing at Axel, who stood like a statue draped in a grey fur coat. Dark hair streaked with silver that matched his beard, and the constellation of freckles across his stoic face gave him a look more powerful than the gods. As the only other person who knew about the gods tormenting their chosen witch, his concern was palpable.

I brushed a loose tendril from Lux's face, dipping my head to get her to look at me, but she wouldn't. This was the most she'd let me touch her since she first returned to the castle. "It's Odin, isn't it?"

She seethed and nodded gently, tugging away from me. "They're so loud after I fight—" Another wince cut her off. She sucked in a breath, straightened, and turned. Slowly, with a tired drag, she made her way to the double doors that led into the hall. "I'm going to pass out if I don't lie down."

I trailed her like a ghost floating in her wake, pulled by her magnetism. "Let me carry you back to your bed."

"This chivalry won't convince me, Drakkar," she said, glancing over her shoulder at me. I frowned. She said my full name rather than calling me Drak. "Not after you threatened to kill me. It's hard to imagine calling you my husband, even if it would be fake."

With that, she yanked the door open and vanished into the shadows of the hall, leaving me to rake my fingers through my hair and grit my teeth. Time to change her mind was running out. The gods' grip on her grew stronger with every fight.

This wasn't just a race to save Yggdrasil, but a race against the madness decaying Lux's mind.

I was already losing her, and I'd never truly had her. That thought left me feeling like I'd taken a fist to the gut as I watched the door fall shut in her wake.

I cleared my throat and, without looking at Axel, nodded toward the servant's door. "Come spar with me," I said.

Like a shadow, he followed me in silence as I strode the opposite way from Lux, taking the quicker route to the training room. The only way to burn off this unease and get my mind off her was with a weapon in my hand. A sword might not save her from the creeping madness, but I took solace in the thought of protecting her from Silver and the other traitors.

Chapter Two

Drak

We marched alongside one another, following the maze of stone until we reached the armory hidden beneath Mara's Keep. A draft pressed icy air against our backs, and even this deep into the castle, the storm made itself known. Another bolt of lightning must have struck the surface because the ground rippled with the following thunder. Though the rain and wind came from the gods, I actually liked storms. They matched the rage within me.

Rage that only heightened at the thought of Lux's rejection.

I swallowed a sigh and glanced at Axel. He'd been silent the entire way, letting me stew, and only when we descended the staircase did his voice mingle with the echo of our footsteps against stone.

"My king, you need to look at the marriage through Lux's eyes," he said. He had always known how I felt, ever since I was a young boy sneaking through the halls of this castle. A home that belonged to a king who hated my existence as much as he was obsessed with my mother.

I released a forceful sigh and yanked a sword off the

mount on the wall. The entire armory was clad with wooden mounts and iron hangers drilled into the stone. Swords, axes, and crossbows decorated the walls. Surrounded by deadly weapons, this was where a vampire king belonged.

Narrowing my eyes on him, I unsheathed the sword. "Nobody else is here, Axel. Why are you addressing me formally?"

"There have been enough traitors infiltrating this castle that I will continue to call you my king at every turn in case they are near."

Fine. It was clear to me that spies were probably lurking in Mara's Keep, but I had been optimistic that the armory, at the very least, maintained the same level of seclusion as the throne room. At least there Axel kept guards posted outside. The curve of his thick hair bounced as he nodded toward the narrow stairs that led up and out of this stony hole. "We must remind our enemies that you are sovereign and will remain their king."

"You're not wrong." I smirked. "But Lux doesn't let them lurk around here for long."

"I'm aware, my king. I've witnessed her skill in their destruction enough times to recognize that she is the true huntress."

I flinched. The *gods'* huntress. She belonged to them, not me.

Axel drew his own sword and positioned himself in the center of the sparring space to duel. I met him at the opposite end.

I didn't love sparring with an older human because if I hurt him after all these years of loyalty, I wouldn't forgive myself. But Axel was the only human who remembered the older ways of fighting. He was the only one, human or vampire, who cared to keep the tradition of dueling and sword fighting alive beyond the executioners. Executioners he trained under King Roderic's command because that lazy asshole never wanted to lift a finger.

As much as I hated the former king, I was grateful that he brought Axel into the castle and into my life. Now he was a part of Mara's Keep, with his slate eyes and cloak the color of the walls.

My gaze flicked from the blade to Axel's face, defined by decades of living in Mara's Keep with a short-cropped beard of the same salt that dusted his once pepper-dark hair. He was somewhere in his fifties based on the fact that he looked twenty when he first came into my life as a boy. He never admitted his age to anyone, not even me. Since he almost never saw the sun, he aged slowly for a human and it was impossible to guess how old he truly was. Serving vampire kings had a few bonuses.

"Aren't you going to remove your cloak?" I asked.

His only response was to lift his weapon in an invitation to spar. If he wanted to trip on the fur, fine. I matched his ready, and steel clashed against steel, but the fight only brought me back to watching Lux battle another traitor.

Eventually, the gods would twist her mind so far that she wouldn't survive another duel. As much as I hated rushing her the same way Odin was, we had to do something—fast. We had to get Silver here, and then take down the vampires, because a fake marriage was better than forging through the wasteland with a vampire army at our heels and madness gutting Lux's mind.

"If Lux wants safety, then why can't she see my plan is the safest option?" I voiced my thoughts. Talking this out with Axel better clear my mind, because fighting wasn't working.

He said nothing and dodged my blade with ease. I swung again and almost tripped over my own damn feet. Before I could react, he pinned me, forcing me to shove him off.

"Listen, son," he said. "You never lied to her, but you did manipulate her."

"For her own good." I slashed at his hip, but he whirled away with all the grace of a lithe swordsman.

"She's rather skilled at addressing her own needs, my king."

"She needs my protection." We charged at one another, striking blades, not caring that this riddled our practice swords with nicks and scratches.

"She needs to know she's protected *from* you."

"Damnit, Axel!" Anger unfurled through me. With vampiric speed, I bolted forward, disarming him in a single blink. Frustration flared in my muscles as I shoved him back, back, back. I almost had him pinned against the wall when his brows lifted, and I immediately regretted disrespecting the only man I truly respected.

Using my skills as an undead was never part of our sparring. That was the whole point of this: to keep my skills as a swordsman, since I wouldn't be a vampire forever. I let my sword drop to my side, and pinched the bridge of my nose. Turning, I strode away from him and back to the center of the sparring circle. "You're right. She needs to feel safe with me, but all she cares about is leaving for Yggdrasil, and she has no idea what it will be like to face an entire army of vampires. I know every single one of Silver's soldiers personally."

"So do I, and though your plan to lure Silver here is solid—"

"You agree she'll fall for it, right?"

He closed his eyes and gave me only the slightest nod. "I agree. Silver's need for control has remained predictable ever since she became a young woman, blinding her to the obvious sometimes. But whether it will work is not Lux's issue with the proposal." I frowned. As much as I didn't want to hear it, Axel was always right. Just like when he told me not to bring Silver back from Drukna Sea. "Lux's entire life and her entire world are fraught with danger and lies, and secrets. She wants safety."

"And I'm trying to give her that."

"Forgive me, my king, but you're one of many who have threatened that. Even if she didn't understand why at the time."

I sighed, and paced the length of the sword at Axel's feet. "Let's go again." I nodded for him to approach and pick it up.

He didn't move.

"Axel," I prodded. "Fight me."

"You, as in King Drakkar? Or the fanged version of the man I know?"

My lips twitched. As much as I wanted to fume at him, I'd requested that he call me out on this. I wasn't supposed to move in a blur, but thoughtfully, building muscle memory the way an ancient warrior would, instead of relying on my vampire powers.

Once I became a god, I'd no longer have the speed or the strength of an undead. Odin's skills were different, more powerful in their own right, but different, and would require months of understanding and learning. In the interim, I'd have to get used to being like a human king again. More vulnerable, mortal.

I pushed out a breath. "Me. Fight *me*."

"Good," he nodded as he strode to the sparring circle. Instead of picking up the sword, he waved for me to attack him barehanded.

The crazy bastard.

I lunged forward, my blade angled to pin him at his throat, but he spun to dodge me, letting his cloak billow out as I thrust it at him. Snatching fur and fabric, he whipped the cloak into his hold and wrapped it around my weapon in one smooth move, both entangling the blade and disarming me without so much as a sword of his own.

I huffed. "Fuck, I'm out of practice."

"Too long relying on fangs," he agreed. I grimaced as I let go of the sword and swiped my fingers through my loose hair.

Marching to a small table wedged in the corner, I picked up a tin pitcher and filled my cup to the brim. Though it wasn't blood, wine would quench my thirst for a few hours, even if the alcohol stung as much as Axel's words.

At least he'd taught me never to shy away from the truth.

"But," he continued as he wiped down the blades, "you're still the second-best swordsman in Vylheim. And when you have Odin's powers, you'll see a trick like that coming moments before your opponent takes action."

"Foresight," I smirked. "And you're sure I'll have this skill immediately upon Odin's death? I won't have to learn it the way I will with calling upon the Valkyries, or command of ravens?"

He dipped his chin. "If what the sagas your father studied say are true, then yes. And your mother's visions confirmed it. Anyone who kills a god will take upon their powers. You will also gain Odin's rune mastery right after you kill him, though I can't say whether creating new runes will take time to learn and improve."

"Foresight is what matters," I said, waving the other skills away. Who the fuck cared to boss around those noisy ravens?

"You should know, though," he said, "that you will not have the strength Lux possesses. That strength comes from Valhalla through Odin; it is not his strength alone. That is how Ingrid explained it. Foresight beyond mere seconds will take time to master, too."

"You said the sagas were clear. That I'll be able to see into the future."

"I suspect you'll see *moments* into the future, but not months or days or even hours. Again, this is coming from Ingrid's confirmation of the sagas, not me. The sagas say that even Odin's sight isn't all-powerful, my king." The wrinkles between his brow deepened. If only Odin could see everything, then *I'd* see everything once he fell dead at my feet. And only then would I be able to keep my promise to Axel.

But finding Axel's son wasn't on a deadline like freeing Lux's mind.

"Odin isn't all-powerful," I echoed. "That's exactly why he's using Lux." I shook my head and leaned both hands on the table. The wine turned bitter on my tongue. "If she doesn't trust me enough for a fake marriage, then what the Hel am I going to do?"

"Give her time to get to learn who you really are, Drak."

"We don't have time. Her mind is slipping."

"Then I suggest you show her the King Drakkar that I know. Not the vampire king you pretend to be for the throne, the real you." With that, he bowed and swiftly disappeared into the shadows beyond the stone staircase.

Who the fuck was I really, except a king weak in the knees for a witch from Skaldir? I didn't even understand why I felt tethered to Lux. Like I'd known her since the creation of the ancient sagas.

Chapter Three

Lux

For once, the gods were silent, but even in a quiet library among the sagas, I felt no relief, something I desperately needed after battling another vampire in the throne room.

Dozens of erratic thoughts raced through my mind. Only a few months ago, the world knew me as Silver, a simple girl from a seaside village. Now, all of Vylheim knew I was a huntress named Lux, and that I'd lied about my past. The real Silver had been buried in a dungeon beneath Mara's Keep, two levels below where I sat today. In a brand-new library, built for me—Lux, the huntress. Living this truth was as intoxicating as it was terrifying.

Heavy expectations came with my life as a huntress: divine pressure and the weight of a kingdom.

I'd tried erecting a wall in my mind to ease the strain of Odin's presence, but it seldom worked to quiet his powerful voice. And when the Gods left my skull silent, my own thoughts continued racing, tripping over one another.

A low rumble of thunder shook the stone like an angry hum. It was clear that the gods disapproved of my hideout. They didn't want me relying on a vampire king, but Freya's visions only came when I pushed my body to the point of collapse.

Even when I had visions, they were vague, rarely clear enough for me to follow a straight path to Yggdrasil. Drak was the only option for finding the tree, and Mara's Keep was my only option for refuge. So the Gods were just going to have to deal with it.

I brushed my fingers over runestones stacked on the shelves, feeling my mind slow as I touched something solid. I relished every second here, even when the wind thrashed against the stained-glass window Drak had installed. It overlooked the former king's graves and the forest behind the castle, and he'd had it built knowing how much I hated the lack of windows in Mara's Keep.

For the past hour, I mulled over his suggestion. Marry him, or rather fake it, and become the pretend wife of a cold vampire king to convince my sister that I was helpless. She would come to kill me the moment she believed I couldn't take down her army, and if we cut off the head, the body would fall.

But I wouldn't gut my sister, even if she was Hel-bent on ending my life. We'd have to take her captive, then destroy her army. To do any of it, I would have to accept Drak's hand and vow myself to him.

Even if it was all a ruse, the thought of coming so close to sacrificing my tether to the Gods—everything I'd been as a witch, now as a huntress trained by Kayn—made my temples throb, worries piling up like stones. Inexplicably, this return to Drak and Mara's Keep had calmed me, but anxiety still raged whenever I thought of Kayn. Even if this potential marriage to Drak were fake, it felt like a betrayal to the vampire who had taught me how to fight.

But I dealt in betrayal and lies, didn't I? I was fucked up that way…

"Stop," I said aloud, commanding my thoughts to halt before I spiraled out of control.

Lightning struck outside, illuminating the dim room through the tinted red and black glass. After one sudden flash, it vanished and dropped the library back into shadows, where the only light came from the glow of the candle in my hand.

With one finger hooked into the bronze holder, I lifted the dancing flame toward the shelves. An orange glow draped over stones and the leather spines of old journals. I moved past the ancient runestones and to the journals of skalds who either gathered information of their era or interpreted old stories of the gods. Poems filled half of the journals with lyrical words about Odin. Others recorded the daily lives of our ancestors.

Another rumble followed the next strike of lightning, and the raging wind threw fat raindrops against the window. As the storms grew worse, Drak had claimed it was the gods' anger, but I wasn't so sure. Yes, Thor was the god of thunder, and as Odin's son, he'd be faithful to his father's plans. But these storms were hurting the people of Vylheim, not the vampires, so I couldn't fathom that the worsening winters were one of Odin's ideas.

A soothing voice crooned at my mind's edge. *"You are what hurts vampires, huntress."* Odin's words confirmed my thoughts, and a warmth akin to pride swelled at the base of my skull, spreading down the back of my neck with prickles.

They chose me to protect the people from monsters.

And here I was, doing a terrible job of it against my sister and her vampire army.

My pulse skipped. I drew a slow, cleansing breath and accepted the truth: I wasn't protecting anyone by hiding in Mara's Keep. Training just wasn't progressing fast enough, especially with my exhaustion interrupting every session. And to face Silver, I needed to understand her better. These records Skalds kept about the first witch from whom Silver received her powers were my best source of insight.

After sliding a journal off the shelf, I padded to the rug in the center of the room. My skirt fanned out around me as I took a seat on the ground with the book in my lap. Deep brown shelves surrounded me in the circular space like towering sentinels, looking over me with the protection of knowledge. This was all I'd wanted when I first came to Mara's Keep: the histories, the truth of witches and gods, and the story of our people.

Now all of it was mine, thanks to Drak.

My heart skipped again. *Ugh.* These episodes always worsened after a fight, but this skip didn't come with a painful halt. Humming with extra beats, it danced as I thought of him building this library for me.

"It's a ploy," I said to no one. Rolling thunder replied, my only response. Rain splattered the glass at irregular intervals, matching my erratic pulse. I let my head fall back and my eyes slide shut. "This gift comes with strings attached." Though Drak had never once referred to the library as a wedding gift, even if he'd been begging for our marriage every day since I returned to Mara's Keep. He swore it was in my best interest.

"Drak will not win me with gifts," I uttered into the stillness, like a vow made to the divine.

"I wish you'd told me that sooner," a deep voice answered. My eyes flew up, and I snapped my head toward the door.

Drak leaned against the doorframe, the door wide open, his forearm raised beside his head. Shadows darkened his thick beard, and loose strands of hair framed his face.

"So having your servants build this for me *is* just one of your many ways of trying to control me?" I straightened my spine, stacking my shoulders as I raked my gaze over him.

A boyish smirk lifted his mouth. Shoving off the wall, he strode into the room. "Wrong, and wrong again."

I frowned, but it didn't deter him. He marched to the

closest shelf, eyeing the space on the stone wall beside it. Even with Drak's height, the shelves dwarfed him.

The library was one of the tallest and roundest rooms in Mara's Keep. Narrow shelves hugged the curve of the walls, lined up side by side, though they didn't cover every inch. Half the room opposite the entrance was filled with them, except where the window pierced the stone. Near the entrance, walls remained unadorned, mirroring the dull grey of connecting hallways.

"Excuse me?" I asked, my muscles tensing at his cockiness.

He ran his palm against the shelf, examining it silently for a second before glancing at me. "You're wrong."

"So you would have had your people build all these shelves even if I wasn't here?" I asked, barely holding back a scoff. "Every one of these records was buried before I arrived."

He chuckled. "And now they're not. Now they're on display in a library, for you."

"What are you doing here?" I switched the subject, not wanting to argue about his tactics to sway me toward him and away from the Gods I worshiped. "I thought every evening you went to sit with your mother." Ingrid had lost her mind to the gods long ago, but according to Drak, she'd occasionally recognize her son.

His smirk drifted into a sad smile. "She's sleeping. Even down in her hideout, she can hear the storms. She knows it's the Gods' anger, and it frightens her so much that she wears herself out. Since the thunder started, she's been sleeping twice as much as usual."

I didn't know what to say to that. Apologize for his loss? That didn't feel right considering it was only her mind that was absent. So instead, an argument edged to the tip of my tongue. I refused to believe the Gods would punish us, especially now that witches were coming out of hiding and people were more comfortable invoking Odin's name and speaking of Freya and Thor and the others. With most of the executioners having defected to Silver's army and Drak not upholding the Blood Council's plans and systems, Vylheim slowly returned to the beliefs of their ancestors.

Before I could say anything, he cleared his throat. "And I thought you'd be sleeping after that fight." He stood over me with his arms crossed. "You need your rest before we train tomorrow. Axel will join us along with Sif and Mista."

"Two vampires?" I asked, referring to the two women. Two fanged women who'd remained loyal to Drak. Like the other vampires still in Mara's Keep, they drank from kept vessels, some courtiers or servants who fed their blood to monsters because they'd befriended them before the Blood Council dissipated.

"You need to practice fighting multiple at a time."

"And why Axel?" I asked. As one of the few humans who knew Drak was a vampire and still trusted him, Axel intrigued me, now that I knew of him and that he had always been a fixture hidden in the halls of Mara's Keep. But when he wasn't busy guarding the castle, I was busy killing a vampire, resting, or reading the sagas.

"Because he's my sparring partner. Even if he isn't a vampire, he'll put up a good fight."

"My strength only flourishes when I'm battling a vampire."

"Exactly. You must learn to fight the humans Silver has recruited too. No doubt she'll drag them into this war." My throat tightened. I couldn't fight humans without tiring. This weakness within my heart was only quieted when a vampire attacked and Odin's strength flowed through me. Drak took a seat beside me, his elbow perched against the triangular tower of his leg while he tucked his other leg beneath it. Resting his head against his fist, he scanned me. "Don't look so worried. I'll fight her army too, and I'll fucking gut any humans who come near you. This is just a precaution."

With his free hand, he fiddled with the bronze chain draped around his neck.

I eyed the chain as I spoke. "What's the point of training me if you want me to marry you and destroy my powers?"

"I suggested a fake marriage this time."

"I don't believe you'd let it be fake," I said.

"All this, and you still don't believe me? I never lied to you, and I never will."

"No," I laughed. "You were just willing to kill me instead." Of course he didn't need to lie to the person he was going to put underground. The dead don't tell secrets.

"I told you *that* was a show for Astrid," he said, tone firm. "She wanted to push us to the point that I'd kill you. I had to let her believe she'd won so she wouldn't do anything drastic."

"And yet, she still did the most drastic thing she could think of." A wry smile shot to my lips, knowing I'd bested him.

When he hadn't killed me as Astrid had hoped, Astrid released Silver at our wedding, and everything went to shit. But the Blood Council fell apart, and their plan to enact the Age of Exploration and send witches to sea was stopped. That was a victory, at least. And I supposed Drak had kept his word. He made no attempt to kill me before or during the wedding. Instead, he warned me to run from my sister's wrath. I couldn't deny that he was almost trustworthy.

A strange sadness swam in his eyes, sparking a prick in my chest.

I peeled my lips apart, dropping my eyes to the book in my lap. "Tell me about Yggdrasil. I should prepare for the Gods' domain as well as I prepare to fight."

His throat bobbed with a hard swallow. "If you could stay here where it's safe—"

"Hel no. I'm not letting you go become a God with some other witch while I protect your ugly castle."

He slapped his palm to his chest as if I'd just stabbed him. "You wound me, Skald."

"Skald?" I snapped.

Shaking his head, he lifted one shoulder. "I don't know, it just felt right to call you that. You're obsessed with these poems and histories just like a skald, a storyteller."

"I'm obsessed with the truth," I corrected, though my voice softened. This was the first time he'd called me something other than his wife or a killer. *Skald.* Even thinking of this nickname on his lips did odd things to my pulse.

My tired mind drifted, and I almost gave in to the temptation of imagining a life with someone who always speaks the truth. A life I'd never known.

I eyed him as we fell into a comfortable silence.

Skald…

A skald was what I would have become if I wasn't a witch and a huntress. I wanted to document histories, preserving my loved ones' memories through time, even as mere farmers and fishers.

Drak's voice was muted as he spoke up, unaware of where my mind had gone. I blinked and tried to focus on his answer. "The Gods' domain is…" he laughed without joy. "Terrible for me. I've only been there once, when I tried to find it. But when I hung from the tree last time, the only wisdom I received was what I already knew."

"And what was that?"

"That to become a God, you must kill a God."

"That's what was terrible about it?" I asked. "That you learned nothing new?"

He laughed again but with a hint of sadness. "No. It was terrible because I suffered. There's a distinct threshold of sunlight between the wasteland and the center of the nine realms where the Gods' power can reach. They used it to get me to leave, but I believe since I did not have a witch with me to summon one of them for me to kill, their attention on me was lackluster at best. I wasn't much of a threat, and I *still* felt their punishments."

"So you came back to Mara to collect witches." I echoed what I remembered of his plan when he first became obsessed with claiming me as his wife.

He didn't confirm this. Instead, his attention had fallen to my lap, where my fingers gripped the journal. Gently, he slid the book from my grasp and dropped it on the stone floor beyond the fur rug.

When he took my hands into his, I pulled back, but his hold only tightened. Too tired to resist again, I relented and let his large fingers bury my hands. The smell of him, spruce wood and fresh snow, filled my nose as he spoke. "You're fucking freezing."

"And you must have just fed," I said, noting his warmth.

"Good thing I did. As I said, you should be in bed after that fight."

"I'm fine." Besides, he shouldn't be touching me. Not after I'd chosen Kayn. Yet, I hesitated to pull my hands free, having been warmed by him. That was all this touching was—warmth for my body and nothing else.

"Your hands are not even ghostly anymore. They're as blue as those damn royal robes Axel keeps trying to get me to wear." Amusement mingled with worry in his voice. A shiver rippled through me but not from the cold.

After a moment of cupping my hands, he pulled me against his broad chest. The warmth of his body seeped into mine. I hated it felt so damn good to lean into him, and that I wanted to curl up and fall asleep right here in his arms.

The wind howled beyond the window, and a strange shape in the stained glass caught my eye. Its design mirrored the Y of the silver tree pendant I always carried. My mouth fell open as I stared. I hadn't noticed this shape until I was in Drak's arms, staring up at the tiny window, and rubbing my thumb against the Y Tree hanging from my throat.

I looked up at him. As pretty as the window's art was, I

couldn't let him lure me in with fake romanticism. Even if he was the first to call me Skald.

Skald.

Fuck, I liked that too much. I was so weak right now, relishing in his warmth, and desperate for touch that wasn't a battle. Wanting company after my sister betrayed me and ripped Kayn, Stasia, and my mother away.

"What did you really come here for?" I whispered as sleep beckoned me. For now, just for right now, when I desperately needed rest and healing, I'd allow him to hold me. Tomorrow would come, and I'd be training to kill all the creatures like him again, and killing him eventually too.

His chuckle was a low vibration against my ear. "When I said you were wrong, I was referring to what you said about the servants building this place." I tried to lift my head to look at him, but his palm fell heavy on my hairline. He rubbed softly at my head, brushing back the hair that had escaped my braid, and petting me slowly as he explained. "*I* built these shelves, Skald, and I came here to measure them to match my next project."

Don't let the nickname sway you.

"Don't even let him touch you." Odin agreed with my thoughts. A bolt of lightning shot through my skull, matching a flash that brightened the sky outside. *"He's tainted. A monster."*

So am I.

That had to be what drew me to Drak. Why I came here, not just for his help, but back into his arms when I shouldn't have…

"You're my huntress and my weapon. Get up and kill him now before I—" Odin's voice grew angrier. I knew I should listen, but exhaustion drained me, and his words slipped from my grasp. Even as he screamed, each shout tugged at me, and I couldn't understand a thing.

My eyelids grew heavier, and the hum of Drak's breath

against my ear pulled me under even faster. Everything about this was wrong, but in his arms, I was welcomed into the darkness.

Chapter Four
Drak

After watching Lux train against Sif, Mista, and Axel, I demanded she take the rest of today to relax while I stole away to my workshop. She would not collapse because of me, and since I swore to be honest, I had to admit that I needed a moment for myself, too.

Smoothing my hand over the black spruce wood, I admired the length of the new shelf for Lux's favorite room. This dark wood balanced the cool feel of the grey stone and brought a deep warmth to the library. I flexed my hand, remembering the chill of her blue fingers in my palm.

Last evening in the library was the first time she'd allowed me to hold her since she returned to Mara's Keep. No doubt she had scolded herself harshly for kissing me when she showed up at my doorstep, and then punished herself for being near me these past few weeks. The gods twisted her every thought and feeling away from me.

Everyone told her not to trust me when I was the only one who didn't lie to her.

Even that bastard Kayn took advantage of Lux's vulnerability and her desire to please the gods her mother had taught her to worship. Though I should probably thank him for helping Lux escape her sister at our wedding, I fucking hated him. He only wanted to use her, but she'd never acknowledge it. Especially not since the gods had the same goal as the Exile.

Blinking, I reached for the drawknife.

If the library was Lux's sanctuary, this workshop was mine. The small room was nothing like the peaked ceiling and open space of the throne room or the armory, but being here quieted my mind. Working with my hands provided a peace unmatched by sparring Axel in the armory or relishing the view from my throne. Building from raw materials was an ancient comfort, something as old as the gods.

Even Odin created humans out of a log of wood before blowing his breath of life into them. Though I despised him, and was nothing like that selfish prick, who the fuck was I to deny this primal instinct to create? I was human once, and the instinct remained.

I flipped the plank of wood over and laid it flat on the table. Gripping both handles of the drawknife, I leaned forward and dragged it across the rough surface. Multiple strokes rendered this side smooth, finally matching its other half.

I swore the rhythm of cutting, smoothing, carving, and even the fine detailing made my heart beat, but it was only the thump of the blade against wood. If I were still living, no doubt my heart would pump from the effort. Now it only pooled with black blood, frozen in time without a pulse.

The work grounded me, as if I were a shipbuilder or a simple farmer. Like a man Lux would have known in Skaldir. Shaping unrefined wood into something polished, exquisite, and *useful* brought me to life more than anything. Except for Lux's touch.

But that wasn't happening again—we weren't happening—because if I allowed myself to touch her more than for warmth, I wouldn't be able to stop myself.

I huffed, leaning over the slab and dragging the drawknife

back. My repeated cuts stripped away layers, their robust rhythm keeping Lux from my mind. Her rejection. Her suffering. Her. Just *her*.

Damn it, why was I so obsessed?

I stopped, jolting my spine straight when her accusation crossed my mind. Did I only want to control her? Was that why I couldn't get her out of my head? From the moment I saw her in Skaldir, I was inevitably drawn to the challenge of her, but like carving, the need for her felt deeper and more primal than something as simple as a challenge.

Palming my forehead, I shoved loose hair back and shook my head. Though the slab was perfectly smooth now, satisfaction didn't come. I tossed the drawknife onto the slab, where the edge of the handle left a nick. Later I'd chisel and carve shapes into the surface anyway.

I dropped back into a chair and scrubbed my palm over my face as if I could wipe Lux from my mind as easily as I wiped the hair from my eyes.

Her pale cheeks flashed behind my eyelids. That last fight left her wincing, and every time she winced, sparks of rage shot through my dead veins. If the gods got louder each time she wielded that stake against vampires, the madness was closer than I thought. She'd put up a good fight for weeks, months even, and far longer than my mother had lasted with Odin and Freya screaming into her skull. But it was all coming to a head now.

I rubbed my eyes and released a sigh. After diving this deep into the gods' games, binding herself to me likely wouldn't work to free her from the damage they'd already caused. It didn't work when my mother bound herself to King Roderic. She was already too far gone, and King Roderic, the fucker, never deserved her.

But maybe if I convinced Lux of this fake marriage, at least it'd draw Silver here. We could get this battle done and over with and then march straight to Yggdrasil.

When I became a god, I'd relish destroying Odin, making him suffer and pay for his sins. For taking *everything* from me, I swore to do the same to him. Fuck, it would feel so good to know he wasn't toying with Lux anymore, using her as his tool, just as Freya did, just as Kayn did. Just as they did with my mother.

My hands curled into fists at my thighs, and I couldn't help but envision what it would be like to free her.

Who would Lux be without their words tainting her? Hurting her? I already knew the answer. She'd still be the same fiery Skald, insistent on spreading the sagas and learning the histories.

A fighter. A survivor.

My eyes snapped open again. I couldn't keep going in circles, thinking of her, obsessing over this damn need I had to claim her as my wife. Each time I got caught in a cycle of these thoughts, I found myself desperate, stiff as the wood I was carving, and only finding relief with my fist.

Now was no different.

The moment the thought of her as my wife crossed my mind, my cock strained against my trousers. I frowned.

Fuck it. I was already hard, and I was helpless to stop thinking of her. Letting my eyes fall shut again, I leaned back into the chair.

"My wife," I whispered.

Images of her face flashed in my mind, and the scent of her followed, along with the lustful thoughts she'd had when she let herself trust me, until a single, clear image overwhelmed my senses: the wedding we almost had. Her walking down the aisle toward me, draped in the dress she was to speak her vows in. I adjusted the fabric of my trousers, freeing my cock from the restraint.

Wrapping my fingers around the length, I tightened my hold, and a grunt escaped me.

"My queen." I dragged my hand up and back. More of

Lux flooded my senses. Her soft lips. The taste between her thighs. When she looked at me like I was a damn Viking hero for having visited Yggdrasil before.

Just like the rhythm of the drawknife, I found a steady cadence of pleasure. My cock twitched, tipping me closer to release with every detail I recalled of our wedding before it all blew up.

Lux was almost mine, *mine.*

I was moments away from her vowing herself to *me*, an undead monster—something I never thought I could really have, not with a woman who saw me as both a monster and a man, but also as a warrior. I wasn't really a king; I was here to fight for revenge, and Lux recognized that the first time she looked at me.

I groaned into the silent room as I thought of our more delicious moments together. Memories of her spine against my chest, her legs bare and splayed open on the outside of my lap, my fingers between them. She'd dripped for me, so wet, so needy.

My clever killer was as dark as me, the same as me. Even her own thoughts acknowledged this, and I'd heard every word. Then she'd forced me on my knees to beg for her hand in marriage.

I'd beg again if it'd work.

I'd kneel in front of her and push up her skirts, licking along her soaking core just as I had in the library when I first teased her. When I first tried to convince her to marry me.

And it'd nearly worked. She'd melted into me, desperate for her own release because she wanted me as much as I wanted her. My cock grew more sensitive, twitching again as I pictured her walking toward her groom.

Voices in the hall almost pulled me from this pleasure.

"To the library, Miss Lux?" Axel asked, his tone muffled by the door.

"That's right," she said. "To study every rune I can find."

As soon as her voice reached my ears, and as soon as she mentioned runes, a strange memory flooded me.

This ripped me away from the present and threw into a dreamlike image of Lux marching down the aisle, dressed in a simple sky blue gown, her hair darker, her eyes no longer a pool of black ink, and this time, she smiled at me. Wanting me. She stopped in front of me, and when she reached up to touch my jaw, pulling me into a binding kiss before an altar, I almost came.

When my eyes shot open, I clutched at my tightening throat, my pleasure cut short with the shock of what I'd seen. "What the fuck was that?"

What had my mind conjured? An end to the wedding that had been stolen away? That didn't make sense. Lux wasn't even wearing the same dress. We weren't in the throne room. The walls, the altar, that wasn't even in Mara's Keep…

A soft knock startled me, even though I knew Axel had been nearby.

"Sustenance?" It was all he said, knowing I hadn't fed for several days. That had to explain this bizarre incident. I was just…hungry. Once I had blood in my belly, I'd forget all about it.

"I'm coming," I said, a smirk on my lips for the choice of words. I was an idiot.

Shaking my head, I quickly cleaned up before abandoning the workshop. Once I yanked the door open, Axel launched into a brief report about my mother. He was trained to be brief and cryptic after moving among the shadows during my entire reign, but I preferred when he gave me more information.

I was so damn glad the Blood Council disbanded, so I didn't have to sneak my advisor around anymore. They'd have hated that their vampire king listened to the advice of a human, even if he was a skilled swordsman who trained the executioners. He was still just a human in their eyes. A vessel.

A bag of blood. Instead of the man who raised me when King Roderic cut down my father.

Our strides matched in pace as we marched past the Blood Council's old meeting room. There, the blood of hundreds of humans who lived only as long as the Blood Council considered them useful vessels stained the stone. Starting with King Roderic, who'd fed on his two chosen vessels in that room. My mother and another woman he claimed and hid away from the other vampires, after which nobody heard from Brida again.

At least my mother had survived his reign. Now I just had to get her to eat more than a diet of thin broth.

I glanced at Axel. "Did she eat this time?"

His shaggy hair bobbed with a curt nod. He marched ahead to push through the door of my private dining room. "She did. A whole crust of bread dipped into the broth. Truly a victory. This is the first solid food she's taken since the storms began."

My mother recognized Thor's anger, even if Lux didn't. This storm was a message that the gods hated us all, not just the vampires. Maybe it was because of Silver. For a witch to defect and find loyalty among hundreds of monsters, no doubt enraged him.

"My mother is at her calmest with you lately," I said. Striding to the other end of a long table, I admired all the food. Roast venison steamed at the center, surrounded by custard tarts dipped in cream and honey, an array of soft cheeses spread over pears and baked apples, and cups spilling over with aged mead. Saliva wetted my tongue in anticipation of the variety of flavors, many combined perfectly as repeated from a recipe created by a former vessel and friend of Lux's. Though Stasia was no longer in Mara's Keep after Silver captured and took her hostage, her legacy remained in our kitchens. And though none of this would satiate me, I appreciated the taste. It was something to relish between gulps of the warm blood pooled in the soup bowl set before my chosen chair.

Axel took a seat at the opposite end. Ingrid seems more relaxed lately; I think her mind is clearer. She actually recognized me today," he said.

"Recognized you?" It was all I could say. My mother rarely even remembered me, her own son.

"I mentioned your father."

Before I could even take a sip of blood, my throat tightened. "What about him?"

Axel sat with his spine rigid, waiting for me to break the fast before he took a cup of mead or a bite. "I told her that soaking his bread was the only way Erik would eat broth."

"That's it?" My shoulders relaxed at this news, and I lifted the soup bowl to my lips. The offered blood tasted both bitter and sweet, but the second it soaked over my tongue, energy spread down my throat and through my torso, giving my limbs a jolt.

"That's it," he said, reaching for a knife to slice into the roast. Eating with Axel was an old tradition from my childhood. One I'd wanted to bring back after the past seven years of feeding on vessels in private. I decided this vampiric life was already only a piece of my past. "She laughed and said that Erik used to insist soup wasn't real food. That only the food you could hold in your hand counted as real food."

He had. My father had said that often, and I didn't recall this until Axel—no, my mother—mentioned it. "Her madness…" My voice trailed off . "Could she be healing?"

Axel set his cup down and swallowed hard. "I'm sorry, my king, but it is still as strong as ever. After that, she screamed at me, saying Thor was going to strike her down. She demanded that I blow out all of her candles because she swore they were pieces of his lightning."

I slammed the bowl down on the table. The porcelain cracked, and blood splashed red stains over the linen cloth that covered the wood. Wiping the back of my hand across my forehead, I cleared the loose hair from my vision. "Why the fuck didn't you start with the bad news?"

"I'm sorry, my king," he repeated.

My anger towards Axel dissipated, given that he was the only person to have consistently stayed by my side without ever betraying me. Though it wasn't my father's choice to lose his head and leave me behind in this world. I ground my teeth and eyed the crack in the soup bowl.

My mind drifted back to the mark I'd left on the shelf. The nick could become a rose adorning the bookshelf's side. Roses always calmed my mother, but I found a sort of horrifying beauty in them after King Roderic had planted them all across the grounds at Mara's Keep. I wanted to keep my hatred for him fresh.

If only I could kill King Roderic again and again for beheading my father and claiming my mother. For denying me food whenever I whispered my father's name. For igniting my desire to become a vampire like him so that I could rip him to shreds and sit on his blood that spilled across the throne.

But that was all in the past.

Lux was my future. Godhood was my future.

And it was nearly time to bring her back into the armory. If we approached her practice slowly and carefully, the madness would have too much time to seep into every corner of her mind, like it had with my mother.

Then I'd lose her forever.

And since she wouldn't agree to this fake marriage, she had to learn to fight off multiple vampires at once.

My throat tense and my stomach churning, I shoved the broken bowl aside. The race against madness had begun, whether I liked it or not. This week's practice would be the last training I'd allow—the last time I'd let the gods scream at her for mere practice. I wasn't like Kayn that way. I actually cared.

"At sunset, you will bring Sif and Mista to the armory

again," I said, meeting Axel's gaze over the dishes of food I could no longer stomach. "And Lux too. Tell her to be ready to train."

I winced, hating how similar I sounded to the Exile. I swore I wouldn't push her too hard the way he had, but time wasn't on our side. This was for her safety, and her safety was my obsession.

Chapter Five

Lux

Two days after I'd nearly killed Sif and Mista and Axel in a three on one practice fight, and the Gods begged me to destroy the vampire women, I stood beside the throne of Vylheim with a weapon strapped to my thigh like I was King Drakkar's bodyguard.

Drak had insisted I sit on the throne and rest, but I wasn't ready to act as queen—or his wife—so I remained on my feet with my head held high to greet the visitors for Supplication Day.

A line of men and women, children even, stood waiting to approach the throne with their concerns. It was tradition. On the first day of spring, weeks after the Polar Nocturne ended, the people of Vylheim traveled to Mara's Keep to kneel before the king and present their requests.

When I was just a village girl in Skaldir, I believed the Day of Supplication was an honest and welcoming invitation from the leaders of our world. After uncovering the truth of the royal court in Mara's Keep, the one run by a blood council of vampires, I knew this day was used to find witches or subjects harboring weapons.

This was the day for vampires to sniff out those they

considered their enemies. Witches would always be first on the list, since our gifts came from the Gods that hated vampires. Anyone willing to shed blood, and waste even a drop of what the vampires wanted to drink, was second on that list.

I lifted my eyes and tried to smile at the woman who limped toward the throne. My face felt hollow even though this was the first Day of Supplication not run by the Blood Council. King Drakkar ran this one, with me alongside him.

Still, the purpose was the same: to dig for information.

Except this time, it was about Silver and her army. I needed to get information about what was happening in Vylheim without leaving the castle and risking her coming after me before I was ready to face a full army. In all of that, though, I insisted we do the best we could to fulfill the people's requests. No doubt those requests would be for food and shelter against the freeze and the unpredictable storms that'd only grown worse since The Polar Nocturne's end.

"My king," the woman said when she dipped into a bow. Her joints creaked as she bent to the cold floor. On her knees, she looked up at Drak, silver hair framing the soft wrinkles of her face. She opened her mouth, but nothing more came out.

Drak leaned forward as the woman forced out a breath, her gaze flickering to me and then back to him. When she opened her mouth again, the result was the same: silence. This woman was afraid, as were most of the people once they stood in the king's presence. Now that they understood he wasn't human.

But Mara and all of Vylheim had mostly taken well to this news. The reveal of vampires allowed many who still believed in the Gods to have hope. Hope for magic. Hope for divine intervention. Hope for change despite the fact that their king was an undead monster, because his actions hadn't aligned with that these past few weeks. He remained loyal to them, and had even pulled back the executioners, reassigning the last masked men and women who hadn't defected to Silver's army to the role of the king's guard.

He allowed my people to have weapons again, which let them defend themselves, and of course, he canceled The Age of Exploration, which would have sent many people to their deaths in the sea beyond Vylheim.

Drak exchanged a look with me before addressing her. "Go on, tell us what you need."

Gingerly, she touched her lips. Her fingers shook as they dropped to the symbol sewn into her cloak. I'd seen it before: the lightning bolt that the people of Torsholt added to their clothing in honor of Thor, the God of Thunder and Odin's son. It was a silent act of defiance in a world that once hushed any talk of the Gods.

Her mouth moved, speaking in whispers. I knew the quiet prayers on her lips, even if I couldn't hear them. I'd whispered to the Gods myself, before they infiltrated my skull and spoke directly into my head.

Now, though, the Gods were quiet. Whenever Drak was nearby, they spoke sparingly in case he could hear them through my thoughts. At least that was what I assumed, but assuming anything about the Gods was stupid. Not even witches could predict their actions. Only the best seers, like my mother, caught glimpses of Odin's true intentions.

"Speak up, I cannot hear you," Drak said.

The woman's fingers closed around her cloak, fisting the fabric tightly at her throat.

I gripped Drak's shoulder and forced him to sit back against his gaudy throne. "She's getting to it," I said, as I frowned down at him. He tilted his head and stared up at me with a furrow in his brow. My voice dropped so that only the king could hear. "Are you so impatient that you cannot even give the woman a moment?"

The cocky curve of his lips fell. I'd struck a nerve with the truth. Now that I had revealed all my secrets, I vowed to speak the truth often and bluntly. It was a gift for him, really, since he'd vowed the same for me and had kept to that promise since I met him.

Turning my attention to the woman, I nodded. "It's safe to speak of the Gods here."

Drak snapped his neck to the side, and I felt his icy gaze needling me. There was nothing he hated more than Odin. I squeezed his shoulder, my fingernails digging into his flesh.

The woman's dark eyes widened, but her tight hold on the cloak released.

"How did you know?" he breathed.

"She looked at me," I said. And there was an unsaid understanding that we were both witches. Though witches were out of hiding now, at least some of them, not every witch trusted executioners would stop hunting them and cutting off their heads.

"It isn't about the Gods," she finally spoke. The quiver in her voice told me she was one of those who still feared the executioners. And why wouldn't she? A lifetime of masked men and women patrolling every village left everyone on edge, not just witches. "They killed my niece."

"They?" I asked. The woman's eyes shifted to Drak, and I understood immediately. "Vampires."

"Not those loyal to me," Drak said.

"You don't control all of them." I tightened my grip on him again.

"Careful," he said beneath his breath. He twisted to look up at me with the crook of his mouth having returned. "I take pleasure in you grabbing me like that."

Shaking my head, I opened my mouth to bite back at him, but a feathery voice interrupted me.

"They're warriors." The woman barely spoke above a whisper. "Acting like executioners against witches."

"I told you," Drak said. "It's Silver's army."

I finally let go of him and stepped closer to the woman. "Your niece was a witch too?"

She nodded. "The warriors dragged her out of her house." Her voice was mousy. "They threw her into the street and fed on her in front of everyone. People ran back into their houses, but not me. I tried to hit him with my walking stick, and he didn't kill me. He said he'd had his fill and that he would come back for me unless I delivered this message."

Drak was on the edge of his seat again. "What message?" he asked.

Reaching out a hand, I offered to help her up, but she did not take it. Instead, she fixed her eyes on Drak and lifted her voice. "That the witches will not only be killed. They'll be tortured, each bone broken and their skin burned before they're bled dry, unless you give up your throne and…" her eyes slid to me. "Her."

Drak shot to his feet. His shadow stretched over her, backlit by the glowing flames in the candelabra hanging behind his throne. "That's never happening." He spoke through his teeth, defiant and impatient, as if she were the one come to steal away his throne right in front of him. "They can fucking try."

I stepped between them and stabbed him in the chest with my finger. "Stop." I kept my voice low. The people here were his subjects. They respected him, even though he had once done horrible things. He wasn't the Blood Council. He hadn't built the fucked up system that hunted witches and beheaded anyone who defied the royal council's rules. Even if the people of Vylheim didn't know all the details, they knew enough to follow King Drakkar. They knew he'd fed on humans, but that he'd become a vampire to overthrow the council. Even if it was for his own selfish revenge, it served all of us well. I searched his ice-blue eyes, letting the chilling anger in them wash over me until they softened. "I know you have an obsession with power, and anything threatening to take that from you enrages—"

He seized my wrist before I could prod him again and tugged me toward him. "Fuck the throne. I'm not giving you up."

I shook my head. "I don't understand why you say things like that."

"The truth is, I don't understand it either. But I've told you before, you are my fascination."

I didn't want to fall into the endless abyss of this conversation again. Drak swore his need to be with me was honest, but it'd never made enough sense.

Fire crackled between us. That was all this obsession was: desire. He'd said he liked how I valued life and saw more for myself than what the law bound me to, but I believed he was just amused by how I handled fear.

Spinning away from him, I knelt and helped the woman to her feet. "I'm so sorry for your loss. The king will address your concerns."

She nodded, eyes still full and round like a child's, though without the innocence. "His army will fight back?"

I bit my lip, resisting the temptation to spew a promise I couldn't keep. Though King Drakkar had loyal subjects, Silver attracted those who hungered most for battle and blood. She promised a force that would provide them with more humans to feed on as she expanded her reach beyond Vylheim. Countless executioners, groomed for brutality, had fallen in line behind her.

Only enough had remained to hold Mara's Keep, and the rest were spread thin, attempting to keep Silver's army out of the vast kingdom of Vylheim.

Drak stepped up beside me, taking the woman's hand in his and giving it a gentle squeeze. "I will fight back," he said. His gaze burned into me, and I turned my head to meet it. "The huntress and I will. Both of us."

"You can kill them all?" Hope laced the woman's words, though I had no doubt she didn't fully understand what it meant that I was a huntress. Only select members of The Blood Council, Drak, and Silver knew the pieces of history that were once buried in the hidden library of Mara's Keep. Only on those pages did a record exist of a witch who had bound herself to the undead, proving that she had been severed from the Gods. And the remaining members of the Blood Council were dead or had defected to Silver's army.

To the people of Vylheim, a union between a vampire king they trusted and a huntress blessed with skills against the enemy army was the perfect hope.

"That's what I became king to do," he said. It was the truth; I knew that much.

Satisfied, the woman bent forward and kissed his cold hand. "You're not like the other vampires."

"And with any luck, I won't be a vampire much longer." He spoke more to himself than to the woman who was now shuffling away from us.

Before the next villager stepped up, I faced him. "When are we leaving for Yggdrasil?"

"When I'm confident that your sister won't be able to kill you. And me, for that matter."

I dropped my eyelids, narrowing in on him. "And what will that require?"

"Well, killing her first would be the best option."

I frowned. "You still want to lead her here."

"I believe I used the word 'lure'. And yes, she'd risk her life for that throne. She'll do anything for it. Why do you think I had to sew her mouth shut? She tried to compel me into giving it to her the moment I became a vampire. She believes all she has to do is sit on the throne and let destiny take its course."

I winced. Witches were dying because of her, sucked dry by rogue vampires, and under Silver's command to *torture* them. Had they targeted my friends in Skaldir yet? Was Ragna safe?

The witches from my home village were on the outskirts, far from where Silver's army camped along the border of the wasteland, but also exposed and with little help from Mara.

The image of my friend, Ragna, dragged from her farm with the vampires shattering her bones and feeding from her in front of her husband and children, knotted my stomach and clawed at my heart. My pulse pushed bile up into my throat with every erratic beat.

So much of my life was based on lies, and Silver knew this. Were these messages more lies? Bait? The woman's pain seemed authentic enough.

Drak turned back to the line of people and addressed as many of the villagers as he could before Axel interrupted. He insisted on a brief break for Drak to consume the offered blood, and for me to sit and eat. He guided the villagers out and returned to stand before us with a bronze goblet for Drak and a cup of stew for me.

The lanky man gave a quick bow of his head before he left Drak and I alone in the vast, echoing room. While Drak paced and drank, I sat on the arm of the throne, devouring the warm beef and potatoes.

"Are you ready to say yes to my proposal yet?" Drak said, turning to me when the door fell shut behind Axel.

Ice hardened in my veins.

"Don't we have to speak the vows in front of Mara according to tradition? How would that be fake?" I asked.

"The blood seal," he said simply. All marriages in Vylheim included a blood seal between husband and wife. This was the true seal that bound the couple beyond mere words. The witness to the vows would present a wax seal with the overlap of the husband's and wife's initials imprinted in the center. Their pricked fingers would bleed into the seal and complete the marriage. "We would use animal blood. Not our own."

It could work. Easy even, if I hadn't already almost married him and our wedding hadn't sent the entirety of Vylheim into chaos.

When I said nothing, he strode back to his throne and sat down. I promptly stood so that I could welcome our visitors.

Before long, the room was teeming with eager villagers again, coming to us with every request imaginable.

Beckoning the next villager forward, Drak leaned against the back of the bronze chair and rested his elbows lazily on the shiny arms. The village man knelt, bowing his head for a moment before addressing the king. I shuffled back to my post beside the throne when the man's words stopped me short.

"I come from Skaldir," he said. I swiveled, heart skipping. "My village experienced an attack." *No.* "Ransacked. All the women have been accused of being witches." *No, no, no!* "I am the first to make it here with this news." What of Ragna? Of the other friends I left behind? My heart splintered in two, like the stories about Thor's lightning cracking the earth open. "Many were fed on until they died. Some of us escaped. Our plea is for Mara to send more help. The vampires came with a woman who said she once lived among us, and for that, she spared us torture, ending those she killed with a swift death. But only for one more fortnight will she allow this reprieve. She promised torture when she returns. I beg you, my king, please send men and women to help us defend our farms. Our homes. Our families."

Drak said nothing, deferring to me as he lifted his eyes.

"Do not stay there," I said.

"We will not abandon our homes." He spoke between tears. "And it doesn't matter, she said she will know us anywhere. She will track us down. The vampires have already scented us."

Fuck, fuck, fuck!

I had to get Silver away from our home. Away from the

village and where I could reach her and her vampires, but only one thing would lure her...

My heart skipped a beat as I dared a glance at the king. A royal marriage would distract Silver from destroying my home, my people; yet something about the thought of being with Drak made my pulse race. Perhaps it was simply that I wouldn't have to face this world by myself anymore. Even if it were a sham marriage, I'd never truly be solitary as long as we were both playing along.

Could I really do this? Could I toy with marriage to a monster just to draw my sister's attention?

Yes. I shivered.

It helped that Drak always told me the truth, and in my opinion, liars were the true monsters. Maybe it was wrong that I could picture myself walking down the aisle with him waiting at the end, even after our last wedding had begun with his threat to kill me.

"Whatever it takes." Odin's voice boomed like the crash of thunder behind my eyes.

What does that mean?

Odin didn't respond right away. The Gods weren't exactly at my beck and call, but I felt his approval. The pain in my skull softened before he explained himself.

"Whatever it takes to bring you and the vampires together."

Shouldn't we go to Yggdrasil?

He said nothing. For some reason, the Gods didn't approve of this plan. At least not outright, and not with words or softening, and of course they didn't, not with Drak leading me there, with his plan to take Odin's place.

This fake marriage was a cleaner alternative to ignite the war between huntress and vampires.

I draped my hand over Drak's shoulder again as I spoke to the man from my village. "Don't abandon Skaldir permanently," I said. "But accept our invitation to come here and visit for a while instead. The entire village of Skaldir is welcome to attend our wedding." The man's mouth flipped in confusion while Drak's anticipation showed in his tense shoulders. I licked my lips and dropped my eyes to him, giving him a faint nod.

He took my hand in his and stood. "Spread the news," he told the man. "Lux Quinn and King Drakkar are to be married here in Mara's Keep before the end of this fortnight. At the full moon."

"A wedding?" he said. "Vampire and huntress?" He was bold to say it like that, but Drak didn't care.

Drak chuckled. "Aren't we the perfect pair? We both have a taste for blood."

"We're the same," I whispered the words Drak had once said to me. We were both twisted enough to pull this off, and knowing it should have made me sick or nervous, but it didn't. The only explanation was that being in Drak's presence silenced those self-hating thoughts. His honesty calmed me.

The man stared at us. I couldn't decide if his eyes held hope or fear.

"For our *enemy's* blood, of course." Drak clarified as he met my gaze and lifted my hand to his lips. "I love that about her."

Despite his stony gaze, warmth unfurled up my neck. The sudden urge for him reared its head like a wild horse, and though I understood little about this traitorous feeling that tugged me toward him. He was a vampire who bled people dry, and yet I didn't notice his fangs.

He'd always looked like one of the ancient warriors described in the stories of our ancestors—like the men I dreamed about while I was alone in the dark. Before the desire building in my core became slick with wanting, I dug my fingernails into my palm.

Drak wanted to kill the Gods I worshiped. And even knowing this, I couldn't deny my desire for a man as determined as a warrior from our history.

The darkness in me calls to the monster in him.

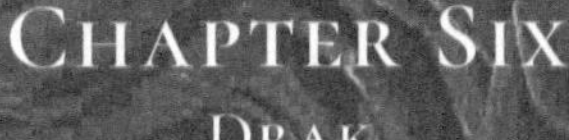

Chapter Six
Drak

Bare shoulders stood out among the ash-brown shelves that surrounded my future wife. I knew I'd find her at the library. She was always here, studying the sagas.

Eight days had passed since she agreed to marry me, leaving one more for the rest of the people of Skaldir to travel here. Surely an empty village would ignite Silver's rage if the wedding hadn't already lured her into Mara's Keep.

It was almost the perfect plan except for only one downside. I didn't want our marriage to be fake.

The pool of her jade skirt rippled out around her folded legs on the shaggy rug. History of all kinds encircled her as runes carved into stone slabs, loosely bound books, and rolled scrolls.

Pieces of our past lay hidden in them, and she was as drawn to the stories as I was to her.

Lux didn't lift her head even with the sound of my footsteps echoing against stone. The journal she studied kept her absolutely enraptured, and the bronze candelabra hanging over her like a high floating crown made her the vision of a fiercely intelligent queen. Wax caught in the shimmering cups at the base of each milky candle, and the glow of pale yellow flickered across the shades of autumn in Lux's hair and clothes. Green and brown fabric, hints of red from her braid. Wild hairs escaped the thick rope of hair and curled inward as if everything pointed back to her.

For me, everything did.

And I still didn't know why I needed her so damn badly. Not just to touch her. I needed her to look at me like she did when she led me to the throne. Lust swam in her gaze, but it was her want for me and the fleeting glimpses I caught of her thoughts about how she longed for me because she saw something in me she hadn't experienced in anyone else that consumed me.

Fuck if I didn't want to know what the Hel she saw.

"Lux," I spoke into the still air. The only sound was the soft turning of the pages. "You need rest before the ceremony if we're going to pull this off. No doubt the fucking army will storm down our doors with Silver in the lead the second you sit on that throne."

At dawn, servants and subjects would prepare for our wedding while Lux and I prepared for war.

"I need to understand Silver, and I keep thinking the sagas will help me," she said, her voice tightening with frustration or desperation. I wasn't sure which.

I crouched beside her, my elbows propped on my knees. "What is it you're looking for?" I searched her face as if I'd find the answers she needed there. Grazing her bottom lip with her teeth, I stared at her mouth. Tomorrow, I'd get to taste those perfect pink lips again.

Though I knew she craved me since the moment she showed up at my doorstep four weeks ago, she held back for some stupid loyalty to the vampire who trained her to become the huntress. The Exile was the bane of my existence after he'd trained her, fucking *trained her*, like she was a damn dog he used to hunt game. She was the one with the claws, and he was directing her how to use them against our kind in some pathetic attempt to redeem himself in the eyes of the gods.

Vampires are irredeemable.

Finally, Lux looked up from the stained pages of the old book. "If I understand the stories of the first witch, maybe I'll know my sister better, and then I'll truly be ready to face her. She and the first witch could be the same."

"You think Myrah was reborn through Silver?" I asked. As we understood it, the first witch tried to reincarnate through Lux and Silver's mother's womb, but since she was pregnant with twins, the witch's powers split. Her natural magic—glimpses from the gods—flowed into Lux, while Silver received the witch's learned power when she'd touched a Valkyrie and gained the ability to alter and control life and death; or undeath.

Now, they shared similar magic after Lux accepted the gods' trials.

She shook her head. "I don't know." Pointing to the scrawled text, her finger traced the ink. "This is a copy of the original story, rewritten only ninety-six years ago by a recorder named Brynhild. This is the writer's interpretation of the ancient runes."

I followed her finger, my gaze flicking over the words. Never had I taken the time to read through every rewritten version of the old sagas. The first witch's story had so many iterations, I hadn't cared to know them all except for what I could learn about Yggdrasil and becoming a god. But there was very little of that information in her story.

Myrah's rebirth in the realm of Odin's children requires her warrior's foot upon the soil.

"Do you think this means the warrior she loved has tried to return to this realm?" she asked. Before waiting for an answer, she read the next line aloud. "*For that to happen, he'd have to fulfill his promise and leave Valhalla. What warrior would ever leave*

Odin's table?" She looked up at me. "According to another record written by Yrsa, Myrah called her lover Rune."

Rune. The name echoed in my mind.

Something suddenly flooded my senses and overwhelmed me with the same feeling that attacked me when I'd heard Lux say this word outside of my workshop. Another episode of surreality or whatever the fuck this was.

My lungs tightened, as if Rune's name, invoked by Lux, had somehow sucked the air from my chest. Though I didn't need to breathe as a vampire, I suddenly couldn't speak. Couldn't think straight. A crushing weight closed in around my temples, and the sensation of choking, strangling desperation overpowered me.

Something inexplicable was happening to my body as the flicker of an old story burst into my memory. A story that seemed to take over me as I lost all sense of this room, of Lux, and of reality.

"Fuck," I breathed as a sharp pain smashed into the soft space between my shoulder and my heart. Pressure and blinding agony bolted up from the spot, like an axe that had embedded itself into my chest before someone yanked it back again. My legs shook, weak even under the weight of my casual crouch.

"Drak?" Lux's voice faded away as if stretching across a vast field.

"Rune." Another voice breathed into my ear. "Come back to me."

I forced my body to move, but the effort was akin to moving through sand and stone. My legs were heavy and almost useless, working only enough to drag me forward. Toward something, someone, a voice.

I didn't know.

"Come back," Lux said.

All at once, the pain lifted. The weight evaporated and the chill of the castle settled over me. I was no longer crouching on the rug beside her, but standing with one hand splayed against the door frame, slumped and breathless as I faced the hallway.

"Are you okay?" she asked. "You just got up and walked away."

Clutching my chest, I straightened my spine before turning to face her, refusing to reveal this strange weakness. She didn't want to be bound to a monster, but from what I knew of Lux, she would hate to be bound to a weak man more.

I had to get this crazy dream under control before she questioned my strength. And since I was bound for godhood, I needed to be ready for this kind of intense pain and the power it would take for my body to adapt to Odin's abilities.

"Come look at this," she said. Thank Hel she was mostly oblivious to whatever the fuck just happened to me. "Myrah was willing to sacrifice anything to get what she wanted. Does that sound like Silver to you?"

Frowning, I turned and shook my head. "No. Silver won't sacrifice herself."

"Well, of course not, then she can't sit on the throne."

"No," I said. "I mean, Silver wouldn't sacrifice herself *for someone else.* The sagas all say Myrah sacrificed the immortality she siphoned from the vampires she created to get to Valhalla. To be with the man she loved."

"But she never made it to Valhalla," she said, her brow scrunched. The wrinkle at the bridge of her nose was enchanting. Despite her ability to catch glimpses of the future as a seer, she still sought knowledge and wisdom instead of relying on the gods. Her curiosity was bewitching, and I feared the tightness in my chest would flare into pain again, but this wasn't like the phantom blade.

"Myrah never made it to Valhalla," I repeated. "But she sure as Hel tried." If she's been successful, she wouldn't have attempted rebirth through Anastasia's womb—Silver and

Lux's mother. Maybe Lux's assessment was correct. Maybe Silver's ability to compel vampires from the beginning meant she was Myrah.

No, I knew Silver. I grew up with her. She loved nothing but herself and the throne. From the moment she saw it as a child, she wanted to be on top. I never blamed her, since I wanted the same thing, though her reason was for revenge against the people of Vylheim who failed her; mine was revenge against the gods.

I wasn't so different from the enemy.

Still, none of this meant Silver was the first witch. "Myrah did everything for her lover," I said. "Silver only does what she wants for herself. They can't be, as you say, one and the same."

Lux chewed her lip thoughtfully. "Perhaps you're right. My mother always said Silver was her own. She couldn't control her, even then. She said that if Silver had been a seer like me and her, she would have seen chaos, and only from Loki's eyes."

Lux winced, that same sign that the fucking gods were in her head again. Loki must have heard his name and come running.

I flexed my hands into fists, wishing I could just reach through her eye socket and rip the bastards out. They hurt her, warped her mind, turned her against herself, and she still followed them.

"Maybe that's the truth," I said.

She blinked up at me; the book fallen open in her hands. Tendrils of soft, burnt redwood curled around her heart-shaped face. For all the huntress that she was, and for all that she'd endured—the lies she had to tell, the heart that often failed her, the nerves that plagued her thoughts, now the gods writhing in her head—Lux looked hopeful, gentle, even knowing she had a weapon strapped to her thigh that could turn monsters like me to ash at the flick of her wrist.

"Maybe Silver's powers come from Loki only," I said, though I didn't completely believe it. All the gods, especially Odin, were as selfish as Silver. They likely all had a hand in her twisted mind.

I gritted my teeth and spoke through my rough voice. "I don't know that you'll understand Silver by learning about Myrah."

She nodded, hope deflating from her eyes. "You're probably right. It doesn't make sense that she'd kill witches if she was connected to the gods."

"But she is connected to the gods. We know that based on her magic." I said it even though I didn't want to keep talking. That pain was sharper than anything I had felt since before becoming a vampire, and I needed to lie down.

"But it's different, the same as the magic that I only got when I passed the gods' trials. Not like other witches' magic. That's why I thought she could be Myrah. Something is different about her."

"That's because she's not truly a witch. She inherited Myrah's learned magic. She has the touch of a Valkyrie, control of those on the edge of life and death."

Lux nodded as she pulled her braid to the front of her shoulder and toyed with it. "A Valkyrie…I should study Odin's maidens."

I strode toward her again. Crouching, I eased the book from her lap. "You won't change Silver. I've known her my entire life, Lux."

"You kept her caged," she said with a frown. It was so damn obvious how badly Lux wanted to call Silver her sister again. The guilt and shame tormented her, but it was her love for Silver that clearly hurt the worst. As much as I hated to see her sad, fierce loyalty and stubborn love looked so fucking beautiful on Lux.

Silver didn't deserve a lick of it.

"The former king did," I said. "And yes, I did too, but only because she was trying to use me, just like she's using her army now." Recognition flickered in Lux's eyes. "Change that drastic is unlikely. I still want revenge on the gods. She still wants revenge on the people of Vylheim."

"Are you saying you're like my sister?" Concern was clear in her frown.

"Didn't you once call me your enemy?" I hated to say it, but it was the truth, and if nothing else, I always swore to speak the truth to Lux.

"And now I don't."

My muscles went rigid. She didn't hate me? "But I didn't change. You've just got to know me. Your sister won't change either. She's only become more steeped in hatred."

"And I want to get to know her."

"You know her. She ransacked Skaldir, and she's killing witches. Fuck, she kidnapped her own mother, Lux." Pain deepened the lines around her pursed lips, and my heart lurched as hurt flickered in her black eyes. The truth. I had to stick to the truth no matter how painful it was. "She wants to see you dead, and I won't let that happen. I won't let her hurt either of us." I took her hands in mine. Sitting here, on my knees in front of Lux, the woman I was to marry tomorrow—pretend to marry—I almost thought of myself as a husband. A human again. A simple man with a simple goal to be with this creature who fascinated me for reasons beyond my understanding. "It'll be easy to take her down if she believes you've given yourself to me."

Damn if I didn't want it to be true. Fuck. This hurt almost as much as the phantom axe.

What was wrong with me? Lux wasn't supposed to be my endgame.

As much as I was drawn to her, I had bigger plans. When Silver turned me, I forged a path of vengeance against the gods. I built my entire reign as a vampire king into a stepping stone to godhood so that we could take control of our own lives. So that nobody would ever have to suffer as my mother had. So that these damn storms, the curse on the wasteland, and every other selfish choice the gods made could never affect us again.

I once fantasized about Vylheim becoming mine. Now I fantasized about Lux becoming mine.

"Take her down?" she repeated. "I will not kill her unless I have to. You know that, right?"

"We can take her captive and figure it out from there." I couldn't disagree with Lux right now. It felt an impossible feat. "Trust me when I say this marriage will bring her here, but we have to sell it. When we walk out of those doors tonight, Lux, you are in love with me. And I—" Something lodged in my throat. But it wasn't an axe this time. "I'm in love with you. Understood?"

"Right," she said. "I'm yours." She repeated the phrase I'd told her when I proposed to her the first time—the moment that only heightened my pull toward her.

I had to remind myself that this was all a ruse. I never lied to her, but she'd lied to me plenty, and now we were going to lie to the entire kingdom.

She wasn't mine.

That was obvious when she dropped my hands and brushed past me, leaving stones, books, and scrolls scattered across the rug. After she disappeared into the hollow hallway, I crouched and scooped up the book. Flipping through it, I scanned the pages until a line near the end caught my eye.

She is the blood. He is the rune.

Rune.

Chapter Seven
Lux

Drak's hand trailed along the inside of my bare thigh, his fingers rough against the smooth skin, but his touch feathery and teasing. My breath hitched as he dragged two fingers over my slick core.

We shared the throne as if we were already husband and wife.

Moaning, I arched into him as he called himself my God. But such words were blasphemous, and each time he spoke ill of Odin and Freya, I flinched.

Except this time.

What the Hel was wrong with me? How could I ache for a Godless creature?

When he brought my wetness to my mouth, I licked his fingers greedily, tasting my desire for him. Drak knew how to touch me.

As if he'd already taken me, he knew exactly what ignited me, and what beckoned the slickness between my legs. It seemed he'd memorized every inch of my body, as if he'd set me on fire hundreds of times before.

Everything about the king was unbidden, selfish, honest to a fault, *free.* And I ate it up. I went from hiding under my sister's name and lying about my entire life to becoming the Gods' instrument of death.

"And you will kill him too," a voice in my mind said. Odin spoke to me, sending lightning pain through my skull as his tone carved into my head. An image filled my mind—my hand wrapped around the stake as I forced it through Drak's chest.

I shoved the thought behind the wall I had built, because all I wanted was to be alone with Drak before the Gods interrupted. They always would because I belonged to them.

"Give me more," I begged Drak.

The tip of his fang brushed against my ear. I flipped around, spreading my legs to either side of his hips. A sly, wicked smile tugged at his lips as his icy eyes poured over every inch of my naked body.

Leaning into me, his breath brushed over the tips of my taut nipples, then found its way to my neck. Stinging pain suddenly shot through the soft flesh just below my jaw.

I did *not* give him permission to bite me.

I tried to jerk away from him, but he vanished. When the throne melted away, I woke with a gulp of icy air.

Absorbing the reality around me, I opened my eyes to a vampire crouched over me, his mouth on my throat.

And it wasn't my future husband.

But I was in no immediate danger, aside from the sting of the bite. This idiot trying to feed on me was no threat; a vampire lost to bloodlust was an easy kill. My heart slowed as my focus narrowed.

I writhed in the tangle of blankets and my nightgown, freeing myself to reach for my weapon and stab him.

The vampire whimpered, suddenly pulling back as he clutched his throat. Feeding on me was painful for all of them, and apparently this idiot hadn't gotten the message. His red eyes widened as his jaw went slack and steam rippled from his burnt tongue.

I ripped the stake from my thigh and slammed the tip into the vampire's ribcage. His black blood spread over his body, turning his skin and bones to ash where it touched. In a matter of seconds, his body disintegrated. Drops of blood stained my nightgown, and the ash scattered over the white bedcovers.

I rolled away from the remains of the vampire I'd destroyed only to catch sight of a figure emerging from the shadows.

Silver sent more than one this time.

I spoke the compulsion into the darkness. "Show yourself, vampire. Your existence ends here." The effort weighed on my eyelids and knotted my throat. I gripped the tree pendant in my other hand, having slipped it from the pocket of my nightgown.

A wiry man appeared in the moonlight, his eyes already glazed from my compulsion. I advanced on him, raising the stake, but after a bout of shallow sleep, I was shaking and weak. Dreams of Drak, the Gods' words cutting through my sleep, and staying in the library late into the night had ruined my chance for rest.

My eye twitched, and the muscles of my jaw ached. I could not hold the compulsion.

As soon as I dropped it, the vampire dashed back into the shadows, but not before I slashed him with the tip of the Y Tree.

After watching his partner's destruction, he must have decided his loyalty to Silver's plan wasn't worth it. I gritted my teeth and stalked after him into the maze of hallways.

This wasn't how I wanted to spend the morning of my wedding.

I hated the endless corridors that led to nowhere, the fireplaces that had the dual purpose of hiding secret rooms, and that damn draft. Actually, as cold as the hallways were, the draft was the part that I hated the least. The icy air that bit at my nose and scraped over my pebbled skin reminded me of home. Every gust of wind took me back to the place I hadn't witnessed with my own eyes in weeks.

The place I'd probably never see again.

My heart sank, twisting in my gut as my best friend's face flashed in my mind. I'd convinced the king to free Ragna, but she'd returned to a different Skaldir, one now torn apart by Silver's army. I shook my head to clear the thoughts and focus on listening for the intruder's footsteps.

Grey surrounded me at every turn. Each corner looked identical to the last, and the only sound was the echo of my own footfalls until the hiss of someone in pain stopped me short.

Creeping to the end of the corner where the hall forked in two, I peered around the edge to locate the source of the hiss and found the dim outline of a figure slumped against the wall.

The silver injured him, making the skin on his cheek bubble from the pure metal cursed to melt his kind. But he would recover fast, and if he didn't fully recover, it wouldn't matter. Vampires had a way of suppressing pain while they fought. The torment of their hunger and anger overwhelmed any distress from a bit of congealed flesh.

I froze in the hall. My fingers had numbed so much from lack of blood flow and the frigid air that the stake in my grip slipped. I snatched it, affirming my clumsy hold around the base of the rough wood, but not before a gasp broke through my lips.

Crimson eyes snapped up. I ducked back behind the safety of the wall, but the pounding in my chest was loud enough to alert him of exactly where I was, flipping me from huntress to hunted.

Fuck.

Vampires had heightened senses in the world around them, but I had a lifetime of learning the nuances of my own senses, knowing my body's every ability and every limitation. Knowing exactly when I would faint and when my nerves would fray.

This awareness led me to Loki's power. I could tame it by naming the sensations the same way I calmed myself in a fit of nerves. "I feel the freezing air; I hear the shaking in my voice." No matter how many times I destroyed a vampire, I'd never be completely without fear. "I see him."

My heart stopped at the sight of the figure upon me. In a single blink, he'd flashed from his place around the corner and pinned me against the stone. Flickers of light reflected from the torch on the wall, catching the fire in his eyes as the base of his palm slammed into my chin and shoved my face to the side.

Saliva dripped from his fangs as he struck, pressing his mouth to the thickest vein in my neck where my pulse pounded uncontrollably. An excruciating sting cut through my throat, hot with the instant draw of my blood to his hollow, sucking fangs.

As he bit me, the focus of my compulsion split apart. The pain, more intense this time because he bit my existing wound. It was too late to talk my way through this, but I'd practiced the angle with which to shove a weapon through a vampire's ribcage hundreds of times, if not thousands.

My wrist knew how to bend, my muscles remembering for me as I tipped the pointed end up and between the bones protecting his dead heart.

He reeled back, but not from the stake. I'd barely pushed the tip into his flesh when he started heaving from the burn of consuming my blood.

I almost rolled my eyes at this blood-lusting idiot as I charged forward. After the second bite, my head was spinning, and collapse threatened at the corners of my blackened vision. My aim was a little off, but I buried the stake into his chest anyway for shock, then pulled back and tried a truer aim.

A hand caught my elbow, and another arm wrapped around my throat.

"Thanks for the bait, Sterak." A woman's voice curled around me, cold and raspy like she inhaled too much smoke from an open fire. Sterak stumbled back, still heaving from the burn of my blood. "Maybe the burning will stop when Lux is dead," she said, pity almost softening her tone.

Still suffering, Sterak fell against the opposite wall and slid down as pitifully as the tone this woman afforded him.

I squeezed my eyes shut in the seconds that she placed her hands on my neck, ready to snap my spine.

Guttural fear pulsed through me with every misstep of my dancing heart, but it was in this fear that my focus sharpened. I'd known fear my entire life. With the illness plaguing my heart, it felt every beat could be my last. My numb fingers and heavy limbs, my tendency to lose consciousness if I pushed myself too hard, the swelling in my ankles and belly, and the never-ending ache beneath my chest bone had prepared me to zero in on every sensation.

And I'd gotten much faster at it after killing nineteen vampires, as long as pain didn't distract me.

I taste blood and smell the acrid burn of flesh.

Her body pressed into mine, bicep against my ear, poised to strike, and in a single breath, I unleashed the compulsion.

"Back away," I said, my voice so unlike my own as Loki's words tainted it. I controlled what I said, but channeled his power through the words. It'd become more muddled lately, with his voice in my mind trying to manipulate my words as he and Odin and Freya argued.

My mind was a crowded place, confusing more often than at peace, but the compulsion worked.

The vampire immediately released me and stepped back. I spun with the stake still in my fist. She was taller, leaner, more haunting in the gaunt hollows of her cheeks than my last kill, and she fell faster when I slammed the stake up into her ribcage. She dropped as I pulled it back, and her dead heart spewed blood toxic to her own body.

In seconds, she would be nothing but specks under my feet.

I turned to Sterak, who was still reeling from the pain of my blood, his lack of control over bloodlust leading to his downfall. He scrambled to his feet as if to fight me, but his attempt to back away really *was* pitiful. Slamming the bloodied weapon into his heart, I ended another undead life, tallying my kills to twenty-one since I'd become the huntress.

But as he dropped in front of me, withering to ash, my pounding heart didn't slow. "Long live the queen," he breathed. "For Silver."

The sound of her name on his lips—of the name I'd claimed for so long—hollowed me faster than his blood did to him. Another shudder rippled through my muscles, my bones.

When the truth came out that I'd stolen her identity, the vampires infiltrating the castle loved throwing her name in my face, even though I never wanted to take it as my own. None of my names had ever felt right. Lux, Silver, Huntress.

I didn't like any of these.

"And that, ladies and gentlemen, is my wife," a voice behind me drawled.

I groaned, because of all the names and titles I despised, being called Drak's wife was once the one I hated the most.

But I didn't exactly hate it anymore…

Relief washed over me when I saw Drak leaning against the wall, concern furrowing his brow. He had threatened me before, like the other vampires, but now I felt safe—he was the first and only person to see my struggles, warm my hands, and insist I rest.

And damn if I didn't need rest right now.

When I took a shaky step toward him, he bolted forward, catching me before exhaustion sent me face-first against the stone floor.

Chapter Eight

Drak

Blood trickled down the curve of Lux's neck, and as torturous as it was not to lick it up, I resisted. She needed bandages, not another vampire's mouth on her throat. Not that I should drink from her anyway. Her blood hurt like a bitch.

"Good girl," I said as she allowed me to scoop her into my arms. "Let me carry you."

"Don't patronize me," she breathed, but it was half-hearted. "You're not controlling me."

"No, I'm not. I'm helping you. And you didn't snap at me when I called you my wife. Maybe we'll pull off this marriage after all." A smirk danced on my lips.

Thick lashes fluttered as she lifted her heavy eyelids to stare at me. Her lips parted. "But it's a lie."

I knew this would come up. Lux hated lies.

"You know lying isn't my game," I said. "But we're in this together." Why did that sound so damn good? I'd never been *together* with anyone. Sitting on that throne alone was all I knew since the gods ripped the only family I had away from me. "I won't lie to you. This marriage will be a lot easier to play off if you'll admit what you thought of me when we…" Now wasn't the time to bring up the desire I knew we both felt, so I cleared my throat and shifted the conversation. "I can heal you." I stared at the bite on her neck.

She tore her eyes away, letting them stare behind me as I carried her down the winding hallway and back to the front of the castle. The dull grey couldn't be that interesting.

"We don't have that kind of relationship," she said, referring to the connection vampires required to heal a human. This connection had to be both sexual and…loving from the human's side…and she had let no one heal her since Kayn. Despite her claim, I knew she was needy for me, because hints of her thoughts flickered in my mind.

"Wanting Drak is a betrayal to Kayn."

"Fuck no, it's not," I said before I could stop myself.

A gasp escaped her as she flicked her eyes up to mine. Her face twisted into a frown, and whatever softness she had felt for me recently vanished in the wake of my blunt hatred for the Exile.

"That's not for you to speak on," she said.

"It's not, but I'm going to, anyway. Kayn used you—"

Her hand shot to my chest, putting slight pressure against me with the heel of her palm. "Stop. You're using me too." My bow furrowed. "You want to keep your throne, right? Then you've got to deal with Silver's army, and that means getting me to summon a god for you." I shook my head and opened my mouth, but she didn't let me speak. "How are you any different?"

"I didn't train you for my own gain."

"No, but this marriage and the summoning will help you get what you want."

I couldn't deny that, but I could show her he was using her in a way that I never would. "The difference is obvious, Lux. You just don't want to see it because you've been brought up to see me as an enemy of witches. The executioners were not my doing. They were part of a system I was carefully waiting to change."

"I know that."

"No, you don't see the difference. That fucking bastard is willing to sacrifice you. From the beginning, he only wanted to train you." She said nothing because she knew I was right. "He insisted you become the huntress."

"And I don't regret that."

"But he had no concern for your mind. Your free will." Her body stiffened, but I didn't let her resistance to the truth deter me. "He watched my mother's descent into madness when I thought he was just another vampire in our court. But he was worse. And now he knows exactly the risk he wanted you to take without informing you."

"Fuck."

Her curse came loud and clear to my thoughts.

"I would never lie to you," I said.

The soft line of her mouth hardened, and she craned her neck to glare up at me. I never should have brought up Kayn. A sharp hiss of air escaped her before she spoke. "If you want me safe, then why the Hel are traitors still finding their way into Mara's Keep? Isn't this place supposed to be fortified?"

"You forget, these traitors were once my council and courtiers. They know Mara's Keep as well as I do. Better than you. And the line between those who are still loyal to me and those who are now loyal to Silver is blurred, which means they've tricked my guards rather easily. I told you your sister was dangerous. You didn't listen." I drew her tighter against me, letting her feel the heat of my chest; she was as cold as she was spent. There'd better be fresh blankets in the healing room.

Maybe she wouldn't be so Hel-bent on destroying us if you hadn't ordered someone to sew her mouth shut.

"So I should have allowed her to compel me?" I laughed, but it was empty. "I would have died. You realize that, right? I have no doubt she would have been used to kill me. And you know what it means to do whatever it takes to survive."

"Fine, then tell me this. Will we be ready to leave for Yggdrasil if Silver doesn't show up after the wedding?" Her black eyes drilled into me, but it was the blood still trickling from her neck that concerned me the most.

I smiled, but it was hollow. "You know, I admire how aware you are of your body's limitations. It takes an intelligent and patient person to reach that point. But for a woman as aware as you, you're dangerously underestimating what the wasteland would do to you."

If the journey took us too long, she'd wither away like those forced to live in the wasteland. It was a miracle that the witches exiled there by the Blood Council had survived at all. Though most didn't for long. Their magic had strung them along, giving them rare chances to cultivate plants and bits of breathable air.

"To no fault of my own," she snapped, fiery with exhaustion. Or maybe it was because of her defense of Kayn. I'd hit a nerve whenever I suggested he was using her, and now she was like a wild animal in my arms, snapping at me as I helped her. "I've never been there."

"And you really should never go," I said as I pushed through one of the many unmarked doors that kept this castle a mystery to outsiders.

"This isn't the way to my bedchambers." She pushed against my chest again, trying to get out of my arms, but I pressed her more tightly against my body. The look of a wild animal exaggerated as she scowled at me. I wouldn't be surprised if *she* bit *me* at this point.

"The servants have bandages stored near the kitchens."

"And what do you mean, '*you should never go there*'?" She repeated my words with a bite in her voice. "Does that mean you're not preparing to go if Silver doesn't come here? Because we had an agreement—"

I laughed. "I made you a promise, Lux, and I'll keep it. I swore I'd never lie to you, so when I said I'd guide you through the wasteland, it was the truth. But first, we'll try my method of taking down your sister."

The door groaned as it swung inward. A small room with dark cabinets lined the walls. The heavy cabinet doors made the space look even tighter. A little table stood against the back wall, and someone had left a bottle open on top. Some sort of citrusy tincture filled the air.

I carried her to the back of the narrow room where two thin candles glowed dimly on a table, the only light in the room.

She twisted in my arms, eyes fixed on the black stains across the floor. They covered the cracked wooden table and the floor beneath it. The stone in here wasn't polished marble like the throne room or many of the bedchambers in Mara's Keep. Rather, it was rough and unfinished, porous enough to soak the blood that spilled there.

She was no stranger to blood, but she still reeled back, every limb in her body tensing.

"What is it?" I asked as I placed her on the table. "You're not usually afraid of blood."

She forced a grim smile. "It's nothing."

"It's not nothing." I breathed as I tore a clean linen cloth into strips. "You can't stop staring at the stains." I tilted my head to catch her gaze. "Lux, listen to me. I can't help if you don't tell me."

"I'm fine."

"It's the gods isn't it?" Vitriol curled around my tongue. "They're in your head again, messing with your mind. I told you not to give them control." I grabbed her arm, and when she ripped it away, she hissed at me like a cornered cat. Worry flashed across her eyes, and my voice softened. "It's not the gods this time. You really think you're betraying Kayn."

Her shoulder twitched in a lifeless shrug. "It's not that. I just—he helped me. So did Stasia, and now they're Silver's hostages because of me. You have no right to say anything about it."

"Fine," I frowned. "But it will be your blood staining the stone if you don't let me bandage you." She said nothing, so I got to work gathering supplies. Yanking a cabinet open, I pulled out a small bottle of brown-tinted cleansing solution and another handful of cloths ripped into strips. When I turned around, I tilted my head. "Lean against me so you don't fall off the table."

"I can sit here just fine."

"That's why you're falling into the cabinet?"

"I'm fine," she snapped as she slipped off the table and hobbled toward the door.

I shook my head, tendrils of deep brown hair escaping from the knot at the back of my head. "Have I told you that you're fucking impossible?"

"Have I told you that your desperation to control everyone is painfully obvious and..." Before she could reach for the support of the cabinet again, she swayed, tipping forward. I dipped at the knees and caught her in one arm. Though the skin around her eyes had turned a sickly grey, she stayed awake and aware as I stuffed the bottle and linens into my pocket, then used both hands to hoist her over my shoulder.

I spun around and walked to the table.

"Put m-me downnn." The words slurred from between her lips.

"No."

My fingers hooked around both of her hips, and I lifted her off me, placing her on the table like she was a doll whose frayed stitches I was about to fix. "You're going to sit here while I put you back together." Her body tipped forward again, losing control of herself and sinking fast toward the ground. I whipped my attention back to her, and hooked my arm around her waist. "Whoa!" Steadying her, I silently thanked the first witch for my vampire reflexes. “Like I said.” I chuckled. “You’re impossible.”

She scowled at me, but I only smirked, and her expression shifted from the fury of an angry animal to vague frustration. I took the tincture that was already left open on the table and spotted a strip of fabric with it. Rubbing it against the linen, I created a sticky white paste.

“So?” she drawled. “You never answered my question. If the marriage doesn’t lure Silver here, will we be ready to follow her into the wasteland?” My brow tightened as I soaked a new linen with the brown liquid and worked it over the holes in her neck. Despite her obvious exhaustion, she continued. “If I know my sister, she won’t wait another week. Not with these storms getting worse.”

“If Silver doesn’t show, then we’ll be leaving as soon as I have the masks and alchemical stones tested and the route is mapped. I’m almost finished.”

“Masks?”

“We can’t breathe in the wasteland for very long. The masks will filter the toxic air and allow us to move through the battlefields when we’re out of the tent. The breathing stones will clear the air inside our tent. They’re created by witches.” I cleared my throat, knowing this would trigger a memory of her mother banished to the wasteland. Something for which she blamed herself. Pain briefly twisted her lips, fading quickly as curiosity knitted her brow. “It’s how they survived.”

“So you stole a witch’s creation?”

“Took inspiration from. Actually. And in case you forgot, I’m the son of a witch.”

She nodded slowly, eyes narrowed. “How do these stones work?”

“When heated, the stone binds the toxins in the air and traps them in the rune.”

A strange laugh bubbled out of her. “My mother headed that creation.” I tilted my head as she continued. “I mean, I can't be sure, but she was working on a root that drew the wealth of the soil into one condensed spot for more successful crops. It was based on a vision from Thor."

I'd forgotten that Thor dealt not only in thunder, but also agriculture. "Why that bastard had done nothing to heal the wasteland, I'll never know," I mumbled. Except I had a pretty good guess—the gods did just enough to satisfy their own selfish means, often for their own amusement, and nothing more.

"The wasteland," she echoed thoughtfully, shifting the subject away from witches and gods. Her voice came out like a ghostly whisper.

"Yes," I grumbled. "You know, where thousands and thousands gutted each other and their blood ruined the entire land, making our most tenable soil the least tenable soil, leaving generations to come on the brink of starvation?"

She pushed out a breath. "You say that like it was a personal attack on you."

"It feels personal."

"And what if Silver shows up?" she shifted the conversation, probably to keep it from turning intimate.

"Then we follow the plan. I hold back her army while you take her down."

"Even though I'm the vampire huntress?"

"Yes. She cannot compel you. She is neither your sister nor your maker."

I didn't know whether the tears she blinked away came from my words or the pain of sterilizing the bite on her neck.

Carefully, I lifted the pasty linen and pressed it to either side of the wounds. I gently tugged at it to test that it would stay, and then slipped the crook of my arm beneath her knees.

"I can make it back to my room," she said. I backed off, but when she edged herself off the table, she stumbled, and it took everything within me not to catch her. She limped toward the door, but even that short walk left her breathless.

"You couldn't be any more impossible," I said as I blew out a breath. "Do you know that? You're going to have to let me pick you up when I carry you to our marital bed. Consummation while the court listens is a Vylheim tradition, and the king always carries his queen."

She turned, letting her limp body press against the frame of the door. Chewing at her bottom lip, she whispered. "I know. You can carry me then."

"But you won't let me help you now?"

Tears welled in her eyes, sharp and sudden and pricking my soulless heart. I bolted toward her, wanting to catch the tear before it slipped over the scar that was slashed across her smooth cheek. Fuck, she was beautiful—more so when she finally allowed herself to be raw and real like this.

She sucked in a breath. "It feels wrong."

"To accept help?"

"From you?" Her brow crinkled. "Yes."

I nodded. "Because of what I did to Silver."

"Because I have to kill you."

My blood stilled. That absolutely would not happen. I would be a god before she eradicated all vampires.

She dropped her gaze and blinked the tears away. "And yes, of course, I saw you as an enemy when you threatened me."

"I was desperate and stupid to threaten your life, but not wrong about the reason behind it. If you had married me, the gods wouldn't be in your head demanding you sacrifice your existence to destroy me."

"Then what would you have done against Silver's army without a huntress?"

"Become a god, and when I control Odin's Valkryies, I'd control Silver's powers."

"You're too fixated on your own plans," she said.

I lifted my chin. "You're right. Now, will you let me carry you?"

"Maybe," she sighed. Not exactly a hopeful sign.

"We're planning a fake marriage, but you forget that I still want you to be my actual wife." Even with her shoulder against the door frame, she swayed. Despite her earlier protests, I caught her, scooping her into the crook of my arm. "Besides, carrying you is more..." my voice faded for a moment.

Her head fell against my chest. "Gentlemanly?"

"Personal. No—" I shook my head. "That's not the right word." She hummed as her eyelids slid shut. *She is the blood; he is the rune.* The words from the sagas haunted me because I could have sworn I heard Lux's voice calling me Rune.

And it felt like I'd lived that moment before. It felt like home—familiar.

"Familiar," I said.

"What?" she murmured.

"That's the right word. This feels familiar."

Chapter Nine

Lux

The second time I walked down the aisle toward the vampire king, my face painted with wedding runes and my body draped in an emerald gown that hugged my hips, my nerves were quiet.

But the Gods were not.

Not only did another storm thrash outside the castle, but the roar of the Gods echoed inside my head too. When the walls I put up in my mind cracked, I heard Freya begging me to gut Drak. Loki giggled maniacally. Odin's voice commanded me to rip the stake from my thigh and bury it in my betrothed's chest.

You told me to get the vampires here by whatever means necessary. Even with the vial of pig's blood in my pocket—proof that I wasn't giving myself to a vampire and abandoning the Gods—Odin still clamored for my attention.

Loki laughed as Odin's voice grated against my skull. *"That was before you dreamed of fucking him."* At this, Loki's amusement became shrill and painful.

It was just a dream.

"It was what you wanted. This isn't worth it."

Too late. I was here, drifting down the aisle toward my future fake husband while hundreds of witnesses watched. Everyone in the court and the wedding guests from Mara and Skaldir focused on me, but I only looked at Drak.

His icy eyes were as sharp as ever, piercing me with a consuming stare. One of them devoid of color since a witch had stabbed him in that eye. No doubt the witch's attack scarred a vampire's eye in such a unique way, leaving his gaze two-toned. White in one and the color of spring fjords in the other.

Drak pulled a chain from beneath his tunic. At the end dangled a bronze ring with a blood-red ruby. Raising it slightly, he made sure I saw it before letting it fall against his sternum.

Sten's ring. Why was he even wearing the ring of the vampire he'd killed, all in the name of some warped mission to avenge me? Sten had tried to kill me, but I hadn't needed Drak's help to survive. When it came to Sten's disgusting comments—lies—about having his way with me, Drak cut off his head and kept the ring.

My eyes narrowed, and my lips parted. He nodded as if I understood whatever message he was trying to send.

And then for some reason, I did.

The ring was a reminder that he'd once promised to protect me. But was this protection from my sister and the vampires, or from the Gods?

He clasped his hands in front of him, never taking his eyes off me. Our shared gaze was like an invisible string, pulling me toward him despite the whispers in my head.

No one else existed as I took him in. His hair mirrored the twist of my braid, but he styled his on top of his head and then tied it into a knot at the back. The angled cut of his beard was as clean as he could get. Drak matched the warriors in the sagas rather than the vampires around him. He opted for a white tunic that fit the muscles of his chest, showing the black ink of jagged tattoos around his collar.

This moment only contained us—the king my family once bargained me away to, and the huntress designed to kill him.

"It is your duty to destroy him."

Odin's demands rang louder than the others, slicing through our moment like an axe. Why didn't the Gods understand that I could die if I ran headfirst at the vampires compelled by my sister? She knew my every weakness.

My slippered feet padded soundlessly across the stone, onward with my plan.

"Kill him."

"Kill."

Freya's voice intermingled with Odin's, and I couldn't discern if Loki spoke too. Their words were a jumbled jolt of pain through my temples. I blinked, trying to focus on Drak around the hammering throb behind my eyes.

My hand flexed, almost reaching for the stake at my thigh without my consent. The connection between my brain and my fingers meant my hands were the hands of the Gods in this realm.

Of course they were. From the moment I was born with the power to receive their visions, I had been their vessel.

But I couldn't kill Drak. Even when I had the chance, I simply couldn't. My reasoning was that he was the only person who had ever told me the truth. Was that enough to let a monster live?

"Turn away." Freya begged.

"Don't do this, huntress." Odin's voice was more oppressive.

A gleeful laugh preceded Loki's slithering tone. *"Stick your tongue in his mouth while you stick the stake through his heart!"*

These messages pulsed, sucking me from reality one second, then plunging me back into this world the next. The whiplash left me breathless, as if the Gods were forcing my head beneath the surface of icy water each time they spoke.

When I stepped within reach, Drak offered me his hand, palm turned up. I slipped my fingers into his hold and allowed him to guide me to stand in front of the one throne of Vylheim. Before these witnesses, and in front of the bronze throne, we faced each other as king and queen. Husband and wife.

My heart was finally quiet, and beating steadily, even as the voices of the divine raged in my head. I pulled my hand back, gingerly touching my temple, attempting to build the wall in my mind that blocked them out. Just for now.

Concern creased Drak's brow. He leaned closer, ignoring the council member who stepped up to face the throne and call for us to kneel toward Mara. Drak's scent of freshly fallen snow and the wood of a spruce tree set me at ease.

"Are you okay?" he asked. I nodded, but he grunted, a low rumble of doubt that made it clear he wasn't buying it. "Don't lie, Skald."

My heart skipped once as I blew out a slow breath. "I will be okay."

Drak's breath brushed over my ear. "We can make this real." I swallowed hard. "You'll never hear the Gods again."

I tilted my chin up, searching his eyes as a whisper slipped from my lips. "And let innocent people get drained by vampires?"

"Let me take care of it."

"You're not a God."

"Yet," he smirked, arrogant in his plan that'd only work if Odin didn't make me kill Drak first. "All you have to do is prick your finger."

I gritted my teeth. He'd better stick to the fucking plan. If he hadn't brought a vial of pig's blood, this entire idea would have been a trick.

But of course, Drak never lied to me. Knowing this, I breathed a little easier.

When we turned, hand-in-hand, and knelt before the

people of Mara—the only time a king and queen would kneel to their subjects—he slipped a tiny glass vial from his pocket and buried it in his fist.

The chosen witness, the eldest council member, presented the wax seal where "L" was imprinted over "D". The red circle fit in the palm of our hands.

When the witness turned, I slipped the vial from my pocket. Drak's throat rippled with a stilted swallow as his gaze flicked from the vial to my face. His mouth was a flat line, and his eyes dropped to the stone beneath us.

"He is my king," I repeated the vows the witness spoke over our heads.

Drak's gaze slid to me again, pinning me as he said his half of the vow. "She is my queen." While the witness invoked the people of Mara to honor the vows, Drak added a whispered vow, a devilish curve on his lips. "My wife."

He tipped the vial of blood into the seal and nodded toward my fist, where my vial lay hidden. I hesitated, glancing as the drop of blood spread through the ridges of the seal.

Drak brought his lips to my ear. "I'll never lie to you."

My heart skipped. This was what kept drawing me to him. It had to be. I was addicted to his constant truthfulness. That he'd always known I wasn't Silver—the woman I claimed to be—and yet he accepted me while ignoring the fucked-up lies I had to tell.

I met his gaze, holding it for a moment as I took all of him in. Drak was many things: a vampire and a king, but I'd always seen the fighter in him. To me, he was just like the men in the sagas because of his wild determination. This truth became obvious when I learned the Gods had twisted his mother's mind, and he sought to avenge her, fighting like the warriors of old once did. Men and women who set out to defend their families. Even if the result ended in a corrupted earth, their courage was admirable.

Finally, I tilted the vial so that the pig's blood smeared across my finger before it spilled into the seal.

It was done.

The witness's voice boomed above us, almost in time with another thunderous roar beyond the castle walls. "King Drakkar and Queen Lux, rise and embrace before your subjects."

Drak helped me to my feet with his palm lifting at my elbow and his other hand holding mine. Releasing my hand, he cupped the back of my neck.

His touch ignited my skin, sending a shiver down my spine. Though we weren't officially bound, the desire pooling in his feral eyes reached my core. I licked my lips, marking them with a heat and wetness like that which was building between my thighs.

"Kill him." Odin breathed.

Drak's face flickered. All desire vanished as rage replaced it. Of course, he'd heard Odin's voice in my mind. Whenever I ached for him, he caught glimpses of my thoughts.

But the mix of anger and worry wiped away as he brought my hand to his lips.

Silence blanketed the throne room. The hundreds of people witnessing our wedding barely breathed because they expected their king to wrap his arms around his queen and seal this marriage with a kiss.

The quiet materialized into something heavy the longer Drak abstained from finalizing this fake marriage. They were going to know it wasn't real, and if they didn't believe it, neither would Silver.

"Destroy him."

I squeezed my eyes shut for as long as it was appropriate, willing Odin to give me this moment with Drak—with my husband. The erratic thumping of my heartbeat slowed. Before Odin could reach into my mind again, I opened my eyes and focused on Drak's lips. *Kiss me.*

Drak pulled me into him, his mouth close enough to brush his lips over mine as he whispered. "What if I wanted it to be real?"

It wasn't a question I was meant to answer because when my lips parted, his mouth covered mine. His kiss was desperate and slow, cleaving my heart in two. I returned the kiss greedily as I sucked his bottom lip between my teeth. When he pulled back, I gnawed my lip, feeling hollow and colder in his absence.

Instead of the joy of a husband who'd just kissed his wife, he looked like a defeated king. As if he'd just lost his throne and surrendered it to the enemy, he clenched his jaw and blinked away the glazed look in his eyes. Empty disappointment wiped his face blank, except for the grim smile he pasted on for the people of Mara.

I slipped my hand into his and intertwined our fingers. *This feels familiar.* His words echoed in my memory. A strange ache bloomed in my chest that I couldn't identify. It wasn't longing, or simple sadness at the sight of defeat twisting his face.

This grief was raw and guttural, a pain I hadn't known since the executioners took my mother.

He lifted his chin to the aisle stretched out before us. "You first," he whispered. "I'll follow you."

That struck me square in the chest, as if he—the king who craved control—was relinquishing it, even for a second, to have me step out first. We stepped forward, hand-in-hand, husband and wife, and I let him guide me to the table of quail eggs, oiled bread, and dark wines. I didn't take my eyes off the goblet while he filled it with deep red wine. The liquid rippled with another tremor from the Gods's storm, threatening to spill and stain the stone between our feet.

I avoided Drak even when he lifted the goblet to loop our arms and drink from the cups. The grief intensified, knotting my insides every time I looked at him.

Where had this feeling come from? What the Hel was I even grieving? We'd succeeded. Everybody believed this was a legitimate marriage.

But what if I wanted it to be real, too? If I did, then I was exactly the stupid, selfish girl my father had always said I was.

The ground shuddered beneath us again, and I knew this was the Gods agreeing.

Chapter Ten
Drak

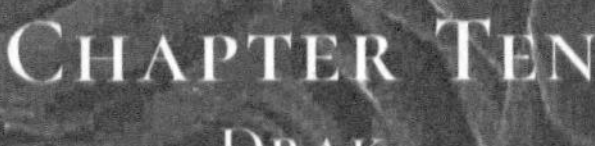

Fucking pig's blood. It was *my* ridiculous idea to give Lux what she wanted, and I'd made it possible with vials of fucking pig's blood.

I'd always longed to give someone what they wanted, a chance I never had with my mother. And now that I had, where the fuck was the surge of victory? And why wasn't I basking in the thought of our coming consummation?

Because none of it was real.

And because my chest *still* ached where the phantom axe had landed.

After slipping her arm from mine, she set the goblet down and lifted her face toward me, holding my gaze with unspoken intensity. This was the moment I was supposed to take her hand and lead her to dance in the middle of the throne room while the witnesses sipped their fill of wine. But I couldn't bear to put my hands on her unless I knew for certain she wanted it too.

Near the throne, a servant plucked the strings of an instrument. The haunting sound caught in the peaked ceiling, echoing throughout the room and drawing every eye toward the newlywed couple.

Lux waited patiently, looking up at me with wide eyes, the same way she'd looked at me in the library when she wanted me to read the saga of the first witch.

"We did it. They think we're bonded," she said, trying to smile, but it didn't reach her eyes. "It's almost hard to believe that was pig's blood in the rune."

Rune? *Shit.* She'd said it again.

Rune, for some fucked-up reason, set off these flashes where the world vanished, and just like before, a memory, a dream, or whatever the hell this was, hit me full force.

Tears of blood suddenly streamed down Lux's face. The white scar from Sten's fang was gone, changing how she looked and confirming that this couldn't be real. When her lips parted, her mouth formed around a familiar name. *Rune! Come back to me.* Her begging carved a hole in my chest, and the pain left my lungs breathless and my vision dimming. Her jaw seemed to unhinge as a shrill sob erupted from her chest.

"Lux," I breathed, grabbing her shoulders to ground myself and pull myself back to reality. But she was just staring at me, her face already normal again other than the aghast expression drawing her cheeks hollow and her mouth in an "O" shape.

The wine must have been too strong, and I hadn't rested at all, too curiously consumed by the pieces of the saga I'd never read before. I hadn't fed on anyone in days either. People loyal to my throne still offered me their blood, rotating so that nobody grew weak or sick from the loss, but I hadn't drunk enough of it. Not that I had any clue what that Hel that had to do with the word Rune.

I rubbed at the pain in my heart, and thrust out a hand. Faking this marriage was my idea. I had to keep playing along even if it felt wrong—or *I* felt wrong thanks to my lack of sustenance and rest.

Lux slipped her hand into mine and allowed me to guide her away from the feast sprawled along the table.

"Are you okay?" she asked when we were away from the crowd. I nodded as the music beckoned our bodies to move in tandem.

Our dance began, and while our limbs followed the rhythm, tension hung in the air between us. Lux was worried about me. I wanted to smirk at that, but after losing control of myself; I didn't dare tempt fate with arrogance.

"Why did you give me that strange look?" she asked.

Shaking off the drunkenness, I pressed my palm to her lower back and drew her into me. "Nothing," I said. But then I caught myself. I swallowed, my tongue feeling like sandpaper with the lie clawing and scratching at my throat. "That's not true." Her brows peaked as I swept her along the stone floor with me. Though she didn't grow up in Mara's court, she followed the dance easily enough with smooth steps and a keen awareness of exactly how to move every part of her body. Fuck if that didn't make my cock twitch. I ground my teeth together, willing myself to settle down and finish my damn sentence. "It's been too long since I fed. I got a little dizzy and thought I saw something."

At the song's peak, I glided my hand up her spine and tipped her to the side; her back arching beneath me. My body was bent, hovering over her in a dance that mimicked what we'd do together as soon as the last of the wine was gone. Once they consumed the last drop, tradition dictated that the royal couple consummate the marriage with the council close enough to listen to every breath and groan as proof.

Her eyes narrowed. "What did you see?"

I lifted her upright again and spun her outward, pulling her back flush against my chest as we swayed. "It's not like your visions," I explained. "There was nothing of the Gods in this. Trust me." Though running my palm up her stomach felt divine.

"What did you see?" she insisted.

"You, crying blood and calling me by another name."

She froze. "And you're saying that's nothing?"

"No, I'm saying it's not from Odin or Freya or Loki."

"Of course not. You're a vampire. Is this some sort of undead ability?"

The saga of the first witch came to mind. Myrah created vampires, and her abilities created me through Silver. Could this be related? *She is the blood; he is the rune.* My skin was covered in runes and tattoos I had chosen, but right where the back of Lux's head pressed against my sternum sat the rune of Yggdrasil, etched into my chest since I became a vampire. Was this the rune the saga mentioned? And what about the mention of blood? I saw it come from Lux's eyes, not Myrah's.

I shook my head. There was no point in trying to rationalize a drunken misunderstanding or something from a stressed mind.

"I don't know," I answered honestly.

She twisted, craning her neck just enough to bring her eyes to meet mine. "Maybe it's just you."

"What do you mean?"

"I'm well-versed in all kinds of vampires now. As far as I know, this isn't part of existing as an undead. So," she held my gaze. "I think it's just you. Maybe it was a daydream. Maybe you're hoping for that in the future."

"Hoping to see you cry? Never. And this isn't a prophecy. It's more of…" I drew her hand up to my lips and kissed the soft skin on the back of her knuckles. We hardly moved as the music slowed. "It felt more like something that'd already happened rather than a coming moment. It happened when I was reminded of a name from the sagas."

"Wouldn't that be crazy?" She let out a little laugh.

"Hmm?"

"If I see the future and you see the past."

My chest tightened with the ache of a moment long ago. Because that was exactly what the experience felt like: a memory.

Drawing my hand over the front of her dress, I stopped at her collarbone, not trusting myself to touch the curve of her neck. The song ended, but I didn't want to release her just yet. Even if this—our vows, our dance, all of it—was only a performance, my body didn't believe it.

Everyone seemed to buy into the facade, especially my fucking cock.

Though every curve of her body was flush against me, her ass pressing into my hardness, it was her words that made me stiffen. She didn't hesitate to believe I wasn't like the other vampires. She knew something more caused the episode. That *I* was more.

I almost told her I loved her in that instant, but she would have seen it as part of the performance, meant to validate our marriage. But damn if it didn't feel true when she looked at me like that.

I held her tightly, dropping my lips to her bare shoulder where I'd craved to kiss her this morning in the healing room. My mouth brushed over her warm skin. The hint of a moan escaped with her exhale, and her thoughts came to me unbidden now.

Like the warrior I'd always wished I could marry. But riding him won't just be a dream anymore.

A smile carved across my face. "You've dreamed of us together?"

"Damn," she breathed. "Every time you do that, it startles me." Ignoring her own words, she leaned closer, and we both forgot the hundreds of eyes on us. We were upright, but she may as well have been writhing on top of me.

"Tell me what else happened in these dreams," I beckoned. The air simmered between us, thick and coating our skin with the sheen of heat. It left us both breathless as I ran my finger along her jaw and tipped her mouth toward mine.

The sharp crash of shattering glass snapped us out of our shared imagination. A chorus of cheers rang out through the throne room. Guests had picked the wedding feast clean.

Lux stepped away from me, and I followed her line of sight to the shards of dark glass spread across the floor by the table. Eggshells, quail bones, and the remains of the smoked pigs from which I'd stolen blood for our vials, were all that remained. A weathered, grey-haired woman smashed the empty bottle at her feet, prompting murmurs and whistles alongside those cheering for tradition.

The last drop of wine had been consumed.

Chapter Eleven

Drak

How quickly my desires changed. All Lux had to do was look at me and tell me she saw *me*. That maybe these insane episodes weren't fucked up, but a contrast to her visions of the future. She didn't look at my fangs, and she didn't care for the crown that adorned my skull. For the first time, she was concerned about me—the cruel and twisted vampire king.

As promised, she didn't put up a fight when I stooped and scooped her into the crook of my arms. The crowd spread like water around a stone, and she even lifted her chin to press a gentle kiss to my lips

A hush fell as two servants opened the double doors. We passed through; the footsteps of the remaining council members trailing behind us. The rest of the guests, the people of Mara and the few who had traveled from Skaldir, remained in the throne room. They'd finish the celebration, cheering and dancing and waiting for the next course of food brought out by my servants while Lux and I feasted on one another.

Her thoughts echoed loudly, though not in the way I had hoped. She was already thinking ahead to our marriage bed.

This isn't a betrayal to Kayn. Forgetting about him was already a

betrayal. Wasn't it? Drak is supposed to be my husband. But I wanted him before that.

Maybe this *was* what I'd hoped for. I couldn't help the wicked smirk that curled across my face. Lux wanted me. Maybe I wasn't alone. Maybe she felt this same string tethered between us, pulling us closer in thought and heat and fate.

Carrying her to the largest bedchamber, I shoved through the door and set her on the bed. Jade fabric draped around her legs, hiding her feet but doing little to conceal the curve of her enticing hips as her thighs parted. I craved to spread them further apart, and bury my face between her thick legs.

First, I had to bid the council farewell as they drew the doors closed, though they would linger nearby, ready to witness the sounds of our consummation.

When the door's hinges groaned and then sealed shut, I ground my teeth together. The heavy oak wasn't enough to afford us the privacy I wanted. This was a moment I'd obsessed over ever since sleeping beside her in the tent on the way back to Mara's Keep from Skaldir. She'd crushed her ass against me then, seeking the warmth of my recently fed body, and I hadn't been able to forget how easily the shape of her curves fit against me.

I spun back around, mouth twisted in an apologetic frown. Her eyes flicked from the door to me.

"It's a fucked-up tradition," I said, hoping she understood I didn't want this to just be a performance.

When she lifted one shoulder, the thin dress sleeve slipped down to her elbow. The sleeves were merely straps, with the strings and cage of the corset keeping the gown in place at her breasts and stomach.

My gaze darted to her exposed skin. The sheen of sweat glistened along her neck from the dance—and from the flame burning between us. Candles flickered a yellow and orange glow from where they were spread in bronze candle plates across the floor. Light framed the bed, sending shadows into an enchanting dance across the ceiling.

Lux's eyelashes fluttered to the spot where I'd fixated. Slipping off the bed, the skirt unfurled around her feet. Slowly, she dragged the other sleeve off her shoulder and then reached for the ribbon binding the corset between her breasts. Tugging it, the bow unraveled and the cage of the corset loosened, but not enough.

I took a step closer. "Are you ready?"

She nodded, pulling another two lines of ribbon loose. The binding spread, exposing more of her breasts. With every tug, my cock grew harder, as if her fingers were closing around it instead of the ribbon. Fuck, I needed her. I needed to rip that damn corset off her and throw her onto the bed.

Striding closer, I tipped my forehead to hers. "Are you sure? Because once this gown is off you, I don't think I can hold back."

Again, she only nodded, but her thoughts revealed what she kept close to her chest. "*Fuck me, Drak. Carve out the darkest parts of me and use them to make me shake.*" All of her worry had sloughed away, and not even the gods seemed to reach her now.

"You know I can hear you?" I breathed.

Her pink lips tipped up. "I know."

Without another word, she unraveled the rest of the ribbon and let the binding fall on the floor at her heels. Green fabric rippled to her feet like a puddle reflecting the shades of the trees above it.

My cock strained against my trousers. I traced her collarbone up to her throat, my fingers wrapping around her neck as I drew her closer.

"Let's give them a show," she said. My gut knotted, unsure of how to feel about a performance, about all of this being a lie. But it was our lie, crafted together. "Fuck me, Drak." She spoke it aloud, and something inside me shattered—every restraint gone.

Slamming my mouth against hers, she released a delicious moan. Her lips parted, inviting my tongue inside. I kissed her ravenously. First her mouth, then her jaw, her throat, the soft rise and fall over her collarbone. Her breasts, fuck her breasts tasted so good.

I sucked a tight nipple between my lips, and she gasped. Smiling against her pink skin, I did it again and again, swirling the tip of my tongue around the bud.

"You're teasing me," she said between breaths.

"Not fast enough for you?"

"I need you inside me."

My hands followed the shape of her waist, her hips, her ass. Palming the back of her soft thighs, I lifted her and dropped her onto the bed.

She lay spread before me, a fucking feast of bare skin and a shimmering, slick center. Her chest swelled and fell as she gulped the heady air between us.

I grabbed the back of my tunic and fisted the linen, yanking the entire piece of clothing over my head in one pull before unhooking the belt at my waist. Dropping to my knees, I ran my tongue over the drips on her thigh. Her panting beckoned me closer and closer to her core. The tip of my tongue ignited a fire in her as it licked up and along her wet lips. Her entire body twisted with the arch of her spine.

I let my trousers fall to where her wedding gown lay and climbed above her.

"Please," she started. "Drak—"

I crushed her mouth with mine, stopping her begging before it made me come all over her stomach. Gently biting her lip, I drew her attention away from the tightness as I thrust my cock into her. Slowly at first, but then without control.

She cried out in shock that quickly flipped to pleasure as

she gripped me. The shape of her body, her fingernails digging into my back, her core clenching around me—everything about her was perfect, made for me.

I'd never buried my cock inside her before now, but none of this felt new. Somehow, I knew the exact speed that'd make her whimper. I knew what she wanted even without listening to her thoughts, but I still did anyway.

More, give me more. Her mind pleaded for me to thrust harder until she came undone all over me. I moaned, desperate for my undoing, and yet not wanting this to end.

"Drak," she whispered. "Rune."

I froze and searched her watery eyes. "What did you say?" For some reason, I didn't lose myself again. Touching Lux grounded me. Her skin on mine. It seemed nothing could rip me from this present moment, not even this strange magic whenever she said that word.

"I don't know." She shook her head. She looked dazed and helpless with pleasure. "Just don't stop."

"It feels like I've waited a hundred years for this..." she thought.

I brought my lips to her ear, biting the lobe, careful not to let my fangs dig into her skin too deeply. "Me too." I pulled my head back in time to see her eyes pop open. A million questions floated in them. "I've waited a hundred years for you."

Tears welled in her eyes, and I kissed her, feeling them slip down her cheeks and run over our mouths. Again, love lingered on my tongue, something I barely understood since this was all so new between us, and this wasn't an actual marriage. I simply got caught up in the moment.

Sudden ecstasy forced pleading moans out of me as I soaked in every ripple of pleasure. I pressed my forehead to hers.

"It sure as fuck doesn't feel fake," I whispered.

She looked up at me, eyes full but glazed with the same

delight coating every inch of my body. "It feels more like its…" I hinged on her next word, not breathing. "Familiar."

Fuck.

She felt it too.

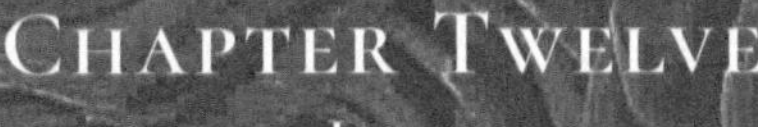

Chapter Twelve

Lux

Hours after we had enjoyed one another, I woke to soft covers draped around me. It was a stark contrast to the hard muscles of Drak's chest and the rigid length pressing against my ass. His face rested in my loose hair, fanning out around me like a coiled crown.

The force with which he'd made me come left my legs weak, even now, hours later, as I stretched them out from my curled position. We'd both collapsed after the ecstasy. My eyelids felt especially heavy after the pressure of the wedding day—the performance we'd put on for a crowd of commoners and the royal court. For Silver's sake.

But in Drak's arms, I'd nearly forgotten about her, and that this wasn't real. Despite the ring on my finger, we weren't actually married. It was just a symbol, a prop in the act with which we entertained our audience.

I carefully rolled onto my back and twisted my head to face Drak. His eyes were sealed shut, and his hair was wild, but a tender peace softened his hard features, and he breathed steadily. Even in sleep, he maintained this human habit despite being a vampire king who'd killed humans and vampires alike.

Though that wasn't unlike the warriors I'd dreamed of my whole life.

Perhaps it was the sagas that made me want to call him Rune, after reading so many runes among their pages. It felt as though I had spent a hundred years waiting for him. Nothing else explained this feeling. Those warriors existed centuries ago, even if I'd only been fantasizing about them for twenty-seven years.

I've waited a hundred years for you. The memory of his words prickled along my skin like breath. The words that'd sparked tears. Even now, the backs of my eyes burned. Why had he said that?

I'd been so lost in the pleasure of his body conforming to my desperate needs I failed to consider it. Unlike sex with Bjorn and Kayn, Drak hit every aching spot. He'd kissed me right when I needed it, and he'd met my gaze the second I wanted connection. It must have been because he was listening to my thoughts.

But couldn't Kayn have done the same? Or had I never truly *wanted* him?

None of that explained why I felt like I'd had sex with Drak before—many times. It had to be the dreams.

I brushed the back of my finger along his cheekbone, and for some reason, it felt as much a habit as Drak's breathing. My hand fell to his bare chest so I could trace the rune carved beneath his flesh in the shape of Yggdrasil. For him, this mark was a cruel reminder of the gods he hated, but as I traced its inky lines, I admired every curve. The other tattoos around the mark formed overlapping runes, something I knew he'd had inked into his skin on purpose.

Runes that spelled his vengeance.

He'd used the ancient language inspired by the Gods to write his revenge so that he'd never forget that it was Odin and Freya and Loki who destroyed his mother and ripped away the only family he'd ever known. But it wasn't the Gods' fault that vampires tainted this realm. That was on the first witch.

His chest twitched from the feathery touch of my index finger. I drew back, observing his restless state as he sleepily reached for me. Even in his barely conscious state, he held me close.

"Drak," I whispered. His only response was a slow sigh as sleep swallowed him again. I chewed my lip, tracing the outline of his face. "It didn't feel fake to me either."

Even now, with his body molded to mine and his arms wrapped around me, we lay as if we had slept side by side for years. But we hadn't been like this since our first journey to Mara's Keep, and back then, I barely knew him. There simply wasn't enough time between us to explain this all-encompassing familiarity.

And why had he seen me crying blood?

Odin himself had shed tears of blood in some of the poetic sagas. I didn't understand the connection, but Drak's vision of me resembled poems written by the ancients. Symbolic and strange and convoluted.

The only way to understand them—even if it was only slightly—was to read them over and over.

I ran my thumb along the arm Drak had draped over my stomach. Carefully, I lifted his wrist and slipped out from beneath him. His mouth flickered into a frown, but he did not continue to stir.

The cold stone floor sent shivers racing through me. I dressed quickly, then reached for something warmer to layer over my outfit: a wolf-skin cloak, left here by Drak. Wrapping myself in its soft warmth, I padded to the door and crept into the hallway. This new bedchamber, chosen by Drak for us to inhabit together, was only a few paces from the library. Perhaps because I spent so much time among the books and scrolls and runestones, he wanted it close.

I pushed through the library's heavy door. A low, rolling

groan greeted me as I slipped into the room I loved. Everything was exactly where I had left it—except for the journal recounting the story of the first witch. It lay page-down; the papers spread, and the spine stretched wide.

I knelt on the feathery rug and slid my fingers beneath the brittle pages. Flipping it over, I slowly smoothed the creases in the paper as I scanned the runes.

The words were nothing new. I'd read this already, so I turned the pages until I did not immediately recognize the runes.

"Last battle," I read aloud. The soft echo of my voice surrounded me, and I suddenly felt hollow, alone, as if Drak should be here listening.

I ran my finger over the runes and followed the story I'd been tracing over his bare skin only minutes before. "The Battle of Sundered Sky. Three hundred and sixty-six men and women die at Freya's feet. Blood bleeds from the stone they wanted to claim as their own." I frowned. I respected the gods, worshiped them, and even admired the battles our ancestors had fought to claim land and protect their families. Those struggles had always been about survival. This one was different. Why kill one another over the ownership of a mere statue?

I sucked in a breath as I pored over Brynhild's words. "Freya, Goddess of Fertility, will bring no children to the wombs of either side." I grimaced. "Fuck." Maybe I'd judged too soon. The survival of their people was also at stake, but like Myrah, nobody else received what they asked the Gods for. "Weeping blood—" Ice filled my veins. Weeping blood, just as Drak had seen on my face in his strange visions. I couldn't read the rest of it fast enough.

Weeping blood, Freya spills her tears over the fallen whom she marks for after life in Folkvangr. Winged women descend, drawing souls from the dead to feast with Odin. Bloodied, Myrah crawls over bodies to her lover.

But she cannot beat the speed of the Valkyries; their wings carrying them with a force unmatched.

They touch him and choose him for Valhalla.

Freya's blood marks her.

They split apart like the sky. Myrah's broken state causes her to curse herself and future generations with her next choice.

Drak must have read this. His strange daydream had mixed with the memory of this saga and confused him. He didn't see me crying blood. It was Freya.

I ran my finger along my lip as my eyes flew across the page. I knew the next part, even if I hadn't read this interpretation of the history. Myrah claimed another dying warrior, Kayn, and using the power stolen from a Valkyrie, she transformed him from near death into an undead. His soul shattered, leaving a creature of eternal existence she could drain from—her path to Valhalla, to her lover.

"But she never made it," I said to nobody. My heart skipped. "All that for nothing. All of this pain and terror was thrust upon us because she wanted to be with her lover."

If anybody was selfish, it was Myrah. How could Drak not see that Silver was the same?

I continued reading, hoping to understand whatever had made him so confident that Silver was nothing like Myrah.

Her love is transcendent. Her love reaches beyond realms. It stirs in Folkvangr, Midgard, Valhalla, and beyond because he first loved her. He reaches for her, soul to soul, and he relinquishes the reward of his afterlife.

"No," I breathed. "No way he chose to leave Valhalla." All my life, I had seen Valhalla as the ultimate reward. To feast with Odin was the greatest honor of all, one no faithful warrior would willingly surrender.

Except Myrah's lover did.

As she cannot come to him, he seeks to return to her.

"Rebirth," I said, before continuing to read aloud. "But the Valkyries have chosen him. Only a sacrifice can bring him forth—"

"And fill his veins with life again," another voice said. My pulse caught in my throat, and the book slipped from my fingers. It fell onto the rug with a thud as I spun around. Blinking, my brain tried to catch up with the sight before me. I almost didn't recognize the vampire who slunk toward me. One foot in front of the other, the cloaked figure stepped closer. He pulled back the hood, revealing green eyes and a clean-shaven jaw. "His heart with the rune of her name," he continued. "The chamber from which her blood flows."

"Kayn," I said, breathless. I stood frozen to the spot, my feet stuck to the rug, and my limbs too heavy to move. Even if I'd wanted to, I couldn't run to him. When Silver took him, I'd thought that once we were reunited, I'd run to him and throw my arms around his neck, but shock—or maybe it was guilt—froze me.

Kayn was so good, so pure. But it was Drak who made me feel like I was coming home.

Why didn't the sight of Kayn feel the same? He wanted to honor Odin and Freya, and he knew the words of the saga. I should have loved everything about him.

"Lux." He stepped up to me and cupped my arms. As he held me, his gaze searched mine, a faint furrow forming between his eyebrows.

"You escaped Silver," I said. Before I could look to see if my mother or Stasia was with him, his grip on me tightened.

Sadness swam in his eyes, and when he opened his mouth, I thought he'd say my mother and Stasia had died. "How could you?" he whispered.

I recoiled. "What?"

He cursed under his breath. "You gave up your powers."

"Kayn—"

Shaking his head, he shook me too. It was slight, not forceful, but enough to cause me to clamp my jaw. "Humans have no chance against the vampires now. You haven't seen Silver's army."

"You don't understand—"

"Neither do you." A vein bulged at his temple. Red lines snaked across the whites of his eyes, and his mouth held a grim smile.

"What's wrong with you?" I asked.

"You're about to see just how bad it is, Lux."

"What do you mean?"

"I didn't escape, I'm here with Silver. She compelled me to track you down."

A ripple of fear, victory, and then raw nerves shifted through me. This was the plan. We had lured Silver here, and she walked straight into our trap, convinced I was powerless.

"Where are my mother and Stasia?"

He shook his head. "It doesn't even matter now—"

"Yes, it does!"

"You'll all be dead soon." His voice cracked, and he wouldn't look at me now.

"Kayn," I dropped my voice as quiet as it could go. "It's a ruse." His brow furrowed until something resembling understanding dawned in his eyes. "It's okay—"

"Stop," he whispered as he moved to the side and revealed my sister behind him.

Silver's arms were folded across her chest, and a smirk played at her scarred lips. Tiny holes, from when Drak had sewn her mouth shut, pierced all around her mouth. She was a mirror of me in so many ways.

This hairstyle was new, though. She'd shaved one side and braided the rest, pulling it to the opposite side of her head in a heavy bun behind her ear.

"Hello," she said, her voice sharp as broken glass. It only heightened the unsettling tilt of her head and the way she stared at me through narrowed eyes. She dropped her arms and stepped into the room, hips swaying and feet arched to near tiptoe. The way she walked reminded me of when we were mere children, darting from side-to-side as we mimicked drunken adults at our father's celebratory feasts. Before Skaldir had nearly starved, and before she'd laid siege to it.

While she circled my library, hawk-eyed and predatory, I slipped my hand into my cloak pocket and closed my fingers around the cold metal of my pendant. She wasn't a vampire, but it was sharp enough to fight her off until I could pin her down and drag her to the dungeon.

I winced.

"Do you remember," she began, "when we were just girls and Father said I would marry a Vyl, likely from Torsholt or Stormdal, while you would always live with our mother?" With a little laugh, she stopped in front of me and finally met my gaze. "I should have known that bastard was wrong. You got married, and I'm the one living with our mother."

I gritted my teeth. "Where is she? Please tell me she's okay—"

"You're pathetic," she said coolly. "You always were. That's why Father let me sit in the Vyl's chair and not you."

"He forbade it only because he was afraid that standing before the crowd would reveal what I truly was."

She laughed. "If that comforts you, you can continue to spin that story for yourself. It's not a lie like most of the words you've spoken in your life." I squeezed my eyes shut as the harsh truth of her words hung between us. "But you know it's not the whole truth. Father prepared me to be a leader. He taught me the tough choices you have to make when you want to maintain that role."

"Silver, listen to me—"

"Shut up, witch." The way she spat the word, as if it was poison in her mouth, was as sudden and startling as a slap to the cheek. My lips parted, and I only stared at her. "I will be the leader he raised me to be."

He didn't even raise you. But of course I couldn't say that because it was my fault they took her. Cruel kings raised her, the dungeons beneath Mara's Keep raised her, and damp, bitter hatred raised her.

But maybe the answers to understanding her weren't in the sagas or her powers. Maybe they were in whatever she remembered from home. From Skaldir.

I dared to speak again. "Do you have any love left for your home?"

"The one throne of Vylheim is my home, Lux. And since you sat on it, claiming this destiny before I could—" her smile spread wider, but it was hollow, haunting even. "You're dead to me." Metal glinted from her fist, but she did not raise her arm.

"You can't take Mara like you did Skaldir," I said.

"Oh, I know. Don't you remember? I grew up in Mara. I don't need my army to destroy the people here. All I need is for the people of Vylheim to witness you relinquishing the throne to me. They're people of tradition."

That depended on how far back you went. Now that it wasn't only vampires ruling Vylheim, Gods and witches and the old beliefs were slowly filtering back into the language of the people, but they'd been stripped of our history for so long. Undead monsters seeking their next human meal implemented half of the traditions, and the sagas hid the other half.

But she wasn't wrong. People clung to these traditions because they were all they knew after our records were ripped away.

"And what would you do as queen?" I asked.

Her scarred lips stretched. "The same thing our father did as Vyl." My brow furrowed. "I will do whatever it takes not to let my loyal subjects starve." Her voice fell to a hush.

"Don't you think the vampires were already trying not to starve? That was the entire point of the bloodshed law."

"And I'll continue it," she said. "Only better. I'll expand. And where we can't expand, I'll have their food source breed more for them."

My stomach knotted at the sick world she described, her twisted views reducing humans to cattle bred to feed the bloodlust of godless monsters. All so she could stay on the throne. All so she could be like our father—no, *more powerful* than him.

"And the last thing you'll see will be me on your throne before Kayn cuts off your head. I suppose if his soul wasn't completely lost before, it will be after that." A single, haunting laugh escaped her. Kayn wanted nothing more than to reclaim the soul he had before Myrah turned him into a vampire, and Silver clearly knew it and used it to torment him.

Pity pinched at the center of my chest. Despite how far his desperation for a soul had pushed him in the past, he didn't deserve to be tortured like this. Everything he did now, he did for the honor of the gods, hoping that one day they might grant him a new soul, though I did not know if that was even possible.

He froze as I snapped my attention to him, but I wasn't the one rooting him with compulsion. Silver's ability to compel vampires had grown so strong she barely needed to look at him to control him. Like a child plays with a doll. Grief punched through me when a flicker of something familiar flashed in my sister's eyes. Her eyes held the same playful glint from when we played dolls as children. Then, in a blink, it was gone, replaced by pure, murderous intent.

"Don't do this," I pleaded. "I know you weren't always like this. Do you remember anything from our childhood? We shared a bed and cuddled every night to keep warm." A well of emotion cut me off, but Silver only blinked at me blankly. "Please, we loved each other once. You wouldn't kill your sister."

Finally, a muscle in her stone-cold face moved. "No, Lux, *you* wouldn't kill your sister. Like our father, I'll do whatever it takes to claim my place." Too many emotions warred within me, grief and fear the most obvious, but I suppressed them as I started to pull the pendant from my pocket. Silver only sighed, as if annoyed by the mild inconvenience of having to murder her twin. "I should have known you'd give up everything for Drak," she said. "I just didn't think it would be this fast."

Every part of me went rigid. "What do you mean?"

She laughed. "You do know he doesn't have his soul anymore, right? The pieces of it are strewn across this realm. He's not like the men in the sagas anymore. Not like Rune in Myrah's story."

"Rune?" I repeated the word as if it took my breath away.

"Not since I made him a vampire," Silver continued.

"Fuck." A deep voice drew our attention to the door. Drak filled the doorway, his broad shoulders pressing against the narrow frame. His face, tight and pale, carried the same weight. His gaze pinned Silver for a tense moment before his eyes slid to me. "You said that name again…"

What the Hel was he talking about? Why wasn't he moving to help me? A million questions buzzed in my tired brain. Silver must have been doing this to him. Holding him back with a compulsion that spread to more than one vampire.

Despite holding power over him, she focused her attention on me. It's time to bow before the new queen."

I didn't even look at my sister. My eyes stayed on Drak as he clutched his chest, sagging forward, breathless, his hands clawing at the space between shoulder blade and heart.

"Stop compelling him!" I begged.

Silver's laugh was shrill, cutting through my ears like blades clashing with blades. "I'm not. Whatever is happening here is simply making my life easier. Now I don't have to compel Kayn to fight him while I haul you to your beheading." She lifted her chin to Kayn. "Bring her to me."

"Kayn, listen to me," I said. "Fight Silver's control." But

he was already lost to my sister's compulsion, and another groan snapped my attention back to my husband. "Drak, please! You're having another episode. Come back to me."

What the Hel was making him so dizzy and faint like this? The last time had been at our wedding, and the dazed look in his eyes told me this was no different.

I'd wanted to blame Silver, but this wasn't her fault.

As Drak sank to his knees, palming his eyes and muttering incoherently, Kayn seized me, rough hands wrenching my arms behind my back. Now was the time to bend him to my will and turn him against my sister. Together, we could drag her to the dungeons and deal with whatever illness plagued Drak.

But I couldn't stop looking at the king on his knees. I couldn't think clearly enough to speak my compulsion over Kayn before he shoved me past Drak and threw me into Silver's rough grasp.

She nodded at Kayn. "Now go to the prisoners. If I'm not out there with my sister in twenty minutes, kill them." A smile contorted her face. "Show her the blood of her loved ones."

My skin iced over. *No, no, no.* How could she kill our mother? And Stasia…

"Kayn, don't do this. Please." But it was no use. Silver's strength in compulsion far outweighed mine. He didn't so much as glance at me before he disappeared into the hall.

Drak's groan ripped my attention back to him. I should have been focusing on capturing Silver and taking control of the situation, but the agony on his face struck me as if it were my own.

"Drak," I cried, as his eyes rolled back to reveal only white, and I shoved Silver off of me, dropping to my knees beside him.

He was the distraction I'd feared.

Chapter Thirteen

Drak

Lux's voice burst through the pain, but it was that one single word that left my chest tight.

Rune.

He's not like the men in the sagas anymore.

Phantom pain radiated through my ribcage as her words settled in my mind: I was not like them.

I was never a warrior, but I swore I felt the axe cut my flesh. A thick blade seemed to crunch the bones at the base of my neck and those that caged my heart. A heart that no longer beat but filled with black blood, ready to push out and poison my skin until I became nothing but ash.

I was the vampire Silver created.

Before that, I was just a young man in the shadows of Mara's Keep. So why did I remember an injury I'd never suffered?

"Rune!" Lux screamed, but she sounded so far away.

I peeled my eyes open to a sea of bodies. The tendrils of her auburn hair were wet with blood and sweat. Clawed hands reached out for me, her fingernails thick and black with tainted magic and the dried blood of the dead beneath her. She no longer looked at me, instead fixated on something above me. "Don't touch him!" Her voice was shrill and stretched with agony.

I tried to reach for her, but my arm was too heavy, and the axe kept me pinned to the earth like I was a weapon mounted to the wall. Something solid, smooth, and shaped to the divots of my fingers was still in my hand.

Twisting my head, I grunted as searing pain radiated through my neck and chest. Still, I forced myself to turn, desperate to see what was in my hand. I was dying, but my grip on the spear wouldn't let go. Blood dripped from the iron tip—the blood of the men and women who lay beside me.

My gaze slid to the woman crawling toward me.

Behind her, gray clouds split like shredded fabric, blazing with red and orange and a swirl of other colors at their center. From where I lay on the ground, the crumbling stone structures loomed, reaching skyward.

Lux heaved herself forward, clutching the limp leg of a dead man and using it as leverage to pull her failing body closer and closer. I dropped the spear and reached for her, the tips of our fingers brushing when her jaw unhinged and a guttural scream erupted from her.

"Drak!"

The pain evaporated.

The spear, the axe, and the bodies vanishing with it.

My eyes split open a second time as if I had a layer of eyelids, each with a distinct memory curled beneath it. Lux leaned over me, at last free of Kayn—thank the stars and skies. Behind her, a slab of solid gray stone rose in place of the sky. In her other hand, the tip of the Y Tree gleamed like light trapped between her fingers.

A shadow cast over her from the flickering of candles mounted along the hallway walls.

Her lips parted. "Drak, I need you." Emotion frayed with each breath, and concern fractured the ease I'd seen on her face last night, when we'd left one another drained from pleasure and full of peace.

The cruel face of her sister filled the blank space behind her. Silver gripped the back of Lux's neck and wrenched her away from me.

I opened my mouth, but Lux's shriek cut off my cry. "Drak!"

Silver threw her sister against the opposite wall across the corridor. The sickening thud of her body slamming into stone filled my veins with rage. Silver was a scrappy adversary, not fast like a vampire, but unpredictable. The most significant contrast between the two was that Lux wasn't willing to kill her sister.

Silver had no such qualms.

This was obvious in the way Silver grasped a fistful of Lux's hair and tried to rip it from her scalp. Lux cried out, shoving Silver off her easily, but Silver never gave up. She slammed the heel of her palm against Lux's jaw.

I bared my fangs and bolted toward them. But as much as I wanted to take her down, Silver was my maker and held immense power over me.

Before I could even touch her, she craned her neck and halted me with her barbed gaze. Every part of me fought against the cage of her compulsion, my limbs moving as if they belonged to someone else. I flexed my fists—the only movement I managed to control.

"Go after Kayn," Lux said to me between heaving breaths. "My compulsion didn't reach him." She launched off the stone and drew the serrated branches of the tree pendant across Silver's arm, the shock enough to shatter the compulsion. The pressure pushing down on me lifted. Silver hissed, but she did not back down, and I knew her savagery had no bounds.

I could not bear the thought of leaving Lux alone with her.

Silver seized Lux's wrist and twisted it backward until Lux cried out and dropped the pendant, but her advantage lasted only a single breath. Lux snapped her arm back, curling her fingers around her sister's, spinning Silver and pinning her arm to her spine.

Silver hissed again, but the troubled smile cracking her face didn't match the tone. A strange laugh spilled out of her. "What is this about your compulsion, sister? You didn't bind yourself to the vampire after all, then? I thought that was an attempt to compel Kayn for a second, but then when it didn't work." Another laugh. "But you wouldn't have tried if it wasn't possible, would you? That means you still have your powers. Of course, I knew that with you, Lux, lying was likely. Or should I call you Silver? You stole my identity and lied about it your entire life." She laughed again. "You figured, why not lie about marriage to the king? I'll give you this: it was a smart move. It got me here. But you don't think I'd come without a backup plan, do you? If I don't walk out of this castle with you within the hour, they'll all die."

Lux ignored her, eyes pinned on me. "Please, Drak. Go after Kayn. He's being forced to kill her prisoners—"

Silver cut in, her voice jagged. "Unless you bow to me in front of Mara."

"You will not ruin Vylheim," Lux spoke through her teeth as she bent Silver's other hand behind her.

"And you won't kill me or imprison me," Silver said.

"Why the fuck not?" I spoke for Lux, though I didn't dare take a step toward Silver. I wouldn't lose control like that again and give her any reason to compel me. It seemed, however, that she didn't even need to. Silver already had control of the situation, and she knew it.

She grinned. "Obviously, because my sister won't let you. She has a soft spot for the people I've brought here to visit her."

Lux grunted as she yanked harder on Silver's hands. A hint of vulnerability flared across Silver's face with a wince.

"What did you do to Kayn to make him comply?" I asked. I didn't trust that bastard Exile, but I knew he wouldn't kill Lux, not when he was so desperate for his stupid soul so that he could *honor the gods*, or whatever the fuck his goals were. He needed Lux alive—as a successful huntress.

"It was either I compel him to kill her, or he kills her friends." She turned her head, forgetting me now as she spoke to her sister. "Kayn is a good boy. He behaves unlike this vampire I made."

Silver flashed a smirk at me. I sank my fangs into my bottom lip, swallowing every impulse to attack her, knowing Lux would not want it. This wasn't part of our agreement. I would fight the vampires, and she would face her sister. Lux didn't trust me not to kill Silver…if I even could. The moment she spoke again, all I thought of was silencing her. "Drak needs compulsion to listen, and I really hate having to spend extra energy dealing with him, but here's the thing." "You and Kayn are equally matched, and he has a head start."

Catching Lux off guard, Silver flung her head back and smashed her skull into Lux's nose. Lux reeled back, but quickly gained control of the fight as she grabbed Silver's wrist and threw her to the cold floor at her feet. Blood trickled from Lux's nose, following the rivulets above her mouth and tinting the lines of her lips like miniature rivers of red.

"Drak," Lux said. "Go!"

I hated leaving her as Silver lunged for the pendant, driving it into Lux's ankle. But this was the fucking plan: I would hold off the vampires while Lux subdued Silver. Since sister couldn't compel sister, Lux would then use her skills as a huntress against Silver's undead army.

What the fuck was I going to do to stop Kayn? Lux would gut me if I killed him, but I was supposed to keep him from executing these so-called prisoners. It was an impossible fight, and I already knew somebody was going to die.

It just better not be Lux.

Everybody else could fall—like the bodies I saw strewn across the battlefield. That image was clear as the fjords, and I knew it was more than just a daydream.

It was a memory.

I just didn't know if it was *my* memory.

I tracked the distant fall of Kayn's footsteps down the corridor and caught the echo of a door slamming at the front of Mara's Keep. Stepping into the widest hallway, I fixed my gaze on the heavy double doors leading outside. I hadn't crossed that threshold in weeks.

We should have fucking expected Silver to show up with hostages.

I struck the heels of my palms against both doors and shoved through. The bright moon greeted me, sharp and uncomfortable to my sensitive eyes. As expected, those still loyal to me stood guard outside Mara's Keep, but Silver's army surrounded the front steps.

Kayn paced before five people on their knees. The captive man's dirty blonde hair dangled in his face, and the woman's neck was stiff as she mouthed something to the three children.

Fuck. *Children.*

When the doors fell shut behind me, the woman's head twisted, and I recognized her as Lux's friend from Skaldir. Her silvery eyes were almost iridescent as they blazed with a blend of outrage and reckless grief.

"Ragna." I raked my fingers through my mess of hair and cut my fang along the inside of my lip. Silver had selected her hostages deliberately. Ragna knelt with her entire family before the vampire chosen to execute them.

Another vampire from Silver's army stepped forward. Every human who had forsaken me as their king to serve her bore a weapon, many plundered from my own armory.

Most of these humans were executioners who blamed me for their lot in life before I'd even come to the throne. The human offered Kayn her weapon—a cross-hilt crucible sword. One I'd trained with beneath Mara's Keep to stay ready for any kind of fight.

A fight like this.

Kayn strode to the end of the line and faced the youngest child, a girl with golden, sun-like hair wrapped in a braided crown. Fuck. He was actually going through with Silver's orders and starting with the little girl. Kayn flipped the tip of the sword to point at the sky and directed the child to put her head down.

I bolted from the steps of the castle in a blur and slammed into Kayn. Gripping his throat in one hand, I threw him to the ground, making his spine crunch against hard-packed dirt. The clash of steel rang out from both my men and Silver's, but Kayn and I were trapped in our own struggle. No one could aid us or harm us.

"What the fuck is wrong with you, Exile?" I fumed as my hands flew to his throat again.

He tried to wrench away. "The huntress must not die. I have to do this."

"Don't you think I fucking know that? I would never let her die."

"You swore to kill her before—"

I shook him, rage blazing through me, though half of it turned inward. Through clenched teeth, I confessed to Kayn, not as the stranger who had entered my mother's life years ago, but as someone I might once have called a friend. "Hurting Lux was a mistake, but at least I can admit it."

Ignoring this, he groaned. "Silver makes good on her promises. If I don't start executing the hostages, she will destroy Lux now that Lux doesn't have her powers. You have to die to sever the bond, and then we can only hope her abilities return—"

"You fucking idiot." I clutched his throat tighter, though it did nothing but detain him. "We lied about the marriage." With my free hand, I snatched the hilt of the sword and released my grip on his neck. Holding the blade at his throat, I shifted my attention to my men who clashed with Silver's army. "Get the prisoners inside!"

"What are you saying?" Kayn's voice strained. "Is she still the huntress?"

I glared at the pathetic Exile at my feet. "How about you ask me if she's okay?"

Kayn's jaw shifted, grinding with impatience or irritation or whatever the fuck was wrong with him. The two armies collided around us, humans toppling first—and there were far too many humans on our side. I winced at how unbalanced the battle had become. The battle didn't matter though, not now that the doors to Mara's Keep swung open and anyone not locked in a fight swept their attention to the castle.

A chill shot through my inky veins as Silver marched out with her fingers clamped at the back of Lux's neck, and a sickly, triumphant smile across her face. There was no way Lux had lost that fight.

Which meant she'd surrendered.

For the prisoners.

Chapter Fourteen

Lux

Unlike my feelings for Drak, which were real, this was a performance. Performing for my sister's sake was crucial to protect the prisoners, so I deliberately failed the exchange and became her hostage, a choice that proved far trickier than I had anticipated.

Silver could see through me as easily as honey cloth, but her hunger for victory and control blinded her just enough to miss what she should have recognized.

She hadn't won this fight.

This was no different from when I gave vampires the illusion of victory and then struck back to seize control. Fighting was much like weaving a tapestry or spinning a story full of surprises and unexpected twists.

"Yes, yes, yes! Kill whoever is in your way. Then go out there and fight, huntress." Odin's voice carved through me with every step we took through the castle.

"Use this advantage." Freya spoke now. Whenever they warred for space within my head, the agony bolting through my temples heightened. *"The vampires believe you're powerless."*

Loki laughed gleefully. *"I love a good trick."*

I have to take Silver captive

"You are our weapon. Trained for vampires only." Odin did not care for my plans. *"Do whatever you must to get to them while their eyes are still blind. I allowed you this opportunity to deceive their leader. Fail to use it, and you'll learn a lesson the hard way."*

The pain grew worse and worse until my vision frayed, and I thought I'd collapse. The Gods' words were final, and the only way to quiet them and block this torture was to do what they said.

So I let her lead me through the castle doors, straight to the prisoners she had dragged here and thrown into the dirt before Mara's Keep, because I couldn't live with myself if I sacrificed Stasia or whoever Silver was using as leverage. If nothing else, I had to at least try to save them.

They deserved a chance at survival, and Drak couldn't guarantee saving them. Not with Kayn there.

Moonlight flooded the stone floor as I pushed through the door on Silver's command. Crossing the threshold, I squinted in the dim flicker of candles. After weeks inside the castle, a rush of freshness hit me, and I gulped it in.

Icy air crystallized in my lungs, and my breath caught when I saw them.

Despite assigning a hundred of Drak's men to protect the castle, Silver's vampires easily overpowered both his human guards and the few loyal vampires who remained. Weapons once dragged out from beneath Mara's Keep now clattered to the dirt as the undead, faster and stronger, took the men down. One-by-one.

My gut knotted, and I couldn't breathe. Among the fighting, a familiar pale blonde braid and angular face caught my eye.

"Ragna," I muttered. Hot breath curled in the frigid air in front of me. Tears seared behind my eyes as my gaze panned to the five people kneeling in the dirt beside her. Her husband, Rolf, and her children, even little Alva—the girl I'd made a promise to. I'd sworn to keep her mother alive back when Ragna was first taken by King Drakkar.

Now, she was forced to her knees in the dirt alongside her mother with Kayn under a command to execute them all. Fear clawed at my heart, stalling my blood and sending shivers through my limbs.

Silver's fingernails sank into the flesh at the back of my neck, and she forced me out into the moonlight. Her palm pressed against the nodules of my spine until suddenly she released me with one quick shove.

I stumbled over the steps and fell to the dirt only inches away from the castle's door. The impact ripped air from my chest, and ragged coughing overcame me. The heels of my palms throbbed from hitting the stiff ground. Dirt clung to the scrapes across my skin, and tiny drops of blood glistened along the thin cuts.

I jerked my attention back up to the family only a few steps away.

In the chaos, Ragna had seized a nearby sword and cut her bindings, then followed suit with her husband. Rolf freed his sons and sent them off running, but before he could turn to grab Ragna and Alva, a human from Silver's army crushed the hilt of his sword against Rolf's head. Ragna hadn't seen yet, too concentrated on trying to sever Alva's bindings before anyone took notice of the entire family's escape.

It was too late.

Crimson glinted in the eyes of a vampire as he cut down one of Drak's guards and left the body behind, bolting in a blur toward Ragna's family. The vampire woman crouched over them, fangs glistening, and snatched Alva's braid, hauling the girl upright.

Before I could even gasp or move a muscle, one of Drak's men crashed into the vampire. The force of his body knocked her to the ground, but it was only a momentary respite because she shot back at him, a blur of fangs and clawed fingernails. She tore him off his feet before plunging her teeth into his throat.

Alva cowered away from them, falling back to her knees and folding into a ball. In the next few moments, the vampire would drain him and turn on Alva again.

Silver's edged voice sliced through me. "Bow before me, sister." I turned to find her standing at the threshold, as if she were already claiming Mara's Keep as her own. Staring down her nose at me, she smiled. "Unless you want little Alva to die." Her smile deformed into a fake pout.

Sickness flared at the back of my tongue, crawling up my throat as a dark and distorted thought formed. I should have killed her. If I had fangs, I would have sunk them into her without hesitation. But she had been no older than Alva when they took her.

I couldn't destroy my sister, but I wouldn't bow to her either. I wouldn't declare her queen.

Sucking in an icy breath, I shoved off the dirt and shot to my feet. Before Silver could grab me, I ran for the vampire bent over Alva. I was chosen for this.

The Gods wanted this, and it felt so damn good to finally make them proud.

"Forget the girl. Kill the monsters. Everyone of them." Their voices twisted in my mind, delight threading through every word with each step I took toward the vampires.

When it came to the undead, I felt stronger than ever. These skills—the visions, the compulsion, the strength—had been crafted and gifted to me to turn them to ash, and I used that thought to drive me. To crush the twinge in my chest and the exhaustion tugging at my bones.

With one foot forced in front of the other, I grabbed the stake from my thigh and advanced. The vampire gripped Alva's tiny arm and wrenched her to her feet again, unaware that I was charging toward her. Summoning all my strength, I ran and drove the stake up, aiming it straight for her side. My weapon struck her, nearly knocking the breath out of me as I buried it into her clothes, her skin, and between her ribs. Reeling from shock and pain, she let go, and Alva fell to the dirt, letting out a cry that tore at my heart.

"Run, Alva," I begged, daring to look at her while I shoved the stake deeper into her attacker's heart. "Get up and run. Find your brothers."

Alva scrambled to her feet, casting only a single glance back at me before disappearing into the fight. I refused to blink until I glimpsed Rolf's features through the chaos.

Alva had found her father.

Before I could savor this relief, the vampire woman clawed at my arm, digging her fingers into my elbow as the black blood within me began to spread. Tension snapped, and my breath finally released as I centered on the fight. Time and motion suddenly whirled around me twice as fast. She lunged at me, but it was useless. Every piece of her flesh touched by blood flaked into ash and caught in the icy gusts of wind rippling through the mesh of bodies. Her body withered away, and she was only the first of my victims.

I drew the Y Tree from my pocket and smashed it against the face of an approaching vampire. Her flesh singed, and she backed up enough for me to rip the stake out of the first vampire and angle it toward the second. I drove it through her ribcage, then turned to another one of the many undead.

One after another, I did as the Gods bid, as Kayn trained me. As Drak taught me.

"Slay every vampire."

"You are the blade we wield."

"Our chosen."

With each vampire that turned to ash at my feet, I craved more. I almost *wanted* to hear the Gods talking now, louder —more!

Do you see that you've chosen well?

I blinked. Where the fuck had that thought come from? I

didn't crave killing. This was simply a duty; that was all. So why did I love watching when their black blood crumbled their bodies?

Because the Gods wanted this and in this moment, I wanted to please them, to make them proud that I was finally fulfilling the destiny they chose for me.

I shook my head and gutted another vampire. This was only to keep Vylheim safe from those who'd chosen violence, and it was working; we were winning based on the number of vampires who pulled back. The fight dwindled as the remaining vampires fell back to heal, hauling off the humans who still drew breath, though I suspected it wasn't out of mercy.

I longed to chase them down and rescue the captured humans, but the vampires' relentless assault allowed no pause. When I finally caught a breath, a single terrible sound froze my blood.

Frozen air carried the cries of the fallen, but Ragna's scream was distinct and tainted with colorful language. It snapped me out of the dreamlike state of the battle, cracking the slow passage of time even as another vampire charged me.

"The Gods will curse your fucking eyes to fall out if you touch one hair on my head," Ragna said between choking breaths.

I heard her, but I couldn't see her. I threw off my attacker and spun around, scanning the thinning crowd of bodies to spot Ragna's sheen blonde braid. Vampires dragged her toward the castle and threw her at Silver's feet. With the blade of an axe balanced between the nodules of her spine, Ragna was bowing to Silver before her death.

And it was Kayn who held the weapon.

I forced my way past the two vampires grappling with Drak and dashed toward the castle.

"It is one person's life. Focus on the vampires instead." Freya's words were sensible, but heartless.

Still, my attention jerked to a nearby vampire. I wanted to show the Gods they had chosen wisely. This was worship, and obeying their commands would make my mother proud. Ragna's ragged voice split through the thought again, and I flicked my eyes back to the castle. They were only a few steps away.

Lining the blade up, Kayn lifted the axe above his head. I'd witnessed a hundred executions. Masked men and women dragged witches, and those who defied the bloodshed law into the streets, and then the villagers were forced to watch the beheading.

"The vampires are escaping instead of dying." Loki laughed with reckless amusement. *"I told you Lux would fail us. You should have listened to* my *plan instead."*

I clamped my eyes shut, trying to silence their voices. I could no longer follow them blindly. Ragna's head was at stake. *Sorry, Mother.* Quickly peeling my eyes back open, I lunged at Kayn with the pendant in my fist, but I was too late. Axe crunched against bone, and a guttural scream erupted from my lips. When I plastered the silver against his neck, he stumbled and dropped the axe.

Wood and iron fell to the dirt with a thud…along with Ragna.

Blood spilled from her spine. She was another limp body with dust coating the surrounding air, but she had not lost her head. I'd interrupted the full strike of the blade even if it wasn't enough to save her life.

My heart plunged to my feet as I fell against the dirt beside her. Cupping her shoulders, I shook her helplessly, as if that could stop the bleeding, as if my desperation could mend her shattered spine.

She was gone.

Tears blurred my vision and all thoughts of pleasing the Gods and eliminating vampires were long forgotten. My fellow witch and friend was dead—used as a pawn in my sister's sick game.

"Ragna, please." Sorrow sucked the air from my voice, and each word hurt my throat to speak, but I kept begging. "Please wake up. You have to watch Alva grow up. I saved her. Please, Ragna. Don't leave me."

My sister spoke from somewhere nearby, but I couldn't see her through the tears swimming in my eyes. "You should have made me queen." A shadow blocked out the moonlight, dimming the area over me and Ragna. Closer now, Silver's warm breath brushed my ear. "Now you know what will happen to our mother and Stasia if you trick me again." She paused, letting this sink in as I shuddered. "I'll meet you in the light of Yggdrasil's fire, where every ounce of your power will burn away. Goodbye huntress, enjoy your abilities while they last."

After wiping away a blur of tears, my head snapped up, but Silver was already nowhere to be seen. She'd fled with the vampires.

I couldn't tell whether a half-second or half an hour had passed when Drak appeared beside me. He was a blur as he ripped Ragna from my hold and sank his fangs into her neck. Her limp arms and legs splayed across his leg, and he propped her torso with his knee.

"Drak, don't!" I screeched.

He pulled back from the bite with bright red blood staining his teeth. "I'm doing this for you."

"Kill him before he makes another vampire." Odin spoke in a low tone, haunting and slow as he instructed me to lift the stake.

I forced my arm back down, keeping the muscles rigid, so that I didn't give in to the temptation to kill Drak here and now. Shaking my head, I tried to free my mind, but Odin's presence was heavy. The only reprieve came from knowing Drak wasn't hurting Ragna.

He's turning her. For me.

But this world couldn't abide by more undead. There weren't enough humans to feed them. Vampires were starving along with their food source, but Drak was creating another one. For. Me.

A quiet, burning rage grew within me as I watched him transform her. He was saving her, in a sick and twisted way, but Ragna would hate becoming the enemy. Most of the Blood Council were vampires, save for some humans who knew and supported them, and Ragna despised those who'd hunted down witches.

She'd despise vampires too, and herself, if she became one of them.

Sounds of battle ebbed. Once Silver's focus had shifted to compelling Kayn and tormenting me, her army had backed down. Too many vampires were lost to my stake.

Except for the one who was once a witch. The woman before me, whose blood drained from her veins and flowed through Drak's.

Clouds passed overhead, obscuring the glow of the moon. Shadows of an approaching storm swallowed Mara in an eerie darkness, even for the night, and the erratic weather was growing increasingly unpredictable.

After a minute, her eyes moved beneath the thin veil of her eyelids. She was coming back, but as a vampire. Lightning struck somewhere in the forest behind Mara's Keep with a crack.

"Now you will have to slay her too."

No, I can't. I won't! But my body didn't listen to my heart. I gripped the stake in my fist. Making the Gods proud—fulfilling this destiny—was the purpose of my every heartbeat.

The battle before Mara's Keep was over, but the war within me had just begun.

"Kill her." Odin insisted.

I pictured Ragna's body succumbing to black blood, like all vampires did when I staked them in the heart. Her skin flaking and fluttering away in the wind. At my hand, her entire existence would be swept away, and in that moment, I wanted nothing more.

Fuck. Drak was right.

Madness had its claws in me.

Distant thunder roared in agreement. Perhaps Odin's son was brewing some madness of his own, for another jagged bolt of lightning flashed, brightening the sky for a moment before darkness swallowed Mara once more.

Chapter Fifteen

Drak

The attack on Mara's Keep left both sides bloodied, but Silver's army would heal—those who survived, at least. Lux had destroyed a dozen of them, maybe more; I hadn't tracked her every move as closely as I wanted.

And while the enemy retreated to tend their wounds, we did the same, though under the shelter of stone. Deep in the castle, where I carved the petal of a rose into the wood panel. Lux would appreciate the flower for her shelf, but this was in honor of Axel's son, too. I missed his paintings.

Thunder rumbled through the castle, but thick walls masked the crack of lightning. Although the weather had delayed our departure by two days, at least we knew Silver and her army wouldn't be moving either. Not even the wasteland was spared from the storm.

No one dared venture out in this, not even the undead. Lightning hurt like silver, and Thor seemed to know exactly how to aim. Or at least that was my guess. Maybe he simply hurled so many bolts that getting struck was not as rare as it should have been, and the fires they sparked were pure agony.

Sure, vampires healed, but that did not mean we did not feel every second of it.

I shaved a curl of wood from the panel and blew it away. It drifted to Axel's feet as he returned, continuing his reports from our network of spies, as he had done every few hours. The enemy had taken refuge in their camp at the base of Mara near the sea, biding their time until Thor grew weary. After all, even gods were not limitless.

He reported on the new vampire too, about how Ragna awoke in a fury and had torn her bedchambers to shreds, seeking blood, trying to kill herself, then screaming for answers about her new status as an undead person before falling asleep again.

I had no doubt that Lux heard Ragna's shrieks and was quietly building a case against me. She had already given me an earful the moment I finished turning her friend, and then for the past two days, she went silent.

Unnervingly silent.

Axel finally got to the good news, and I focused on him again. "The masks and alchemical stones have been tested and returned. They're ready for the wasteland." He hesitated, waiting for…something.

"Axel?"

"My king, I'd like to make a request." I raised my eyebrows and gave him my full attention, urging him to continue. "While you're in the wasteland, will you keep one eye open for him?"

That was the only place Axel's spies did not venture, at least not deeply enough, so it made sense that he believed his son could hide there. But it had been fifteen years since anyone had identified Soren, and it broke my heart to think that if he was in the wasteland, he might no longer be alive.

"Of course, Axel." I nodded and offered him a promising smile. "With Odin's foresight, that will be my first order of business."

Axel bowed in gratitude. After I thanked him for the intel, clapping his shoulder with reassurance, I stalked down the dark hall. Storms inspired me, so I abandoned the workshop for a room with a window: my study.

I snagged one of the masks I'd created for the wasteland and turned it over in my hand. Kicking my feet up on the table, I ran my thumb over the smooth ridges of the mask as my gaze wandered out the window. Blinding bolts struck deep into the village.

Thor was a bastard, but I admired his performance even if I hated the gods used their powers to fuck with us. He could intimidate an entire village with a single strike.

I squinted at the jagged shaft of white light. After a few moments, thunder growled loud enough to shake the foundations of the fortress. Even Mara's Keep was not entirely solid against these new storms, each one growing steadily worse. We were once a kingdom plagued by crop failures, buried under heavy snow and bitter freezes. But the gods grew impatient with this tactic because starvation was neither fast nor effective enough. Even if it weakened us vampires, it did not kill us.

Another bolt collided with Vylheim, closer to the castle now. The thunder overlapped, and the ground where the Exile executed Ragna burned. The charred pattern rippled out several yards, stretching in a single second as the spiked lines scarred the earth.

The mark looked far too familiar.

I dropped my feet to the floor with a thud and sprang up. With my hands splayed on the cold stone windowsill, I bent over and scanned the ground below. The jagged lines almost matched the lifeless branches of Yggdrasil.

After a moment of staring, I shook my head. "It's not Yggdrasil," I said. "I'm going as mad as Lux."

I flinched. My wife refused to believe the gods were destroying her as easily as Thor's lightning set fires and slaughtered livestock. She would see the truth soon enough, in the desolate, terrifying wasteland.

She would see the same things I did: that we were meant for each other and that she was not meant to play the gods' games.

I shook my head, letting the tension roll through me as hair fell into my eyes. It had grown long and unruly over the past few weeks. Since becoming a vampire, it grew exceptionally fast, so I usually shaved the sides and tied the rest in a knot at the back of my head. Now it hung loose, and I almost welcomed the curtain of dark brown that blocked my view of Thor's mark on the land.

It would remain there, a reminder that the gods were at my doorstep.

I curled my hands into fists and pressed against the windowsill until the rough stone bit into my knuckles. Another crack of lightning lit up the sky and struck just outside the window. Intense brightness left my vision temporarily dark. Thunder shook Mara's Keep so violently that I had to scramble blindly to grab onto something.

My heel hit the chair behind me, and I caught myself on the table to my left. The masks clattered to the floor.

"Fuck," I breathed. "I hear you, Thor."

I bent down and grabbed the mask at my feet, my vision clearing. The black clay was molded to cover the entire face, with gauze stretched across the mouth and strips of leather layered over it to hold the mask's shape.

The same black gauze framed the eyes and covered the forehead; it was attached to the clay to block as many of the thick, tainting particles in the wasteland air as possible.

Lightning exploded at the corners of my eyes, and I glanced at the window. "Tell your father I'm coming to kill him."

"Drak?"

I spun around to see Lux in the doorway. Beneath the thick cloak I'd given her, glimpses of her white nightgown hung loosely over her curves. Her wavy hair was left untethered from her usual braids and cascaded over her shoulders, reaching to her hips.

I grazed my fangs over my bottom lip as I took her in. "You're supposed to be resting. We'll be leaving for Yggdrasil as soon as the storm passes."

I didn't doubt the gods would try to trick me first, muting the weather just long enough to lure me out—the same way we'd lured Silver here, but I was prepared to deal with Thor's storms with our protective tents.

Lux's bare foot peeked out from beneath the gown as she stepped into the small study. "I've been watching Ragna sleep. I hate that you turned her."

"So you've said. I'm sorry, Lux, but she's not dead, so she can move and speak and even return to her family."

"And now I have to kill her. Plus, she'll hate herself."

"I doubt that," I said. "Yes, it takes time to come to terms with this existence, but like I said, she'll be able to return to her family this way. And I saw the way she looked at her children when Kayn was about to execute them all. She'd do anything for them, even if it means becoming a monster."

Lux's frown merely twitched, but she knew I was right. "That doesn't change the fact that it sickens me to hear her screaming for blood. And if it upsets me, what do you think it will do to her family?"

"The panic will calm once she gets used to the bloodlust. She'll be herself again, just faster, stronger."

"She was plenty fast and strong. She always won every race I ran against her—" A sudden choking in her voice cut her off, and sadness filled her eyes. "Even in sleep she mutters about blood."

"I told you to leave her. When she wakes again, she'll be ravenous and won't have the self control not to attack you."

She nodded, toying with the ends of her hair and twisting the waves around her bluish fingers. I wanted to comfort her, but after turning her friend, now wasn't the time.

After a long moment of silence, she swallowed hard and met my gaze. "I know she'll be better off guided into this by the vampires who remain here," she said, padding past me to the window. She stared out at the storm and let out a sigh. "Also, I came to you because I can't stop thinking about your…episodes."

"Memories," I said. "They're memories."

She turned on her heels and tilted her chin up to me. Pitch-black eyes searched mine, the ferocity in them always causing a pleasant jolt to my senses. "How do you know?"

"I can't explain it. That's how they feel."

"Memories from when?" she asked.

I forced out a breath. "Another life."

"You truly believe that? I thought you believed the gods didn't give second chances, and that's why Myrah took it upon herself to attempt rebirth."

"I saw *you*, Lux," I said. The hint of a wrinkle appeared between her brows before quickly vanishing again. "In a battlefield. Like yesterday's fight, but so much worse. You crawled over a mass of bodies to get to me."

Her mouth dropped open as she drew a sharp breath. "That's in Brynhild's journal." The wrinkle on her forehead deepened, and her hands suddenly shot to her temples.

"The lightning is in your head right now, too, isn't it?" I ground out between my teeth. As powerful as I was as king, I couldn't take away her pain. I couldn't stop the Gods until I became one.

She blinked slowly. "What was I saying?"

"The recording of Myrah's saga."

Confusion twisted her mouth until she finally nodded. But it was half-hearted. "Right." Distracted now, her gaze dropped to the mask in my hand. She slipped it from my hold and turned it over, examining the carved clay. "This will protect us in the wasteland?"

I sighed. "It should. The clouds there formed into thick

particles. Breathing them or getting them in your eyes burns and blinds you ."

"You don't need to breathe. Will your mask cover your mouth too?"

"It's a habit I can't break now. So yes, we will both cover our faces unless we're inside the safety of a tent." She hummed in understanding, brushing her fingers across the mask's smooth clay forehead. Taking her chin between my thumb and forefinger, I tipped her head back to guide her gaze to me. "What was it you were saying about Brynhild's recording?"

Her eyelashes fluttered for a moment until she blinked fully. As if that'd cleared her mind, she nodded. "Yeah, um, Brynhild wrote about that. Whatever you said."

I took the mask and set it on the table so that I could slip my hand into hers. "Come," I said. "Let's look at the record again."

"What about in the gods' domain?" She asked, blinking up at me. For whatever reason, the gods were distracting her from thinking about that journal. "Across the threshold closer to Yggdrasil, will we still need to wear the masks?"

"Not you," I said. "For me, it will protect my flesh from the sunlight. But for you, I suppose you'll thrive being so close to their power. The veil between Asgard and Earth is thin there."

She nodded slowly, taking this in. "And how will you feed when we're traveling?"

It was a good question, even if I was far more curious about what she was about to say regarding my memories and the histories. This wasn't like Lux. Surely, if the gods allowed her space to think and be herself, she'd be obsessing over the sagas and stories of our ancestors rather than concerned with my access to blood.

"Axel has fashioned leather pouches full of offered blood. If I drink from them regularly and keep them close to my body with the glass cap tight, the warmth circulates and keeps the blood fresh."

"Blood bags?" She grimaced. Yeah, I guess that sounded pretty sick to her, but it worked, and her frown quickly flipped. Her eyebrows ticked up. A sparkle brightened her midnight eyes. "Do you think Silver's vampires will use something like it?"

"Yes, Axel got the idea from the spies we have watching them. They use the blood bags because vessels cannot always keep up when vampires move from place to place."

"We can use that against them." Lux spoke while staring blankly out the window. "Drain their blood, fight them sooner if we find them."

"Maybe," I said, sucking in a breath. "But fighting them when we're at our strongest and they're at their weakest in the gods' domain is our best chance. The gods will make sure any vampires near Yggdrasil suffer. Odin has a lot more control there."

Concern flashed in her gaze as she flicked it back to me. "But you'll be weak too."

"I'll be ready for it. I'll be able to track them by sound more easily than her vampires can track us. An army will make a lot more noise than we will. And with any luck, we'll arrive long before they do. I'll have time to become a god and gain some foresight, and you'll thrive so close to Asgard. Once they're all dead, we can end this madness by burning Yggdrasil to the ground."

"No way. I will not disrespect the gods like that."

"It's the only way. We have to stop their influence over your mind if you ever want to be free again." She jerked her head to the side, her chest heaving rapidly. It was the first hint that she truly realized she was trapped. My tone softened. "You will have already killed most of Silver's army, so you won't need the powers. Whatever vampires remain, I can deal with them. I'll be a god, Lux, in *this* realm."

"Then, as a god, you can convince the other gods to retract from my mind if they have not already. Once the vampires are dead, I trust they'll let my mind rest."

"Then your trust is misplaced," I said. Fury twisted her stunning features into abrupt angles. When rage burned in her veins, she looked too much like her sister. Before the gods reminded her to hate me, I changed the subject. "Show me more from Brynhild's records."

With our hands still intertwined, she led me out of the study, another flash of Thor's fury flooding the room behind us. The door fell shut behind us, sealing away all sight of the gods's storm. As we snaked through the castle's corridors, only the rumble of thunder could reach us now.

A draft of icy air unfurled around us, and Lux pulled closer to me. With her free hand, she clutched the cloak tighter at her chest, burying her breasts beneath the wolf's skin. She was always so cold, and I wished we could spend our nights lying side by side so that I could keep her warm after a fresh feeding.

I opened the library door and motioned for Lux to go in first. Without hesitation, she darted straight for Brynhild's journal.

"I remember what we were talking about now," she said, her voice lighter but shaken with the chill. Tugging the journal off the shelf, she flipped it open in her palms, and I slanted my head to see the pages over her shoulder. She craned her neck to look up at me. "You saw Myrah crawling to her lover."

"No, Lux. I saw you as you were crawling to me."

Silence fell between us as she gazed at me. The emotion swimming in her eyes was one I couldn't name. Did she understand what this meant?

Did I?

I couldn't be a warrior reborn. According to all interpretations of the saga, a warrior would never choose to leave

Valhalla. Once he was feasting at Odin's table, he would hardly remember his lover.

Worlds apart, it would be *her* task to find him again.

But as certain as the records were, it didn't feel right because it didn't match what I had witnessed. In the memory, I reached for her. Even with the spear in my hand, knowing I could die and be chosen for Valhalla, I had dropped it to reach for her, willingly giving up my passage. Then the damn Valkyries chose me anyway.

I flexed my fist, remembering the smooth handle of the spear against the palm of my hand.

"What are you saying?" she asked.

"I don't know." It felt too insane to speak aloud. Like I was losing myself to the same madness that kept interrupting Lux's thoughts. I scrubbed my palm over the back of my neck. "Maybe the memories were just memories of reading this interpretation."

Her face fell. Had she wanted it to be true?

"What is it?" I asked.

"I've always thought you were the only man I've ever seen who resembled the warriors in the sagas. Not just because of the way you look, but your balance of brutality and determination. Your ability to be both fierce and caring at the same time. I mean, you threatened to kill me only a day before you were going to allow me to kill you. That courage, to do what you must, even if it is contradictory…I've only ever seen that described in the stories of our ancestors. Men in Skaldir, or here in Mara, aren't like that. So when you said you saw yourself in the saga." She shook her head. "I don't know, it almost made sense." A little laugh escaped her, but I could have sworn tears filled her eyes. "But I guess my thoughts are so scattered, what makes sense to me probably doesn't to anyone else."

I cupped her chin and brought her face to mine. The scent

of her, citrus and sage, beckoned me closer. I hovered my mouth over hers. "This makes sense to me, Lux."

"What does?" she whispered.

"That we're meant to be. That we've already been." Because I loved her. *I think I love you now.*

"Myrah and…" her voice trailed away.

"Rune."

Every muscle in my body screamed at me to scoop her into me. To taste her lips. This close, the aroma of her desire tinted her every breath, and I wanted to soak it in. I needed to touch every inch of her and watch the prickles alight over her skin with pleasure as I listened to her moans.

She pulled back, her lower lip curling inward. "It's too insane. I don't have Myrah's powers. If—" she slapped the journal shut and gripped it so tightly her knuckles turned white. "If I'm Myrah, then I created vampires. I created Kayn. Wouldn't he remember this? Wouldn't he have told me?"

"I don't know. He's lied before."

She released a curse with a breath. Her arms hung limp at her sides, defeated. "I can't wrap my head around this."

"But you want to," I said. Or did I just want it to be true? This was insane. She was right, but I didn't know if I cared how insane it was. If this story—this ancient saga—brought us closer together, I'd accept the insanity of it all, because she challenged me to be better, but more than that, she saw me. She gave me a place in this world that wasn't just the forgotten-boy-turned-vampire-king. Even Axel didn't give me that.

I brushed the back of my knuckles along her chin and then cupped her jaw. Dipping my head to her, I beckoned her to me. All at once, she melted into me, her body molding to mine like the mask that'd been shaped for my face. Maybe we'd been together hundreds of years ago, maybe not.

But we fit together now.

Fuck, was I falling in love with my fake wife?

I pressed my mouth to hers, slowly, gently, and building to an all-consuming fire. Her lips parted, inviting me inside. Need tightened across my body. My cock grew stiff with the taste of her, and when she released a soft moan, I buried my fingers in her loose hair and kissed her harder.

Her moaning built with urgency. Hungry kisses told me she needed more.

I sure as Hel needed more.

Bending my knees, I cupped my hands around the back of her thighs, and she lifted herself with me, throwing her legs around my hips as I held her.

When she pulled back again, her lips were swollen and tinged red. Breathless, she begged for more. "I need to feel you." I pressed her against the wall between bookshelves, desperate with the need to grind myself against her. But fabric still separated us, and it wasn't enough for her. Not for either of us.

I slipped my fingers between her legs to catch the wetness dripping from her core. Carefully, I brushed my thumb over her most sensitive spot, sparking a gasp from her. I ate up every sound of her pleasure. Teasing, I pulled my finger back, then brushed over again and again.

"Please," she breathed. "I need all of you."

"Not yet. I'm playing with you."

"Fuck you." A frustrated laugh danced in her voice.

"Come for me, my wife." She was teetering, not right on the edge yet, but slowly building with tension and greedy pleasure. I felt her need when I slipped my fingers inside her and her pussy clenched around them. "Then I will reward you."

"Please." Her begging didn't stop. "Please, Rune."

My heart stammered, but just like last time, Lux's body kept me grounded. The strange, dreamlike memories couldn't pull my mind away from her, even if she had spoken that magic, fucking word.

Chapter Sixteen

Lux

Why had I said that? The name slipped out.

This was a wishful hope—not that I was Myrah, but that being with Drak couldn't be selfish. If destiny forged us from a twisted past, then our actions weren't wrong, regardless of the gods' warnings in my mind.

As a witch, my upbringing taught me to view the king of Vylheim as a monster.

As the huntress, I was molded to destroy him.

Freya's words were on repeat, even if they were short. *"Be the weapon."*

"Fuck first then kill him. Then use your dominance for your pleasure again." Loki spoke more chaotically and with vulgarity between unsettling laughter.

Odin said nothing. His silence was heavier; a weight on my mind that caged my temples and squeezed my skull. Disappointment, anger, and hatred were evident in the pressure convulsing through my head.

Even when Drak and I first came together, the gods hadn't been this loud. Perhaps it was because only our bodies had intertwined, not yet our souls. Back then, my heart and mind had only just softened to him.

But now I remembered, or at least I remembered the excruciating grief of losing him, lodged in the hollow of my gut, as if we had been one soul torn apart by Freya and Odin's choices. I had no idea where such grief had come from.

I'd never lived this.

"They're not memories, girl, that's what madness sounds like." Odin finally reached out. *"Kill him, and the rest of them before you lose yourself."*

"Don't listen to them." Drak's whispers slipped through the cracks in my mind. I heard him, even if he felt distant—like the Gods were standing between us.

It wasn't until he softly bit my bottom lip that I was pulled back into the present.

Succumbing to him was exactly what the Gods didn't want because it put barriers between them and me. Walls erected in my mind when I fully allowed myself to enjoy his touch and think of nothing else. With his lips brushing against my neck, Drak opened his mouth again, but it was Freya's words I heard.

"A weapon is as much for protection as it is for aggression. Didn't he once deny you weapons? Deny you protection? Deny your loved ones any hope?"

She was right.

A rope cinched around my heart, tugging it lower in my ribcage. Every beat hurt, and every one of Freya's words matched the erratic rhythm. She didn't speak all at once, but with pauses and skips, just like my pulse. It was off-tempo with the rumble of Thor's storm outside. Each strike of lightning reverberated with the following thunder.

"If you don't kill him for us. Do it for your mother." Odin's voice cut like a serrated blade along the back of my skull. I seethed at the sting. "*Don't fail me. You selfish witch.*" His tone grew sharper, more tense, making my heart skip. He would not stop haunting me, and the back of my eyes ached, tears burning at

the edges. Still, I resisted. *"Your hands…give me control, Lux. Give me all of you. NOW!"*

Breath sucked from my lungs, and my throat tightened with a raw scratchiness.

"Lux, I'm here," Drak said. Focusing only on Drak's voice, the pain receded with Odin's fading voice. "I'm here." He coaxed me out of the spiral with the same phrases I'd used to call him out of his episodes. The more I experienced this life alongside him, the more I realized we were what we'd once said—what I'd once vehemently denied. We were the same. "Come back to me."

My eyelids fluttered as I met his intense gaze. The white of his scarred eye was like snow, while the blue in his other eye mirrored the fjords. Together, they held an all-consuming beauty, the kind I had adored gazing at since I was a young girl.

Taking in every mark on his face, I sank my fingers into his hair. Drak dragged his thumb across my bottom lip, parting my mouth before he crushed it with a greedy kiss. I wrapped my arms around his neck, and he lifted me higher, propping my legs on his hips.

Everything within me scrambled for this moment of reprieve. Never would I understand how Drak beckoned me out of my head, but he'd been able to do it with my frayed nerves, and now that the Gods's voices were louder than my panic and self-hatred, he pulled me away from them too.

His hand slipped over my core, eliciting a sudden gasp from my throat. Arching my neck, I let my head rest against the wall. The feather-light touch of his finger had me writhing, trying to press against his hand, but his rhythm was a steady tease.

Drak tipped his chin back, and with one brow arched up, he smirked at me, eyes roving over my face. "You're so fucking beautiful when you're needy."

My needs should be second—

"Stop," he interrupted as he ceased teasing me and grabbed my jaw to force me to look at him. *Really* look at him. "I will not let you put yourself last. Everyone wants to use you. The Exile, the Gods, even the people who came here on Supplication Day."

You do too. For Godhood.

He let out a breath. "Fuck." Stepping back, he released the pressure of his body against the wall. His arms slowly went slack as I slid down his hips and straightened my legs. As he turned away, his fingers raked through his wild hair, and his broad shoulders tensed.

Every muscle in his back seemed to tighten.

"Isn't it true?" My voice was quiet.

He nodded but did not turn around. When his arm fell to his side, he let out another sigh and stared across the room at the opposite bookshelf. "Maybe."

"Maybe?" I stepped closer to him, reaching out but not letting myself touch him just yet.

"I don't know anymore. Yes, I have plans for more power, but your safety comes first."

"What changed?"

Spinning around, he pinned me with a desperate gaze. "You, Lux. You are what changed for me." I searched his eyes as he towered over me. "Fuck, can't you see that? The first time you looked at me, I swear you didn't see a king."

My mind flickered back to that day in Skaldir when he'd strode into my village flanked by executioners. Though he looked the part of a royal, I saw something else. Angling my chin up at him, I said, "I saw a warrior."

"You saw me."

"I don't understand," I said, even as I remembered his grin that day. How he looked at me with a crooked smirk I interpreted as a threat. Of course I'd been wary of his smile; he was the crown in a kingdom that executed and exiled witches.

"You didn't listen to me either. When I told you to fight back. Everybody listens to their king whether out of fear or respect, but even at your own execution, you didn't listen." I tilted my head. What the Hel was he getting at? "I couldn't control you."

A strange laugh forced its way out of me. "And you've hated that."

"No," he stepped closer. The back of his finger grazed my chin as his eyes took me in. Suddenly, his gaze dropped to the space between our feet. "But I can't say I don't want your help at Yggdrasil. So you're right about me using you, and I don't think I would have done that..." He jerked his head to the side. "In the past."

After a moment of silence, he stepped past me and strode toward the door.

Why was he leaving now, when my body still ached for him?

I had agreed to lie about our vows, but when we consummated it, nothing about our relationship felt fake. Now we no longer needed to prove our marriage with our bodies. No witnesses waited outside to confirm the sound of our climaxes, and yet I wanted nothing more than the pressure of his body against mine again.

My hand shot out and I gripped his wrist. "Drak." He stopped, but didn't face me. "You made me beg already, so you know exactly what I'm going to say now." He said nothing—did nothing. He only waited. "Please." I tugged him toward me. When he obliged, I matched the energy his desire had given me. Trailing my fingers along his rough jaw, I followed the line of his beard to the back of his neck. I snaked my hand around to cup his head, my fingers tangling in his overgrown hair. With a pull, I beckoned him to my face and kissed him with the same intensity he always offered me. Taking a breath, I whispered, "demand that you're the only one I worship."

His hands found my face. The space between his thumbs

and fingers framed my ears as he held my head. It was all he did.

He simply held me, looking at me as if I were the one who had him frozen in place.

"Please," I said.

A single twitch flickered over his lips, and then the dam broke.

We consumed one another. One moment we were kissing, the next he ripped his shirt over his head. I dragged him onto the rug so that I could climb on top of him. His need was obvious from the strain against his pants. I freed him and drank in the sight of his cock.

Taking all of him into my mouth, I wanted to tease him the way he had me before I straddled him. His moans beckoned me to lick up and down his shaft, swirling my tongue at the tip. It was the only thing I could focus on.

Being entirely absorbed in the moment shut everything out; the pressure in my head, the skipping in my heart, even the voices—mine and the Gods'—were deliciously silent.

I could remain here forever, drawing desperate groans from Drak's throat, focusing only on his pleasure, and then mine.

The only other thing I was aware of was the storm. Roaring thunder grew more frequent. We couldn't hear sheets of water falling from deep within the castle, but the weather made itself known by shaking the stone.

Drak grabbed my wrist and pried me off him, dragging my face to his.

"Let me feel that needy pussy, Lux," he breathed, then refused to let me respond as his mouth devoured mine.

I spread my legs around his hips and pressed myself against his tip. A small cry escaped me as I sank lower. His cock split me open and I suddenly needed all of it as deep inside of me as possible.

Reading my thoughts again, he gripped my hips and

slammed me down against him. I cried out, both pleasure and pain threading together in perfect harmony. I tilted forward and back, soaking in each rising ripple deep within my belly.

His hands guided me to grind harder, faster, and with as much fervor as I could. Rocking with the rhythm of the storm, ragged breaths burned hot in my throat. Bjorn—Kayn too—had pleasured me, but this, with Drak, destroyed me. The closer I came to the edge, the more tears collected in my eyes.

"It's because we're destined for one another," he said, addressing my thoughts without a lick of the jealousy he once expressed for Kayn. "You're so perfect, Lux. So perfect sitting here on my cock like a fucking queen on her throne."

I absorbed his words, using them to build my pleasure until I couldn't keep going. The tension was too much, too intense, so I let him take over. His fingers sank into the skin at my hips, and he held me against him, guiding me to lift and arch and writhe until my breathing became desperate panting.

Ecstasy unfurled within me, and I couldn't stop the words spilling from my lips. Again. "Rune!"

"Say my name again, baby."

I could hardly speak with the ripples undulating throughout my entire body, but I managed a whisper that made him explode. "Rune…"

All at once, our storm ended, and outside had become quiet, too. The earth stopped shaking sometime during our ecstasy. Mara's Keep was still, which meant Thor's storm had finally ended.

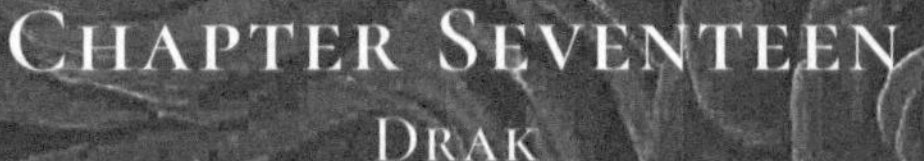

Chapter Seventeen

Drak

After the thunder silenced and the sky cleared, the aftermath seemed to lay bare across Lux's sagging body. Lying with her legs and hips and ass curled into me, I let her rest.

Deep sleep pulled her away from me, but I held her tightly and watched her rise and fall with each breath.

She had called me Rune, but there was no recognition in her eyes. She didn't fully believe it; she only said it because I had beckoned her to use the name.

Lux saw me as a warrior from the sagas, as if that were my true self. But I had no proof. The idea of claiming myself as part of the sagas—Myrah's lover—was almost madness, even for me. The thought that I had once been valiant and strong enough to leave Valhalla behind was everything I wanted to believe about myself. Yet I had been alone and for my own goals for too long to truly think I would have walked out of Valhalla and returned to this realm for someone else.

Sighing, I brushed a wavy tendril back from Lux's face. Once she woke, we'd leave for Yggdrasil, and everything would change. Tonight was our last moment of peace together before she turned her full attention to hunting Silver's army, and then—then I'd have to convince her to burn the tree.

The simplicity of sleep blanketed her features. Instead of tension in her jaw, Lux's face was relaxed, her lips parted slightly. There was no crease between her brow, and the vein at her temple didn't pulse because, in sleep, the gods seemed quiet. Only sleep and sex protected her from them. That much I could tell from her thoughts.

But once she woke, they'd return louder.

Freya would chide her.

Loki would laugh at her.

And Odin would wrap his fingers around her mind and control her like the fucking doll Kayn and his stupid gods convinced her to become. I couldn't blame her for falling into the role, not with the power of the divine speaking through her own thoughts.

It was either rise to the challenge, or watch everything fall to the vampires. I had chosen the same thing as Lux. When the gods ripped everything away from me, I rose to the challenge.

I became the undead creature they hated.

Footsteps echoed in the hall, then stopped outside the door. Axel wouldn't dare bother us, and no one else knew the library's location, buried within the maze of Mara's Keep and hidden beyond my bedchambers.

I'd chosen an old, forgotten bedroom deemed too drafty and at the end of a winding corridor for privacy. Anybody could have followed us here, but they didn't. I would have heard them, scented them.

So who the Hel knew?

Silver.

Kayn had tracked Lux here and led Silver straight to her sister. I didn't dare blink as I listened. Only the soft rise and fall of Lux's breath filled the air until this intruder moved again, a shadow dancing beneath the door.

I bared my fangs. Another of Silver's vampires was likely the culprit. One who'd returned immediately after the battle at the castle, knowing Lux would be weakened. She'd fought so well, taking on multiple vampires at once. Pride swelled within me, but it was quickly dashed by the flicker of the shadow.

No damn way they were interrupting her sleep.

Lux didn't need the practice right now; she needed as much rest as she could get before we left for the wasteland.

"Sleep well," I whispered, grazing my thumb across Lux's cheek. Carefully, I eased myself off her and padded across the room, leaving her to rest, curled beneath my cloak.

I waited at the door, biding my time for just the right moment that wouldn't wake Lux. When her breath rose, I would yank the door open and silence the bastard on the other side before he even had time to flinch.

Matching the rhythm of her inhale, I gripped the handle and twisted, bursting through with lightning speed. A snarling face met me as I lunged for the vampire's throat, pinning him against the hallway wall. The door shut behind me with a soft click.

The young man bared his fangs and hissed at me, his eyes glowing red as his fingernails clawed at my forearm. I tightened my grip around his neck. Though he didn't need to breathe, his eyes widened at my hold, betraying a flicker of fear beneath all that anger…anger at being bested before he even came close to Lux.

I tilted my head. "If it isn't little Alfie. Wasn't it just yesterday you turned into a vampire?"

His hissing dropped an octave, and I couldn't help but laugh. He was barely twenty, a boy who had begged to become a vampire to avoid being chosen as an executioner. Coward. Though I couldn't blame him for not wanting to serve as a vessel for the Blood Council, even if he had to sacrifice his soul to do it.

I swallowed any pity for this traitor before I spoke again. "Why would Silver send someone so…inexperienced with their own abilities? Does she want you dead? Or was it because you were the only one stupid enough to volunteer to try going after Lux, again, when so many of you have already failed spectacularly?"

I let up on my hold so that he could speak.

The red in his irises flared. "If you must know," he seethed, spit gathering at the corners of his mouth in foamy bubbles.

My fingers tightened again. "Speak quietly. Whispers only."

He continued, frowning, but speaking at a lower volume now. "Silver trusted me to send a message."

"Oh?" My eyebrows ticked up. I feigned interest by releasing a little more of the pressure on his throat.

"She's set forth for Yggdrasil. The tree will be burned in a fortnight, and your wife will be powerless once the gods can no longer reach her to grant their powers."

My wife.

My *wife*.

Hel, I loved that he called her that, even if it was fake. About as fake as this shit Alfie was trying to sell me. I snorted. "You're such a fucking liar. Just like you were as a human, always sneaking around."

When he smiled, I cringed at how ugly betrayal looked on a once handsome young man. In my eyes, he was just a snake now. "If you want to stop us, you have no choice but to leave your little hole."

"It's a trick," another voice joined us. Axel marched up, calm as always, hands clasped in front of him. He dipped his head quickly to pay his respects, then spoke. "Several vampires are hiding in the forest behind Mara's Keep. They're lying in wait to capture you, and of course, the new queen."

I loved Axel even more for calling Lux that. As one of the

few who understood that binding a witch to a vampire stripped her connection to the gods, he knew Lux was never truly my wife, having recognized the gods' madness in her after years of seeing it in my mother.

I grinned at Alfie and squeezed his neck again. "Good attempt, I guess." My words came out lazy, bored, and it made him stiffen under my hold, frustrated that he had done nothing but march toward his own destruction, though Silver had already expected it.

Alfie was definitely a sacrifice, bait to force us out of Mara's Keep while Lux was at her weakest. Silver was relentless, but this attempt at least showed her desperation. She had failed so many times to draw us out. There was no way she was braving this storm to travel back to Skaldir in search of Ragna's family again. If they even returned there. The only thing that would work was when they finally left for Yggdrasil.

Because she knew the truth about that tree.

Thanks to the hours we spent together as children, reading the records and sagas stored in Mara's Keep, she was the only one besides Lux who knew how treacherous the gods' domain was. For vampires, at least.

Fear took over the anger in his eyes now. Poor little Alfie. I almost felt bad for what I was about to do. The idiot should be dead before I took another breath; his neck snapped and then removed with the sword that Axel had hanging in a scabbard across his back.

But I released him instead.

Alfie lunged at me, but I smashed him back toward the wall. Axel drew the sword and tossed it to me. I held the side of the blade to Alfie's throat, pinning him only with my eyes now. The sword didn't touch him, but if he moved, I'd cut off his head. "I'm going to let you go." The stupid bastard didn't know Silver's way of killing him would be so much worse. I grew up with the girl, so I knew how twisted her thoughts were. "But you will tiptoe back where you came from so that you don't wake my wife. Not a sound. Got it?" When he didn't nod, I let the silver blade dip into his flesh, singeing the pale skin at the knot bobbing with his every swallow. "Got it?" Finally, he nodded, and the sword cut deeper with the movement, flaying his flesh. "And then you will remind Silver that she has lost. Again."

A shudder rippled through Alfie. Poor guy.

I let my arm fall to my side with the sword, and Alfie shot down the hallway in a blur, running with his damn tail between his legs. Such a shame he had chosen to follow Silver. When she and I were children, she'd always had an affinity for reading the sagas that spoke of torture. Full of ways in which our ancestors tormented their enemies.

And Alfie would be her test subject.

I shook my head and offered the sword back to Axel. "As always, thank you. You're one of the few people I can trust."

"I came to tell you both." He paused and nodded toward where Lux was still asleep in the library. "Ragna, the fresh vampire, has completed her transformation. She is asking for Lux, and your mother is asking for you."

I snapped my eyes to the closed door. "Give Lux another hour of sleep, and then I'll bring her to Ragna. For now, I'll say goodbye to my mother."

With a quiet nod, Axel accepted this and retreated down the hall.

I slipped back into the library and let out a sigh. Lux was still out cold, curled beneath the coat, her long lashes brushing her rosy cheeks. She looked perfect asleep, but the room itself was incomplete. I wished I could finish the shelves and give her a chance to see her favorite room whole before we risked the journey to Yggdrasil.

But there wasn't enough time to return to the workshop, and I wanted to savor every moment of my mother's clarity before she forgot me again.

Chapter Eighteen

Lux

R*agna is a vampire.*

Repeating it didn't help me wrap my head around it, and though my gut churned at the blood staining my friend's teeth, I didn't look away. I didn't treat her like a monster or act disturbed. When the man she had fed on left, Ragna seemed like the same person she had always been, just with a stronger thirst for blood.

Really, Ragna had always been bloodthirsty, even if not in the literal sense. She was the one pushing for illegal battle training.

And I loved her for it.

I perched at the edge of her bed, sinking into the soft fur. Ragna had undone her braids, and while one side of her hair fanned out like a horse's mane, she had shaved the other half of her head close to the skull.

My tough-as-a-wild-boar best friend didn't exactly have tusks, but the gleaming white fangs in Ragna's mouth made her look as terrifying as I knew she was on the inside. Red pooled in her gaze, and though she struggled to talk around her new fangs, she hadn't shut up since I sat on her bed.

"Alva will get away with anarchy," she said. "I just know it.

She has Rolf wrapped around her finger. That child can do no wrong in his eyes." She clicked her tongue.

A smile cracked my tense, stony expression. Vampire or not, Ragna was the same matter-of-fact witch I had always known, more concerned for her family than for herself. Fierce but protective, and a lot like Drak, if Drak didn't have his self-ish-ass side.

"This is all so freaky." She ran the pad of her thumb against her fangs.

"You only just woke up," I said, even though we had been talking for almost an hour. She had told me everything that had happened in Skaldir. How it felt when Silver's army raided and threatened them when the vampires took her entire family captive. My heart pinched painfully.

"Okay, but why the Hel can't I hide these things?" She tapped a fang with her finger. "It's true I've only known about vampires for a couple of months, but I swear I've seen them retract their fangs back into their mouths like a tongue."

"As I understand it," I said, "you'll learn how to do that with time. You're a new vampire."

"Great, a baby Draugr." She rolled her eyes. "Just what I always wanted to be." A laugh escaped me, but it died as her lips tipped downward. Ragna rarely frowned, only when she was concentrating while tilling the fields, scolding her children or husband, or focusing on a fight, especially back when sparring was still illegal and we had to hide beneath her house to practice with fake weapons. Now, she frowned easily. "In all seriousness, I felt it happening." Her hand splayed across her chest with her palm pressing heavily against the center of her ribcage, beneath her breasts.

"Felt what?"

"My soul."

I drew a sharp breath. "What do you mean?"

"When my soul broke, horror came over me. It shattered. I know I felt it. My whole body, my mind, everything froze as if I had fallen into a fjord in winter, yet I was also on fire, and across the back of my eyelids I saw an impossibly bright light." Her eyes went blank, unblinking. "It cracked like ice and shattered like glass."

She winced as if she were experiencing it all over again.

"That sounds…awful."

"And now I no longer have a heartbeat." She grabbed my wrist and forced my palm against her chest. "Do you feel that? Do you?" I shook my head, giving her the response I knew she was looking for. "Exactly. Nothing. My heart and soul are both gone."

"I'm so sorry, Ragna. It's my fault."

"Don't you fucking blame yourself, Lux Norn Quinn. I'm still here, not in the afterlife." She jabbed a finger at me like a weapon. "I'm still here, and for that I am grateful. I will learn how to use these, as I learned to use any other weapon." She tapped her fingernail against the tooth again. "And I will protect my family."

She reacted just as Drak had predicted. He didn't know Ragna like I did, but I had forgotten that he understood how tempting and powerful it was to become undead. He recognized that same fierce determination in her, so I should have known he'd be right about this.

"But I am the Gods' huntress, Ragna. I'm chosen to *kill* vampires." She only knew as much as the people of Vylheim had gleaned from the fragments of information about vampires, the Blood Council, and more, but it was enough.

"You are named after the Norns, Lux. I know you will thwart whatever destiny you do not want, because you weave your own destiny."

I laughed again until Odin's voice crooned at the back of my skull. "*She will be destroyed. There is no destiny but death for all vampires.*"

My stomach curled in on itself, but I forced myself to focus on the present. I didn't know how much longer I'd have with

Ragna before we left for Yggdrasil. Vampire or not, I cared for her.

A skip in my pulse left me momentarily breathless, and as hard as I tried to clear my mind, Odin's words ground through me. As if he'd imprinted his will on my very bones.

"Listen, listen huntress…kill her now. Listen!"

I forced out a harsh breath and blinked. "I wish I could be as sure as you are."

"You don't need to be sure," she said. "I remember when you were a teenager. Weaving records into the tapestries with your father's new wife. Remember when you wove the image of a whale into the winter tapestry? And then, someone spotted a stranded whale on Skaldir's beaches just weeks later? We ate well all that winter, and you were the one who made that happen."

I smiled. "It was just a tapestry."

"Perhaps," she said, nodding. After a moment, she smirked. "I can use your guilt about this to make you weave again, can't I?" I gave her a look of mock anger. "Like maybe you should weave a tapestry for me with an image of a soul."

My brow furrowed. "And what would that look like?"

"What I saw was a beautiful crystal." She snorted, tapping her chest. "As if anything inside here could be called beautiful."

"Rolf would say everything about you is beautiful."

"My face? My body? Definitely, but with how much I hated the executioners, I expected my mind and soul to be a little uglier."

A soft knock rapped at the closed door of the bedchamber, and I turned toward it as Axel poked his head inside. Usually, his soft-spoken voice and steady demeanor soothed me, but a frown was fixed across his lips now.

My nerves hummed.

"What is it?" I asked.

"We've come upon the time to embark," he said, using the

phrase of our ancestors who often traveled by sea. Another reason I liked Axel so much.

According to Drak, Axel had always known that young Drak was sneaking into the library to read the sagas and rune-stones. But he'd never stopped him, and he'd never dared tell King Roderic that Drak wasn't hiding out in his room where he was meant to stay.

"Leave Mara's Keep?" I asked, more to hear it aloud than to confirm what he was saying.

When he nodded, his white-streaked hair bounced. "That's right, my queen. King Drakkar has summoned you to the study. He will meet you there to prepare for the journey once he is ready."

I squeezed Ragna's hand before slipping off the bed and facing Axel. "What is he doing now?"

"Saying goodbye," he said. My mouth popped open again, but before I could ask for more detail, he answered. "To his mother."

With that, Axel's head disappeared and the door fell shut. The hollow bang of it reverberated through the room.

I turned to Ragna, but she too spoke before I could. "Weave your own destiny, Lux, as you always have."

"I'm sorry I can't make you human again," I said. If it was as simple as weaving a crystal into a tapestry, Freya and Odin would have told me, and I'd be a weaver, chosen to restore the vampires' souls rather than kill them all…right?

Odin hummed low, a vibration through my mind that sounded like Thor's thunder. But I hadn't heard the crack of lightning or the howl of wind since Drak woke me and took me to Ragna. The storm must have stopped.

Now we could forge a path to Yggdrasil and fight Silver's army in the Gods' domain.

I was ready.

Ragna gave me a sad smile. "How about this? Weave a set of teeth for me so I can learn to harness all of this. The sooner I master this monstrosity, the sooner I can return to my babies. And if I'm being honest, I'm not sure I even want to be human again."

My pulse skipped at her words, but I understood completely. The power coursing through Ragna's veins gave her newfound hope to defend Skaldir and her family from Silver and the vampires. She could tear wild animals to shreds and feed Alva, Rolf, and the others.

But she didn't have a soul; none of them did. Those were long shattered, destroyed, lost.

My heart sank slowly, dragging my stomach into a tight clench as I thought of Drak, hollow and devoid of a soul. Ragna had only just turned into a vampire, but Drak had been undead for years, feasting on human after human. Even if they hadn't all died from his bloodlust, Odin's voice at the back of my head confirmed my fears.

"Monsters cannot love."

But was this the truth? I had a soul, yet I was a monster in my own right, and I knew how to love.

Listening to Ragna now, I realized just how fiercely I loved her, how I loved my mother and Stasia, and, as wrong as it felt, how my heart found comfort in Drak. Especially when he had told me he'd waited a hundred years for me, though his claim made no sense, since Drak had only been on this earth as long as I had.

Whether or not it made sense, my heart, or perhaps my soul, relished his words.

Chapter Nineteen

Drak

Every weathered walkway on the path to my mother's room was etched into my memory.

I knew the maze of Mara's Keep from a childhood spent sneaking through its corridors, and when I first discovered the stairs leading down into the depths beneath, I wasn't even seven years old.

I found myself drawn to the dungeons below, drawn to Silver. Not because of who she was, but because I recognized something within her, and it brought a strange comfort, even if the dungeons were cold and damp and Silver was angry and unkind. Back then, I didn't blame her for her unhinged behavior. She was a little girl trapped behind bars. I would have been furious too.

And I grew angrier the older I got, and the more murderous she became.

In front of the heavy door, I drew a steady breath before gathering the strength to enter. The door let out a yawning groan as I pushed through and stepped into the dusty bedchamber. I'd abandoned this room when Lux returned to Mara's Keep, only returning to visit the one who dwelled beneath the creaky hatch.

My bed lay empty, dust settling over the rumpled covers. Large stones filled the fireplace, which had once been a passageway leading outside the castle. Now, I blocked it off to keep the enemy from sneaking through.

I strode to the wooden hatch that I no longer kept concealed by a rug, and crouching, I pressed my hand against the splintered oak.

"Mother?" I said, my voice cracking. After several moments of silence, stirring echoed from the deep. "Mother, it's Drak."

The latch on the other side slid with a clunk. That was a good sign of her stability.

I gripped the handle and wrenched the hatch open to see my mother climbing back down into her bedchamber.

Her room was nothing unique, aside from it being hidden. A large bed occupied one end, with a chest at its foot. A wardrobe stood open, revealing her nightgowns, all the same drab beige she wore daily. Down here, she didn't even know the difference between day and night.

Tall candles sat on the shelf of the open wardrobe above the hanging gowns. Their quivering flames cast a narrow shaft of light across the stone floor, and she crossed through it like a ghost.

"Come in, my boy," she said. My mother shuffled back to the bed where she let her hip sink into the side. The bed was too tall next to her slight body. I made a mental note to have the servants bring her a stool to climb into the comfort of her blankets more easily. Maybe I should have them bring a whole new bed.

I climbed down into the room, using the curves in the stone to guide my hands and feet.

She stared at me, holding a fragile smile full of sadness. She rarely greeted me with recognition, but when she did, she always came to me, cupping my face in her frail fingers.

Today, she couldn't even summon that strength. My skin

grew colder than usual, and a dull soreness spread through my throat and lungs. I should have been grateful that she was well on the day I came to bid goodbye, but her physical weakness pressed a heavy weight onto my chest.

Her prominent cheekbones, once marking her as one of the most beautiful women in Vylheim, now jutted sharply across her hollow face. A plate of lamb's leg and bread crust, soaked in the juice from the meat, lay uneaten on the chest. It was obvious she hadn't touched the food since the bronze fork was clear of fingerprints and the plate was full.

"Mother," I said as I marched toward her. "You have to eat."

She only shook her head and let her chilly eyes fall to her knobby feet. If the world saw her, they'd assume she was as old as our ancestors based on the twist of her bones and exhaustion in her eyes, but she'd been a young mother when I was born twenty-seven years ago—strong and intense—before King Roderic sentenced her to the life of an executioner.

I scrubbed a hand over my face. "You're not doing well."

"I am okay."

"The madness you're dealing with—"

"I'm not mad!" she shrieked. Her skeletal hands shot out to either side of her forehead. Thin, twisted fingers resembled branches stripped of their leaves.

She was a dying tree.

I stepped closer and gently wrapped my hands around her wrists. Pulling her hands away from her face encouraged her to meet my eyes, and I spoke softly. "You know that when you acknowledge the truth it helps you."

"No." Her chin quivered. "No, don't say it. I'm Ingrid."

"Yes," I brushed my thumb over the back of her hand. They were far too cold, even against the chill of a vampire who hadn't fed in too long. "You're Ingrid."

"Curses. Cursed Ingrid. A cursed weapon."

My grip tightened on her hand. "No." This was the same

narrative the gods fed Lux, and I wasn't about to hear it from my mother too. I couldn't bear it now, not when I needed her to see me off. "You're my mother."

"The spawn, living dead, evil."

"No!" I squeezed her fragile fingers too hard. She shrieked and whipped them back, clutching her hands to her chest as she jumped to her feet. Curling into herself, she retreated step by step until her back met the wall beside her bed. "I'm Drak, your son." I swallowed hard. "Little Drak."

"So big. Bloodthirsty." I breathed a quiet curse when she raised a crooked finger at me. "Have to kill you."

No matter how many times I heard her say this, it still gutted me. I clenched my eyes shut and let the darkness fill the space beneath my lids before opening them again. "You won't kill me."

She shook her head harder, eyes unblinking. "I won't?"

I sank onto the bed, sitting low so I wouldn't intimidate her by standing over her. Like a little boy again, I sat at the end of her mattress and stared at her, waiting for her to see me as *myself*—not as a vampire she had once been chosen to destroy.

Her wide eyes stayed fixed on me for too long, and though she was upright, she looked lifeless as she stared blankly. Neither of us moved. Even the twitch of my mouth could cause her to flinch or attack.

And I hated having to subdue her.

I hated the feel of her skeletal body in my arms as I lifted her struggling frame and laid it in the bed. I'd wrap the blankets tightly around her until she finally gave in from exhaustion and fell asleep, only for the servants to return later with warm broth and help her out of bed.

Finally, she blinked. Her eyelids cleared the tinted glaze from the whites of her eyes, and the hard line of her wrinkled lips softened. Tears welled in the pale pink corners of her eyes as she stumbled toward me, arms outstretched.

"Little Drak," she sobbed as her fingers curled around my beard and jaw. "My little Drak."

I leaned into her touch for the minute that she was with me. "I have news, Mother."

She struggled to climb back into the bed, so I cupped her elbow and let her use my arm for leverage. "I want to know how my little boy is."

"I'm going to become a god, Mother."

The lines between her brow deepened. "Evil?"

I nodded. "I know, but I have to because I have to stop them from doing more of what they did to you."

"You can't." Childlike, her voice trembled as she placed her hands in mine. So frail were her fingers that they felt as though they might crumble under my touch. I moved as gently as possible, even as the truth of her words cut deep. "It's too late."

"I failed you," I said. "I know. Becoming a vampire was only the first step. I couldn't move everything fast enough. I couldn't control Vylheim with The Blood Council in my way, but now I have a witch to bring Odin to me." She blinked at me. "To become a god, I must kill one. That was what you saw in your visions, a long time ago."

"That won't fix anything."

"As a god, I can do almost anything, Mother."

"You can't fix me. The gods' abilities are very specific, and I've never heard of one that could heal the mind. Maybe the body, but not the mind. So no, you can't do just anything."

She had spoken more than she had in a long time, and I was grateful, yet the harsh truth she shared still hurt. "Damn."

"Language, Little Drak. I know you're an old soul and a grown man, but our father didn't like angry words. They reminded him of King Roderic."

I lifted my eyes to meet hers again. Cold and scared, yet fully aware. She was the only other huntress left alive. Even if she never fully embraced the role, the gods had claimed her mind ever since her skills as a seer drew their attention.

What had she seen of me before they took her from me? This wasn't the first time she'd referred to me as an old soul.

"Mother," I licked my lips, tentative, but also tempted to ask. "Back when you were a free witch, what did you see of my future?"

"Witches are never free."

"I know." I nodded. "But free of this madness the gods left you with. Did you ever see anything different in me?"

Her eyelids fell slowly, not sealing fully shut before they opened again and her lips parted. "What do you mean?"

"Is it possible that I am someone other than Drak?"

Damn if I didn't want proof before we left Mara's Keep.

Proof I could show Lux that we were meant to be together, even after godhood. When she no longer needed me.

"Other than Drak?" she echoed. "Someone other than Drak. Little Drak. My Little Drak…"

Shit. Once her repetitions began, her mind spun out of control. I lifted her hand to my jaw and brought her attention to me again. "You said King Roderic named me Drakkar." That bastard. He wasn't even my father. Although he had slept with my mother many times, he showed no interest in her until she was pregnant. Then it didn't matter who my father was, because she became one of his mistresses, and he forced her to forget the other men and women she loved. "What did you want to name me?"

"Drakkar," she whispered. "Drakkar is the king. But I've never met him…"

No, don't lose reality. "Mother."

"I hear of him." She yanked her hands back and tapped her ear. "Cruel things. Blood drips through the door." Pointing to the hatch, she referred to my feedings. Panic crawled into her eyes, and she scooted away from me, head shaking. "You."

"I'm Drakkar, your son." Frustration clawed at my ragged

throat. "Listen to me, Mother. You didn't choose the name Drakkar because you wanted to name me something else. I remember you saying that once. So what name did you want, and why? Did you see someone else in me?"

This was too much. Her eyes widened until they seemed to bulge, like the body of a fallen soldier on a battlefield, lifeless and bloated.

I'd pushed her too far thanks to my own damn desperation.

I swallowed my questions and turned my palm upward, revealing the scar that traced the natural lines of my hand. She'd once called it my battle wound, even if it came from the little girl imprisoned beneath the castle.

The first time I went to the dungeons was with my mother, when the executioners threw Silver behind bars. In a burst of unhinged rage, Silver lunged at us, raking a sharp rock across my hand as I raised it to block my face. The wound gushed blood, and my mother whisked me out of there for a bandage.

My mother cried for hours, mourning that her son had been hurt and also because she had to leave the little witch alone and cold in the dungeons. To ease her worry, I memorized the path and returned to visit Silver, so Mother would know the witch wasn't truly alone.

"Do you remember this?" I asked, while flexing my fingers over the scar, and then opening my fist again.

She hummed. "That poor witch." *That poor witch* was now trying to murder everyone, adding only to our enemies. My mother's whisper cut through my thoughts. "She was just scared." She could believe whatever she wanted, but Silver wasn't just scared. Rage defined her, even at that age.

"What was the name you chose for me?" I asked, now that she was back to reality. "From your visions?"

My mother curled her lower lip inward and then shook her head. "I don't know. I—I think your father named you. Yes, yes!" Recognition and joy lit up her eyes. I felt the corner of my mouth twitch, almost smiling. "Erik swore he'd already met you. He said he knew who you were, even before you were born."

Hanging on her every word, I didn't dare move a muscle. I didn't dare do anything to frighten or distract her. Why would he have said that? Did he think I was another family member reborn, like so many others of his time believed?

If only I'd had more time with him.

"But the name he wanted…" her voice faded, and her brow pinched. "I can't remember. I'm so sorry, Little Drak."

I nodded. "It's okay."

She turned my hand over and patted the back of it. "It doesn't matter what your name is; I love you all the same. Whatever you are."

Rarely did she remember anything new from our conversations. Even minutes later, her mind would wipe away the words, but this time, she had been aware enough to see me as her son and a vampire.

I dragged my eyes back up to her face, but when I opened my mouth to tell her I loved her too, her eyes darkened.

She shot to her feet and backed away from me. "Leave me. Leave now. Leave, please!"

"Mother." I stood.

Cowering in the corner, she pressed herself into the shadows, hands clutching her head. "Rip these thoughts out of me. Rip them out and take them with you!"

My teeth ached under the pressure of my clenched jaw. The distant echo of the gods—the memory of their voice still plagued her. I could do nothing to help her, so I curled my fingers over the scar in my palm and strode away.

This was the last time I'd see her as a vampire, because when I returned, I'd be a god who killed everyone who'd fucked with her.

Chapter Twenty

Lux

I ran my hand over the ridges of the black mask. After half a day of sleep, I wrapped myself in the leather and thickly woven linen meant to protect my skin in the wasteland.

"It's time," Drak said, interrupting my thoughts. "Put it on."

I snapped my gaze from the mask to the vampire king, who filled the study doorway with his broad shoulders. My heart skipped. The clay had already molded the mask tightly to his features, fixing it to his face. Thin strips of leather, sliced in columns at his mouth, had thin, gauzy fabric webbed through each strip. Only his icy eyes pierced through the combination of clay and leather.

"We're really leaving?" I asked.

He nodded. "Someone spotted Silver's army moving across the border. It's now or never."

I sucked in a breath and pressed the mask to my face. "We need to catch up."

"We will. Two travelers compared to fifty or so vampires will be much faster."

"She's not taking her entire army?" I asked as I followed him from the study and through the winding stone.

I wouldn't miss Mara's Keep, but I'd miss the quiet we'd enjoyed here and the library. Sitting on that rug, surrounded by the books of our history and sagas recorded by our ancestors, was akin to the one throne of Vylheim for Drak.

Maybe for Silver, too.

I didn't understand the obsession with that hideous bronze chair. Of course, I knew the hunger for power was the real draw, but even that never attracted me. I wanted a place for the witches, a safe world to live in, and enough to eat, not to tell others how to live their lives. There was already too much of that control in my past.

"Of course not, she thinks she doesn't need everyone," he said. The low timbre of his voice echoed through the stretch of hallway. "If she burns Yggdrasil, your powers burn too. You won't even be able to fight one vampire, much less fifty, but thankfully, she's taking most of them. The strongest of them."

Forcing out a huff, I picked up the pace. "We should have left sooner. Why did we let them get ahead?"

"Because we're not insane enough to risk being struck down by Thor's storm."

I let out a little growl. Last night, while we should have been enduring the storm, we were wrapped in each other's arms, lost in a foolish fantasy about our romantic future.

Even if the impossible were true, and Drak and I were in this realm to find each other, we were bound to fall apart again. Once my sister destroyed our chance at resisting her army, we'd be ripped away from one another—me chosen for Folkvangr or Hel. Definitely not Valhalla after failing the gods.

And Drak would turn to ash when she compelled him and staked him with a branch from Yggdrasil.

"You don't regret it," he said, shooting a smirk over his shoulder at me.

"What?"

"Last night."

Pursing my lips, I looked away so I didn't give him the satisfaction of being right, even if I succumbed to him whenever he kissed me.

And when he promised to protect me by wearing Sten's ring around his neck.

And when he kept me warm both last night and in the tents during my first trip to Mara. Every one of those moments was etched into the rhythm of my pulse.

Drak took care of me, bandaging my wounds, giving me plenty of rest—no, *demanding* that I rest. He was the only one who saw my blue fingers and took them in the warmth of his hands.

So no, I didn't regret last night.

Gnawing at my lip, I kept quiet and let Drak's pride squirm a little. Even if he could read my thoughts when I ached for him, that didn't mean he could see through me like a ghost haunting these halls. We turned a corner, marching with purpose while my mind explored this.

What a strange thing it was to want to be known as myself, and nothing more than myself. Not the huntress or a witch, or the name I went by almost my entire life. I wasn't Silver, but I didn't know if I was truly Lux either. Whoever Lux was supposed to be, I never got the chance to find out before everyone else told me exactly who to be.

How could I long to be known and yet recoil at the thought of being perceived?

Drak's stride quickened. I almost had to jog to keep up, but I didn't complain. Moving fast was exactly what I'd insisted on. Besides, it had been so long since I ran, and running had once been woven into the fabric of my life.

I hurried ahead and matched Drak's pace. He tilted his head and gave me a careful look, a small smile flickering beneath the mask.

Finally, an oval door of black, nearly rotten wood came into view at the end of the hall. This wasn't a dead end or a new turn into a seemingly endless corridor, but our exit. Wood scraped against the stone frame as he shoved it open, and the hinges seemed to whine at us for leaving them behind.

I stepped up to the threshold, drawing the deepest breath I could. Hiding in Mara's Keep was over. This was a new beginning, like the calm after a storm, when we would have to leave our shelter and confront the mess the wind and rain had left behind.

We were cleaning up Silver's mess, the vampires' mess, and Myrah's for creating the undead in the first place. I winced, never having blamed an ancestor so easily before.

Yes, they fought and bled and tainted the wasteland with their battles, but my mother had raised me to respect their fervor and bravery. Their imperfect humanity pushed them to the edge, but they'd fought in the name of the Gods, so it couldn't be entirely wrong.

But Myrah…Myrah abandoned the Gods and sentenced our realm to suffer the plague of the undead. A twitch forced my left eye to flutter at the same time my mouth involuntarily pulled down at one side.

"Now you see." Odin's voice scraped through my head like the rough wooden panels too large for the doorway's cutout in the stone.

"Lux." Drak's call feathered through my thoughts.

He reached for me, beckoning me outside. I slid my fingers into his hand and let him lead me into the moonlight. The thin crescent offered only a faint glow, casting a dim blue light across the hill behind the castle.

Axel and Sif greeted us, carrying heavy packs filled with the provisions we needed to survive: dried meat, fresh water, and hide tents we could close tightly enough to block the thick particles drifting in the fog.

"Thank you, Axel," Drak said as he took the pack and

lifted it to his shoulders where a sword already hung across his back.

Axel didn't exactly smile, but his expression was always warm. A pleasant contrast to the cool white streaks in his peppered hair. "You can trust that both Mara and your mother will be in good hands."

"Right." Drak frowned, his voice sarcastic.

"King Drakkar, you've selected me and Sif to step in for you in the interim for a reason."

Nodding, Drak gave him a grim smile. "As much as I trust you, you know I hate leaving my throne. There's just something about it..." He shook his head, cutting himself off. "I could swear it gives its own power."

Axel coughed and cleared phlegm from his throat. The knot in his neck bobbed. "I thought you should know of this news as well."

Drak pinned him with a stare. "Yes?"

"Observers have spotted Ylva and Darius conspiring closely with Silver."

Drak cursed, clawing his hands through his hair. "I should have known." He shot me a loaded glance I couldn't read. I remembered Ylva and Darius from the old Blood Council—they hadn't trusted Silver either, but these were desperate times. Ripping his eyes from the ground, his gaze landed on me again, almost as if he had heard my confusion. "They've always had a strange power over Silver. That's how we get to know her better. Through them. They're almost like…parents to her." A strange, hollow laugh escaped him. "If parents simultaneously hated, respected, and were terrified of their own child."

I frowned. This solidified my desire not to kill my sister. My mistake had torn her away from her real parents, and she'd had no one to look up to. No one other than two bloodthirsty, power-hungry vampires.

Axel coughed politely, his face revealing no emotion. "There's more."

"I already know plenty about Ylva and Darius," Drak said, waving his hand dismissively. "I have no doubt they're leeching Silver's power and quietly manipulating her now that they have no other way to control her."

Axel shook his head. "Not about them. The other vampire has escaped from Silver's captivity." We exchanged a look before Axel explained. "Fishers at Einnland's shore spotted The Exile heading toward the old Hall of the Gods—"

Kayn.

"Do we know how he escaped Silver?" Drak asked.

"Unclear," Axel said. "The only information we have is that he is, indeed, free of her this time. He did not appear to be under any compulsion, and she and her army were miles away when he was spotted there.

"Was anyone else with him?" I asked, interrupting the interim ruler of Vylheim. "Two women, perhaps? Young and blonde, and the other older and possibly sickly looking?"

When he shook his head, my heart sank. My nerves stretched thin, and old thoughts threatened the wall I had built in my mind to keep the Gods at bay. It rarely kept them out, but it helped temper the intrusive thoughts that needled me whenever my nerves became threadbare.

Now, they filtered back in.

How many times have I failed my mother? And now Stasia too. I hadn't allowed myself to think of them often. I couldn't, not when worry for them stripped me of all rational thought and my entire being became nothing but a raw, exposed nerve.

If you can't do this, you're worthless.

Stupid.

A husk of a human.

No! I didn't need to waste time tearing myself apart.

"I'm sorry, my queen," Axel said, reading the torment on my face. "If it is any consolation, our understanding of the timeline is that he had escaped a few days ago and we did not have eyes on him until recently. Perhaps he could have had others accompanying him before we caught sight of him."

Kayn might have helped them escape and stashed them somewhere, like the ruins of the old temple. My mother had once taken refuge in the Hall of the Gods.

"So he was definitely alone?" Drak asked again, his gaze slicing to me. Concern softened the edges of his chilly eyes.

"Yes, my king."

"Now use some of your spies to locate Soren," Drak said. "And if they don't before I return, you have my word that I'll repay you for everything and use the foresight to find him." With a slap against Axel's back, Drak thanked him and tilted his head. "Lux, come."

That was it. We left Axel and Sif at the threshold of the arched entryway and pressed onward. Equipped with fresh blood donated from one of the humans at court, Drak would keep his energy up whenever mine waned. I'd keep my strength with regular rest and plenty of meat and water.

As we walked, I inquired about Soren, but when Drak only shared that he was a relation of Axel's that he'd lost track of years ago, I turned my attention to the path ahead.

From this height, we glimpsed the dull, unnatural clouds hanging over the wasteland. But once we descended the peak Mara's Keep rested on, the thick tree cover blocked our view. It didn't matter. Soon we would cross that threshold too.

I'd never been to the wasteland, but the skin on my neck and shoulders already prickled at the thought of navigating through toxic fog.

What would Yggdrasil look like? Drak had said it sat at a peak, like Mara's Keep. Did its branches stretch above the sickly clouds? How fast would it burn in that environment? Too fast for me to stop it if Silver sparked a flame?

If it became ash before I killed her army, I would have failed not only my mother and Stasia but also the Gods I worshiped. Odin, the Allfather who created us. Freya, mother of love and death and fertility. And all the girls in the villages across Vylheim who dreamed of simple lives weaving and gathering. Many of them caught glimpses of what it would be like to train as a warrior and shield-maiden now that the bloodshed law withered with the collapse of The Blood Council. Perhaps they'd learn to fight, and we could expand beyond Vylheim to find better soil and safer land from the storms.

Now that vampires were exposed, so many possibilities emerged—if *only* I succeeded and saved Yggdrasil.

The heat of Drak's gaze burned through the images in my mind. "What is it?" I asked as I eyed him. The forest welcomed us with deeper shadows.

Drak hefted the heavy pack higher on his shoulders. "I want to know what you're obsessing over." His lips split into a sardonic smile. "I would know if it were me consuming your thoughts because I'd be able to hear it. And I'm greedy—"

"Jealous, I'd say." I returned a flash of the grin he gave me.

"Yes, I'm fucking jealous of whatever you can't stop thinking about. So, tell me."

I lifted my chin to the thin stream of light filtering in through the branches overhead. "What if we don't make it?" His eyes narrowed. "What if Silver destroys the tree?"

"Then she can't stake me," he said with another mischievous grin.

I huffed and rolled my eyes. "Sure, but you can't reach Godhood either."

At that, his eyes darkened. "We'll make it. Silver's only guessing at its location, and I've been there before. Besides, once we catch up with them, you'll gut half her company. How likely is she to get away from us again?"

"She can compel multiple vampires at once, so I'd say it's possible."

"You need a little hope."

"Like some ridiculous dream that we were both warriors in a past life, destined to fight and fuck and love once we found each other in the next life?"

Drak ran his tongue along his exposed fangs. Clearly, that had made him mad, since his fangs only emerged when he was starving, aroused, or furious.

Ripping his gaze from me, he fixed his eyes on the path ahead. He barely breathed, even though his usual rhythm was always steady, a simple habit that rarely wavered. Perhaps he wasn't as angry as he was…disappointed?

I squinted at him, catching dim glimpses of his face in the slices of moonlight that broke through the forest. Did he truly believe that he was Myrah's lover, and that I was…her?

While we ducked branches and climbed the slight ascent toward the wasteland, I mulled this over for the next few hours. I was probably the closest she'd ever come to being reborn, inheriting her abilities while Silver took on her learned skills after creating the first vampire. Witches shared many powers, but that didn't make us the same person.

Still, I'd had the urge to call him by a name I'd never used before.

Drak stopped abruptly, and I blinked at the cloud before me. The forest gradually transformed from tall, sturdy trees with lush leaves to thinner trees with darker wood, burned and leaf-bare. Further out, only stumps remained, and the earth was no longer covered in leaves, moss, or life, but cracked like splintered logs. Black veins snaked through the reddish-brown soil, and further still, the dirt held the crimson stain of our ancestors' blood.

Thick fog, gray and brown, and tinted red in places, carried spots of black. My stomach churned, and the throbbing in my head expanded.

This was the last step from the forest of Mara to the wasteland. Once we entered, our survival became uncertain. Drak was moving closer to the tree that held the only wood capable of destroying him, and I was risking the land our ancestors had fled after it claimed so many of their loved ones.

Nervous tension pressed against the walls of my mind, threatening to collapse them as scattered thoughts slipped through the cracks.

Worthless failure.

Just turn around, you'll never beat her there, you're too weak.

"If you don't listen to me, you will fail. Kill him, wild little weapon." Odin's voice was shrill, unsteady, grating at my raw nerves.

I need him to show me the way.

"Then swear on your life, your mother's life, and every life, that you will do what needs to be done once you glimpse Yggdrasil, or I'll meet you there, beneath the tree, and make sure you suffer."

You would threaten me? My heart hurt when Odin didn't respond, but in his defense, I'd been listening to him less and less…

I gnawed at the inside of my cheek, biting down hard as I tried to give him the promise he wanted. I couldn't swear on their lives as much as I couldn't imagine killing Drak now. The ice cracking inside my skull confirmed Odin's disappointment, anger, or perhaps even hatred.

Whatever it was, I shuddered.

Drak took my hand in his. "Lux, look at me." Peeling my eyes from the black specks, I met his gaze. "Whatever shit you're thinking about yourself, or whatever poison the Gods are feeding you, isn't true. You're just afraid, and you fucking should be. There's no shame in it. Fear tells lies because it wants to keep you alive."

"And shouldn't I want to stay alive?"

His eyes narrowed with a thoughtful look. "You know you're meant for more than merely surviving. That's one of the many things I've always found fascinating about you. You take control."

I scoffed. "You can't control everything, and I don't care to."

"That's not what I mean. You don't listen to me. So don't listen to the lies in your head either."

My body failed me often, but that didn't mean I was weak, and even if I was one of the slowest at the footraces, I loved running. I loved the challenge. I loved the witches and Skaldir and my mother more. For once, Odin's disappointment didn't curdle in my gut and cling to the recesses of my mind. Somehow, I blocked him out.

Perhaps I could care for Drak, and refuse to hurt him, while also refusing to summon Odin. They could both exist, right? Hel, I hoped so because when Drak looked at me with softness warming his icy gaze, my heart skipped.

He placed his foot on the cracked earth, crossing the threshold into the wasteland. Dust puffed around his black boot, leaving a hint of red.

Reaching out, he offered to guide me beyond Vylheim for the first time in my life. A strange smile tugged at my lips as I took Drak's hand. He was right here with me. Even if he had his own twisted goal, right now it seemed he saw nothing else, cared for nothing else. He was only looking at me.

The pride in his eyes swelled in my heart, and I thought, perhaps I loved Drak, too.

With that thought curling in my mind, Odin's anger surged. All the effort I'd made to calm my nerves and the peace I'd felt with Drak by my side withered away. I felt naked and exposed to the elements of fear and frustration.

"Monsters don't know love."

Chapter Twenty-One

Drak

After just a day's travel, I already hated not being able to see the creases of concern on Lux's face. The mask gave only fleeting glimpses through the mesh, and that wasn't enough, especially as I watched her struggle.

Something had unsettled her the moment we crossed into the wasteland, evident in the irritation behind every word she spoke. What I wouldn't give to hear her thoughts right now. But even if I could, I needed to focus on listening for Silver's approaching army.

With each step, red dust rose into the air, settling on our boots and clothes. Lux's ragged breathing grated on my nerves because I couldn't help her. All I could do was keep walking and guide her toward Yggdrasil, to the east where the bloody sun rose.

The clouds were the only good thing about this damn place. The dust and fog blocked the sun, letting me move freely in daylight. Through the haze, the deep red sun hung high, not lighting the wasteland but dangling like a massive, dirt-streaked apple in a wild tree.

Lux slipped over the hard-packed earth, her ankle twisting in a crack. I caught her elbow just before she fell, preventing the snap of her bones, but she remained breathless. The air here only made it worse. Adding to her struggle, her entire focus was on tracking Silver's army, a task guided by nothing more than Freya's vague visions.

She wriggled free of my grip and pushed on.

"Let's rest again," I said.

"No."

"Lux, come on." When I reached for her arm, she shoved me off and almost lost her balance. I couldn't blame her for the rising frustration. Nobody moved through the wasteland unscathed, not even the gods' chosen witch.

"We can't stop again already."

"Your body will force you to."

She craned her neck and pinned me with a haughty stare. "What if I want to collapse?" Her voice was edgy, irritation rising to the surface with exhaustion. "That's how I receive visions, and maybe we need a vision to show us a faster way."

"There is no faster way."

She continued as if I hadn't spoken at all. "Freya can only reach me when I'm between consciousnesses. So if I collapse, it could actually help us."

"That's fucked up."

She shrugged, her arms falling limp with the weight of Vylheim. "That's how it works."

"The gods are lying to you then."

Whipping around, she poked me in the center of my chest with her finger. "The gods don't lie. We're the liars."

When she turned and kept forcing one foot in front of the other, I placed a hand on her back, urging her up the slanted ground. The dust and hard ground made it difficult to gain purchase at the angle, and though she slipped with every few steps, I wasn't about to let her fall.

"I don't lie," I said.

She scoffed. "What about our marriage?"

"Fine, I don't lie to you, but the gods clearly do."

"How can you talk so poorly of them when they gave me the ability to protect everyone, including myself?"

"I'd argue that hunting them is less about protection and more because Odin hates that he can't reach the undead. In no realm does it make sense that you have to destroy yourself for answers when the gods are already speaking directly inside your mind."

She fell silent.

Hiking through the fog of blood and war and remnants of our ancestors felt like a hundred years had passed—for both of us. I couldn't see the nuances in Lux's expressions to determine how much she was suffering, but of course I didn't need to. The shaking of her hands, the blue fingers, the tightness in every breath she drew was enough to know she was at the edge of collapse, and she would not let me do anything about it.

Fuck if I didn't despise watching Lux push herself to the breaking point.

"We're headed to Yggdrasil," I said. "That's enough for now. We'll make it there faster than Silver."

"We don't know that for sure, and cutting down as much of her army before we get there ensures the tree's safety. So if you'll let me focus, I'm going to spark a vision and find out where they are."

Her foot slid backwards, so I increased the pressure at the small of her back. After a few deep huffs, she steadied herself and took another step. The crimson cut through the earth grew darker and wider now.

"How do you know Freya will even show you what you need?" I asked.

"Because I'm requesting it. When I asked the gods how to help my mother, they sent me to you."

As much as I wanted to relish the thought that she considered me helpful, I had to speak the truth. "And? Your mother is Silver's captive."

"But they gave me access to the sagas. They supplied me with information that had been withheld from witches and the people of Vylheim for hundreds of years."

"I gave you that."

As I kept pace with her, her gaze flicked toward me from beneath the mask. A shiver ran over my skin whenever she looked at me, as if she knew exactly what I was thinking and feeling. Like she knew me.

"Greedy, jealous king you are," she said. Despite her irritation, I could've sworn I heard a playful note in her voice.

"Can't a husband take credit for giving his wife a library full of the answers she wanted?" I teased her, and though she said nothing, the smirk beneath the mesh gave her away. Not even the shadow of the mask could hide it—or the connection I felt.

I grinned, knowing I'd won. This little game was my way of pushing back against whatever the gods had done to leave her so frustrated.

The edge of her foot bent sideways when another dry crack in the ground crumbled beneath her boot. Dirt eroded away, and her bent leg sank deeper into the hollow. It was no different from the dozen other times the ground had given way beneath us, but the twist of her ankle seemed to drain the last of her energy.

A sudden gasp yanked me from my thoughts. Lux's breath hitched again as her knees buckled, and her body slowly sank to the earth. Tiny rivulets of red stained the dirt beneath her, frozen in time from the deadliest battle in our history.

"Lux." I caught her before the heels of her palms hit the ground. Worry iced over my dead veins. When she didn't respond, I gently eased her onto her hands and knees. The black in her eyes tilted back until nothing but white and slivers of red were visible. "Lux." I gently shook her shoulders, calling her back to me, only to remember that this loss of consciousness was exactly what she wanted. But I. Fucking. Hated. This. What if she didn't wake up again?

Her eyes lolled, her body going limp. *Fuck!* Breaths grew shallower, each one more strained than the last. Every ounce of me fought the urge to grab her and force my healing on her. If I had my way, I'd bite her, turn her—anything to stop her suffering.

Instead, I tilted her onto her back and pulled her into my lap. Her breathing quickened, strained and desperate. Could she survive a collapse in the wasteland? What if the poisoned air made it impossible to wake up? I didn't claim to understand her illness, but I saw what it did to her. Her lips parted as she gulped sickly air, and her eyelids finally folded over the white, sealing shut.

My fangs descended, ready to sink into her and stop her from slipping away from me, but I resisted. For what felt like an eternity, I sat hunched over her, her body across my legs, letting her suffer.

Finally, her eyelashes fluttered. "Drak?"

Relief eased the tension in my jaw, where my teeth had been grinding. "You fucking scared me," I said.

"Do you—" she sucked in a quivering breath and spoke without opening her eyes. "Do you know where the statue of Freya is?"

Heavy pressure suddenly sank into my shoulder, and I grunted at a strange, all-consuming agony that followed. Lux kept speaking, but her voice became muffled and faded, and I drifted into a sort of unconsciousness of my own.

Lux's voice broke through. "That's where I saw Silver. In the vision."

A memory enveloped me, and though I felt the pain of a phantom axe in my chest again, I didn't faint. I was fully awake, and remembering another moment from another time.

Another life, maybe.

A massive stone shaped like a woman flashed before me.

The goddess of fertility stood, molded in grey and stained with wetness. Tears, thick and red, slid down her rough surface, like the blood I'd fed on, dripping onto Mara's Keep floor.

Except I didn't see Freya as clearly as everything else in the memory. She was a distant image of cold lifelessness in the middle of a field of bodies, a battlefield. She stood at the helm of the battle, the goddess of war, weeping not for the lost lives but for something else. At one point, I knew what made her cry, but I hadn't cared for the gods and their woes in a long time.

Crumbled stone structures surrounded the statue with bloodied warriors scattered among ruins I recognized. Ruins that I'd seen surrounding Lux as she crawled toward me.

I knew this place; this was Skaldir—the first Skaldir. Battle decimated the original home whose name had been stolen by Lux's village hundreds of years after. When I blinked, the memory and the pain dissipated, coming and going so fast it seemed Lux hadn't even noticed.

"I… don't," I said. If only seeing the statue in my memory could lead me to it.

Lux licked her lips, creating a sheen that caught the sun's dim red glow. "It's okay. We can follow the stains."

My eyes flicked to the red lines in the dirt. "The blood?"

Nodding, she blew out a slow breath and peeled her eyes open. "The statue wept blood and stands at the site of the Battle of Sundered Sky. If we follow where the stains grow darker until the ground is all red, we'll find it."

A strange little laugh bubbled on her lips.

"What?" I asked.

"That's the same thing Freya told me to find you. Follow the blood. Except yours was because you're a monster and a messy eater."

Fuck. Should I thank Freya for bringing her to me? No, if we were meant to be, we would have found each other, no matter what. I was the one who sought her out in Skaldir, the one who felt the string pull taut between us the moment I saw her, fiercely focused and competing in a footrace. She smiled up at me.

"Feeling better?" I asked, though exhaustion clearly tugged at her eyes.

"I guess…I guess my mind is clearer after a vision."

Meaning the gods were quieter. When they weren't toying with her, I caught glimpses of Lux as she truly was, echoes of joy and playfulness, the person she could be without this world and the gods weighing her down.

"Carry me?" she whispered.

Her throat rippled with a swallow, and my eyes shot to the vein pulsing along the curve of her neck. Drinking from her was forbidden. The huntress's blood burns those she's cursed to kill, but in that moment, all I wanted was to taste her. Not her blood, though; I just wanted to taste her desire again.

"You're asking me to carry you now?" I said, resisting a smirk. "I had to force you into my arms back at Mara's Keep. Maybe I like what the wasteland does to you." Of course I didn't enjoy watching her suffer, but this vulnerable side of her allowed me to see all of her.

Her mouth curved. "Do you want me to beg?"

"I do love hearing you plead for me," I said, relishing this glimpse of her playfulness again.

She released a soft moan as I slipped my arms beneath her legs and neck and rose with her in my hold. "Follow the blood," she said.

"Yes, my queen."

I carried her in silence for a long stretch, her body sinking into my chest. The soft curve of her neck angled out, exposed beneath the leather hide and cloak draped over her shoulders. Her head propped against the dip between my shoulder and breastbone, the same spot that'd felt on fire when the disturbed memory flooded me.

Despite the steep climb, I cherished the moments when she rested, letting me support her entire weight.

After a time of nothing but fog and Lux's shallow breaths, the stained cracks deepened in color. They spread wider, turning the dirt from familiar brown with hints of red to a bright crimson, like fresh blood spilled in a dry pool across the land. But nothing about the wasteland was fresh. Ancient was a closer description, except that it felt as familiar as a memory.

Lux stirred in my arms, eyes flickering. "You should—you should see structures soon."

"Ruins," I breathed. "I know."

"I can walk now."

"Lux."

Her muscles stiffened. "I can walk. Thank you, Drak." The softness in her eyes was new. Even when I'd bandaged her, she hadn't looked at me like that. Lux had always been wary of me from the start. When we exchanged our fake vows, she looked at me with curiosity and a hint of sadness. In the throes of ecstasy, her eyes were wild with pleasure. But never had she been so soft like this.

Glimpses of her came through in these moments, until the gods fed her lines about my monstrous state. About how stupid and sick and disturbed she was to even play at marriage with one of the undead.

The gods must have been quiet now, because she held me in her gaze as carefully as I'd lifted her into my arms. I helped her to her feet and followed as we crept deeper into the ruins, hiking through the clouds until the echo of voices halted our progress.

We froze, exchanging tentative, curious looks. A human cry echoed from deep within the fog. Lux's hand shot to the weapon at her thigh, and laughter filtered through the mist—until the cry turned into a whimper.

Lux inched forward, her boots light where the ground evened out. No longer did we climb at an angle. The land leveled near the ruins, dipping slightly like a faint valley that collected a pool of the ancestors' blood.

The closer we came to the dark, roofless structure, the more I felt the need to touch it. The stone wasn't cold like Mara's Keep; it pulsed with a sickening warmth, out of place beneath the endless storms and ice we'd endured for months.

A blur darted behind another structure, and the whimpering went quiet. Another voice, this time female, let out a curt laugh. That meant two vampires, one vessel. The human was probably drained and would leave them to decay in the ruins.

"Drak, they're here," she whispered. "We found them."

"And there goes our plan to ruin their source of food. Clearly they have more than blood bags." I frowned. "They brought humans."

She seethed, her chest heaving with rising rage. "I hate this. I hate blood-thirst and knowing that the people of Vylheim are fucking tormented. Hel, I can't wait to turn every one of those vampires to ash."

I grabbed her arm before she could take another step. "Let's do this carefully before Silver realizes we're here and runs."

Her eyes flashed with a hint of impatience before she finally relented and spoke. "Vampires often feed in small groups for privacy, right?" I nodded, and she continued. "When they break away like this, I'll pick them off one by one. Before they feed, so they're at their most desperate."

I smirked. "Torturous little killer you are. Making them die hungry."

She only arched a brow, disappearing behind the mask. When my gaze shifted to the structure behind her, her face flickered. The mask vanished as a memory seized me.

But she hadn't spoken the magic word to trigger this…

I didn't have time to dwell on the details of how this episode came about, because Lux suddenly stood bare-faced before me. Not covered in clay and leather and mesh, but painted with runes across her forehead and beneath her eyes in the smudges of black coal. The runes were messy and hurried, completely different from the modern wedding symbols, yet still strangely familiar. They spoke of vows of love, untouched by the language of today.

A simple gown woven of crystal-blue fabric replaced her dust-covered clothes.

I took her hands in mine, and she tilted her chin up. Her eyes were bright and clear and searched mine when she spoke. "Follow me?"

"I'll follow you," I echoed. "Into every life."

As another cry ripped through the air, it swept away the memory, and the truth hit me.

Every strange memory I'd had was finally confirmed. We weren't just at the site of the first Skaldir—we were at our home. This was where we'd married, where Rune had married Myrah. Maybe that was why I no longer needed to hear my former name, my true name, to recall the memory.

Now I knew how to control it.

Chapter Twenty-Two
Lux

Drak repeated the words he'd spoken to me at the altar of Vylheim's throne. Though simple and spoken while he suffered another strange episode, they left me breathless. *I'll follow you.*

"Lux, listen to me," he whispered as he came back to reality. "This was our home once."

We didn't have time for his wild theories, and the Gods made that clear, pounding at my temples. Another scream swallowed Drak's next words.

My gaze shifted to a structure on the right. The spire of what might once have been an altar or temple was severed in half, the crumbled stones scattered. A jagged tip pierced the fog, its charred stone dark against the mist.

I listened intently, waiting for my sister's voice—or the voices of others nearby—but none came. This vampire and their victim were alone.

I twisted my neck to glance back at Drak. Shock hung from his jaw, or at least what I could see beneath the mask. His two-toned eyes were wide and unblinking, and his lips parted. "Drak," I said, snapping him out of it. "Do you hear Silver?"

After a minute, he nodded. "Yes, she's not close, but she's here. Maybe a hundred paces away."

I hummed my acknowledgement. "Let's keep this up as long as we can. Don't let them know we're here." His brow furrowed as I gestured toward the other structure with a flick of my wrist. "Grab them so that when I attack, they can't run off and warn Silver. We'll pick them off as we make our way to her, and if I get locked in with the vampires, you go for her. Capture her only."

Drak was already nodding and turning away from me, unsheathing the sword at his back. He stalked into the clouds, his broad shoulders disappearing as the fog swallowed him. Split up, we could pick off more of them without alerting the head of the snake.

"That's it." Crooned Odin's heavy voice. *"This is what you're made for. It is your purpose."*

I winced. Was I really nothing but a weapon?

The human's cry forced me to focus. I stepped forward, following the side of the structure and the faint whimpers. Clearly, the vampires no longer cared about the comfort of their vessels during feeding. That was a courtesy of the past—a courtesy only granted to them because vampires wanted to stay hidden, and secrets required a little bait.

I edged my feet forward, fingers curling around the stake strapped to the outside of my clothing. My loose pants gave me freedom to move, though they bunched awkwardly where the stake was secured. It wasn't ideal, but it was the closest to comfort I could manage.

Each breath the human took grew more labored, short and jagged as they struggled to inhale, choking on the particles clogging their throat. I wasn't sure if I could save them, not with the wasteland swirling in their lungs, but I freed the stake from its binding and didn't hesitate for a moment.

Peering around the stone, my eyes locked onto a bald vampire, fangs buried deep in a man's muscular neck. The skin on his throat was a mottled red and purple as he struggled to breathe. Not that he'd live if he could breathe. Not one, but two vampires drank from him. The other, a female who'd twisted his arm back and licked at the blood spilling down his wrist. Soon, his red and purple skin would be entirely pale and devoid of life.

When I stepped out, the female vampire jerked her attention to me, and I immediately whispered a compulsion. Her friend was slower to the draw, still enraptured with the taste of the man's blood as he desperately and greedily drained the poor vessel.

"I feel the stake in my hands," I whispered. "And the breath in my throat." I pinned her with my gaze when Drak's words popped into my mind, and I wanted nothing more than for them to be true. For him to have followed me and fought beside me. But I had to focus. "I'll feel your ashes blowing in flakes over my hands." She bared her fangs at me with a hiss, but it was all she could do before I turned her into my puppet. "Slash at the vampire," I commanded, voice sharp with compulsion. "He's draining your vessel."

She did as I bid, lunging over the man's body at her friend. It was just enough to throw the bald vampire off of their shared vessel, but it was too late for the human. His body lay limp and sprawled in the crimson dust, his neck twisted unnaturally after he'd rolled out of the bald vampire's arms. I only hoped he'd fainted from blood loss before he felt the panic of choking.

The bald vampire threw off his attacker and shot to his feet in a single blink. I barely held to the compulsion, like a single thread fraying more and more as my focus turned to the bald vampire. I held the compulsion, forcing the female to remain still. It was all the energy I could muster as my focus stretched thin and I fought to control the situation.

Perhaps it should have intimidated me that the bald vampire was nearly two heads taller than me. He stood like the spire itself, his head in the clouds, his body bent over me and his hand wrapping around my throat as if I was as small as Alva. Just a child in the hands of monsters.

But I wasn't.

I was chosen, trained, and had fully draped myself in the body of a killer, so smashing the stake into his ribcage was nothing. It was even satisfying when his blood withered his body to nothing but ash.

I didn't wait around as he disintegrated, and the flecks of him scattered over the blood-stained earth. The woman was my next target, but the thread of compulsion broke, and she was free to attack me.

She was scrappier, sharper, and far smarter than her arrogant companion who thought he could end me with nothing more than a careless grab. He definitely would have snapped my neck if I hadn't had the stake perfectly angled at his heart. Kayn had made sure to train me to precision.

The vampire woman forced herself against me, throwing us both to the ground. Air knocked from my lungs and the mask dislodged. Sucking in a breath, chunks of something bitter passed over my tongue and caught in my throat. I coughed, trying to force them out, but it was no use. Time was slipping away as she tightened her grip, one hand clutching my chin, the other pressing against my shoulder. This vampire was intent on snapping my neck.

With the last of the air in my chest, I whispered a weak compulsion. "I feel breathless but you feel even more desperate." Scrambling for breath, I couldn't fight back. I had to get her off me and fix the mask before more of the black particles filled my throat.

Trying not to draw in too much air, I commanded her to kill herself by feeding on my poisoned blood. "Drink from me."

Wasting no time, she sank her fangs into the base of my neck, just above my collarbone. The sting of the bite left me gasping, but no air came. The toxins in the air suffocated me, and the shock of it all hit like a wave, drowning me in helplessness. Nothing but the burn of the wound registered in my mind. At least that was quiet. No Gods, no questions, no wondering what might come next.

Only pain. My world was all pain thanks to the wasteland's lack of fresh air heightening every feeling.

After what felt like hours without air, she drew back. A horrified expression twisted her flawless face. My tainted blood turned her tongue and lips and tinted her veins black. Soon, she would join her partner as I used the last of my strength to plunge the stake into her heart.

Once she fell away, and her body was already disintegrating, the stake clattered from my hold, and my hand shot to the mask. I adjusted it back over my mouth, desperate to breathe, as if the clay, leather, and mesh could somehow undo the damage, clearing the particles already choking the air from my lungs. Thin streams of air slipped between what felt like rocks sitting in my throat.

I refused to die like this. The wasteland would not take me before I took my mother back from Silver. If I died now, I'd never have the chance to ask what else Drak had said to me earlier.

I'll follow you.

I'll follow you.

Drak filled my mind, and I couldn't make sense of it. I should have been focused on the fight ahead, on getting to Yggdrasil or stopping my sister before she reached it. Instead, all I could think about was him. The way he'd said it felt like a knife carving a hole in my chest. He'd follow me. Nobody followed me. I wasn't a leader, and I sure as Hel didn't want to be.

But I wasn't alone either. He was with me, physically and in every truth he bore for me. Suddenly, I couldn't bear the thought of leaving him alone either. I couldn't die breathless and abandon him in these ruins.

I rolled onto my stomach, using the little air I had left to force out another cough, straining to stay as quiet as possible. My lungs filled halfway before a fit of uncontrollable coughing overwhelmed my body. My throat was raw, and the muscles across my stomach and chest ached from the effort. Tears slipped past the clay plastered to my skin and dribbled down the sides of my face, spotting the dust beneath me in fat droplets.

Somewhere nearby, Drak's voice rang out, cursing another vampire as bones cracked and crunched. Snapping necks was easy enough for Drak, and then he could finish them with a beheading using the sword on his back. But none of that reassured me when he grunted, and then after another thud, he fell silent.

Drak…

I struggled to my feet, each breath coming in shallow gasps, pain flaring every time air brushed over my scratched throat. But I gripped the stake and forced myself upright.

This had only just begun.

Loki's gleeful laugh echoed through my mind, and I felt Odin's pride swell through me like a blessing, but that was all I heard from them about this. Freya didn't grant me another vision, and Odin said nothing. I'd just destroyed two more of their enemies, but they weren't going to encourage me to save Drak.

"Now you're getting it." Loki's voice slithered around my skull like a snake hissing in the grass at my feet.

I focused on breathing instead of his words. When I stepped out from behind the structure, a wave of relief washed over me at the sight of Drak standing over a headless vampire.

"You're okay," I breathed. It felt so good to have enough air to talk.

"You were worried about me?" Drak turned at my approach, the thick hilt of his sword clasped in his fingers.

"Yes." Worried about whatever he said that I'd missed.

You are a weapon. Though I didn't hear them speak it this time, the Gods' intent still echoed in my mind, clear as ever. Bitterness swirled at the top of my belly like foam threatening to fill my chest and throat and mouth with filmy bile.

"What a show it will be to watch you kill the man you love."

No.

I couldn't tell if I argued that I wouldn't kill him, or that I didn't love him. Trying to figure it out felt like a distraction I couldn't afford. I stalked toward the next shadows, the next sounds, the next vampires who'd slipped away to feed on helpless vessels.

Drak followed me.

He was right by my side when I staked another of his kind, effortlessly throwing off a vampire who had grabbed my forearm. One minute the vampire was hungrily pulling me toward him and the next, his head was rolling across the dirt.

We pressed on, picking our way deeper into the ruins. Structures surrounded us now, reaching their crumbling spires into the stained sky. If I squinted, I could make out the silhouette of a towering human—no, a God. Freya stood at the center of the ruins.

This was it.

This was the true site of the Battle of Sundered Sky, where she cried tears of blood and tore Myrah from her lover, claiming Myrah for Folkvangr, even though Valhalla had already marked the warrior for its own.

A haze came over Drak, or perhaps it was the fog that was growing thicker.

"Drak?" I called, but another vampire appeared, pulling me into the fight.

When the undead were finally destroyed, we counted twenty-seven vampires down from Silver's army, and by then,

I couldn't push myself to my feet anymore. After wrestling with the vampire, the world spun, and I couldn't find the strength to rise. I'd pushed my body too far. This sudden collapse didn't drag me into unconsciousness, but I was teetering on the edge.

"Lux," Drak's voice coaxed me to peel my eyes open. "Silver is gone. While you were fighting, I found her and their stash, and I cut open all their blood bags. But she ran."

"To Yggdrasil?" I mumbled.

"No, she fled with Ylva and Darius, just as Axel said, but they'll have to backtrack. The vampires have no vessels left, and now they have no stored blood. Ylva and Darius are nothing if not gluttonous for blood so they won't last long without it." His thumb brushed over my cheek, and the crook of a faint smile bent his face. "You did it."

A flood of relief surged through me, warmth spreading through my veins. It wasn't just because we'd won the battle, but because this victory felt strangely familiar, even if I couldn't understand why it felt so damn good to fight alongside Drak. And hearing the result of our efforts spoken aloud in his voice? The praise? A smile tugged at my tired lips.

"We did it," I said, correcting his statement.

"Fuck yes we did." A wicked grin spread across his face. Perhaps it was silly to celebrate such a small win, but we needed this. Hel, we needed any small sense of victory we could grasp while stranded at the broken heart of a wasteland, in the center of a world torn apart by monsters.

And Gods—according to Drak, anyway, and I was almost starting to believe him, but I dashed the thought away before Odin punished me for it.

"Our victory is only temporary," I breathed. "She'll be back with more vampires. So we did win…but only for now."

"For now," he echoed, "you have to rest. We're staying here tonight. We'll be safer hiding among the ruins, anyway."

Shuffled movement happened around me, but I couldn't so much as lift a finger.

Drak carried me back, unpacked the skins, and set up the tent while I sat in the dirt, my head drooping with exhaustion. The sound of his swallow told me he'd paused to consume some of the blood he'd brought with him into the wasteland. Once the tent was erected, he beckoned me inside, instructing me to curl up beneath the furs and sleep while he stood watch.

I gratefully accepted, eager to slip into the quiet and let my heart and other muscles finally rest. But before I could close my eyes, I couldn't help but notice the way Drak raked his fingers through his hair. A heavy sigh escaped him as he pushed the fabric of the tent aside and stepped one foot outside.

"Drak?" I said. He paused and turned back to me. "Don't you also need rest?"

He shook his head. "No, there's just…" he drew a sharp breath. "There's a truth I haven't exactly admitted to you." I pushed myself up onto my elbows, holding his fragile gaze as his throat rippled with a heavy swallow. "I couldn't get to Silver; there were too many vampires."

"You already told me that. It's okay, we'll stop her when she shows up at Yggdrasil."

"No, Lux, listen." He glanced outside again, his jaw working with anticipation. "Even after all that Silver's done, I won't be able to kill her either."

"But isn't that what you've been pushing for?" Confusion cracked my voice.

Flexing his jaw, he mulled this over, his eyes on me the entire time. "It is, and I'm sorry. I should have understood that you couldn't kill her. But I really thought I could. I thought killing her was best for everyone until…" His voice trailed off, his focus sharpening. He stared at nothing, as if seeing an answer invisible to me. "Until I saw her running away today. She didn't look arrogant the way she did after the attack on Mara's Keep. Fuck, she looked scared, Lux." I had never seen Drak like this before. He was always honest with me, but this was different, like he was tapping into a well of sympathy he didn't know he had buried inside. "The only other time I've ever—ever—seen her afraid in her adult life was in the seconds before she made me a vampire."

Breath was ripped from my lungs, as if the alchemical stone had failed and the toxins in the air were draining me dry. But inside the tent, the air was almost completely clear.

A grim expression flattened Drak's lips before he continued. "She saved my life when she turned me. I'd been planning to turn into a vampire for quite some time, but the final choice came when we were traveling across Drukna sea."

I still couldn't breathe. Drak and Silver dared to travel Drukna? "How did I never hear of this?" I asked.

"Before I became king, hardly anyone knew me. King Roderic made sure of that, since I wasn't his son. Only when you and your obsession with history showed up did I start to believe I could be seen as more than just a vampire king—fuck." He shook his head again. "That's not the point. I want you to know that I shouldn't have told you to kill your sister when I wouldn't hurt her either. Imprisoning her will have to be enough."

"She saved you?" I almost didn't believe it. Even as a child, Silver was…harsh, and though I forgave her for it and loved my sister, the other children in the village didn't always do the same.

"She did. We were The Blood Council's test subjects before The Age of Exploration. I told you before that was always their plan, not mine. It had been in the making long before I became king. They used Silver as a witch to guide us to West Anglor so we could cross Drukna Sea and capture vessels for the council to feed on. More people to grow our numbers, all for the sole purpose of filling vampire bellies. King Roderic sent me with her and several executioners, hoping I'd die on the journey and be forgotten, and I almost did." He sighed and waved at the furs. "You're supposed to be resting."

"I can manage." I propped myself up a little higher. "Tell me more."

"That's basically all of it. Drukna is called The Drowning for a reason. On the way back with the people the executioners had taken captive, the Gods raised the waves, attempting to drown us all and prevent the vampires from gaining more vessels. Half the executioners and nearly all the captives were thrown overboard. I almost drowned too, but Silver dragged me back onto the ship. I couldn't breathe with all that water in my lungs, but she knew what to do because I had said so many times before that I wanted to become a monster to overthrow King Roderic. Being sent to sea pushed me over the edge." He laughed without joy. "It literally pushed me over the edge. My fate was to drown in Drukna until Silver changed everything by turning me."

"She was your friend," I said, noticing what he did not say.

"As a child, yes, I would say that she was. But she became something else on that trip across Drukna too. Unrecognizable. Once I turned and she realized the power she had over vampires, that power consumed her. I still stand by the plan to bring her down, just not by killing her. Her place is in the prison beneath Mara's Keep."

"On that we agree."

Drak forced a smile. "Now you know another story. Sleep, Skald."

I didn't argue with his command. Sleeping sounded divine, and despite being in the wasteland, I felt safer than I ever had before. Drak had shared a side of himself I didn't know existed: sensitivity, true empathy, or something along those lines. Exhaustion blurred everything, and I drifted into a dreamlike state, Drak at the forefront of my mind and a faint smile on my lips.

I woke, reaching out with Drak's name on my tongue. I quickly swallowed it, not wanting him to know how often he filled my dreams. As I propped myself up, I saw him sitting at the edge of the tent, his attention fixed through an opening, keeping watch just as he had promised.

When he noticed I was awake, he pulled me into him, and my body naturally curved against his. The warmth of his recently fed skin enveloped me, offering a sense of comfort I hadn't realized I needed.

"Do you remember this?" he whispered.

I hummed through the haze of sleepiness. I remembered my body molding to the shape of his when we traveled from Skaldir to Mara's Keep. "Drak?" I said. His steady breathing was broken by a sharp intake of breath. "What was it you said before we invaded Silver's camp?"

"I said that I'll follow you."

I hummed again. "I know. What else?"

His hesitation was clear from the clench of his muscles. Something held him back. Had he suffered another one of his strange episodes?

"Into every life, Myrah," he said.

Myrah? The sound of this name on his lips left me dizzy. A fire ignited in my skull. Sudden and awful and strangely different from the pain of the Gods' voices. It felt as if the Gods were trying to burn the name out of my mind, but it lingered there, a memory from the sagas that wouldn't fade.

"I think…I think I remember," I said. But what I remembered was a story from the sagas, told to me as a child. A tale I had often pictured myself in as I grew older, imagining myself in the role of the bride.

As the bride, I pictured Freya towering over us in a mask of unmarred stone. Drak—or a warrior—vowing himself to me. Real vows, spoken in the language of ancients. An axe hung at his side and the hilt of a sword crossed his back. Runic ink covered my fingers where he closed his hands over mine.

"My wife," he said, as if he could see it too.

Our wedding.

"My weapon." Freya's stone mouth split open in my mind's eye, but it was Odin's voice that emerged. Claws closed around my heart. *"This isn't real. You're descending into madness."*

Odin cursed.

No. Tears burned at the back of my closed eyes. I needed it to be real, but even Drak had said my madness would get worse. I had to accept that these weren't memories, but desperate thoughts strangled by the fear of more days like today. The mindless battles and ash at my feet left my heart and body raw. Even if I rid this realm of monsters, killing took its toll.

I had wanted nothing more than to dream of a simple life with a man I loved—one of the warriors from the sagas I'd adored as a girl. But Freya was right; this wasn't my life, not now, not ever. And it hurt too much to wish for something that would never be mine.

Nerves and frustration swelled within me. "Don't call me your wife again," I snapped.

"You said—"

"I'm tired." I shut the conversation down, and that was it for the night. I would not speak of it anymore. I would not allow the madness to take me.

And when I woke the next morning to the Gods whispering gently, their pride soft and low in my mind, I knew I'd made the right choice.

Chapter Twenty-Three

Drak

We'd won, for now. But the victory was marred by Lux's denial.

Even if Silver fled and had to backtrack to find more vessels for her vampires, it still didn't bring the satisfying sense of success I'd hoped for. Not when I'd failed with *her*.

Lux lay beside me, breathing raggedly through a fitful sleep. I never closed my eyes; instead, rolling the painful truth through my mind.

With Odin constantly interrupting her memories, telling her they weren't true, I saw no way to convince her we had been in love in a past life. That she was the witch who created vampires, and that I had left Valhalla for her. Each time she started to remember, they fucking ruined it.

I had loved Lux long before these past few weeks, but saying it while Odin kept taking her away from me only made the pain worse.

I rolled onto my back and stared up at the tent's hide, stretched tight against the stone to block out the heavy air. The rest of the fog and particles had been bound to the alchemical stone. Thanks to witches, I could stare up at the mottled hide with clear vision and breathe free of the mask.

Lux's lungs expanded and shrank with each breath. After our crawl across the ruins, destroying every vampire in our path, she'd sleep for hours. But lying awake, with everything I knew and the way she'd denied it, did nothing to help me rest. I was here, in the ruins where I'd first lost her. Surely, there had to be something here I could show her to prove who we truly were.

Once she believed it, we would make this marriage real. Our past would be enough to bind her to me, to erase the gods from her mind and have her sit beside me on Vylheim's throne. We'd continue the life we once shared, and maybe, just maybe, I could fill the damn hole she'd left in me.

If she wanted to finish this quest to kill vampires first, fine. I could wait for the woman I loved. I'd done it before.

Shoving off the fur blankets, I climbed to my feet, fitted the mask over my face, and took one last look at Lux's peaceful expression before slipping outside. The clouds were as heavy as always, pressing down on me with the weight of thousands of lost lives. The ashes of our ancestors. And the ashes of my own body, but not Lux's—or Myrah's. Thanks to her undead creation, she continued on, passing to the afterlife long later in a death documented by the sagas.

Moving through the ruins, my memories flooded back, one at a time, though always in fragments. I surveyed what looked like a temple with half of a steeply pitched roof that remained. It was the only building not made of stone, but timber that'd withstood the test of time. Carved into the front of the roof was a boar's head. Now, the skull had split open and was crumbling.

I walked through the vast structure as if it were one long hallway. At the end stood a crumbled altar where we had once offered sacrifices. There would have been a massive table at the center, long and made of the same wood as the temple itself, meant to hold feasts in the mirror image of how warriors dined in Valhalla. Along the sides of the structure stood carved figures, nearly as tall as me. The wooden gods seemed to watch me, despite many having lost their heads.

Hundreds of years ago, they witnessed Lux walking this same path with the wedding runes painted across her face.

I stopped in front of the altar where we'd said our vows—real vows. The memory was as clear as the air in the tent I had left Lux behind in. I saw her across from me, tears slipping down her face.

To mimic the past, I stepped into my place as if I were Rune on my wedding day. I reached out to the distant memory of my bride, wiping at tears I couldn't feel. The echo of her voice clung to the corners of my mind.

"What if it doesn't work?" she asked. "What if our vows aren't enough to change Freya's vision?"

I opened my mouth, as if I could comfort her now and tell her we'd find each other again. She just had to remember me.

Instead, Rune responded. "That will only be determined by the Valkyries. You don't know what afterlife I'll end up in."

Fuck, I wanted to punch that bastard. He knew nothing. We'd be separated, no matter what, and it didn't matter that in death, I let go of my weapon so the Valkyries would pass me by. They still chose me for Valhalla and ripped me away from her.

When Myrah's tears did not stop, Rune finally said something useful. "If we can't change our fate before we fall, we'll change it after."

Her face flashed with that same furrowed brow Lux always had. Myrah didn't look exactly like Lux because subtle differences made Myrah gaunter in the cheeks and with more wiry muscle. She wore her hair, which was lighter and more fiery, in several braids twisted across the top of her head and joined at the base of her neck. Even if their faces weren't identical, their expressions were the same. This was the woman I knew.

What Rune was about to say was all too familiar, so I formed the words in my mouth as my former self spoke.

"I'll follow you back to Midgard by rebirth if I have to."

Midgard. This realm we used to call the center of the gods' focus. Now it was simply Vylheim, a place that we understood in modern days was not the entirety of this realm. There were kingdoms and more of Odin's people beyond Vylheim.

"Follow me?" she said.

"I'll follow you. Into every life."

The memory wavered as my fingers tried to catch the tear slipping off her jaw. In an instant, it was gone, and nothing in this temple remained to prove that the moment had ever existed. Unless this place could spark Lux's memory, I didn't see how any of this would change her. Odin wouldn't allow her these memories because any distraction risked a divergence from her task.

Unmake the vampires.

Destroy them all, including me. Fuck, I had to get to that damn tree.

Leaving the altar behind, I stormed out of the broken temple. Every step through the ruins brought painful memories of the life we'd once had, before the Battle of Sundered Sky. Before West Anglor invaded, seeking revenge against our leaders to strip us of power and end the threat we posed to their wealth and churches across the sea.

This was where we'd lived and loved and fucked. Fields we'd tilled side by side. She may have been a witch, and I a warrior, but first, we were farmers. Simple people stupidly worshiping gods who didn't care if they tore us apart.

And for what? Their own amusement?

I blinked up at the dark sky, staring through the mesh in my mask. Freya's face was still intact as she stood over the ancient battlefield. Red rivers carved lines through her cheeks, the blood having faded to black in the cracks.

Frowning, I spat out the thought that circled my mind. "What the fuck was the purpose?" Of course, she said nothing. It was just a fucking statue and the real Freya would never—could never—reach me in this form.

I shook my head and stomped across the battlefield with dust curling at my heels. Even if Lux would not believe it, I'd try anyway. Discouragement never stopped me before. Not when my mother begged me not to become a vampire, and not when Silver herself warned me against it.

Becoming a vampire led Lux to me. Without the throne, I never would have found her, and I never would have had the power to stop her execution.

So fuck every discouragement.

I pushed through the opening in the tent and pulled it tight again. Stripping off my mask, I turned to see Lux awake and sitting up. Her black eyes were both bright and clear as she looked up at me.

"What is it?" she asked, worry wrinkling her brow. I dropped to my knees on the fur beside her. Searching her fierce eyes, I held her in my gaze, wholly absorbing her curiosity and concern. "Has Silver returned with more—"

"No," I said, my voice rough. "Listen to me, Lux. You won't want to believe this, but I. Never. Lie to you. Never. I never have, and I'm not starting now." Her lower lip pulled inward as she absorbed my desperation. I probably sounded pathetic, like a beggar, but I didn't care as long as it kept her attention. Taking her hand, I continued as if I were about to speak the vows we had said at the altar in that ancient temple. "I know now. What I was seeing in the library when you read to me from that record. In your voice. I had read from some of those books before, but it was your voice that sparked it all. You changed it for me."

She shook her head. "What are you talking about?"

"I followed you."

That stopped her. Lux's hand went to her chest the way it always did when her weak heart danced around. The gods were likely to blame for that, too. "What do you mean?"

"You know what I mean. The rest of what I said earlier was that I'd follow you into every life. This life."

She shook her head again, blinking rapidly. "Drak, I—"

"I felt the memories, Lux. Twice in the library, and then after our wedding. And here. They're clear as a breathing stone here. You *are* my wife."

"Drak."

"You are. Or…" I mirrored her movement, shaking my head. "You were once. Years ago."

"That's insane."

I seethed, my free hand clenching into a fist. "What's insane is the gods in your head." Her lips parted as she recoiled, pulling her hand from mine. She was slipping away from me, right out of my grasp. "I don't know how to say the truth any plainer. You are Myrah, the first witch, and I am Rune, the warrior she asked to follow her. You asked me to follow you, and I did. I'm here. I left Valhalla for you and I'd do it again."

Her fingers touched her temples gingerly. Agony was obvious in the pulsing vein above her brow and the red streaks in her strained eyes. The damned gods grew more persistent. "You're not a god, Drak. There's no way you've left Valhalla, because you've never been. You don't know what you're talking about." With a wince, she gasped and rubbed her forehead.

"You would remember if it weren't for Odin. Lux, Myrah—"

"Stop!" she shrieked. "It's too loud. You have to stop."

My fingernails dug into my palms until I grabbed her hands again. She had to listen. She had to hear me, damn it! "I won't stop until we're actually together again."

With a grunt, she shoved away from me and ripped the silver tree pendant from her pocket. This was a warning. If I came any closer, if I tried to touch her—my own wife—she'd burn me. The silver couldn't kill me, but it'd hurt like an axe dipped in flame.

"You *will* stop," she gritted. "You can't control me with something you conjured up as memories. It's not true."

"I don't lie."

"I'm sure you believe it," she said. "You'll believe anything that will convince me to do what you want. The gods warned me of this. They told me vampires would do anything, anything at all, to strip me of my identity."

"This isn't who you are."

"I am the huntress, Drak. Accept it."

The quiver in her voice revealed that even she didn't believe what she was saying. She was once Silver, and now the huntress, but none of those roles truly defined *her* because no one had ever allowed her a life where she could be herself, free from hiding. A life free of the gods where she could choose whatever the Hel she wanted to choose.

But I supposed right now, she was choosing the gods. Even if they were forcing her by twisting her mind, I had to honor her choice until I could drag Odin out of her mind. When I fucking destroyed him. The ghost of a smile twitched on my lips.

"Fine," I said. "But I won't give up. I swore to follow you."

She eyed me. Maybe she recognized the promise, maybe she didn't, but this was the same interest she'd had when I said it the first time. Something about that particular phrase piqued her interest.

Finally, the harsh lines of her mouth softened before her lips parted. That phrase was definitely my clue to calming her and reaching past the gods. "This obsession you have with calling me your wife..." she drew another breath, and I waited at the edge. "It's more than just taking my powers, isn't it?" A sliver of recognition cleared the red lines in her eyes. Somewhere in there she knew the truth.

Instead of answering her question, I went deeper because

I didn't need to confirm what she already knew. "Being the huntress is a defense against Silver's army. It's admirable." She lifted her chin slightly. "But it's not all that you are. It's a part of you. Everything you choose to be is you. I just want you to remember the part of you that..." Fuck. My voice choked even though the air in here was clear. "That was mine."

"Drak—"

"No, I mean, the part of you that loved me."

Her brows knitted together in a weak attempt to hold back the tears welling in her eyes. Wetness pooled at the base of her eyelids, then spilled over, as if clearing the fog from her gaze. Of course, that was all in my mind. These were just tears that finally slipped over her eyelids and down her cheeks.

I reached out, finally able to touch her and actually brush them away.

Pink bloomed across the bridge of her nose and the peaks of her cheekbones. "Drak, maybe in another life—"

"That's the point, though; this is another life."

She shook her head, then leaned into my hand, resting her jaw against it as her eyes fluttered shut. "Like our marriage. We can pretend this is another life, for now."

"I don't want to pretend, Lux." I cupped the curve of her jaw, feeling her soft, warm skin against my palms. Holding her here, I forced her to meet my gaze, our eyes lost in one another. "In this life, and the last, I love you."

Her chest pressed tightly against the fabric with every gulping breath, and a flush of crimson deepened across her cheeks, making her more radiant than ever. Both sharp and sexy at the same time, the perfect queen to challenge and hone a lost king. I loved her so fucking much.

He doesn't lie, so when he says he loves me...

"It's the truth," I finished her thought. Thoughts I could only hear when Lux was...wet for me.

Desire flooded my veins, and before I could catch another one of her thoughts, her mouth crashed against mine.

Chapter Twenty-Four
Lux

For now, we weren't the huntress and the king of Vylheim. In this moment, I didn't care to be called Lux or Myrah because I didn't feel like either. I just was.

"You are mine." The burning rage of Odin's voice pulsed at the back of my skull, but his tone was different, almost giddy. Strange. I expected that from Loki, but this tone from Odin disturbed me.

If I belonged to the Gods, then I was nothing more than a weapon chosen to kill their enemies.

"And a savior." Freya interjected with a cool sentiment amidst Odin's fire.

No, not right now, I'm not. I didn't belong to anyone, and as much as I wanted to save the witches, my mother, Stasia, and Ragna's family…this moment was mine. One where I relished the peace Drak's presence brought me.

The Gods chose a selfish huntress. What did they expect?

With Drak, or Rune, or whoever he claimed to be, my past and destiny didn't matter. My mistakes weren't at the forefront of my mind, and I could just *be*.

Slipping my hand to the collar of his tunic, I gripped the fabric. He followed my cue and tugged it off, tossing it into the corner of the tent where our masks had been discarded. Together, we disrobed, and when he pulled the pants off me, the leather no longer rubbed against my thighs.

Pink marred the skin on the insides of my legs. But with my body bare now, I could move freely. And Drak could admire me freely. His gaze brushed over me as his hand trailed to the tie at his trousers. Before he loosened his pants, his eyes stopped at the pink flesh. He reached out, brushing his palm over my thigh with a careful, feathered touch.

"You're hurt."

"It's nothing," I said. "The clothes keep me warm, so a bit of discomfort is worth it."

"When I'm a God, I'll find a way to take all your pain away."

With my head tipped back, I let out a huff. "That's not how the Gods work."

"Not Odin, because he doesn't care enough to figure it out. But I'll find a way to help the blood flow more freely through you."

I flexed my stiff fingers. From the minute Drak saw my tinted fingertips and heard my ragged breaths, he'd been concerned about this weak heart that plagued me. Something I had to hide when living in Skaldir. My father had made sure of that. The leader of our village couldn't have a weak and sickly daughter. Perhaps my life in Skaldir would never have been the simple life of a village girl, even if the royal court had never hunted witches.

Even if vampires didn't exist, my survival was tentative.

At least in all of this suffering, I'd found pleasure and release and…fuck…did I really feel safe with Drak? How long had I truly felt at ease with the vampire king?

Glimpses of the comfort he offered—not in the castle, but through his touch and his words—had been appearing since the first time we slept side by side. That night he kept me warm on the way to Mara's Keep was the first glimpse.

The way he aggressively insisted on warming my hands as we rode from Skaldir. He had recognized what I needed from the start. Could it be because he already knew me? I suppressed the thought because the past didn't matter right now.

"It matters greatly. You must forget this distraction—" I blinked, staring at Drak again, letting my desire for him push Odin from my mind before I lost control, and wanted to rip my eyes from my sockets and smash my head against stone to stop this agony.

I scratched at my temple too forcefully, and the sting of my fingernail jolted me. *Focus on Drak.*

I drank in the sight of his broad chest. The runes etched in ink. The glowing tree of Yggdrasil that marked him as a vampire, created by Myrah's power. None of these could hold my attention when he looked at me the way he was now. He pinned me with his gaze, both gentle and fierce and heavy enough to leave me breathless.

Need fluttered at the base of my belly.

Drak clutched my wrist and tugged me into him, his kiss rough and desperate. He tasted each one of my breaths as he gripped my thigh and marked me with his fingerprints. I climbed into his lap, pressing my nipples against his chest. The brush of his skin against mine left my heart skipping. He leaned back just enough to run his hands over my chest, stopping at my nipples. They tightened at his light pinch, and with his head tipped forward, he sucked one into his mouth. My core tensed with anticipation.

I was eager to taste him, but before I could disrobe him completely, a jolt of lightning radiated through my skull. A gasp escaped me, and I recoiled from Drak, curling back over my legs on the fur.

"Lux..." he said with worry straining his voice. "We can stop."

"I'm okay."

He tilted my chin back with two fingers. "You're sure?"

"Do. Not. Deny. Me." Each word Odin spoke into my head was laced with fire.

Please. Let me have this.

"You can have all of me whenever the fuck you want," Drak said, unaware that I was pleading with Odin. He ran his hand up the curve of my neck and drew me to him, nipping at my throat. When he stopped at my ear, his lips hovered, grazing my skin when he spoke. "I'm yours. I always was."

"Drak—"

"You were mine, too."

My heart pricked. If our marriage was fake and I'd never vowed myself to him, why did all of this feel so real? I would have given my blood to the seal that day.

When wetness slicked between my legs and Drak's tongue parted my lips with each kiss, the Gods couldn't interrupt my thoughts. They couldn't call me their weapon now, or perhaps they could, but I didn't hear them.

Not until Odin screamed and it felt his bare hands were ripping my skull open.

"You are mine!"

Please. I just want this. And then I'm yours, Odin—

Drak grabbed my throat and forced me to focus on him. "No!"

"Drak," I begged, but the harder he squeezed and cut off my breath, the more distant the pressure from Odin became. The strength of his hold matched the tightness building in my core. His desperate need to claim me only had me dripping for him. Normally, I wouldn't let him control me like this, but in sex, I couldn't deny how his intensity only made me want him more.

He blinked and released me. "I'm sorry. I can't—" he forced out a breath. "I won't let him take you away from me again."

"Huntress…" Loki's voice purred.

Please stop. My thoughts descended into begging.

If only they'd shut up, just for now, just for a little while. With my eyes on Drak, I drew a heady breath.

"Do it again," I demanded. His brow flickered. "Grab me." To guide him, I pinched his wrist between my fingers and placed his hand on my collarbone. He licked his lips and ran his palm up my neck. Slowly, his fingers curled around my throat while he guided me onto my back.

His other hand splayed over my belly, and then carefully found its way to my core. Two fingers brushed over my nerves, sending tentative ripples through me. He swirled his fingers over my clit, and I tried to gasp, but he gripped my throat harder. I moaned faintly as he rubbed my core with a rhythm that coiled me tighter and tighter. With every swirl, his grip squeezed harder until I was right at the edge, helpless, desperate, a puddle of desire in his hands.

"You're mine," he whispered, right as everything unraveled. As soon as he tipped me over to the other side, and ecstasy rolled through me in undulating waves, he released my throat. I sucked in air, sweeter for my need of it.

Dizzy, I arched back, letting my eyes fall shut for a minute. I soaked in each wave that rippled through me with Drak's name on my lips. After catching my breath, my eyes popped open, and I pushed him from his side onto his back. Tugging his pants off, I finally freed him.

"Lux, breathe first—"

I responded by burying his cock in my mouth. Wrapping my fingers around his cock, I returned the pleasure he'd given me, tightening my hold as I licked at the tip. Every tease drew delicious moans from him that only had me sucking harder when I took all of him between my lips.

"Fuck, you're so amazing. You're everything." Drak didn't need to breathe, yet his words came out scattered and breathless. "My everything."

Encouraged by his moaning, I took him deeper down my

throat. His hands tangled in the mess of my braids, and he tugged, the satisfaction becoming too much. To tease him, I pulled back, giving myself breath while he paused on the edge. But he couldn't wait. Immediately after I took him in again, he used my hair to guide me gently. With a careful push and pull at the base of the braids he'd gathered in his grip, he led me in a rhythm that had my thighs slick with desire again.

I lived for every sound he made, and I hoped to drink him in, but he drew my head back just in time to come across my breasts. My chest, wet now with the proof of his pleasure, heaved from the effort of sucking on him.

With his hand still intertwined with my hair, he led me to him, having me crawl up from his cock to his mouth where his lips crushed mine. I collapsed onto him, our bare bodies molding to one another.

Tucking my head at the base of his neck, he held me, one arm cupped at my head, fingers still tangled in my braids. I could have fallen asleep again, but before my eyelids became too heavy, I tilted my chin up to look at him.

Odin would make me pay for this, but I wanted to say it—no, I wanted Drak to hear it—just once before this was all taken away from us.

"I'm yours," I said.

He stroked my hair quietly for a moment. A strange sound came from his throat when he finally spoke. "I'll take all of you, but you belong to nobody except yourself." Breath caught in my throat. A wicked smirk curved across his face. "Still, I'd like to actually call you my wife."

I opened my mouth, unsure of what I was even going to say when a noise outside interrupted.

The steady thud of something striking the hard-packed dirt grew louder. Footsteps were approaching. Had Silver's army returned? All the muscles that pleasure had just relaxed stiffened in anticipation of a possible fight.

We both jolted forward, sitting up with our clothes strewn

around us. In a blur, we threw pants and tunics back on, quickly strapping the weapons to our backs and my thigh as the footsteps stormed up to us. Sealing the masks over our faces, I stood and gripped the edge of the tent.

I glanced at Drak, who gave me a quick nod before peeling back the hide.

Through the fog, a familiar face emerged. I blinked, my mind struggling to catch up with what I was seeing. Dark eyes, wheat hair, and only the barest shadow of hair on his chin. My heart stuttered at the sight of him, free of Silver's compulsions. I could see the difference in his stride and the clarity in his heavy brown eyes.

Dust swirled around his ankles with every step. Kayn marched up to me, bypassing Drak, and wrapped his arms around me in a sudden, all-consuming embrace.

Chapter Twenty-Five

Drak

Why the fuck were the Exile's arms around my wife?

I buried my fingernails into my palms and resisted every urge to plant my fist across his face. If Lux didn't want Kayn touching her, she could easily whip out her pendant or use the stake against him.

"I'm here now," he said with a glance at me. Baring my fangs, I narrowed my eyes at him. Was he suggesting that he was here to save her from me? Little did he know, she'd just been on her hands and knees, crawling to me, and that I'd had her long before he did. Centuries before.

Except, according to Kayn, he'd been a vampire for that long.

I'd never given it much thought before, but he was the first—Myrah's undead vessel, created by her experimental power, as recorded in the sagas. Unless he'd also left Valhalla, or Folkvangr, or wherever he'd spent the afterlife, he'd always been here.

The sagas never mentioned Kayn being destroyed, and of course, he couldn't be, unless someone fashioned a stake from Yggdrasil and drove it through his heart. My mother hadn't been a successful huntress, and as far as we know from history, nobody else had either.

That meant Kayn had always been here. While I'd just learned of our past lives, he always knew. He knew exactly who I was—who Lux was.

Who he was.

I gritted my teeth, letting my fangs protrude and bite into my bottom lip. Even knowing Lux was Myrah, he was willing to sacrifice her to his cause to please the gods.

Maybe I should have paid more attention to Kayn, but from what I knew of him from The Blood Council, he was an abomination of a vampire, one who foolishly worshiped the gods who despised us. I gave him little consideration, except where Lux was concerned. I wanted to believe he was nothing but a drop in her ocean, but his presence here was about as tumultuous as Drukna Sea.

Lux's braids tumbled over his arms as she craned her neck. He wasn't letting go.

"You're really free this time?" she asked, her breath still quickened from the effort of taking my cock down her throat.

When Kayn's dark eyes dropped to her, he conjured a weak smile. "I'm really free." He brushed a palm over her hair and it took everything within me not to break his fucking fingers.

I ripped my gaze away from them, twisting my neck to stare at Freya's feet. Just beyond her stood the ruins of the temple where I'd vowed to follow Lux into every life.

Unfortunately, Kayn was part of her life now, and no matter how much I hated it, she had chosen him before. Although it was from the influence of the gods and Kayn's lies that led her there, but I couldn't deny that it was my actions that pushed her into his arms too.

I had to play the Blood Council's game. I'd wanted so badly—too desperately—to convince her to give up her powers and bind herself to me. That desperation made me impulsive and stupid, and I never should have threatened her.

Knots tangled in my chest, heavy and thick around my heart and throat. All at once, I remembered the truth of Kayn's past, about who he was…my choices in this life had inadvertently led Lux to my best friend.

"Fuck," I whispered.

The smash of the phantom axe shattered the bones in my chest again. Even though these memories came quick and easy now, the pain still occasionally accompanied them. At least whenever the memory of that last battle resurfaced.

Agony parched my throat, and I saw Kayn as he had been hundreds of years ago. Kayn, covered in blood, barely alive, lay only a few feet away from where I had died. Back then, his hair was long and clotted with fabric woven through the thick tail of blond.

Even close to death, his dark eyes maintained their stare on Lux—Myrah. He watched her crawl to me. He winced when she dragged me into her lap and looked away when her tears splashed over the crusted blood on my cheekbones.

Just as I'd looked away when he embraced her centuries later.

Clarity revealed everything about the last moments of his life before Myrah used the touch of a Valkyrie on him and turned him from near-dead to undead. I didn't have to be alive to know he'd been a willing participant.

Kayn had always loved her. He'd coveted my wife long before we exchanged official vows. Nearly brothers, we'd grown up together.

Flickers of Rune's childhood lifted the pain of the axe as the memories shifted. I was no longer at the Battle of Sundered Sky, but in this part of Vylheim where I'd lived as a young boy, as Rune.

A frail blond boy, Kayn, sat in a hay cart at the base of Freya's stone statue, watching the others play at war. My father stood behind the boy and his wagon, shouting at me that he would return from fishing soon. A cleft split his top lip, and he was identical to Erik. *Erik.* My father in this life…

Somehow, my father in my past life was the same man as my father in this life.

Heavy sorrow buried deep between my ribs. I had the strange sense that this was the last time I saw Erik as a young boy. As Rune.

And as Drak, I'd suffered the same fate, only knowing my father for a short time before death took him from me. He was a good man. In both lives, I suspected, he was a good man.

Before I could make sense of this, he turned away, and my attention fell to the other children around me.

The others and I, two boys and three girls, swung sticks at one another in mock battle. Snowflakes drifted around us in a soft dance, nothing like the brutal storms that plague Vylheim now. Nearby, two men marched past, discussing the construction of ships. A woman tugged several sheep along with a rope. In step beside her, their thick wool seemed to rock side to side like the ships the men spoke of on an unruly sea.

The frail boy shouted at us to pull him closer so that he could watch our fight. I jumped as another boy, taller and thicker than me and with a knot of hair at the back of his head, swung his stick at my face. Barely dodging it, I sucked in a breath before I laughed at him. He'd come so close to landing his blow, but he'd missed.

That only twisted his mouth. He came at me with all his force, barreling toward me like a wild and angry horse. He was easily three or four years older than me, and with age came size. Ducking, I spun around, but before I could swing at him, a rock struck his shoulder. He turned toward a boy and two girls who were giggling furiously.

Another whine came from Kayn, claiming he could not see the fight from where his wagon was by the blacksmith's building.

Rune! Rune! His cries echoed in the surrounding air.

Winded, I blew out a puff of white air among the crystalline flakes and turned to him. My shoes crunched on the freshly fallen snow as I ran to him. I grabbed the handle of the wagon he sat in and pulled as hard as I could. It rolled over ruts in the uneven ground; the wood grinding and the wheels squeaking as I brought him closer to where we played.

"Here," I said as I thrust a stick at him. Turning it over, he stared at the branch as if it were gold. "Come on, Kayn." I whacked my stick against his weapon. "Fight me."

His wide, dark eyes fell to his leg. Strips of cloth fastened the splint to his thigh and knee, and ankle so that he could not bend his leg. Until the broken bones healed, he was bound to the wagon, but that did not mean he couldn't fight.

I slammed against his stick again. "So the ice made you fall. Do you think a warrior would let that stop him?" His bottom lip thrust out for a moment as he pondered this, but I would not let him pout or give up. Clashing my weapon against his, I ripped his attention to me. "Your arms still work, don't they?" When he finally scrunched his nose and growled like a wild animal, I smirked.

The older boy marched up to the wagon and kicked the wheel. "I doubt it," he said.

I hissed at him as if I, too, were one of the beasts we hunted in the woods. "Do you have eyes?" I waved the stick in his face.

Where his thick brow protruded over his eyes, a wrinkle formed, deeper and deeper as his brow furrowed. Like the hogs penned up on our farm, he grunted. His scowl worsened, if that were even possible, and a shadow cast over his deep-set, beetle's eyes.

"What's that supposed to mean?" he spat.

I stepped up to him. "It means you should be able to see that his arms work perfectly fine."

"Doesn't mean he's a warrior."

"Then what does?" I challenged.

His only response was to bend at the waist and grip the edges of the wagon. Before I realized what was happening, he flipped the wagon, and Kayn tumbled out. A pained groan came from Kayn, and the older boy released a chuckle laced with venom.

Rage bloomed hot in the center of my chest. I threw the stick aside and lunged at the bully, gripping the back of his tunic as fury surged through me and sharpened my strength. In that moment, I understood the tales of warriors who lost all fear in the heat of battle. Berserkers fought wildly and without abandon, as this loss of senses gave them inhuman strength. I channeled the energy of every story I'd heard my mother and the other men and women tell of berserkers, throwing myself at this bastard.

I yanked him toward me with one hand while planting my fist into the side of his face. The meaty thwack left an angry red mark in the shape of my fist by his hairy ear.

The impact only fueled his rage. When I ducked away from his swing, I grabbed the stick and jabbed the end into his gut.

It wasn't until Kayn's cries pulled me from the fight that I allowed the bully to land a hit. Once he did, I knew he'd leave. All he wanted was to appear victorious and walk away with his twisted sense of dignity. So I let him smash his fist into my stomach, knocking the air from me, before I scrambled for Kayn.

Another child stood with him, a girl our age with fierce eyes and white lines painted beneath them in branching streaks of bone ash, mimicking the war paint of shield maidens.

She grunted as she tried to push the heavy cart off him. Joining her, we forced the wagon back onto its wheels and freed Kayn. I grabbed his arm and threw it over my shoulder, hefting him up and over the edge of the cart. Gripping the wood, Kayn pulled himself in the rest of the way. His bulging eyes peered around me with a wild look.

I craned my neck to be sure the bully had vanished in the crowd of bodies milling about the village. In shades of brown, green, and blue cloth, men and women went about their duties, some conversing lightly, others busy in work, spinning wool into thread, or chopping wood.

"He's gone," I said as I turned back to Kayn. He nodded slowly. "Are you hurt?"

"My leg is broken," he said.

I rolled my eyes. "I knew that. And it'll heal in a few weeks, then you'll be faster than me again."

"Give me my sword," he demanded.

I bent to pick it up, but the girl snatched it away from me. She tossed it to Kayn, who caught it easily. Though I knew most of the children in our village, I hadn't seen her before, maybe because she worked on one of the farms farther out, or perhaps her father built longships and they lived closer to the sea.

"Who are you?" I asked.

She smiled and only responded by lifting her own makeshift equipment. She used a web-like shield of woven sticks to block Kayn's blows, then pushed back against me when I struck her shield with my stick. A smile spread across her dimpled cheeks, and her free-flowing auburn hair blew into her face, sticking to her lips as she turned and ran from me.

Our battle resumed with gleeful shrieks from the mysterious girl.

Laughing, I chased her down, trying to grab at her shield, but she used it to push me away. I darted after her and grabbed her wrist. She let out another shriek, spun, and slammed her shield into my chest, then tossed her long hair over her shoulders. A gust of wind carried it out behind her in a dance of soft, rusty tendrils. Her brow furrowed, and she poked a finger at me, scolding me for grabbing her arm but it wasn't a second later that she flung herself at me, and our play battle began again.

"Show me you're a warrior," she said. Her pink cheeks bubbled as she returned my smirk. "Don't play easy."

So I didn't. I slammed my sword against her shield again and again, and she carefully angled it to protect her fingers. Though I pushed her back step by step, she didn't seem to mind.

"Rune! Rune!" Kayn's voice was an echo behind me.

I was so absorbed in the rhythmic clash of my weapon against her shield that I no longer felt the snowflakes tickling my cheeks. Kayn's shout fell away from my focus, and I wanted nothing more than to rise to the challenge this girl gave me. I would prove to her that I was a warrior. I'd show her I didn't tire.

The whack of the stick became my battle cry. Her laughter inspired me to try harder and harder to break her shield. This is how the warriors trained. They practiced and fought into the wee hours of the morning until their weapons cracked or the shield-maiden's defenses splintered.

I pulled my stick-sword back, preparing to hit with more force than I had before. Bringing the weapon down, the girl dodged out of the way. When she stepped to the side, my sword smashed against the stone base of Freya's feet. The stick shattered into a dozen splintered pieces.

For a moment, I stared at the remnants of my destroyed weapon until the girl's voice plucked me out of the stupor.

"Protecting others," she said.

I couldn't help but notice the way the white war paint concealed a few scattered freckles on the apples of her cheeks. "What?"

"That's what it means to be a warrior." Her dark eyes flickered to where Kayn's shouts echoed. Shrugging, she continued. "And protecting our land, and all that is ours.

What the gods have given us. All of it. That is what I will record in the poems when I become a skald."

"What is your name?" I asked, intrigued by her compliment. She'd nearly granted me the title of a warrior by suggesting that I was there to protect Kayn. Of course I protected Kayn because his damn leg was broken.

The blush blooming beneath her bone-ash spread across the bridge of her nose and down the curve of her cheeks. "Fight for it," she said, giving me another challenge. "My father says that's another thing that makes a warrior. Earning the right to something." Her eyes sparkled with mischief, and I grinned.

"Rune," Kayn yelled. I turned to him in time to see his arm rear back. He hurled the stick I'd given him into the air. Catching it, I beamed and spun on the girl.

"Follow me?" she asked with a giggle as she darted away from me. Throwing me one last look, she ducked behind the statue of Freya.

I charged after her with my newly gained weapon. After a few solid whacks, she pushed me back harder, and I slipped on the slick earth, now coated with a sleek layer of snow.

When I fell to the ground, she stepped up, standing over me with her shield. Looking down her nose at me, she smiled.

"I followed you," I said as if I were the one who earned the right to speak triumphantly, even though she towered over me. "Will you tell me your name? Or should I just call you Skald?"

"Myrah," she said. "But I am whoever I want to be. Maker of longships. shield-maiden. Winner." Her lips pursed in a mischievous smile before they parted again. "But I'm called Myrah."

Kayn's childlike voice called out again. "Myrah's just a fisherman's daughter."

She shot him a look full of vitriol. "I'm whoever I want to be, *Kayn*," she snapped.

He just laughed and begged me to pull the wagon closer to us again.

"Shall I show you I can be more than a fisherman's daughter?" She whacked the wooden stick against the edge of his wagon.

I took this as an invitation to duel again. Raising my little weapon, I advanced on her. She smacked my stick. Then again and again, but it wasn't as hard as it was the first time.

"Are you going easy on me?" I asked. She shrugged, but the smile that ghosted across her face betrayed her. I lifted my chin and mirrored her smile. "Hit hard, Skald."

That was why it felt right to call her by that name.

The memory of my childhood vanished, and I knew why I'd given Lux the same nickname. My Skald. Myrah…

This was a name Kayn had known all along, for hundreds of years. Even if he wasn't sure who Lux was at first, just like we hadn't known, he definitely knew now. There was no way in Hel he stood amongst these ruins, the same place we'd played at battle as children from another lifetime—no, the *same* lifetime, for him—and didn't remember.

Blinking away the memory, I lifted my head. Tendrils of hair the color of oak hung in my face as I dragged my eyes up to stare at the bastard who'd kept yet another secret from us. We'd been friends. He'd been there since the beginning, always vying for Myrah's attention, though not always in the best way.

Whenever Kayn found out Lux was Myrah, I couldn't be sure, but I had no doubt he knew now. Since Lux and I had reincarnated, we had to fight for the memory of our former selves, but he'd been in the same body and the same life the entire time. With the same damn envy for the woman I loved.

When Kayn placed his hands on Lux's face, I gritted my teeth, letting my fangs scrape painfully across my bottom teeth.

"You must try harder," he said. My mouth twitched. What the Hel was he asking of her now?

"I am," she insisted.

He shook his head, a look of almost fatherly disappointment coating his nearly black eyes. "No, you're not. You're here, with him."

"We're going to Yggdrasil. I can't let Silver take away my powers."

"Right, but you can kill them all now. Just be done with it."

"I know—"

"You don't," he argued. "If you knew, you'd be moving faster.You'd be destroying vampires for every minute you had the strength to move."

"I am, but Kayn, we can't…I can't," she stuttered. "I'm tired, and my mind is so muddled."

Something flashed in his eyes. Irritation, worry, and maybe anger. "Exactly, you have to push through it. A human mind —even a witch's—cannot handle the weight of the gods's voices. That's why you have to move faster. You've lasted so much longer than the other huntresses. They never made it long enough to kill any of us."

His gaze flicked to me, no doubt because he was thinking of my mother. Ingrid's mind distorted long before she ever came close to hunting the undead. Like Lux, Kayn had tried to train her, or at least that was my assumption when she vanished for days at a time. Then Kayn reappeared in my life as The Exile, the vampire who had offended the former king by spending too much time with my mother. After that, I'd only heard rumors of who Kayn was. That he knew my mother, that he was the only vampire who still worshiped Odin and Freya and wanted his soul back.

"We tried luring Silver in so that we could cut her off from the vampires, and they'd be scattered without their leader," Lux explained. "She got away. So our next best bet is to beat her to Yggdrasil and fight her army there. By the time they make it there, they'll be weak from the gods' realm and hunger. There's no way they can protect enough human vessels to last all that way."

He stared down at Lux, determination setting his bare jaw. "I see the gods within you, Lux. You won't have control of yourself much longer."

She tugged against his grip, but he did not let her go. "Kayn, I'm fine."

"You just said it. You're tired and your mind is slipping. Before it's lost completely—"

"Fighting makes it worse!" she cried. Shaking, her hands planted against his chest. I nearly broke my fangs as I ground them harder and harder. My jaw throbbed as I held back from attacking him. He needed to hear this from her mouth.

With every fiber of my being, I kept my fists at my side instead of wrapping my fingers around that liar's throat. Just like when he was a young boy, he needed to be reminded that she wasn't who he said she was.

Lux was whoever she chose to be. Whether that was the huntress or…my wife.

Chapter Twenty-Six

Lux

Two midnight eyes stared down at me, seeing what I didn't want to acknowledge. He was right; I was losing myself…

I drew a quick breath, desperate for any relief, and for help to gather the courage I'd need to admit the truth. I was so terrified. Terrified of being alone again.

I'd clung to those who'd accepted me: my mother, Stasia, Drak, and even Kayn when he sought me out and trained me. But losing my mind would lose all of them. My mind would erase all memories, and I would be submerged in the solitude of my own world. Except, I supposed, I wouldn't be entirely alone, not with the Gods' screams echoing through me.

Suppressing Odin's demands and Freya's vague statements proved tricky before, but now…now I didn't know where they ended and I began. And should it even matter? Beyond them, I didn't know if my life had purpose, or if I should even want for that purpose and an existence outside of them.

My mother raised me to worship Odin, revere Freya, and be cautious of Loki. But my mother praised all the Gods, especially the Allfather, even if she did so in secret.

This was for her.

I held onto my resolve and imagined my mother's face as she was finally free of my sister and the vampires she'd employed, but by then I'd be living in fear, my mind frozen, jarred, and in an eternal state of confusion like Drak's mother.

"I'm sorry, Lux," Kayn said. He sounded sincere, but the hard line of his mouth remained flat. Specks of black fluttered around him, and the thick air pressed down on my shoulders and chest.

He pulled me into him again, embracing me with all the warmth of a vampire who'd just fed on a human. But Kayn had broken off his fangs and sworn himself to a life of animal blood.

He was a good man because even without his soul; he wanted to make this world right again. Myrah's desperation and grief sentenced our realm to the existence of the vampire she created in him, but Kayn created the others, who then created more. He plagued Vylheim with the undead crawling across it.

Kayn may have made a horrible mistake, but I didn't blame him. Who hadn't made a mistake? Who was I to judge Kayn? Who was I to want to pull away from him when all he wanted was to correct his mistake?

He was even sacrificing himself. He knew that he, too, had to be staked and destroyed like the rest of the vampires in order to make the Gods happy and completely wipe this realm free of monsters.

The undead monsters, at least.

Despite it all, I still didn't want to meet his gaze. Good man or not, a dull ache throbbed behind my eyes whenever I had to listen to him urge me to push harder and move faster. I swallowed, my throat raw and dry as the wasteland's dirt. My voice came out gritty, rasping like sand dragged across the edge of the tumultuous southern seas. "I'm scared," I whispered.

"Then you have to do it scared," he said. "The Gods will do everything to keep you alive."

As victorious as that sounded, it wasn't the entire story, and I knew my saga ended in tragedy, in the shadows of my own mind.

"I'm not afraid to die, Kayn. I'm afraid of everyone else dying."

Drak made a sound behind me, something between a grunt and a gasp. I glanced back at him to see his bottom lip curled inward and darkness swimming through his icy eyes. It took me too long to realize the shadow in his gaze was sorrow, because if it were anything else, he wouldn't be holding back right now.

His hands clenched into fists at his sides, a sign that Drak resisted the urge to strike the one he blamed for my madness. When he lifted one fist, I held my breath, but he simply relaxed it and let his fingers brush over Sten's ring, a silent reminder of his promise to protect me.

Unaware of our silent exchange, Kayn's voice cut through our gaze. "You're saving the humans, not actually killing anyone because undead cannot die, again… This is merely a cleansing." I closed my eyes and turned back to him. Relishing the blackness behind my eyelids, I drew a deep breath, already difficult through the mesh pressed against my lips. Once I peeled my eyes open, I fixed my attention on him. Before I could speak, he continued. "You knew this was where your fate would lead. Drakkar and I are monsters, and you hunt us. That is the way of this. There is no way out—"

"That's not true." Drak spoke low, his voice gritty and quieter than usual.

"There is no way out," Kayn repeated.

"Listen to the one who stands in front of you." Freya joined the conversation, though Kayn could not hear her support of him. If he could, he would take joy in the Gods still acknowl-

edging him, and maybe even hope they would help him forge a new soul.

Her voice left a dull ache digging into my temples.

There is no way out. Old nerves that I'd learned to contain rose with a wave of bile, and my heart fluttered with scattered thoughts that I wasn't good enough, I couldn't do this, I hated myself for being this huntress, and for not being enough of a huntress. I didn't know which.

The back of my neck prickled with Drak's gaze. I tensed, holding back from spinning around to look at him again as I silently repeated what he'd told me. *Everything you choose to be is you.* That was my way out. I would do this on my terms, following the plan I had already laid out, no matter how much Kayn pushed.

Tears welled in my eyes as my stomach recoiled. A swath of sadness mixed with frustration for Kayn's impatience. Drak and I had crafted a delicate plan that had given me a sliver of hope, but now it felt as if Kayn had ripped it apart by voicing the Gods' demands aloud. Giving breath to their words made it so much more real. *Do it now.*

My head was already shaking. "No," I breathed.

His deep brown eyes darkened. Thick, dirty blond hair swooped over his forehead, where wrinkles bunched in shock. His expression finally fell into disappointment. "No?" he echoed.

Shaking my head more firmly, I repeated myself. "No, I will do this carefully. I can survive this. I *will* survive this and come out whole, both of us together. I'm giving you the end you deserve, with me."

With that inhuman vampire speed, his hands shot to my shoulders. Gripping me tightly, he shook me once, enough for me to tense every muscle in my body.

"Wholeness isn't an option for you or me, Lux. Do this, and you'll be welcomed into Valhalla where you can be whole at Odin's feast."

"And until then?"

"You will suffer; no one can take that away. Give yourself fully to the huntress—"

A blur whipped between us, and in the blink of an eye, the pressure of Kayn's grasp vanished. Fog swirled from the rush of movement, and once I processed what I was seeing, Drak had Kayn pinned against the massive square slab beneath Freya's stone feet. Drak's fingers bit into Kayn's throat. Both had their fangs out and their eyes burned as red as the stains in the ground beneath us.

"I can," Drak breathed. Kayn's strangled voice gurgled something unintelligible before Drak continued. "I can end her suffering."

A grimace contorted Kayn's flawless face. "No," he managed. "It's too late. You know this. Because of Ingrid, you know this."

Drak hissed. "There are other ways besides a binding."

"There is nothing but our fate, Drakkar."

Drak tightened his grip, pressing the back of Kayn's skull against the hard stone. Perhaps I should have moved to free him immediately, but none of the urgency I once felt to save Kayn stirred this time. He was already free of Silver…

I frowned at Kayn. "How did you escape Silver?" Without a word, Drak released him, letting him speak. "Don't lie," I said.

"I slipped away after she was weak from the siege on Mara's Keep."

"Did you try to save my mother? Stasia?"

His hesitation said enough, and my stomach sank. Still, he had the audacity to admit it aloud. "If they do not survive, their sacrifice will not be in vain. I had to find you and help you—"

"Fuck you," I said. Instinctively, I stepped back to put distance between us, though Drak's actions had already separated us. I shook my head, fighting back frustrated tears. "Tell me, could you have at least tried? Was there any opportunity?"

Instead of answering, his dark eyes drifted to the black specks hovering in the fog at my feet. Hot grief simmered alongside a fury rising in my throat. Tears threatened to sting my eyes again, but I swallowed the emotion.

"All you speak of is sacrifice, yet you always get exactly what you want." My voice tightened with every word.

"Sacrifice is what a warrior does."

"No. A warrior doesn't just throw themselves away without cause." From the corner of my eye, I caught Drak's head whipping toward me. "They do it to protect their people, their land. You've cared for nothing but killing all the vampires."

"The Gods—"

"Exactly," I interrupted him. "You only want to impress the Gods. That's what it was when you came to me at Mara's Keep and told me you'd had a change of heart about taking my soul, wasn't it? To impress the Gods. To show them you didn't act like the monster you are." Again, he stared at my feet, refusing to speak. Silence was in his best interest, with the rage climbing up my throat. My fingers flexed, reaching for the stake at my thigh. "Did you think you didn't need my soul because behaving as if you had one was enough?"

"This is our fate. We were always both doomed for exile, and now to serve the Gods. You and I, Lux."

"Call her by the name you know," Drak said.

My spine shot straight, and I drew a sharp breath. What was that supposed to mean? Kayn was well aware of the fact that I didn't go by my sister's name anymore.

Kayn slid his eyes to the only other vampire strong enough to kill him. His jaw rippled with consideration. Finally, he peeled away from Drak and faced me. "Myrah, this is your fate."

My fingers unclenched from around the stake and shot to my mouth. "What?"

"He knows," Drak said. "He's always known who you really are."

"Not always," Kayn said. "If it'd been clear sooner, I would have found her years ago."

I couldn't process this extra layer they piled onto this conversation, so I shook my head and steeled my resolve. "Get the Hel out of here, Kayn." I spoke through my teeth, but he didn't listen.

Instead of leaving, Kayn shoved past Drak and stepped up to me again. Everything within me withdrew, but I remained steady. "Myrah—"

That was enough. I dropped my hand to my thigh and slid the stake from the leather scabbard. Lifting the weapon, I stabbed the tip into the center of his chest. Even if it was fashioned from Yggdrasil, the stake wouldn't kill him at this angle, but it was enough to show him that I was willing to hurt him. "Leave, Kayn. Before I turn you to ash."

Of course he didn't listen, because when had he ever listened to me? And why the fuck was I just now seeing it? Was it the Gods' influence? Before I could form that into a full thought, the Gods interrupted again.

"Just kill him now." Loki's laugh followed the snake-like voice slithering through my head.

"Heed his words, but I agree with Loki. You've heard what he has to say, so now you will kill him." Odin immediately amended Loki's words. *"Do it now. Now! Be the weapon you were born to be. I won't wait much longer. You will do as I say, because if I must walk the ground of Midgard myself, you will regret it."* His voice turned shrill, desperate, wild. Odin was basically begging me now, while also demanding. Screaming.

Hel, it hurt. My head throbbed as they spoke, but if I kept my eyes trained on Drak, I could focus on my plan.

Even if it angered the Gods.

No, I am more than your weapon—

"Fuck you, you weak little bitch."

My mouth fell open and every muscle tensed. I'd done so much for Odin, and this was what he'd called me… The Allfather's words resembled my own father's too closely. He, too, had considered me frail and a failure in many ways.

But I wasn't weak or worthless; Drak had shown me that.

Sadness and shock settled quickly, giving way to something brewing deep within me. Nerves pricked along my spine and the hair on my arms stood on end. Forcing out a breath, I straightened. I would get through this. Selfish as it might be, I wasn't ready to sacrifice everything the way Kayn wanted.

His face twisted into something unrecognizable, or perhaps I was only now seeing him for the first time. Kayn tried everything to control me: lies, secrets, and now demands, and though I didn't have Yggdrasil's stake to destroy him with, he deserved it.

Something inside me seemed to snap as his lips twisted into a haunting scowl, turning his youthful vampire face into one of ancient evil. "Turning to ash is my fate, and unlike you, I accept it gratefully. But before I die, I'll get my soul back, and since you won't help, I'll do it myself."

What the Hel did that mean? A shiver stole through my bones.

"What are you going to do?" I whispered.

Kayn's eyes flashed red. "For my soul? Whatever it takes."

At that, my blood hardened to ice, and I couldn't take one more second of looking into his blood-red eyes. The cruel eyes of a man who'd abandoned my mother and friend to the enemy, and then claimed to care for me.

Finally—finally—he backed away. With another look at Drak, he peeled back his lips and spoke around his broken fangs, where the snapped-off bone was shaped into an odd curve. "The Gods will do everything to stop you, of this I am sure. I just hope that when you fall, you don't take Myrah with you."

Drak opened his mouth to respond, but Kayn vanished into the fog, and we were alone again.

All at once, the grief of losing someone I'd wanted so desperately to trust, and learning he'd left my mother and friend behind to die, piled onto my heart. It hung heavy in my chest, beating once, then stuttering.

The weight of the anger and loss left my legs weak, and Drak didn't need a warning that I was about to collapse. He simply knew. He darted to me, letting me fall against his chest as he scooped me into his arms.

This time, I didn't argue when he carried me back to the tent. I couldn't, not with unconsciousness dragging me into Freya's vision.

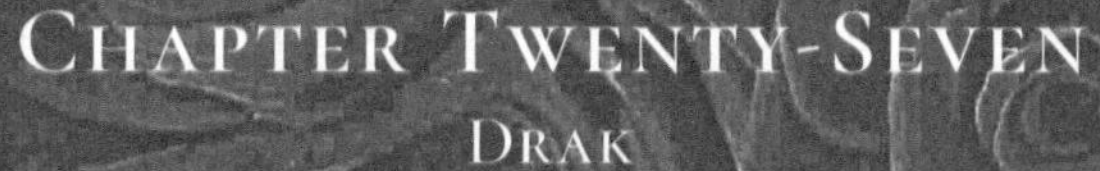

Chapter Twenty-Seven
Drak

Lux's arm fell limp, her pale wrist exposed to the sky. The sun's glow tinted the drifting fog orange, casting an eerie light across her skin.

My jaw tensed, and it was everything I could do not to curse at Odin and Freya. Shouting into the wasteland was a foolish use of the energy I needed to preserve the closer we drew to Yggdrasil. At the base of the gods' tree, they could almost reach out and touch us. At least that was what I remembered from the first time I saw it, when I bowed before the trunk and begged Odin to release my mother's mind.

That was so long ago, before I knew of Lux, and before I remembered Myrah. Back then, I was just a boy, desperate and alone in a court teeming with monsters.

I tore my mind away from the past and focused on Lux in the present. Her unconscious body felt light in my arms, but I hated that the gods had stolen her control. Her eyes had rolled back before her lids fell heavy over them, lashes fluttering to reveal glimpses of white streaked with red. If this was the gods' only way of reaching their people, then they weren't as powerful as they claimed. And if it wasn't, then why the Hel would they choose collapse and unconsciousness as the means to give people answers and glimpses of the future?

Instead of carrying her back to the tent, I carried Lux to the ruined temple. Her body twitched every few seconds. When a whimper escaped her, I curled my lower lip between my teeth, channeling my anger somewhere safe. I sank my fangs into my lips to keep from doing something reckless, like marching straight to Yggdrasil. The path was clear, but the journey would be painstaking. For both our survival.

Lux needed rest she couldn't get while I carried her, and I needed to prepare for what lay ahead.

Inside the temple, the headless gods stood like silent sentinels. I knelt before the sacrificial altar, not because Lux was a sacrifice, but because I imagined this was where the gods could reach her. Maybe if they saw her here in this ancient place of worship, they would stop tormenting her for the rest of this vision.

Nothing changed, however. Lux still seized, then fell limp again. I cupped the back of her head and brought her forehead to mine. "I'm here," I whispered.

Finally, her eyes opened, heavy-lidded and clouded with a haze, as if the fog had permeated her. But they were transformed, no longer painted entirely with a film of blackness. "Drak?" She murmured, her throat rippling with a grim swallow. "Drak…"

"I'm here."

With effort, she shook her head, tears slipping through the corners of her eyes. "Not for long," she said.

I furrowed my brow and drew her closer to my chest, letting her cling to my neck. "Lux, just breathe," I urged, my voice steady against her ragged breaths.

Hiccuping, she forced out the words. "I saw you die."

"I did," I said. "But that was many lifetimes ago."

Her fingers curled around the fabric of my collar, fisting the material with a desperate grip. "No. You will die."

I couldn't help the chuckle that escaped me. "Lux, you're the huntress destined to destroy me. Surely, you've thought of my death many times."

"Not like this. It is torture that you'll suffer over and over."

I examined her face. What the Hel had she seen? "It won't matter, I'll be a god."

She shook her head again, eyes welling. "You won't make it there. Death will find you first. The sun, starvation, and a spear of gold will strike you down." Tears spilled over her cheeks, each drop carrying the weight of the vision and blurring her gaze.

"I can't die except from a stake fashioned from Yggdrasil. You know this. Whatever fucked-up vision Freya painted on the back of your eyelids is a lie."

"This isn't a lie, Drak, and I won't watch you suffer the way you did in my vision." Her eyelashes brushed upward as she looked up at me, still cradled across my lap. Flecks of gold and brown dotted her black eyes. The concern lacing her gaze captivated me. If she wanted to protect me, she truly was a warrior. She drew a breath and pulled herself up to sit across from me on her legs. We faced one another in front of the altar. I'd never bow to the Gods, but I had no problem being on my knees for my queen. "I don't think I can bear to watch you suffer."

I swallowed. The burden in her voice wasn't just from the weight of the vision. Even if Lux didn't remember our former life, she was finally trusting me—enough that she no longer saw me as her opponent. We were together, a team, almost as if this marriage were real.

"I know all about the risks in the gods' territory," I said. "You forget that I've already been there, and I'm not stopping now. But you're getting worse. You were out for so long, and don't tell me you're not in pain now." She flinched because she couldn't deny it. The gods were trying to carve out her very soul. "When I'm a god, you won't have to listen to them. We'll cut a place for ourselves in this world, and the vampires will be gone."

She folded her hands into fists, but she didn't fight me. "What if you don't make it?" she asked.

I shifted my gaze to the altar. Back then, I hadn't known the death that awaited me on the battlefield. Fragments of myself emerged, recollections of my arrogance even when staring down the wrong end of a weapon. At least I knew I hadn't changed much.

Shifting my eyes back to my wife—because, fuck it, she was my wife once—I held her fragile gaze.

People only worried about those they loved, and Lux damn sure looked worried right now. With my arm outstretched, I cupped her jaw and tipped her toward me. I kissed her with the weight of two lifetimes and the strength of a warrior who had abandoned Valhalla for her.

Myrah chose me, and Lux knew me, from the second she recognized the warrior within. The person I was in the past.

When we parted, I stared at her perfect lips, swollen with the hard kiss, then dragged my eyes up to meet hers. "If I don't make it, then I'll follow you into the next life."

Chapter Twenty-Eight

Drak

My wife stared up at me, her thoughts brimming with desire that I didn't want to stop listening to. The kiss left us both wanting more, but giving in and absorbing Lux's lust would pull me under her spell, leaving me weak to her needs and unable to focus on reaching Yggdrasil. Kayn moved with the precision of a predator, and though we had no idea what he planned, I knew it wouldn't be good.

I tore myself away, extending my heightened senses beyond the ruins to catch the vibrations of Silver's coming army. If the sounds were any indication, she was closing in on us.

"You need to rest." I refused to look at Lux as I said it, because sensing her desire and feeling her gaze on me was already too much. I balled my hands into fists and pressed the tips of my fangs into my bottom lip, but the sharp prick did nothing to stop my cock from stiffening.

"Right." Her voice was a desperate pant. Fuck, it took everything within me not to spin around, wrap her legs around my hips, and take her right here.

"Silver has crossed back over the border of the wasteland," I said, keeping my eyes trained on the cracked earth. The sight of the dry, bloodstained ground helped my cock finally get the message, but when a little gasp escaped her, I cursed under my breath. "We're still a day or two ahead, assuming Axel's estimate of her army's speed is right. So you will rest." And we were safe from Kayn because even he wasn't stupid and reckless enough to come near us again. I'd behead him, no holding back.

"Fine," she agreed, "but not for long."

I glanced over my shoulder without letting my gaze meet hers. Swallowing hard, I added, "I'll wake you soon."

Her fingers brushed the back of my arm, and though fabric separated my skin from her touch, my muscles went taut. I ground my jaw and pulled away, scrubbing my hand over my beard. Finally, her scent of warm honeyed wine faded with the sound of her footsteps, and my body relaxed, though it took my damn cock a couple of extra minutes.

I lifted my head to stare at the altar. If only she could remember our vows there, maybe everything would be different, though I couldn't see how it would change our plans. Those memories had ruined my plan to lure Silver, and because of that distraction, Lux and I had missed our chance to work together and capture her.

Of course, we hadn't expected Kayn to fall so easily under Silver's compulsion. He was the oldest vampire we knew and the only other one marked by Yggdrasil, placed by the first witch's power. Lux couldn't destroy him before, too torn by her emotions then, but things were different now.

I spread my palm against the altar, feeling the cool ridges of the wood against my skin. "Please remember, Lux," I breathed. "Myrah."

Hel, even Kayn had admitted she was Myrah, but Odin was too damn loud for her to accept it. The gods ignored her plea not to split us up in the afterlife, so she created Kayn out of desperation, and of course he allowed it. I was gone, and he would have done anything to please her—to win her heart—after failing the first time he tried to take her from me.

My fingers dug into the wood, scratching the altar like an animal tearing at its prey. I remembered him standing beside me at our wedding as more of that night came back in flashes. He had pretended to honor his best friend's marriage. "You were there, you bastard."

He showed up at our wedding after boldly approaching Myrah the night before and claiming she belonged with him.

Rage coursed through my black-stained veins. Fuck the Exile. He had always moved in secret, and I still let him into this temple after he betrayed me. I had held a soft spot for far too long for the boy I once called my best friend.

I turned my back on the altar and stormed out of the ruined temple. The wasteland offered no fresh air, but I marched on without stopping, heading straight to Myrah's old home.

I wanted to remember everything he said that night because I didn't yet have Odin's foresight to know what Kayn would do. Maybe, like Lux thought she could predict Silver's next moves by understanding her, I could guess at whatever reckless shit Kayn would try after Lux finally rejected him. But to do that, I had to recall Kayn's reaction the last time she had rejected him in our former life, to glimpse how he might behave now.

Old Skaldir was falling apart around me; the walls of Myrah's old house shattered and strewn across the floor. Dust hung heavy in the air, but in the spot where I had overheard Kayn's pleas, everything snapped into focus. I saw it all as if I were there again, fully Rune and feeling every desperate word as though it were my own.

Snow crunched under my boots, but the shouting inside Myrah's home drowned my footsteps. I didn't slow down until I heard it was my closest friend who was shouting.

"Kayn?" I whispered as I halted outside the door. The

small house of a retired fisherman stood with only thin, timber walls, old and creaking each time the icy wind blew through the village. Disease ravaged Myrah's father's lungs, forcing him to quit fishing and not long after, he died, and we carried him miles and miles to the shore, to send him off to sea, Myrah having shot the flaming arrow that burned his body and fisherman's boat.

"I deserve you," Kayn said.

Like fuck he *deserved* her. What the Hel did that mean? I almost ripped the door from its hinges, but I forced myself to stay calm. Myrah preferred to stand on her own two feet, and Kayn was her friend as well, so I had to let her take control of the situation.

Myrah spoke firmly and with the steady strength of the queen I saw within her. "I'm not sure what you mean, Kayn, but you're drunk and I don't appreciate you coming to me the night before my wedding."

"We belong together."

"Explain yourself," she said. *That's right, demand more of him.* One side of my mouth lifted in a crooked half-smile. I couldn't see inside, but I knew she stood with her arms crossed and her lips pursed, expecting to receive what she insisted upon. She always pushed others to be as honest as possible, and that was exactly what I loved about her. She challenged me.

"You're a fisherman's daughter," Kayn said. I scoffed at the exact time Myrah did, and I couldn't help smirking again. "Neither of us is of high status here, M. We understand each other."

"Because I didn't bring back gold from my time across the sea?" she said. "Is that what this is about? You know that isn't what our village invaded for, we were sending a message for the West Anglans to stay out of Vylheim."

"And you almost died there. You almost didn't come home to me."

"You're not my home."

"I should be."

"Rune and I went there together as warrior and shield-maiden. He's my—"

"AND HE LET YOU FALL!"

"Exactly," she hissed. "Rune lets me fight my own battles. He doesn't tell me he deserves me either, or insist that I do what he wants—"

"M, please, I love you."

"You love controlling me. But I won't pity you anymore. If you show up to our wedding tomorrow, you will keep your mouth shut and respect my marriage."

Damn right. Whatever Kayn described wasn't love at all.

Somebody whimpered, and it better not have been her, or else this house was about to lose its door.

Finally, he spoke. "I'll be there to remind you that you're making a mistake." I backed away from the door as his foot-steps pounded toward me. The door slammed open, and he strode into the night, oblivious to me hidden in the shadows.

But Myrah's eyes immediately landed on me. She eyed me with a knowing smile from her spot at the threshold. Kayn's words could not extinguish her spark, showing her fire that would always blaze, for challenge, for story, and for me.

The rest of that night we discussed our village's plan to invade West Anglor. Even in the shadow of what was coming, there was a warmth between us. We had always known battle would follow our wedding, and we wouldn't have traded a single moment of it.

Except for Kayn's presence.

I would have changed that. Even as the memory faded, I wished I could go back and erase him from our wedding. But that night taught me one thing: Kayn would return. I didn't know how, because centuries of experience made him impos-sible to predict, but I had no doubt we would see him again.

And when we did, I'd make sure Lux was ready with a stake from Yggdrasil.

Hel, no wonder my attempts to force Lux into marriage had triggered her. Deep down, even if she didn't remember, my need to control everything must have reminded her of Kayn. I had been unbearably and stupidly desperate.

It was time I learned from the Exile's mistake. Everything from here on out had to be her choice. I'd give her the tools to fight the gods, and I'd give her the *truth* whenever she was willing to listen, but she was strong enough to fight the madness.

I had to believe this, or I was going to go mad myself.

Chapter Twenty-Nine

Lux

Sleep claimed me quickly, but I had told Drak to wake me after four hours, and he'd kept his word. I jolted awake, drenched in sweat.

Kayn's threats hammered through my mind with each one promising he would do whatever it took to reclaim his soul. My chest burned with the implication, and I couldn't stop asking myself what that would mean for us. Nerves prickled along my neck as if he were here and watching me, even though I knew he left when he could no longer use me to sway the Gods.

Glimpses of my mother and Stasia were woven into the nightmares like gruesome images of death upon a tapestry. Despite my sweat soaking the furs, a violent chill shook me.

Drak urged me to sleep longer, but I threw the furs off my legs and pushed to my feet. With Silver forced to backtrack, we held the lead, but I had already spent too much time resting. We needed to continue climbing to hold our pace ahead of her, and if she caught up, we would have no choice but to start the fight early.

In silence, we packed up the tent and the furs, and Drak

drank a carefully portioned swig of stored blood. Unable to drink from me and with no vessel to carry, this leather pouch was all he had to survive until Yggdrasil. He certainly wouldn't have enough for the return trip if he failed to ascend to Godhood and remained a vampire.

I didn't let myself think about it for too long. It was all only a distraction from our meticulously laid plan. Pick off the vampires, protect the tree, return to our old lives. Drak on the throne and me living in Skaldir. The thought that I might be Myrah, and that Drak and I belonged together, barely formed in my mind before Odin's voice shredded it, grating through me like bone against bone.

We pushed on quietly and with determination, and thankfully, Drak said nothing about my misreading of Kayn. He refrained from boasting, enabling us to settle into a comfortable silence as we proceeded at a pace that kept my heart rate stable.

Time was hard to track through the fog. The sun seldom glimmered behind red clouds, and I had to count our stops to make camp. As night fell, the fog shifted from pulsing brown and red to drab gray shadows, marking the slow progress.

We forged ahead for another two days without incident. No collapse, but also no sign of Silver's army. At least when we fought them at Yggdrasil, Silver wouldn't be able to compel Drak. Nobody could compel a God.

And as one of them, he could make the Gods retreat from my mind, freeing me from the weight of their screams. I didn't even care if he had other plans with his future Godhood, because at the very least, he was willing to try to help me. Instead of facing this fate alone, he stood by me. He took every step, pacing with mine when I slowed, watching in case collapse threatened me.

He was always here. The question remained: for how long? How long had he been following me? I peeled my lips apart, ready to ask him about Myrah and Rune, but the bolt of pain through my head stopped me.

Right. I could focus on nothing but my duties as a huntress. I'd endured pain before, so I pushed past the ache and forced out the question. "Is all of that about our past lives really true?"

As if he'd been waiting for this question, he stopped walking and faced me. "You should know, your eyes have changed."

"What?" That had nothing to do with my question.

His gaze wavered between my eyes, intent and all-consuming. "The blackness over your eyes. I can almost see the center. They're…" He squinted. "I think they're golden brown."

"That's not possible." They had always been purely black. No whites, no tiny red veins, just black. Silver and the other children used to call me an animal, teasing me for how bizarre my eyes looked.

He bore a sad smile. "Nevermind. You were asking about our past. So, will you believe it if I tell you about the first time you became my wife? With real vows?"

I skimmed my teeth along my bottom lip, considering this. How much was I ready to hear? How much could my mind endure before the Gods brought me agony?

"Were we actually married?" I asked. I'd start there, at least.

He curled his forefinger and tipped my chin up. "In another lifetime. I was drawn to your ability to spin stories from our daily lives." He winced and fell quiet for a moment before sucking in a breath. "Stories were the only way I kept my father alive in my memory. He died when I was a young boy. The same day I met you, actually."

My heart skipped a beat, and the world began to spin. I wanted nothing more than to believe this, but the implications of what that meant were too heavy. If I were Myrah, then I'd have created the monster I just sent away, and I'd have done it all for Drak.

For Rune.

A bolt of lightning seemed to flash behind my eyes, striking the soft spot at the back of my neck where the base of my skull balanced.

I squeezed my eyes shut as tears flooded them. "I want to remember, but I can't."

He dragged me closer to him, resting his chin against the top of my head. "We met as children. You told me…" I felt the ripple of his swallow. "You told me that a warrior protects others, just like you told Kayn." I pulled back to look up at him, but he was a blur in my swimming vision. "It's true. The memory came back to me when we found the ruins. I think it was because it was you who read the sagas to me that first sparked the memories, and then each time you said my true name, it brought more memories. Coming to the place where we'd met, and the place where we married, also filled in the missing spots. The ruins were of a village once called Skaldir. Old Skaldir, I've taken to calling it. Your hometown in Vylheim is named after it.

I wished I could recall it all.

I wished I could think about anything besides this fate. But Kayn was probably right. Even if we followed the plan precisely, fate had already sealed my destiny, and imagining a life with Drak only made the pain worse.

Still, my mind drifted to it. Would we have found each other and resumed a love that stretched across time? Would we have been farmers? Yes, but I had a strange inkling that he'd also build longships like he built my bookshelves, and we'd live near the sea. That I'd bring up our children to train for battle and protect our land. Perhaps they'd enjoy footraces and weaving and telling sagas aloud over the fire, like I once did.

My stupid heart stuttered, and the back of my eyes

burned. Now was not the time to crumble into tears for a life I'd never have. We didn't have the past or the future, only this moment, and in this moment, we had to move forward.

I pressed on without speaking, at last escaping the heavy fog and entering the light.

Chapter Thirty

Drak

Memories of Erik from my boyhood kept me company during the long, treacherous climb up the sunlit mountain, though Lux's presence was the better comfort. She eased the grief in my chest—grief that shouldn't have existed, since my father, in this life and the last, had died long ago. But the memories made it feel fresh and immediate.

I grieved not only for Erik, but for the farm we once lived on and the longships he built before he died at sea. For the path I'd wanted to follow in his footsteps, building ships like him to impress the fisherman's daughter. Fierce little Myrah. Skald. My warrior friend.

Lux seemed to understand that my silence came from some ancient pain as she walked beside me, her hand brushing the back of mine.

Yggdrasil stood at the summit of Vylheim, the highest point on this known land. We couldn't see it yet, but its presence surrounded me, pulsing like the beat of the heart I did not have. Pressure mounted with every step, and my limbs grew heavier. I silently cursed Odin for hating me just because he didn't create me.

Myrah created me.

I stole a glance at Lux. Despite her weak heart, she remained fixed on the path ahead, moving over dry ground that no longer looked like scorched stained earth. It looked more like the soil of a world I could recognize. The fog lifted as we neared Yggdrasil.

At the tree, Odin and Freya didn't have to rely on witches and battles to access this world. Even miles out from the base of Yggdrasil, the sagas foretold the gods' reach. Like the outstretched arm of the divine, they could influence the elements here.

This was the center of the nine realms, the place of knowledge, where Odin hung to gain wisdom, and I'd do the same. The image of grabbing him by the throat and ripping him out of Lux's mind kept my feet driving forward.

The sun's weight tied itself around my limbs like an invisible force pushing me back, back, back. I ground my jaw, my back teeth nearly cracking as I fought against the gods' influence. Nothing beyond Lux gave me relief.

Only her voice eased the hours spent ascending the steep slope to Yggdrasil. Her questions kindled a fire within me as she processed the former lifetime I'd shared with her.

"You really saw us," she hesitated, "at that altar?"

I saw far more than just us at the altar. After recalling our childhood meeting, hundreds of memories flooded back. Memories of training together for battles to come, my sword crashing against her shield. Memories of firelight flitting across her face as she recounted stories of us as Odin's chosen, envied by those who lived across the sea. Memories of taking her on the floor of our home, our bodies entwined over furs, and then sharing a cup of mead before drifting to sleep with our hair and limbs tangled.

My jaw was tight with the ache of sunlight piercing the fog, so I just nodded instead of saying all of that to her. The dense air faded, and the sun's rays grew harsher, battering down on us with ruthless intensity. It never changed, never wavered from its stagnant spot in the sky. I squinted against it, thankful for the mask and leathers shielding my body.

Though the sagas alleged vampires burned beneath the sun, it was far less a firestorm than the skalds described. Our flesh steamed, and the wound was a persistent sting, eroding our strength hour by hour. The sun felt endless here, as Odin had apparently instructed Sunna to prolong daylight.

Night might never come.

At least the perpetual winter's chill afforded some respite, cooling the skin the sun grazed, but it was barely enough to ward off the weariness dragging at my bones.

"What's wrong?" Lux asked.

I pinched my eyes shut and forced my foot in front of me. "The sun…"

"So it begins."

My eyes strayed from the sky to her face, the sun permeating through her auburn braids and setting them alight. She grew stronger and healthier as we neared Yggdrasil. A faint radiance illuminated the patches of her skin visible beneath the mask, and as soon as we spotted the tree, she'd probably be able to remove it entirely and breathe freely.

"I'm fine," I insisted, knowing Yggdrasil was on the horizon and she'd come alive.

She let out a laugh. "You're fucking impossible, you know that?" Her eyes sparkled with mischief, and I couldn't help the smirk twisting my lips. She had spat my words back at me, and for that, I loved her. Nobody else dared to argue with me. Nobody else cared whether I lived or died. Now I had a shield-maiden, a woman who knew her worth and who worried about my suffering.

Lux had a fire for life that this fucked-up world had robbed from the rest of us.

She survived and persisted in a way that I once did when I chose to become a vampire. Where others were dull and gray, she was orange and red with brilliant shades of black and white. Nothing about her personality was hazy.

Even if she didn't know exactly who she was, I did.

She was my wife and the same woman I vowed to follow into every lifetime. Lux became what the occasion required—dark for rage and death, blazing with fury when survival demanded it, and calm when stillness was necessary. Even before the gods intervened, she met her execution with composure, finding peace in her fate rather than fighting it, despite her mental turmoil.

She saw all my pain, even the parts I fought to hide with every pulse of Sunna's rays.

Fuck, I loved Lux. For seeing everything I suppressed. I'd loved her when we were training together a lifetime ago, and I loved her for seeing the warrior in me, even before she knew I was the only vampire king who maintained an armory and trained with a sword.

"And when we married, you said you'd follow me?" she asked. Did she remember? In that moment, the sun's oppressive weight felt as if it had lifted. "Like you did for our fake wedding?"

I swallowed and peeled my lips apart. "I swore to follow you, yes."

"Why?"

Her curiosity appeared, shimmering like tears of joy at the base of her eyelids. The red lines that shot through the whites of her eyes had faded, and she appeared brighter and more voluminous than ever.

"Because I would have given anything for you." I *would* give anything for her.

She hummed thoughtfully. "Because you were my warrior, and I was the shield-maiden."

My jaw went slack. Was I losing myself to the sun's fatigue, or was I just desperate to hear what I wanted? Not wanting to face the possibility of her not remembering, I didn't find the courage to ask why she had said that. There was already enough tugging at my limbs and dragging me back.

This could be another one of her lies because she knew I wasn't strong enough for the truth right now. But her lies never bothered me. The opposite, actually. Recognizing her worth, she acted for her safety and survival, and I had immense respect for her darker nature. I craved to see more of that darkness in her almost as much as I craved to know what made her say that.

Fuck it.

"Why did you call me Rune?" I asked. *Ready or not.*

Her chin tilted up, her mouth hanging open as she panted from the effort of climbing. Her legs must have been screaming by now, especially since I could no longer carry both her pack and my own. Didn't the gods recognize that this damn sun was causing their precious chosen witch to suffer too?

Not that they cared for her suffering. They only wanted her for what she could do for them. I curled my fingers into fists and fumed as the fog cleared altogether. Winter air bit through the mesh in the mask, but the sun's rays were just as aggressive.

If I wanted to follow Lux, I had to keep moving.

Her answer came at last. "I don't know."

"Is that the truth?"

"Why would I lie about that?"

"Because you don't want me to know that you remember."

Her brow creased under the mask, fine lines appearing around her eyes. "I'd have no reason to conceal that."

"Except then you'd have to admit you loved me once, too." Hel, I wanted that. I'd almost do anything to hear her say it, but nothing I did or said could control her feelings. That was entirely up to her.

"I'm Lux. I don't know Myrah."

"Good thing I love you no matter what you choose to call yourself."

"I don't remember any of this."

There it was. A slight crack rippled through Lux's voice every time she lied, like an iced-over lake splitting under the weight of a boot. It was more obvious now that she didn't lie daily. She was slipping, on the verge of sinking beneath the surface and drowning in deceit. More deceit would destroy her. That much I knew about my fake wife.

Her cheek trembled, and the scar etched across it pulled taut with the movement.

"You're lying," I said, holding her attention as if it were as fragile as the fractured lake. She jerked her head forward and shattered our tethered gaze. "You can't look at me."

"I don't enjoy watching you suffer."

I smirked. At least that wasn't a lie. Her voice was as smooth as the ice's surface this time, and when she snuck a quick glance, I chuckled.

I allowed us to fall into a comfortable silence for the next few hours, and sure enough, the sun didn't budge. Night was not coming. I clenched my jaw, swallowed the pain, and wouldn't allow Lux to witness her vision unfold.

But I could tell from her repeated, lingering looks that she remembered when we were together.

Chapter Thirty-One
Lux

Pieces of the past slipped through the wall I built every time Drak said that name. *Myrah.*

Every fragment of the past stirred questions I couldn't ignore. With Drak's memories as a guide, I could finally assemble the picture that had long haunted my thoughts.

Like images of our hands intertwined flashing through my skull, or of us before the altar at the ruins. Of us marching into battle together, side by side beneath a shield wall. The images were a source of encouragement, driving me forward, knowing that I could make a life like this a reality for someone else in Vylheim. Perhaps Stasia would enjoy this freedom and simplicity with Finan someday. Instead of training with an axe and shield, Stasia would be a cook in a safe village with Finan, liberated from vampire control and no longer forced to be an executioner.

In an instant, the memories were swept aside by the sight of branches reaching up into the sky.

Like spiked fingers, the ash tree reached for Asgard above. Even miles from Yggdrasil, we could glimpse the core of the nine realms, stretching out beneath its colossal branches.

Blinking, I almost didn't believe that this was truly Yggdrasil. An odd feeling, both hot and cold, coursed through me; my blood's flow unusually slow even as my heart raced.

I squeezed my eyes shut, but the sight of the branches penetrated beyond my eyelids. Even in my own mind, I wasn't alone.

The presence of the Gods thickened around and inside me. A curious sense of liveliness and buoyancy washed over me, even as my muscles protested and my jaw tightened inexplicably. "That's really Yggdrasil…"

"We haven't made it yet," Drak said. The rasp in his voice echoed the dust-laden air at the heart of the wasteland. I blinked hard and ripped my gaze from Yggdrasil. Despite my throbbing feet and burning thighs, Drak's misery was far greater, apparent in his split, pale lips and the black blood marring the cuts on his dry flesh. His icy blue eye faded to a dull grey that matched the sickly color of the sky, except for the sun's faint orange glow. When he spoke again, arid anguish laced his words. "We have to keep moving."

He weakened with each step, and I slowly drifted closer to him. I had no power to ease his suffering, but I could at least try to catch him when he tripped. That much I owed him.

Despite my longing to reach Yggdrasil, I hated what the Gods' power did to him. Hel, what had become of me?

This was Drak, my fake husband, the monster who had held me hostage in Mara's Keep and threatened both my life and my sister's. Of course, his reasons were obvious now. The Gods despised him, and their venom occasionally pierced the walls of my mind, but I did not feel the same hate.

Not only did I *not* hate Drak, I couldn't bear to consider how my heart might break when we went our separate ways. If Silver and the vampires were defeated, and Drak ascended to Godhood, Mara's Keep would be his domain. Vylheim would capture his gaze, and the throne would own his heart.

My neck arched, eyes rising to the sky. The clouds hung

dull and grey, yet the sun glowed a stubborn orange, endless and eternal, a presence as inexorable as the Gods.

Whenever the sagas spoke of the end of the world as we knew it, I grieved, not for myself and my kin, but for Odin and Freya, Thor and all the Gods I worshiped in secret. Every day. Every story surrounded them, and everything my mother taught me turned me to honoring and respecting the Allfather and the others in Asgard.

My gut knotted. Where had that grief gone now? Drak spoke of summoning one of the Gods and killing them, and I'd simply pushed this goal of his out of my mind. Until now.

Now that we had climbed the hill to Yggdrasil, its craggy branches clawing at the sky, I couldn't ignore the sensation rising in me. Bile pushed up my throat, bitter and stinging at the back of my mouth. My tongue dried and expanded heavily behind my teeth as the truth swelled within me. It'd become impossible to suppress.

Drak was going to kill Odin.

He never had to say it aloud for me to understand. Odin despised Drak, and his voice rang loudest in my mind. This was who Drak planned to leverage as a stepping stone on his path to becoming a God, and as much as he had claimed it was for the power to lead Vylheim to safety and prosperity, I knew it was personal.

The Gods had destroyed his mother and now…me.

Hel, did I really believe Odin was willing to destroy his creations? My heart skipped and breath was suddenly sucked from my lungs. Did I dare to consider that the Gods were hurting me?

No.

This can't be their fault. It is we humans who are the hardest to reach. That was what my mother would say: that their power was simply too much for my fragile mind to handle. Right?

I couldn't voice this question aloud. Drak would dismiss it at once, claiming Odin was a cruel God and that all of them were selfish. He would respond only with his warped perspective, and I couldn't help but wonder had my mother's views been just as warped?

The madness clawing at the back of my eyes came from the Gods. Thor's storms raged in Vylheim like a punishment to the very people who were daring to emerge from their secret worship. It didn't make sense.

Sickness sloshed in the pit of my gut. I reached for the leather pouch carrying my water reserve and wet my thick tongue. Swallowing, I buried these traitorous thoughts and glanced at Drak.

I gnawed at the inside of my bottom lip as I watched fatigue and desperation pull at his flat mouth and his hands clench into fists at his sides. I recognized that look: the desperate suppression of pain. How many times had I ignored the sharp twinges of my erratic heartbeat only to be forced flat on my back for days? When my father demanded I push through, wasn't it the same as Freya granting visions only after I finally broke?

My head jerked against my will, as if the Gods had seized my skull to shove my thoughts aside. These were among the truths Drak had been offering me. He was the only one willing to speak them, the only one who noticed my frozen fingers and recognized my need for rest. The only one who truly saw me…

"Drak," I blurted.

He came to a stop, and the tension at the corners of his eyes finally eased. A brief rest would benefit us both. I flinched as his cracked lips parted, and my heart sank at the pain etched across his face. Still, it was not my place to hold him back from pursuing his own goals, no matter how much I ached to shield him.

"What is it?" he asked, his eyes narrowing with a concern he always reserved just for me.

Oh, Hel. I think I trusted him. I think…I loved him. This

was the vampire king, and the man I once considered an enemy for the way his council treated witches. How could this be?

Impossible.

Impossible.

Gods aren't selfish, girl, you are.

Were these thoughts mine at all, or did they come from Odin? Perhaps my father's and mother's voices, each so distinct yet equally powerful, had merged into one. Whoever they belonged to, I could feel the same sharp, twisted weight behind them.

Calling me selfish was a lie, and it stung after all I had sacrificed to become their huntress. I had obeyed their visions and carried out their commands. I had denied Drak. Every glance at him since our sham marriage denied the truth stirring within me, and I had done it all for the Gods.

It wasn't that I couldn't marry a monster—after all; I had once been one—but Odin would never allow me to be with a vampire. For him, and for all of Asgard, I denied Drak. And that definitely wasn't a selfish choice. Perhaps Myrah had done a terrible thing, but I was no longer her.

I drew a breath that sliced sharp through my throat and locked my eyes on Drak. "When you said it was fucked up for the Gods to force us to sacrifice and suffer for their aid…" my voice trailed off. I watched him, noticing tendrils of steam rising from the few places the sun touched his skin. The mask had openings in various places, and flesh was visible on his neck where his tunic and the mask didn't quite meet.

The Gods told me they would make him suffer, the same way they had made me suffer. The same way they were making the people of Vylheim suffer from howling winds and lightning that destroyed the last of the winter-stricken crops.

"Lux?" he prodded.

My tongue swelled in my mouth, as though Odin himself were blocking me from admitting the truth. I opened my mouth, but my veins froze, and the wall in my mind split apart, shattered by an invisible strike like Thor's lightning.

"He is a monster, and we're protecting you from him." Freya's voice held a strange sob.

My heart stuttered, and the tightness beneath my breast sent dizziness swirling through my head. Black spots flickered at the edges of my vision. I gasped for air, willing my blood to flow again, but invisible claws gripped my heart, squeezing with relentless force until I shut my eyes. Then my pulse surged, racing in sharp, uneven beats, each one trying to reclaim the time my heart had stolen from me.

Pulling the mask off, I let it fall to my side, still grasped lightly in my fingers.

"I'm sorry it took me so long," I whispered. Drak's brow pinched, and the slight tilt of his head endeared me to him.

I'm sorry I didn't remember.

I'm sorry I didn't listen.

I'm sorry I called you a monster when all you've done is tell me the truth..

"You never lied," I said absentmindedly, as if my voice was a tangible bubble that could float away and pop under the intensity of Sunna's rays. "I've been so grateful for that. I–I love that you're always honest. I…"

His gaze suddenly flicked beyond me. Sharpening, his eyes shifted from their icy blue to a bright gold, and then the sharp crimson of hunger and fury and…was it fear?

I whirled to follow his line of sight, my lungs burning as the air ripped away. My throat ached, raw and desperate, while a shadow slid across us, dulling the sun's fierce intensity.

I blinked, trying to make sense of what moved across the sky. A faint silhouette formed against the swath of grey, and I made out the impossible expanse of wings covering the length of the sky, as if a crow had expanded to the size of Midgard itself. My mind could not process the human-like face plastered over the crow's head, but my pulse pounded faster and faster as the creature approached.

Free-flowing hair, longer than the longest river I'd ever laid my eyes on, billowed behind the creature. Blindingly bright silver armor covered the voluptuous shape of a woman. Her body seemed to stretch to the size of the universe, blocking all light and plunging us in the shadow of her being.

A scream split the sky, jagged and merciless, hammering at my ears. I pressed my hands to my head, imagining that if nothing else, my hands would stop the flow of blood that surely poured from my ears.

The woman raised a shield toward us, catching Sunna's rays and reflecting them to strike with even greater intensity. In her other hand, she raised a spear that looked as large as the trunk of Yggdrasil. Though I'd never seen one before, I recognized this being from the descriptions in the sagas. This was a Valkyrie, come to claim the dead for Odin's halls.

Except neither of us was dead. I still had breath in my lungs, and Drak was undead.

Drak.

The Valkryie wasn't looking at me.

She swooped down on us, slamming against the surface of Midgard with the heels of her golden boots. I followed her line of sight, my heart skipping with understanding as I watched the creature pierce Drak with her gaze.

On the ground, she still towered at least two feet above him, though she no longer seemed impossibly massive like the sky itself. My mind couldn't track her motion. She flowed like water, faster and more fluid than anything I had seen, and she surged straight toward Drak.

"No," I breathed.

Valkyrie slammed vampire, and Drak hit the ground on his back in an instant.

"Don't touch him." My tongue shaped the words, but I wasn't sure they had left my lips.

A strange, floating haze washed over me, as if I'd been here before, watching a Valkyrie descend upon Drak.

Yes, I'd already experienced this. I'd seen this before.

Hel, this was just like Myrah's saga, but I'd *lived* it.

I lunged forward, hand stretching toward her wing. The instant my fingers brushed the blazing feathers, I recoiled from the shock of the heat that scorched right through my gloves. Leather sloughed away, dripping to the ground between my feet, and blisters bubbled at my fingertips.

The Valkryie released another ear-splitting cry, and I snapped my attention to the weapon she raised above her head. Her hands wrapped around the thick pole as she struck him with the sharp, golden tip, bearing down full of divine weight.

I lunged forward, but it was too late. A cry tore from my throat as she drove the spear deeper into the ground beneath his back. His flesh around the wound singed just as vampire skin burned at the touch of my silver Y Tree.

"Stop!" I begged, because it was all I could do. Everything blurred around me, and I did not possess the Godlike power I commanded against vampires. The Valkyrie was unshakable, impervious. Neither Odin's might nor Loki's manipulations could touch her, because she wasn't an undead.

Her gaze locked on me, irises alight with fire. The taut lines of her cheekbones deepened as she parted her lips, and her voice scraped against my ears like shards of glass. She spoke in a language I'd never heard, but I understood enough.

"I do what you will not." Her voice was nothing like a human's; instead, it rang like runes carved into glass that scraped against the tender flesh of my ears.

Her enormous wings unfurled, nearly grazing me as she arched her back and lifted her chin toward the sun. Something in her grasp caught the sun's light, flashing so brightly it nearly blinded me. I barely had time to dodge her searing feathers before darkness swallowed the sky above. She was no longer a woman but a force and a shadow in motion above me as I sank to my knees beside Drak.

He lay pinned against the earth, the golden spear piercing the center of his chest. How deep it went into the dirt, I couldn't be sure.

Drak writhed under the weapon, a low and desperate moan slipping from him. I bent over him and swept his long hair from his face. His fangs gleamed, the white tips curving low, nearly grazing the beard beneath his lip. A gurgle shuddered through him as pain and fury erupted from his body.

And then around the blood, he managed three words. "I love you." He said it as if this were his last breath. Wet spots dotted his beard and splashed against his pale, distorted face, and it wasn't until I blinked and more droplets fell on him that I realized these were my tears. A sob clutched at the center of my throat.

His eyes rolled back into his head and his body went limp.

"No," I cried. "No, Drak." I cupped his jaw and tilted his head toward me. "Drak, please."

This couldn't be the end.

Not now, not when I'd just—fuck, I'd *just* remembered. I was finally ready to listen to him and tell him how I felt.

A sob caught in my throat. Pressing my forehead against his, I barely managed to whisper my plea. "Rune, come back to me."

Chapter Thirty-Two
Drak

A torment unlike anything I'd ever experienced tore through my muscles, head, and heart. I could only compare it with the gnawing ache of watching Myrah crawl toward me across a battlefield of our friends, slain for the gods. But that was a lifetime ago.

And once again, I slipped away from the grasp of the woman I loved.

The grief and desperation clawing at Lux's voice weighed heavy on my bones, and something wet dripped down my neck. Each drop soothed the exposed skin where Sunna's rays slowly turned my flesh raw and red, and steaming.

"Rune, come back to me," Lux pleaded.

Rune? *Rune.* What made her use my former name?

I refused to let myself believe she remembered. If the ruins of Old Skaldir didn't convince her, and if the details of the memories I'd shared with her didn't help her remember… nothing would.

Despite the burn of the golden spear and the sharp ache of it piercing my flesh, this anguish was minimal compared to the pain in her voice. The pain of this separation.

I tried to flex my fingers and lift my arm—to reach for her

—but my hand wouldn't move. Consciousness disembodied, and I became lost and unaware of my limbs. The only thing keeping me from darkness was the sting of the spear perpetually searing through me.

Peeling my eyelids back, I tried to meet Lux's gaze. I opened my mouth, desperate to ask her what had changed, but she faded from view, her face distorting, becoming vague and distant with the sound of her breath.

"Lux?" I said into the empty space that replaced the feel of her presence beside me.

The weight of the spear and the grip at my chest faded, and I let my eyes drift closed as relief washed over me. All the pain in my body melted away, and I glimpsed my time in Valhalla.

Then, the full nightmarish memory of waking in Odin's realm without my wife came rushing back.

RUNE
VALHALLA

I reached for the spot between my shoulder and chest where the enemy had lodged the axe. The last thing I remembered was being pinned to the ground by the enemy's weapon. Now I woke in a bed, my body completely free of pain.

How was this possible, and where was my wife?

Wooden beams made from some strange combination of Blackthorn and Yew formed the longhouse surrounding me. Small, scattered flames drifted through the room, unattached to any wax and not burning from a candle. Though minuscule, they were fiercely bright, enough to pierce the darkness. Something about them was ethereal, unexplainable.

A woven blanket separated me from the voices echoing in the beyond, but none sounded like her.

"Where are you?" I whispered as I planted my feet on the floor. I couldn't feel the cold wood against my bare skin, nor the ridges of it against my heels.

Raucous laughter burst from the other side of the tapestry. I stood, marveling at the effortless motion of my body, and soon I was at the edge of a table that stretched infinitely, dissolving into the ether.

Hundreds—no, thousands—of men and women gathered around the yew table, shouting, drinking, arguing, and slapping each other on the back. All manner of warriors feasted on leg of lamb dripping with decadent juices. Crisp chunks of bread steamed from plates placed along the center of the table. Countless horns, ceramic cups, and small wooden bowls held foamy ale and mead that was potent enough to fill my nose with the scent of sharp rye and honey. The smell reminded me of a simpler time, as if I was home working the farm Myrah and I built at the base of Freya's feet.

A bolt of lightning shot through my heart.

I lifted my hand so slowly it still felt detached, but when I palmed my chest, my awareness of my body solidified. The rhythmic pump of a beating heart thumped beneath my hand.

Dizzy, I leaned forward and lifted a ceramic cup from the table. The mead inside teetered at the brim but didn't spill. I brought the edge to my lips, feeling the cool, smooth surface of the ceramic against my mouth, as warm mead spilled down my throat and heated the center of my chest.

When I emptied the cup, I set it down and saw that the mead still reached the rim, pooling to the very edge as if I had never drunk from it. The cup was brimming, just like the legendary horn from the saga that recounted Thor's drinking challenge in *The Tale of Utgarda-Loki*.

Blinking, I took in the longhouse's vastness—the impossible blending of two types of wood into one, the endless stretch of the table disappearing into shadow, and the weapons: axes, swords, arrows, lances, and spears, held in the hands of men and women or strapped to their clothing.

The ethereal glow of floating flames shone against their healthy, radiant skin. Despite the loud arguments and the clash of blades, the warriors fought with gritty smiles etched across their faces, and none of their strikes ever landed. Blades and axes came close, whistling past an opponent's head, but never struck. In Valhalla, they trained to stay sharp for Ragnarok while never harming one another.

When the warriors decided a fight was over, they returned to the table, downing ale and tearing into the flesh of roasted boar, spiced and cooked to tender perfection.

I fixed my gaze on the far end of the table, and everything I had taken in since opening my eyes seemed to pass in a single, fleeting breath. Two beats of my heart at most.

I couldn't see Odin, but I sensed his presence.

This was Valhalla.

I did not hold a weapon like the other warriors around me. My sword remained strapped to my back, heavy and familiar, just as it had been before the Battle of Sundered Sky. Its presence anchored me with the reminder of fighting alongside my shield-maiden. My muscles tensed, and my pulse fluttered painfully beneath my skin.

This was the end, and Valhalla had become my final resting place.

"Myrah," I whispered. Nobody around me noticed or cared that I spoke to the open air. The clink of weapons drowned my voice anyway. "Myrah!" I shouted this time.

I drifted through the battles and the throng of drinkers, ignoring the tempting aroma of sizzling, mouth-watering meat. Shoving past still more warriors, I found my reflection in a bright mirror staring back at me. My hair was long and woven into a thick tail that reached down my back. The sides were shaved short, and my clothing reflected a time long past.

I tore my eyes away from the mirror and pushed through

the endless onslaught of bodies, people, warriors clad in leather and gripping the hilt of their swords.

"Myrah!" My voice seemed to suck away as soon as I gave breath to it. Tears pricked my eyes because I already knew it didn't matter how far I ran or how loud I screamed; she'd never answer.

Myrah wasn't in Valhalla. She was either still alive, or she had gone to the place her vision had foretold. While I had been chosen for Valhalla, Freya claimed Myrah's afterlife for Folkvangr. But we refused to be separated, so seeking to bargain with the gods, Myrah made her offering not at a temple altar, but at the very roots of Yggdrasil. Together, we'd ventured to the center of the nine realms, the peak of Vylheim, and she'd called upon Freya, petitioning for Freya to choose me too. Or to release her.

When her pleading was not answered, Myrah wept, but tears did not fall from her eyes. Blood did. Blood, the same shade that later spilled from the eyes of Freya's statue.

I knew all of this not as a memory, but as a perpetual awareness that existed both in the present and the past. In Valhalla, I knew all that I'd experienced without having to recall it in pieces. Knowledge was all at once, forever, and disembodied, like a part of my mind existing outside of me.

Awareness struck me with agonizing clarity.

Myrah had sacrificed her heart to Freya so that we could be together. But Freya did not change the vision; all she did was cry tears of blood while speaking over us with one horrible promise—"If Myrah tries to leave Folkvangr, her rebirth will be cursed. Her blood, my tears. This is my reminder that her fate is with me."

I was in Valhalla, and Myrah was bound to Folkvangr. But that was in death. She'd survived the battle. She was *alive*, and I had to find a way to her.

I had to.

I wasted no time considering whether to wait for her here. Leaving was my destiny.

"I'm coming, Skald," I said. "My wife."

Gripping the hilt of the sword strapped to my back, I yanked it upward, then grabbed the blade to unsheathe the length of the enormous weapon. Despite a lifetime of mastery, I could not direct it toward me; the weapon seemed to resist my will. For some reason, it was impossible to slit my throat. No matter how hard I tried, ending this existence was out of my grasp. Impossible, yet frustratingly close.

I couldn't end my existence here on my own. Yet somehow, I knew there was a way to leave. A path existed, and I damn sure would find it.

Letting the sword fall to my side, I formed a tight grip around the hilt and pinned my gaze into the ether. The table stretched endlessly, and though I could not see its far end, I knew Odin sat there. The god who hung from Yggdrasil for all the universe's knowledge that one being could hold. The god who traded his eye for this wisdom would know the process by which I could end this afterlife and return to Midgard, to Earth, again.

With the sword in my grasp, I forged ahead, driving forward through bodies and battles, ever tempted to stop and drink and eat and relish in the joy of this eternal feast. The celebration pulsed around me, swelling with victories, aromatic glory, and the near-tangible force of happiness in triumph, each essence the same and yet distinct in how the individual warrior absorbed their own success.

With Myrah's face fixed in my mind, I fought against the pressure of the celebration, pushing onward and onward and onward for what felt like an impossible stretch of time. Myrah may have become an elderly woman, shriveled and near death by the time I reached Odin. She may have already passed on and gone to Folkvangr to exist alongside Freya.

And yet, she may have found a way to leave Folkvangr.

Myrah had always been determined. No matter where she was now, or the moment I was reborn in Midgard, I'd grow up and scour Vylheim for her, even the memory of her. Maybe I, too, would age and die before I found her, or before I found a way to Folkvangr, but then I would simply do it again.

Again.

And again.

For my wife.

Days passed on, years, maybe hundreds of thousands of years or hours or countless beats of my spirit-heart, but I did not reach the end of the table. I could not even glimpse Odin.

Delectable smells beckoned me to reach for the plate of roast boar. Thirst for ale parched me, like a fruit sucked dry and withering. But I did not stop. I never stopped.

Odin had what I wanted, and I would find a way. I'd promised her, which meant I'd burn this whole fucking place down if I had to.

My gaze shot to a flickering candle perched between two roasted boar's heads. Valhalla would turn to ashes. Everyone here sacrificed if I could just. Get. To. Her.

"I'll follow you," I said, seeing Myrah's face painted with runes behind my eyes. "Into hundreds of lifetimes, no matter how long it takes and no matter what it takes, I will find you."

Though I never made it to Odin, never even laying a single eye on him, the endless stretch of time brought new awareness. Forging a path through countless warriors cleared my inner sight. Wisdom dawned from the journey itself.

I didn't need Odin.

Without stopping, I examined the faces of the men and women. I observed their source of joy: a fight won, a feast earned, a battle well-fought. Valhalla was glory, and glory was Valhalla.

To leave this place was to be humbled. Leaving was loss. I had to lose a battle, to let my opponent's blade strike me as it had during the battle that brought me here.

I didn't stop moving, but instead of forging forward, I turned and raised my sword. Slamming the hilt against the shoulder of a man, I challenged him to a duel.

The man spun around, wielding a massive axe, one that seemed impossible for any human to have lifted, but he was large, muscular, and the perfect person to best me. A cleft left his upper lip open, split from the lip to the base of his nose.

"Father," I said. Looking at his short facial hair, chiseled jaw, and hard eyes, my awareness expanded, transcending the present and past into the future.

"Rune," my father finally responded. "Rune, my boy." A sense of coming home swelled within me. My father, this was *my father.* The man who named me. The man who once loved my mother, and the only other person in my family.

"It is a pleasure to be in the presence of my only son," he said, grin widening, reflecting a smile I would see in the mirror once I returned to Midgard. I looked so much like him.

This was the future, my destiny, and I'd found a way back to her. My family would help me; I had no doubt.

"You loved my mother?" I asked, though I didn't know why.

"I love Ingrid."

At the sound of her name, my mind froze.

"But you do not return to Mother." My brow furrowed, suddenly knowing that going back to Midgard was possible. Or maybe I just wanted it to be. I needed it to be so that I could get back to Myrah, as I'd promised.

"I clawed my way out of Hel twice already for rebirth in Midgard, and your mother did the same, but leaving Valhalla is impossible." Hearing my father say this made rebirth feel so much closer, so much more *possible*. Energy pulsed through my veins, anticipating the opportunity.

"No, I know the way."

"You would leave me, my son?"

"For my wife." I didn't need to say more. He nodded,

seeming to understand. Whether the conviction inspired this understanding in my voice or something else, I wasn't sure. My father just knew.

And maybe it was me he knew.

"Rune." His palm landed on my shoulder. After a moment of shared gaze, his fingers sank deeper, and he pulled me into him. His embrace broke something in me. Something long buried. *No,* it wasn't his embrace but his recognition. When we parted and he leaned back, eyes searching me, I was seen. I wasn't just Rune; I was a man slaughtered and flayed open on an altar before my wife.

I was a farmer turned warrior. A simple man who wanted a quiet life.

"Fight me to my end," I said.

"This is what you want," he said, without question. He knew me well enough, though how he knew, I could not fathom. Like my wife, he simply understood me. He saw the man under the body. A familiar sting pricked my eyes, and tears welled up .

I raised my sword and planted my feet, ready to strike at my father, and he mirrored my stance. The duel began, and I poured everything into each move, the primal drive to win surging through my veins.

With every beat of this spirit-heart, I longed for victory—but I *craved* my wife.

And finally, I let go of glory and all that came with winning, with control, with security, and allowed my father's axe to land a final blow against my skull.

Conscious, though unable to lift my eyelids, I heard my wife's voice. Lux's cool skin pressed to my forehead, and in that instant, I knew—I would die for her again. I'd let my father gut me and rip my soul out of Valhalla.

Erik had done it for Ingrid and she had done it for him. My parents had paved the way for reincarnation, and I would follow in their footsteps, except this time I would go armed with the knowledge of how to leave Valhalla.

I'd return to Midgard and to Vylheim. To Myrah, or Lux, as many times as it took.

Chapter Thirty-Three

Lux

Tears dripped down the groove beneath my husband's cheekbone. His ashen face blurred, and my vision swam with another swell of tears.

With my eyes brimming and overflowing, everything inside me suddenly cleared.

I blinked the wetness away, swiping my knuckles at the tears spilling over my cheeks. I remembered Drak in this same position once before. In the memory, no spear struck through him, but an axe had been embedded between his shoulder and collarbone. Back then, the light faded from his eyes. As I shoved the sword into his hand, he let go and lifted his arm, brushing his fingers across my jaw. Where I once begged for Rune to come back to me, I now fell silent.

Because he had. He'd come back to me as Drak. He had found me, just as he'd promised.

Everything came back as clear as the crystalline water in the fjords surrounding Skaldir. Long before storms whipped the water into foam and ran red with my people's blood, and long before they stained the wasteland, we lived here.

Drak and me. Rune and Myrah.

Our wedding day was a vibrant memory that consumed

me now. All I could see was myself in a dress the same icy blue as his eyes, my body marked with wedding runes that glowed across my skin.

And Hel, it'd taken hours to paint those runes just right. Hours upon hours with a shaking hand, the muscles in my arm tired. But I married him as a farmer and fisherman's daughter turned shield-maiden, and I wanted the runes to reflect both sides of me, showcasing my whole self.

I was back in that moment, that life, living as Myrah for one brief and beautiful moment, though it was only in my head.

On the night of our wedding, we fucked and fought, honing our skills as warriors for the battles to come. Rune's eyes glittered with admiration as our weapons clashed. I shoved him with my shield, but he didn't budge.

"Give me everything," he said, grinning. "Like I'm the enemy." I grunted and pushed with most of my weight. "Come on. My wife is wilder and fiercer than this." He lifted his sword. "Hit hard, Skald."

I laughed, and we sparred until the heat of the battle led us back to our bed, and we made love once again. Later, in a haze of pleasure, he followed me into the darkness where the dying fire cast an orange glow on the low-hanging fog.

Out there, my mind cleared with the sharp edge of the winter's chill. Cold and awake, stories lingered on my lips. I craned my neck and smirked at Rune. He loved listening to my storytelling as much as I craved to share them.

Sagas of Loki turning into a mare to seduce a giant's horse. This one always made Rune laugh, which was a warm sound, deep and full of a life he lost on the battlefield.

Sagas of Thor attempting to drink all the mead in the world, rivers and lake-fulls. The first time I recounted this story, Rune downed nine horns of ale and then fell asleep tangled in my hair, drunkenly drawling about how much he adored my 'bedtime stories'.

Sagas of men and women like us, most notably a famous warrior who'd died only a few years earlier named Ragnar Lodbrok and the shield-maiden, Lagerda, who brought him to victory. They trained and fought in honor of Odin and Freya, just as we prepared to do. The more other villages pushed into the rich land of Vylheim, the harder we trained, ready to defend our home. What did we have if not a home to share the sagas, put down roots, and raise livestock?

Alone in bed after our first full day and night as husband and wife, I curled into Rune's arms, a sigh of relief escaping my lips.

"Tell me another story," Rune said as he lay with his arm beneath my neck. I arched my neck to look up at him, our naked bodies draped in soft furs. Tomorrow, we would rise with the sun and march into battle against the kingdom of West Anglor, defending Vylheim from their king's claim. We would not allow ourselves to fall prey to someone else's rule. And we'd fought West Anglor once before, having crossed the sea to battle on their shores. This fight would be easy enough. We'd won before, returning to Vylheim and Skaldir with gold and honor for our leaders.

Now they came to us.

I laughed. "Aren't you sick of all the sagas by now?"

"I never tire of the light in your eyes when you bring another bedtime story to life." He slid his arm out from under me and propped himself up. With his free hand, he brushed a lock of loose hair from my face, tucking it carefully behind my ear.

"It's history," I said, feigning irritation with the crook of my brow. "Not just a story."

He leaned forward and whispered. "I know, Skald." A shiver ran along my spine at the nickname. I loved it when my husband used the title reserved for poets and storytellers. Every time he said it, he was acknowledging what I cherished most in the world—aside from him. "I'm poking the bear," he added. I smirked and released a ridiculous-sounding growl, bunching my nose into what probably looked more like a rabbit's face. "When will you realize for yourself what it is you love about storytelling?"

I blinked at him. Where had that come from? "Do I need to consider why I love it? I simply do."

He chuckled and leaned forward, planting a gentle kiss where my forehead met my hairline. Loose waves of hair tumbled over the furs beneath us; my braids long undone. "Yes, my fierce Skald. You need to think about it."

"Why?"

His icy gaze held mine, bright and clear, but chilling in its honesty. "Because then you'll see yourself as I see you."

I stretched my neck and lifted my mouth to his jaw. I brushed a light kiss over his rough beard, smiling as my lips lingered against his face. "And what is that?"

"Raw perfection. The most important woman in history."

I laughed. "You're too much."

"I'm hardly enough. For you."

"Lagerda is far more important," I said.

"She is also important. But without skalds like you, she would be forgotten, and her importance erased. You are what keeps her alive, even in death. In the sagas, nobody truly dies."

"And if we don't die," I started, quoting a phrase we'd shared with each other before.

"We'll never be apart," he finished it. He propped my chin on the inside of his index finger and guided me to him. He kissed me slowly, his tongue brushing mine before he pulled back to search my eyes. "Never apart," he repeated.

"Never," I echoed.

His mouth crashed against mine again. Ripples of excitement ignited my entire body. My skin pebbled with tiny bumps and warmth flourished between my legs.

With his fingers sinking into my hair, he cupped the nape

of my neck. I ground my center against his solid length. Pleasure tingled along my core, and I sought more and more and more while I writhed and squirmed against his warm body. He grew thicker and more in need of me. Moaning, he softly nipped at my neck, and my body rewarded him with my slickness.

"Skald," he said between gasps. "You're going to end it before it begins."

"But we just fucked not an hour ago."

His eyes flared open. "So what? Just thinking of you is enough to unravel me."

My lips curved into a wicked grin, and I lifted my hips, positioning myself over his cock. Agonizingly slow, I sank onto the tip of him, letting his hardness split me open. I dropped another inch, desperate for him to be deeper.

In his own desperation, Rune's hands found my hips and his fingertips dug into my skin. He pressed my body down farther, filling me. I cried out, frustrated that he wasn't buried as deeply as possible and yet clinging to the slow tease of it. My arm shot out and my fingers wrapped around his throat.

"I'm in charge, Rune."

His eyes flashed with feral desire. "You always are." A smile crooked his mouth. "You're the only one allowed to tell me what to do."

"And it will be that way forever," I said as I sat lower. Only another inch and I'd be full of him, stretched to the brink and shaking on the edge of pleasure accompanied by a delicious twinge of pain. He should have been too much for me, but my desire coated his cock with just enough to fit him all the way inside of me. I squeezed his throat, my eyes pinning him as I sank one more inch, pressing the inside of my thighs against his flesh.

Rolling forward and back, tension built both deep within me and at the nerves rubbing against his skin. Unencumbered pleasure always made me come at the same time as him—an ecstasy only possible with Rune.

As soon as pleasure rippled through me, Rune exploded, his low growl an animalistic release. I bent forward, lying across him, and feeling the sensitive tips of my nipples brush his bare chest.

Brushing hair from his face, he stared at the ceiling. His voice was feathery, barely a whisper after the intensity of what we'd shared. "Tell me the saga of Freya's tears."

"That's a sad one."

He smoothed his palm over my wild hair. "I know, Skald, but I want to remember that not even the gods have found a way to stay together forever."

I scrunched my nose like a rabbit again. "Why?"

"Because it is motivation." He paused, sucking in a breath. "To become a god someday and be better than them. They squander their power, Skald. I will not waste it like Odin wastes his wisdom. I will give up my eye and endure longer than he did hanging from Yggdrasil, just to see the past and future and find the path that will keep us from ever being apart."

My brow twitched, but I settled back against him, muscles melting into my husband's warmth. I licked my lips and plunged into the saga of Freya's husband, Odr, the Aesir god who brought her heartache.

"Odr wandered often," I began, my voice soft as I nestled into the gentle wave of his chest. "Leaving Freya alone to cry tears of red and gold. Blood-filled tears. Tears that will someday rip the very foundation of Midgard apart. Perhaps during Ragnarok, or sooner, she'll flood the earth with proof of her anguish, crying over Odr's decisions to abandon her, choosing other women over her and disrespecting their marriage."

Rune's breathing quickened. He hated this story. Something more than the simple recounting of Odr's betrayal and

Freya's pain deeply disturbed him. Almost as if it directly affected him.

"Soon, Freya sought to punish Odr. This desire for punishment stretched and stretched like a Valkyrie's wings expanding across the length of the sky. And Freya grieved, wanting others to share in her pain. She took mothers from fathers, husbands from their brides. And warriors from…"

The words slipped away from me, and I blinked back to the present. I hadn't realized I was whispering the saga I told to him a lifetime ago, but now I spoke it over Drak's limp body.

Was this Freya's punishment? Having reached into Midgard? She'd already cried tears of blood that destroyed the lush land of the former Vylheim. The prophecy—the saga—was fulfilled. So what was her punishment?

I winced. "The gods are cruel." My words came out in a whisper despite how raw and honest it felt to say this. I was still too scared to give it my full voice.

Hel, these were the gods I'd worshiped alongside my mother.

The gods I'd so desperately wanted to bring back to the forefront of our culture.

The gods I'd given my life and purpose to hunt for were cruel and untrustworthy.

I grimaced and lifted my eyes to the grey sky. "You did this. All of you." Odin had convinced me to take up the mantle of this madness, and Freya forced us apart. That was why she chose me for Folkvangr; she *knew* the Valkyries would take Rune to Valhalla.

We weren't only separated; we were torn asunder to grieve the loss of one another until the end of time.

Tears pricked my eyes. When I blinked, they spilled over my cheeks, rolling in fat rivers. "I hate you," I breathed. "I hate what you've made me." Foolish and daring, I defied Odin and Freya, yet they stayed silent, watching the storm inside me. Pain shot through my jaw as my teeth clenched, and I lifted my eyes toward Yggdrasil's looming branches. The gods were near. I'd almost reached them. "If Drak does not kill you, I will."

Pain lanced across my skull like lightning, forcing a ragged cry from my throat. I shut my eyes tight and dropped my chin.

Freya moaned with a strange, haunting grief, and Loki laughed cruelly. But it was Odin's silence that disturbed me the most. He didn't scream at me and he made no move to resist as his silence was absolute, like his voice and very being had been erased.

A shiver rippled through me.

I shoved the laughing and moaning behind the walls in my mind so that I could focus on Drak. I pressed my ear to his broad chest beside the spear. There was no heartbeat, though there hadn't been one even before the Valkyrie had struck him.

If I trusted the skald who recorded my actions as Myrah, I knew that the only way for Drak to die was from a stake fashioned from Yggdrasil itself. This spear was gold, which cursed him to suffer, but not to die. I had to trust another skald over the gods.

My spine went as straight as the spear. Climbing to my feet, I wrapped my fingers around the golden weapon. Though it was white-hot and seared the flesh of my palms, I gripped as hard as I could and pulled.

No matter how hard I tugged, it refused to move. Sweat beaded along my hairline. Rivulets of my effort trickled down my temples as I stood over Drak with one foot on either side of his broad body. I pulled harder, desperate to release him.

Even if I collapsed, and Silver's army found us first, I would not leave him.

"Never apart," I grunted as I tugged. My palms went numb from the overwhelming pain, but I bent my legs and pulled again, finally jarring it slightly. Hope flooded me despite the tears that had dried salty and tight against my cheeks.

With another fierce pull, I ripped the spear from his chest, and as soon as it released, I tossed it to the ground. It clattered against the dirt and rolled off the path and into the brush, looking dull and lifeless now that it'd lost its purpose and the one who wielded it.

"Drak," I crouched over him. His eyes didn't so much as flutter. "Please." Drawing my legs beneath me, I pressed close and tucked the hair from his face. "Let me tell you the saga of Myrah and Rune."

Chapter Thirty-Four

Lux

As I spoke our ancient love story over Drak's body, I could almost see him standing before me. It was enough to feel real, like a memory pulled from the depths of my past, clouded by battles and pain. Not a vision from Freya, not a godly glimpse of the future, not imagination—just a plain, stubborn memory dredged from years long gone.

I could not picture everything perfectly, but I felt the scene around me as I told him the saga of *us*. The quiet wedding between a love-struck skald and the farmer boy she had taught to fight at the base of Freya's feet unfolded before me.

I saw a life well-lived until he was taken from me.

I saw our old home and described it to Drak's limp body. Where he'd built a fire at the edge of the wood so that we could be alone, two young adults tempting a fate of pregnancy, before we'd said our vows. Where he'd given me a flat bear's bone to carve runes into, calling it Myrah and Rune's saga.

Where I'd chased after him. We were only children when he stole the wooden sword my father had carved for me and taunted me, telling me I couldn't best him in a fight if I didn't have a weapon. At first, he hated that I could fight better than him. Later, he said it was one of the most fascinating parts of me. I wasn't afraid to spar with him, with a sword and shield or on the furs with our naked bodies intertwined.

A memory of our home and the life we had brought me back to the edge of the farm. One of our sheep was missing, and I knew she was hurt based on the blood soaking the bent weeds beneath my feet. With winter approaching, every loss felt catastrophic. Every animal played an important role when frost coated the ground and crops died out. Each ewe provided wool for extra blankets and milk to fill our bellies.

It was increasingly important now that we prepared for battle to defend Skaldir. As West Anglor pushed into Vylheim's villages, the other kingdoms pushed into Skaldir, threatening to take our homes and displace us, or worse, force us into slavery.

Glancing back at the house, I squinted beyond the peaked timber roof and toward the village. Rune would come from that direction, marching through the heart of Skaldir with his spoils after the hunt, but he wasn't here yet. I'd have to find the ewe quickly if I wanted to greet him upon return. We'd promised one another an evening just for us after so many days and nights toiling and preparing for winter's arrival in Skaldir, working with the other men and women to gather and store food with salting and drying. Tonight, I'd sit under candlelight and carve runes into bone to record the lives of the people in Skaldir, and Rune would lie beside me, listening to my story. His open palms would rub across my bare back until he could no longer resist kissing my neck or brushing his fingers over my nipples. After that… a blush warmed my icy cheeks.

Snapping my focus back toward the sheep's trail, I forged ahead, following the smashed weeds. The poor creature must have limped away or was dragged by wolves.

I pulled the axe I'd used for chopping wood from the hook

at my belt. Gripping it tightly, I crept along, keeping my eyes peeled for any sign of white wool among the brown and green in the faded shadows of dusk. The further I tracked it, the less blood I found. I clucked my tongue, calling out for the sheep with a gentle tutting.

Dusk slipped into night as darkness coated the fields. A howling wind picked up, slicing across my cheeks with an icy edge. Droplets of the ewe's blood led me to the opening of a cave where she either dragged herself to shelter from the wind and the dropping temperatures, or a predator brought her here. I wasn't about to go near the home of a pack of wolves or a bear. The ewe was lost.

I turned and picked my way back toward the farm only to realize it was no longer in sight. I had gone too far. The wind dried out my eyes, and with the remnants of the sun gone, the air turned frigid. As my boots crushed the brittle leaves beneath me, another noise cut through the forest.

A low growl sent my heart racing, and I spun to face the cave's entrance. It didn't matter that I'd been careful to stay away because the predator had already heard me. I lifted the axe and held my breath as I scanned the shadows, the bushes, and the edge of the woods to my right. Two glowing eyes stared back. They drifted closer and the growling swelled around me as the creature emerged from the brush.

I steadied myself, ready to strike the moment it lunged. Time seemed to stretch as we locked eyes. Surely it wanted another catch for its den, but I could fight it off. It sank back onto its haunches for a single, tense breath, and I did not dare blink.

As soon as her hind legs jerked and her body launched toward me, I swung. The axe's blade landed with a muffled thunk near the wolf's neck. The beast recoiled, blood spreading across the thick cream-white fur on her shoulder and neck. She was far from defeated, snarling and baring her fangs at me.

I barely had time to raise the axe before a blow from behind knocked the wind out of me. My hands splayed out, instinctively dropping my weapon to catch myself before my forehead slammed against a rock. Claws tore at my back, and the heavy weight of another animal bore down on me.

The wolf had brought her pack.

Scrambling for the hilt of the axe, I barely brushed it when a horrible pain shot through my shoulder. The wolf's jaws clamped down around the bone, and a piercing cry ripped from my throat. The thud of a dozen paws pounded around me as they closed in to take a bite of their latest catch.

But I wasn't going to die searching for a damn sheep. My hand shot out toward the axe, and I wrapped my fingers around the hilt. Twisting as much as I could, I swung it at the wolf bearing down on me.

Whimpers erupted from him as blade met skull, but victory was short-lived before another wolf snapped at me, so close her saliva dripped across my eyebrow. Her jaws split again, and her sharp canine tore a fiery line across my cheek just as I rolled the other way—toward another wolf.

No. This couldn't be the end of my life. How foolish and unworthy of a saga. Rune would find my remains here and record the briefest story.

Darkness enveloped me, and I saw my friend who'd fallen through ice and drowned. I saw my older brother who died defending Skaldir from another village's attack. I saw a flesh and blood version of the stone statue depicting Freya.

She stood before me with something wet and bloody in her hand. My mouth dropped open as I understood it was a heart, still beating, and pushing blood from inside it to drip out over her fingers. My heart.

Flicking her eyes up, she met my gaze. "Myrah, Folkvangr is your fate."

I shook my head, the words of denial stuck in my throat.

Rune and I were to defend Skaldir, and if we died in battle, our afterlife was meant to be Valhalla, together.

"Myrah!" Rune's voice jerked me out of the vision. My life wasn't over yet.

Rune ran as fast as he could, axe overhead as he threw himself at the wolf on top of me. His wild, animalistic look matched the predators that hunted me. As soon as his weapon hit the beast, I was free to breathe and grab my own axe.

A wracking pain burned at my shoulder, and my arm almost went limp, but I forced myself to move through the pain. I kicked at the first wolf who was still bleeding over me. She doubled back when my foot planted against her wound.

Agony in my shoulder made my head spin and my vision blur, but watching Rune cut down another wolf flared my determination. A yell tore from my throat as I got to my feet, swinging repeatedly; my blade struck fur and flesh, but every blow was in vain. The wolves were stronger than ever. Each wound healed quickly, and they bit back with twice the ferocity, as if Freya had called upon Odin's wolves, Geri and Freki, to lure me into this vision.

I heaved a breath, peeling my lips back to scream at them. "Leave! Go, Geri, Freki. Run back to the gods!" Rune snapped his attention to me, but I faded fast, my voice trailing into weakness and my legs buckling beneath me. But by the will of the gods, every wolf obeyed. They clamped their jaws shut and backed away, yellow eyes still fixed on us before they turned and threw themselves into the night.

Darkness encompassed me as Rune ran to me and fell to his knees. I woke to the steady rhythm of his stride. With my head against his warm chest, unconsciousness beckoned me, but the searing pain in my shoulder kept me alert.

"I can't be a shield-maiden like this," I said, my voice squeaking with effort. "The battle—"

"I'll fight for both of us."

"No, Rune, I—I had a vision." He looked down at me

with eyes full of curiosity and worry. I'd never had a vision before, but I had feelings, sensations, plenty of times, and I'd proudly claimed my title as a witch, though I wasn't exactly a seer—yet. "Freya has claimed me for Folkvangr."

He denied this with a simple "no." "We're going to Valhalla together," he said.

"How? This isn't the will of the gods."

"Fuck the gods," he said.

"Rune…"

"I made a promise to you when we married: we won't ever be apart."

"You don't have a say in that."

"You didn't die today, did you? I'll find a way to you again, just as I did today."

I didn't want to think about it anymore. Rest and recovery were my only focus now. "I wish I had never left the farm," I said.

"You were only defending what was yours. As you always have." A smile softened his face. "And I'm here now, Myrah, sleep."

Except right as he instructed me to sleep, the memory and saga faded away, and the reality of my husband's lifeless body struck me. The story was over. I had nothing left to tell of our saga right now. Tears blurred Drak's ashen face as I leaned over him and pressed my head to his chest.

"You're not here now," I whispered.

Chapter Thirty-Five
Drak

An ethereal voice permeated the surrounding space, and I absorbed the words, unsure if they came from my imagination or from outside me.

"They dreamed of living a simple life on a prosperous farm in Vylheim. Husband and wife. Farmer and skald. Your Skald, Rune."

Rune.

Was this a trick of my dreams? Or had Lux found her way back to me?

Stirring, I tried to lift the impossible weight of my eyelids until they finally peeled open. I swore my head was split open and bleeding all over the ground, but it was my chest that had a hole in it. As soon as I took in the sight of my body, I shot forward, sitting up with my palms clutching the empty space in my torso.

Slowly it sealed shut as my skin knitted back together. The fabric of my tunic had no such ability and remained torn and ragged, baring my flesh to the elements, namely the sun. Tendrils of steam rose from my healed skin. I swallowed a curse and tensed, finally realizing both where I was and who was breathing fast behind me.

I twisted, and my chest tightened as she came into view. Her eyes were entirely clear now, beautiful and brown with flecks of gold. None of the blackness remained, but all of her fire did.

In the grey shadow of a looming tree, Lux sat on her knees. She must have dragged my body into the shadows and peeled off my mask, because only where Sunna's rays filtered through in a few narrow streams did the light reach me. Though her back was bent, her neck curved to look up at me. Strands of dirty red hair hung in her face, and her lips were parted. I thought maybe I'd heard the echo of her voice, but she wasn't speaking now. Tears gave her cheeks a sleek and shimmery glow but shot her eyes through with scarlet lines. Puffy skin swelled around her eyes, and I had no doubt her lips tasted of salt and sadness.

She'd been crying for me? Hel, I wanted those tears to be for me. Seeing her cry fucked me up, but if it was over losing me… damn it, I was a self-serving bastard if I ever knew one. And yet I still couldn't help but wonder if her eyes were clear now, was her memory?

Her lashes dipped in a slow, wet blink. "Rune," she whispered.

Before she had even finished saying my name, my hand shot out. My thumb and forefinger gently pinched her jaw, but I didn't have to draw her toward me. Lux straightened, and I met her on my knees. Our arms tangled around one another, grasping for the firm feel of our bodies in this present moment.

Right now was all we had, so I kissed her hard, desperate to taste her and to relish the fact that this was my wife. Not the other half of a fake marriage, but the wife I'd married lifetimes ago.

The wife I left Valhalla for.

Whether she went by Lux or Myrah or shield-maiden, or witch, or Skald, she was the same. Broken by this world, but healed by the sagas and stories she loved, keeping history alive even in modern Vylheim where The Blood Council had forbidden it. *That* was what fascinated me about her. She dared to seek truth amidst the torture of the lies that'd been thrust upon her. And she'd done it for the protection of those she loved: her mother and the other women beaten down for their ability to know the gods.

They weren't to blame for the gods' reach, or the gods' selfish and power-hungry cruelty.

And then, the deeper part of me knew her. From the second I saw her, I had no choice but to bring her into my life, not because she looked vaguely similar to Silver, but because Lux captivated me. The gnawing inside me had never let go, only worsening when I saw her back in Skaldir.

My jaw tensed at the memory of how I'd approached her. I'd been too fucked up by The Blood Council and my obsession with controlling every angle of my life and the lives of others to see that she deserved better.

Her lips were warm and swollen, spreading to let my tongue between them as my fingers sank into her hair. Tearing myself from her, I placed my forehead against hers and listened to her breathlessness.

"You remembered?" I asked. She swallowed gently, her head bobbing almost imperceptibly. That single nod almost broke me. "They tore us apart," I said.

"I know. Freya wanted me to join in her suffering because of what Odr did."

"I recall every terrible detail of the saga. You tell it well, Skald. And then she cursed the blood of your rebirth to flow with her tears. I suspect that is why it burns vampires. Why your heart… struggles. She wanted you to remember that if you found a way out of Folkvangr, your fate still belonged to her."

Her lips parted, and the horrified expression on her face

melted into recognition. "That's why I only get visions when I collapse. She wants me to suffer."

Was she finally recognizing the gods' cruelty?

Curling her lip inward, she chewed on it for a moment. "You really left Valhalla?"

"With my father's help, yes."

Her brow twitched as she processed this. "I wish I could recall how I escaped Folkvangr. Because if I die again—" her voice fell away.

"We'll be separated."

She didn't confirm whether this was her fear.

The world fell quiet around us as we both climbed to our feet. My body had gone too long without sustenance and fresh blood. Even my bones felt brittle, barely holding my body together after the Valkyrie's attack sapped the rest of my strength. I felt like a boy again, weak and hungry, when King Roderic withheld food to punish me for speaking my father's name.

We turned to Yggdrasil and stepped into the light. I replaced my mask, though hers remained unnecessary.

Lux moved easier, fluid in her footsteps through the gods' domain, while every step I took grew heavier. My very skeleton seemed shot through with the quiver of weakness. Fuck, I didn't want to have to crawl the rest of the way, but my legs shook. I almost grabbed my thigh and used my arms to drag my leg forward, but my arms were as useless. This wasn't going to work. I needed rest that we didn't have time for.

I stopped, ears straining as a distant crowd-like murmur reached me. Down the mountain, the brown haze clung to the valley, and at its edge, the fog stirred. I sharpened my gaze, honing in on the spot where shapes moved among the haze. Silhouettes emerged from the toxic fog, advancing into the gods' domain. The sun and fertile earth slowed them, but not like they slowed me. With human vessels at their side, the fresh blood gave them an extra boost of strength.

Silver's army was still miles down the mountain, but they were closing in, slowly gaining on us after the Valkyrie's attack. If we didn't pick up the pace, I wouldn't have time to hang from Yggdrasil before they attempted to burn it, and Lux would be left alone to fight all of her sister's sworn vampires. Whether a Valkyrie would try to stop them too, I didn't know. I couldn't depend on it. The gods certainly weren't going to make this easy for any vampire, but especially not for me.

I kept to Lux's footsteps, moving as she moved, eyes fixed ahead on our destination. Every muscle in me tensed, aware of Silver trailing behind us. I didn't need to tell Lux. Her focus was sharp, but the danger at our backs hung like a shadow we both felt. It was only a matter of hours before they'd come into view again.

As I dragged at her side, she finally addressed my admission. "You said your father was in Valhalla. Does that mean he died before you were born?"

"No, I barely had any time with him, but I knew him. I knew him better because my mother spoke of him often. She's not unlike you in the way she gives life to words. Or she used to be before Odin fucked her up." I swallowed my rising anger. We couldn't afford distractions, not with the little time Lux and I had left. "I don't know how to explain it. But once you're in Valhalla, you know both the past and glimpses of the future. Maybe it's because there, you're at Odin's table. You're in his presence, and he has the eye of wisdom. That's what I made sense of when I was there. Before I left…" My voice suddenly tensed.

I'd left for her, and I'd do it again and again.

"Drak," she murmured, frowning. Even in her sadness, I adored her face. The scar across her cheek, the rose warmth of her skin, and the faintly crooked canines that hinted at fangs like mine. "The gods are…" Her breath grew shallow as she denied the gods she had devoted her life to. She was stripping away the heart of her faith, realizing that the gods only looked after those in Midgard when it pleased them.

"They're selfish," I said, helping her come to terms with this. My knee gave out, and I had to steady myself by reaching for her arm.

Her brow pinched tighter, forming a deep crease above her soft nose. "They're as good as dead." Anger coiled through her voice, and her hands curled into fists at her sides. "If you don't kill them, I will."

For a second, I just stared, and then a smirk formed. "You want to kill the gods, huh? And you told me not to call you a killer." Her anger was new and fierce, and it lent power to my steps.

"I wasn't yet. But I can't bear this madness anymore. I don't want to forget everything again. Sometimes, I can't hear anything but Odin, and he tells me—" the words caught on something in her throat, and her palm splayed on her chest. "He's obsessed with me killing you."

"I'm well aware." It felt as if the gods themselves had struck me. My legs gave way without warning, folding beneath me, and the world pitched sharply. The hard bone of my left knee slammed against the ground first, followed by my other leg. Lux spun around, hands flying out to help me, but she wasn't fast enough. Defeated, I let the heels of my palms catch me before I was completely flattened against the ground. I shoved off the dirt and to my knees. "Hel," I breathed. "I know we have to keep moving, but I can't." I swallowed. "I have to stop and drink and let the blood give me strength before I can get up again." Reaching for the pouch I'd secured into the pack on my back, I waved my free hand for her to keep moving. "I'll catch up."

"No," she said. "I'm not leaving you behind. Silver's coming."

"I know, but once I feed—" My voice fell away, swallowed by panic as I palmed the pack where I'd tethered the neck of the leather pouch, dread twisting in my stomach.

"What is it?" she asked, her eyes wide, witnessing my sudden panic.

I ripped the pack off my back and scrambled through the makings of the tent, searching frantically, but no matter how carefully I looked, the pouch of blood was gone. "It's not here," I said, my throat tight.

"We didn't drop it," she insisted. "I would have seen it. It has to be—"

"The Valkyrie," I said, my words tight with suspicion. "Did she take it?"

Lux sucked in a quick breath, her voice trembling. "That's what was in her hand! I saw something with glass. I didn't think—I'm sorry."

"Skald, it's not your fault." I forced my voice soft, despite the rawness that clawed at my throat, though once my strength began waning, even that small control slipped from me, falling away like charred skin.

I dragged my eyes to Lux, offering a weak, broken smile. "You keep moving."

"What?" Shock lifted her brows, and for a moment, her disbelief was almost tangible.

I tried again to squeeze my fingers into fists, but it was no use; only one hand still obeyed, and even that would soon follow the others into numbness. One by one, sensation vanished from my fingers until even my thumb refused to bend, and the weakness compounded relentlessly. I wasn't making it to Yggdrasil.

The gods had won this battle, but not the war.

Lux was no longer their puppet, and now that awareness had shifted her beliefs, she remembered us…My chest squeezed even if my hand could not. Fuck. It hurt to think we would have to endure this again. But we had found our way back to each other once before. We could do it again.

"Lux."

"We have to keep moving. Silver is right behind us, and she'll compel you the moment she sees you."

"I can't," I said, defeated.

"Drak, come on." She offered me a hand.

"You keep moving."

"And what will you do? Die?"

A hollow smile curved onto my face. "Not until Silver gets a branch from Yggdrasil."

"She'll just use the compulsion to drag you there and then kill you. I'll be too busy fighting the rest of her army to save you."

"I know."

"So that's it?" Frustration ground through her words. I knew it well. The anger that came with the loss of control. "Are you really giving up after all this time?"

"I'm telling you to stick to the plan."

"The plan includes you. You have to drink," she said, yanking the sleeve of her tunic up and baring her tender wrist. "From me."

"Your blood is poison."

"But it's still blood."

"It is Freya's tears. They flow through you because you made a sacrifice asking her to free you from your fate in Folkvangr."

She pursed her lips. "It's still blood, no?"

I nodded. "It'll burn, but it's still blood."

"So drink. My blood certainly cannot kill you. We know that much. Nothing but a stake from Yggdrasil can do that, and I refuse to let Silver reach the tree before us. If she does, she will find you and destroy you. You can't die." Her voice splintered. "Not now."

It didn't take a genius to know what she was thinking. Not now that she remembered.

We were finally together. Fucking finally. But the gods would not have it. Freya wanted company in her grief, and Odin just wanted to control Lux and everything in Midgard through her and the other witches.

"I'm sorry if this hurts, but you threatened to kill me once. You can survive a little burning."

I smiled again, this time not wholly hollow, and used the last bit of strength I had to grab her wrist. I tugged her toward me and let my fangs descend over my bottom lip. In a single breath, I sank them into the thin skin covering her delicate veins.

She didn't complain, only gasping once before falling silent. My tongue immediately bubbled with dozens of swelling blisters, and a wretched burn dragged down my throat with every swallow. Her blood tasted bitter, not sweet like the life flowing through most humans. Despite the acrid taste and the sweltering pain of it washing over my tongue, the blood left my thighs tingling with energy and the fingers of my lifeless hand finally twitched.

We would keep going together.

Chapter Thirty-Six

Lux

It felt strange to see Drak weak and to be the one leading the way to Yggdrasil. He was the ever-powerful vampire king, and I was only a simple witch from Skaldir. Or so I wanted to be: a woman with a quiet life and a simple marriage instead of a fake one.

Could we ever have that, or had this life changed us too much?

"It's not yours to have," Freya spoke while Loki laughed, amused by my pain. I winced and snuck a glance at Drak, who pressed his fingers against the mask to hold it closer to his face and block the sun. The hard line of his mouth told me he was both determined and hurting. My blood barely kept him going, but he was back on his feet, and that was victory enough for now.

Nothing had stopped him from charging into battle to secure our home in Vylheim. Nothing had stopped him from finding a way to leave Valhalla and return to Midgard. And nothing was stopping him now.

The catalyst was always the same—me.

A shiver trickled down the nape of my neck and spread

over my arms. Perhaps Drak hadn't changed from Rune at all…when he was with me.

My gaze raked over the thick muscles of his upper arms, honed from hours of training with a sword in the armory beneath Mara's Keep. Training he maintained because deep within him, he'd always known he was once a warrior for Vylheim, not a soft king. But it wasn't until he found me that he remembered all of it and stepped into the truth as a man not Hel-bent on only vengeance, but vengeance for the sake of us.

The way he'd grasped at control, desperate to grab onto everyone and everything in his life, was an echo of how helpless he felt losing me.

No, Drak hadn't changed.

It was me. I had one goal in mind: to save my mother and the other witches. Then the gods infiltrated me and I focused on killing vampires. But now I wanted all of it and none of it at the same time.

My mother's survival and the lives of innocent witches would always take precedence, but dedicating my life, sacrificing my mind and peace to kill for the gods was an outlet for me. But who was I? Did it matter? Witch or not, huntress or not, I was really only a girl who loved history and my husband.

Too many questions clouded my mind as we climbed the last stretch of the mountain to Yggdrasil. With Drak beside me, a strange peace settled over me. It wasn't me against the executioners, the vampires, or the gods.

It was us against our fate.

And I would not lose.

Warriors who find meaning in dying in battle always emerge victorious. We'd found each other once, and we'd find each other again. If Silver's army cut us down, or the gods twisted my mind beyond recognition, we'd start over.

This was the only thought that kept my feet moving, and

my screaming muscles from giving out. The gods' domain strengthened me, sloughing away the exhaustion and skipped heartbeats from my illness, yet the climb to the center of the nine realms still took its toll. I could not imagine the pain Drak endured with the blistered simmering inside and out of him.

Sucking breath in through my teeth, I drew energy from the crystal-clear air. Forging ahead, I crested the peak of the mountain.

At first, Odin's silence unsettled me, pressing against my chest. Now it felt different; relief and curiosity brimming in the recesses of my mind, twisting together in ways I didn't understand. I had thought he would push harder, especially with me so close here in the gods' domain. But he gave up on me…

Yggdrasil loomed into view, and my breath caught in my chest. Relief and happiness coursed through my veins at the sight of the gods' domains, and thoughts of glory, honor, and sacrifice surged, courtesy of Odin. Part of me wanted to sprint toward its magnificent glory, while another wanted to fall back to the vampire at my heels.

War raged within me. This was the tree giving the gods access to my mind. Yggdrasil made it possible for their power and influence to infiltrate Midgard, sending Valkyries to rip loved ones apart. This was the source of all our pain, and yet the answer to ending it.

Fire burned at the center of my chest, slipping through my veins like venom. The sagas told of a massive serpent coiling at the base of Yggdrasil, of various animals gnawing at the roots and the branches that touched Asgard and the other realms, but I saw nothing so menacing.

My heart flipped upside down, and slowly sank deeper to the base of my ribcage.

Yggdrasil grew larger before us with every step, looming over us in both power and physical enormity. It was impossibly tall, reaching into the heavens beyond my sight. The thick trunk stretched farther than my mind could make sense of it. If I could guess the time it would take to walk around it, it would span a lifetime.

Drak shuffled up beside me, the sun finally blocked as we stood in Yggdrasil's shadow. Even so, the power of the gods pulsed around us, and Drak fell to his knees. He still cupped the mask to his face, doubling forward with one hand braced on the mossy ground.

I crouched at his side and whispered. "We're here." Now there was only one thing left for him to do before he would be free of this pain and suffering.

"We don't have much time before Silver gets here," he said. He slipped his hand into mine, letting the mask finally peel off his face and fall to the ground. Without it, he already looked freer. "I'll need help to the tree."

"Of course," I said, even as Freya and Loki's shrieks echoed at the back of my skull.

The heel of Drak's hand pressed against my palm. Helping him to his feet proved difficult, but we got him upright and limping toward the tree. We dodged the thick roots that broke through the surface of the ground. The closer we drew, the darker the shadows became. Some branches reached into the heavens, while others hung low, draping around us like the icy embrace of ash.

We had entered the true center of the nine realms, encircled by Yggdrasil's branches and roots. From within the tree's embrace, low branches stretched out, thick enough for Drak to climb. There, he could hang with a rope around his throat and absorb the same wisdom that Odin had gained centuries ago.

I squinted, trying to make sense of the shapes in the dim shadows. Trying to spot a place for him to hang.

Drak froze beside me, the muscles of his arm suddenly rigid.

"Drak?" I glanced at him, but his gaze fixed on something I couldn't yet see through the shadows.

"Fuck," he breathed, and nerves flayed open within me at the disturbance lacing his voice.

Blinking, I made out a man dangling above us. After another moment, I could see the curve of his short hair and the cut of his bare jawline. My heart jolted.

"Kayn," I said, acknowledging the vampire hanging over us. His arms were stretched above his head, tied at the wrists to the thick branch above him. A gasp died in my throat as I took in his vacant eyes, open and staring at nothing. "He's dead."

When Kayn blinked, a strange film suddenly covered his eyes.

"Not dead," Drak confirmed.

Kayn's black gaze slid toward us with an unrecognizable glint in them. When he blinked again, the glint vanished, and his attention focused on me, suddenly as sharp as it was clear. "I do what you will not," he said. Those were the same words spoken by the Valkyrie. A trickle of unease swam through my veins.

"What is that?" I asked.

"Thank you for showing me the truth, Lux." His voice was monotone as he avoided my question. "I thought I loved you, but you never listened to me. You never deserved me."

A vein in Drak's neck bulged as he stepped forward. "Deserved you? Don't you mean she never let you control her? So now you're throwing an eternal tantrum like an immortal child? Now answer the fucking question, Exile. What are you doing?"

"This is my final act." Kayn almost smiled. "For my soul."

Drak released a curse. "Explain yourself. Are you becoming a god?"

Kayn frowned. "I'm becoming a vessel. For my soul," he repeated, almost as if in a trance. "For the gods."

"Cut him down," Drak said as he shoved off me. He waved his arms, weakly pointing at the tether around Kayn's wrists. "Cut him down, Lux."

I glanced between them, my heart fluttering and my mind racing with whatever Drak apparently understood that I did not. "What does that mean?"

Drak shook his head, mouth twisting into a grimace. "I don't know, but I have a guess." He ripped a small silver dagger from the pack on his back and thrust it toward me. "Cut him down now! You have more strength than me."

I scrambled to take it and reach for the lowest branch. Climbing to Kayn would be easy enough, but before I hefted myself into the tree, a low, vibrating laugh stopped me.

The laugh curled out of Kayn, taunting as it echoed against the trunk and filled the air around me like the gods' power, almost tangible as it was invisible. "You took too long, Lux. You missed your chance at hunting vampires. Odin can't wait any longer with Silver coming. He has to do this before the tree burns."

Waves of horror washed over me as I stared at him, absorbing the words like icy water into my skin.

"Lux! Cut. Him. Down." Drak spoke slowly and clearly, yanking my attention from the haunting look of the man hanging before us, and back to the task at hand.

With my heart hammering, I tucked the dagger into my pocket and climbed onto the branch. I reached for the next branch—the same one holding Kayn's body. Carefully, I crawled out to where his hands were tethered.

His laugh came again, twisting through me and stealing my breath with its sickening edge. I fumbled for the dagger. The hilt of the blade caught on the fabric at the edge of my pocket, and a curse escaped me. I yanked it out and angled it over the rough tether holding his wrists. Bringing it down with as much effort as I could, it broke the cord, and his hand shot out, grabbing my wrist before the weight of his body tugged him to the ground.

I cried out, losing purchase on the branch, and the rest happened so fast. Kayn tore me down with him, my hip slamming against the ground, my ankle smashing against the hard bump of a root. The impact shot a vibration through the bones in my lower leg, but the worst of it all was the wind that was knocked from my lungs.

It was then that I realized night had finally come. Sunna's rays no longer filtered through the branches in scant, bright cones. The gods allowed the sun to set and the moon to take precedence in the sky, even though vampires were marching here.

But why pull back on their torment now?

Kayn straightened beside Drak, landing easily with a strange, newfound strength despite being a vampire in the gods' domain. I glared up at him, struggling to catch my breath beneath his shadow.

"You're too late," Kayn said. But the voice didn't sound like Kayn's, and though it wasn't his, I recognized the heavy tone that had haunted my mind for months.

Horror chilled my stomach as I stared at Kayn's twisted face. This no longer looked like the vampire who had trained me, or the man I had once thought cared for me…

The filmy texture over his eyes thickened, and his blond hair faded away to a dull grey that matched the sky. Wrinkles formed, folding the smooth skin around his mouth and eyes, and aging the body that had once been a vampire. In a matter of seconds, his bare jaw filled in with wiry hair and a thick beard full of scraggly grey hair hung down the front of his chest.

"Odin," I murmured.

Even before the change in his appearance, I recognized the Allfather by his voice alone.

My chest tightened with understanding. *This* was why I no

longer heard Odin in my head. This was how I'd been able to recall more memories of Myrah's life when he went quiet. Not because I'd successfully kept the madness at bay, but because he was occupied elsewhere.

From the moment Kayn climbed Yggdrasil, Odin's attention must have shifted away from me. This was what Kayn meant when he called himself a vessel. He hung from the tree not for wisdom, but as a sacrifice.

In the end, had the gods granted him another soul?

I didn't have time to dwell on it. Wings fluttered above me. Two ravens, black as night, swooped down from the highest branches. They settled on either side of Odin's head, tilting in unison as they tittered, one eye on me each. Odin mirrored them, his single eye fixed on me, now inhabiting Kayn's body.

"I do what you will not," he repeated, his voice heavy but no longer painful now that it came from outside my head.

Breath stagnated in my throat, growing warm. The sudden coming of night made perfect sense now. Odin took the place of a vampire's body, and he certainly wasn't going to make himself suffer.

Having him here was far worse than hearing his voice in my head; I knew even without words that he would strike me down along with the vampires. I'd already sworn to destroy him if Drak didn't.

Kayn—or Odin—had been right; we were too late.

Odin was going to kill both of us.

Chapter Thirty-Seven

Drak

Odin? Had Lux just called Kayn by a god's name? Wide-eyed, she stared up at him, almost as if in a trance. All color drained from her face, and the skin of her cheeks, formerly pink from Sunna's rays, turned to bone ash.

Rage flared in the center of my chest at the way she looked at him. Horror pulled her lips apart, and shock left her chin quivering. I fixed my eyes on the bastard who was tormenting her, my fangs sliding down as I prepared to fight. The hardest fight of my life, likely, but a fight it would be after he taunted her with that disturbing laughter.

I found myself staring too.

Though he bore the same cropped hair, dark eyes, and smug mouth, the man standing before me was no longer the same. I couldn't pinpoint exactly what the difference was, but Lux clearly saw it. Maybe because she was a witch, or maybe because I never had it in me to care about the gods. Not in this lifetime, so even if the Allfather were standing before me, I wouldn't recognize him.

"Odin?" I echoed.

Kayn's lips pursed as if he held the secret close to him.

"Drak." Shivers rippled through Lux's strained voice. "He's—he's here." That confirmed it; I stood before a god wrapped in the body of a vampire.

It was both deliciously and sickeningly ironic that Odin inhabited one of the undead creatures he hated. Of course, I didn't see any humans or witches lining up to sacrifice themselves just so a god could step into Midgard.

Curling my hands into fists, my knuckles ached and my fingernails pricked the soft skin of my palms. "Perfect," I said, responding to Lux while keeping my eye on Odin. "He's here just in time to kill Silver's army."

That taunting laugh rolled out of him again and it took everything within me not to choke him, especially when a little gasp escaped Lux. I didn't care that he was making my blood boil, but tormenting her, as he had since he took over her mind, was too fucking much.

"And why," he began, licking his lips, "would I not start this cleansing with the creator of vampires and the reason for which she created them?" His eye flickered from Lux and then back to me. She was the creator and I the reason.

She was the blood. I was the rune.

The skald who recorded the most recent version of Myrah's story must have mistakenly interpreted it. Or maybe there was yet more that we did not understand. Myrah's story—our story—wasn't over after all.

Odin's eyelids feathered as he faced her. "You refused to listen. You forced me to come here and save Yggdrasil, and for that you will suffer."

Lux didn't move, didn't blink. How shocking it must have been: the god she had worshiped and then been ensnared by now stood before her, vowing her death.

I understood the reason for it, but her paralysis definitely wasn't ideal. She froze when I needed her help the most.

The creepy ravens perched on Odin's shoulders cocked their heads in unison, like horrifying puppets. Their sleek black feathers gleamed in the scattered moonlight breaking through Yggdrasil's canopy. Slowly, Odin angled his head and fixed his attention on me. Hatred welled at the center of one of his deep black eyes.

King to king, we glared at one another in the calm before the storm. If I moved, I had no doubt he'd take it as a threat. If he moved, I damn well was taking it as a threat. So we froze for another second, caught in the interim and simmering with the all-consuming desire to slaughter one another.

I always knew I fucking hated the Exile. But giving his body for Odin to inhabit was a recklessly stupid act even I couldn't have predicted for him. Anything for his soul back, I guess. One man's obsession was with himself; mine was with my wife. Maybe I couldn't blame him because I knew I'd do something as stupid if she needed it.

I already was.

Odin was going to die tonight. And though I wasn't sure how, I was willing to take a wild guess and a wild risk.

With night shrouding the gods' domain, I stood taller and strength flowed through my muscles again. No longer did the sun beat me down, and though drinking from Lux hurt like a bitch, I'd fed on my wife's fresh blood, thrust upon me with her fierce determination. A smile almost ghosted across my face.

Kayn must not have fed recently, and though we were in the gods' domain, Odin was in the body of a vampire. Who would have thought it would be Odin who finally lost his mind?

Fuck this standoff.

I grinned, having made the first move. There was no turning back now, so I ripped a thick branch from the ash tree and readied for the fight of my life. It wasn't sharp, but with enough force, it would make that bastard implode from the inside out.

As a vampire and a god, Odin reacted just as quickly. He

grabbed Lux by the throat and picked her up with one arm outstretched. The muscles in his forearm flexed, but he lifted her with ease, leaving the tips of her boots to brush the mossy floor beneath Yggdrasil.

I snapped off the small branches at the end of my makeshift stake, preparing to plunge it into Odin's chest. Choking gasps tore from her throat, and where her skin had once been pale, it was now mottled pink and red from the desperate effort to breathe. She kicked and writhed, fighting as bravely and fiercely as she could, but her effort wasn't enough. Color drained quickly from her rosy neck and face.

I shot forward, gripping the branch so tightly that my joints ached and the rough wood dug into my palms. The damn moss was slippery beneath my feet, but in a single heartbeat, I was nearly upon Odin. But my rescue didn't matter because Lux had already freed herself in the half-second that it took for me to close the distance between them and the tree.

Odin cried out with a painful grunt that echoed against the trunk, seeming to pulse around us like his power. Clutching his arm, he quickly recovered, but his skin bubbled in the shape of Yggdrasil. Lux had managed to thrust her silver pendant against his arm, forcing him to drop her. I almost smiled again. How long had it been since a god felt pain?

But he was still a god. Killable as a vampire…maybe, hopefully, but as powerful as a god. And with foresight, damn it. He knew what I was going to do before I even moved. The moment I was within reach, he whipped around, a blur with the speed of the undead, and wrapped his fingers around the branch. From the tension of our struggle over it, the branch splintered and then snapped into two blunt, useless halves. Without it, I had to use my fists.

I tried to plant a blow to his chin, but he easily blocked it with a wiry forearm. The meaty thwack of my knuckles against his muscle only stoked my rising frustration. I tried again, to no avail. Odin knew exactly what to do and when. Every swing of my fist was perfectly countered, and he knew where I would step or hit before I did. I was fast, but I couldn't see the future. Damnit.

Fighting him was an impossible feat. If only I'd had the chance to hang from Yggdrasil and gain such knowledge. But I didn't. This was what we had to work with, and I damn well wasn't going to let Lux die.

Head down, I barreled into him, finally knocking him off his feet and slamming him against the slick floor. His skull bounced off the thick hump of a root that'd broken the surface of the ground. I pinned him against the root with my hands around his throat.

And then it became obvious he'd allowed me to take him down. Of course he fucking had. With the blunt piece of Yggdrasil still in his grasp, he smashed it against my ribcage, breaking through the fabric of my tunic and crushing my ribs.

A grunt escaped me as I reeled back. Freed from my weight, he shot to his feet, stalking toward me with venom swirling in his single, focused eye. The other looked as if it had turned to glass. Kayn, Odin, whoever the fuck this bastard was, had his singular gaze fixed on me, and good thing too. He was focused on killing me.

I tilted my chin as if to say, *go ahead.* Kill me, not her.

But Lux appeared behind him, the pendant in one fist while she held her trusty stake in the other. Dull agony still throbbed across the lower half of my ribcage, but my body was already knitting itself back together.

Lux angled the stake and drove it into Odin's back. The fire in her eyes made my breath catch. She was terrible and beautiful all at once, just like the shield-maiden who once fought at my side. Ruthless and full of rage as she had been when she protected Vylheim, our farm, and our home.

Now, she protected herself, and I was damn proud of her for it.

Odin bent forward, wincing from the same pain I had suffered moments before. Lux hadn't gone as deep, but with her stake's sharpened tip, I prayed it hurt just as much. If she'd killed him, she'd become a god herself: powerful, divine, endless. This thought tormented me, racing through my mind as I bolted for a branch that I could reach.

Endless. Eternal. We'd never get another lifetime together if she became a god but if *I* became one, I imagined returning to Vylheim with the power to see the future and finally shape our kingdom, securing it under my control. How perfect would it be to bend people to my will the way the gods had done with witches and those who worshiped them?

But if Lux became a god, where would she go? We weren't married, and though she remembered, she had never said she loved me. She hadn't let me die to Silver on the path, but there were no promises, nothing to keep her by my side. The thought of losing her again made my chest tighten and my breath catch.

As a god, I'd have more sway to try to force her to stay with me. I could glimpse the future and understand her reasons for leaving and know where she went, so I could always follow her and keep watch over her.

But none of that was *having* her. None of that reflected the life I'd died defending on our farm in Vylheim. A life where I sat bent over smoky fires, listening to her weave the sagas with a rhythm like music.

With another branch in hand, I snapped off the twigs and lunged at Odin, taking advantage of the distraction Lux had caused with the stake buried in his back. He ripped it out and tossed it on the ground. Now that his focus was narrowed on her future movements, I had the opportunity to slip up behind him. He didn't turn around when I angled the branch at his heart.

But before the stake even brushed against him, I froze. I almost let go of the branch, then flexed my fingers around it in a tighter grip again. What the fuck was wrong with me? I was right here, ready to destroy him with a mere second to end his life and this fight and save both of our lives.

Then I knew.

I couldn't shake the thought of Lux becoming a god. As much as it terrified me to lose her, she'd be eternal. Though gods could die, and this fight was proof of it, it was only by the hand of another, not by age, not by sickness, nothing. She would finally be free. Selfish as it might be, if she lived, and I remained a vampire, we wouldn't have to wait for future lifetimes to be with each other.

We wouldn't risk being ripped away from each other, one taken to Valhalla and the other chosen for Folkvangr. If we weren't together, it would be by her choice only.

And the gods would no longer have a say.

Death would no longer have a say.

Lux could ascend to the power of the Allfather, and if she chose this, we could reign as an endless king and queen. Or maybe not. Maybe we'd grow weary of rule and find a quiet farm.

"Endless," I breathed.

But none of it was guaranteed. I couldn't make her stay with me, and all I'd wanted since turning into a vampire was this vengeance—Hel, *before that*—since my mother had lost her mind to madness.

Vengeance for everything Odin had done to my mother, and Lux pulsed at my fingertips. The power to foresee the next moments and shape their outcome. The power of a fucking *god*.

And yet, I did not push the tip of the stake into him.

Shutting my eyes tight, I felt the discomfort in my joints and the burning in my chest. *Just kill him. Do it.*

No.

I refused to take this opportunity from Lux. This freedom. As a god, she'd no longer have Freya and Loki echoing through her skull. When I peeled my eyes open again, my breath was swept away.

In the time lost to my hesitation, fire engulfed the base of the tree. Licking and crawling up the trunk faster than I could make sense of it. Wood snapped and crackled in the flames, each pop mirroring the fire in my chest.

Suddenly, it hit me. Silver had arrived. Hidden in the shadows, she had slipped up to Yggdrasil during our fight with Odin and set it ablaze, just as she had promised. With my eyes sharper now, I caught silhouettes approaching in the shadows, only brightened when the fire cast a glow against them. Her army was right behind her.

This was it. With each flicker of fire, Lux's huntress powers were being stripped from her. Everything we'd fought to come here for was stolen from us.

Except for the opportunity for godhood.

Odin shoved Lux forward once. Then twice, then again and again as he drove her further and further to Yggdrasil.

I bolted for them, the branch still in my grip, but this time, I did not angle it toward Odin's heart.

"Lux," I said, knowing this would draw Odin's attention. He predicted her movements, but when his focus switched to me, she had a second to break free.

"Drak! He still has the branch—" her ragged voice cut off when I tilted my chin in a quick nod.

"I know," I said. "Hit hard, Skald."

Understanding sparkled in Lux's midnight eyes. They widened, huge and round and suddenly full of fear. I hated seeing fear in them, but it was that fear that would trigger her to know what to do next. The same fear that we fought through together at the Battle of Sundered Sky.

For once, I could predict what Odin was going to do next. He would take this opportunity to slam it into me again, harder this time, in an attempt to pierce my ashen heart.

Struck by the blunt stake of an ash tree, how ironic. I smirked. At least it wouldn't hit deep enough.

The second blow from the branch sent me doubling forward, pain flooding my midsection and rattling my bones. Just as it hit, I let go, sure Lux would catch it when it fell.

And she did.

Of course she did. It wasn't so different from what our love had survived before, even if we hadn't. We knew this fight. Maybe I couldn't see the future, but I knew the past. Lux snatched the makeshift stake just before Odin knocked me to the ground with another blow.

"Drak!" The echo of her scream pierced through me.

I slammed the front of my skull against his nose, but Kayn's nose—Odin's now—only dribbled black blood. The impact didn't so much as distract him. Shoving harder and harder, the blunt branch broke through skin, then crushed my bones. Pain overwhelmed me, and I could not hold back the grunt that came out of me. He bore down on me with more effort, pinning me with his knees to a gnarled root.

Odin's eye reflected the flames, burning with so much hatred that I couldn't look at him. My gaze flicked away. He was going to kill me. It didn't seem possible with the small piece of a branch, but his determination scared the fuck out of me and I felt death drawing closer. He was insane, a god possessed with the thought of murder and nothing else.

Lux smashed against him with all her strength, but he did not budge. "Get off him," she cried.

"Lux," I garbled. "Kill him."

"No," she breathed.

Odin pushed against me, the blunt end pressing down on my heart and the weight of all nine realms pounding against my chest. The Allfather had made up his mind. I would die first. He didn't spare any attention for her, likely assuming she didn't have the guts to kill the one she'd worshiped for so long.

"Lift the stake," I said.

"No—" A sob seemed to cut her off. "The impact will push him down harder on you."

Fuck. She couldn't kill him, and he definitely knew it. She wasn't going to let me die by the force of her own impact against him, so he was going to keep pushing, hoping to destroy me, knowing he was safe from her while doing it.

"Lux," I said. "You have to do it."

"No."

"Yggdrasil is burning." My voice was weaker. The edge of the stupid, blunt branch angling against the dead center of my heart. "It is now or never."

"You'll die."

"Lux, Skald, my wife—" this time a sob cut me off. Fuck, it hurt so bad, but that wasn't the source of the emotion welling in my throat. "I love you."

"But you don't have a soul, Drak, you'll be lost."

"I. Love. You. And that's enough for me. Become a god."

Odin still didn't believe she would do it because he did not stop bearing down on me; his eye flickered orange with the mirror of the flames. Ravens screeched from somewhere above us, circling in the recesses of my vision like flies buzzing around the dead. They knew what was coming.

So did I.

But Odin knew Lux wouldn't let me die. Being inside her head, he knew better than anyone what she was thinking. It couldn't mean that she…was she really going to sacrifice a perfect chance of relief, and power, *freedom*, for me?

My throat went dry and my mouth chilled.

Tears rolled down Lux's cheeks as she stood over Kayn's body, Odin's vessel. She shook her head slowly, letting the tears slip off her chin and splash against Odin's back where she should be forcing the stake. She kept it angled perfectly, but never pressed down.

"I can't," she said.

A smirk ghosted across Odin's mouth, and if I had any

strength left to care about him, I would have raged, but Lux was the only one who held my attention. She was the only one who mattered.

"I wish we had never left Old Skaldir," I said, "but we did and we're here now. This is your freedom. Your life."

"Not without you," she said. "I can't, Drak. I–" she licked her lips. "I love you."

I could have sworn my black heart started to beat, but it was just Odin's stake pressing down on me, breaking through the surface.

"*What?*" I tried to speak, but I could not give voice to the word.

Somehow she still seemed to understand, maybe from reading my lips. "I love you," she repeated.

But just as Kayn had said, it was too damn late.

Odin gave it one more heavy shove, and the edge of the blunt branch pierced my heart. All at once, every trace of strength left my body. Black blood burst from my undead heart and spilled out of my chest, staining the pale ash branch.

Once the blood forced out and reached my skin, it spilled with a vampire's speed, withering every bit of flesh it touched. My body was turning to ash before my eyes.

Instead of watching my own death, I dragged my eyelids up and stared in awe of the woman I loved, or rather the woman who loved me. Hel, she was perfect, even riddled with tears and sorrow. She fucking loved *me*.

My vision filled with a creeping blackness that spread like blood, but I refused to look away from her. Yes, this had been reckless, but it'd always been exactly what I wanted, even if I didn't know it when I came to Yggdrasil. As clearly as I saw the past now, I didn't know the future—that I would die for her freedom. I only knew that I would die for her again and again.

Blackness enveloped me, and in the last moments of my life, I saw my wife kill a god.

Chapter Thirty-Eight

Lux

I kept my promise as I bore down, pushing the stake further and further into Odin. Though he did not die easily. He was a god, after all, both divine and a force of creation and wisdom.

But his need for control was his downfall. His hatred for vampires had driven him mad, and I had felt it. And now I felt him resisting. Resisting death. Resisting the stake.

Keeping one hand with the stake steady at Drak's ribcage, Odin twisted and tried to grip the stake sinking into his own back. I cried out when his grip found my wrist, and he wrapped his fingers around it so tightly that the bones crunched. Another sickening snap came from where he crushed my hand, but I let out a feral scream, channeling every ounce of strength to drive the stake deeper and deeper.

A jolt of agony rippled from my cracking bones. My hand almost went limp, but I tightened my grip with my uninjured hand. Finally, forcing the stake deeper, and with the weight of my push, the weapon sank into Odin's back.

And then, Odin's stake bore into Drak.

Drak's eyelashes fluttered, and black blood bubbled between his lips. A horrible gurgle came from his choking, and a sob ripped from my throat as I killed both of them at the same time. I killed Drak.

I killed my husband.

And I couldn't bear to watch, so I fixed my attention on what was left of Kayn's body—Odin—as he withered at my feet. Just as any other vampire body, his blood ran black, burning his flesh from the inside out. Every inch of him flaked into grey nothingness.

Flecks spread across the moss, catching on the grooves of my boots. Because I'd angled the stake just right and forced it all the way through his heart just as Kayn had taught me, his death was quick, over within a single breath.

Who could have predicted that Odin would be the one to lose his sanity? To come down here as one of the creatures he despised just so that he could speed up the eradication of vampires. So he could *reach* them. Finally.

All of this I knew as my mind adapted to the pieces of Odin's wisdom I absorbed through his death. And through my hand, being the one to have destroyed him.

A sudden, terrible pain tore through me as godlike power surged through my veins. All at once, I saw the strange and wonderful things I could achieve someday with time and practice. I hadn't had the chance to hang from Yggdrasil and awaken this wisdom as Drak had planned, so my reach as a god wasn't what he had expected for himself. But it was enough. More than enough, and Drak had made it possible.

My Drak... He'd sacrificed himself to give me all of this—power to change my fate. Power over myself and my own thoughts.

Glimpses of the moments in the immediate future were the most obvious ability I'd gained, because it was the only power I could feel now. Odin's other powers brushed by my consciousness, but I did not understand them yet, and I knew I wouldn't without learning how to wield them. I shoved the thought of them away.

I could only focus on Drak now.

His death…

My knees buckled beneath me. Slamming bone against root, I fell to the ground and crumpled over Drak's body. When the pain and the shock of my body adapting to Odin's power subsided, I found myself still touching Drak's arm. My fingers dug into his bicep with desperation.

"How?" I whispered. He was still here, not withered like all the other vampires.

And then I simply knew the answer.

Odin's wisdom was a bright and clear pillar in my mind, showing me that my hold on Drak, my touch, kept the human pieces of him from disintegrating. This was another one of Odin's abilities: creation, and the human side of Drak was once a piece of Odin's creation.

But that meant if I let go, my husband would wither away instantly.

A massive hole ate away at the center of him, but it was slow. Roots and moss became visible from where his heart should be. The stake, no longer held by the muscle or wedged between rib bones, fell away as I grabbed at him.

Creation power or not, imbued touch or not, my husband was still disintegrating in my arms.

Anguish tore at my heart, each beat dragging and stretching time. I moved sluggishly, like thick blood flowing through the carved channels of an ancient altar. The crackle of Yggdrasil's flames faded behind me, and Drak consumed all of my attention—what was left of him.

I barely heard my own cry, but the burn of it tore up my throat. Dragging his head into my lap, I brought my forehead to his. How many times was I going to lose him?

How long would it take me to remember him in the next lifetime? That thought struck me harder than anything else, crawling through my skull and poisoning every inch of my battered mind with grief. I was immortal now, but that didn't mean a god couldn't be killed. That I couldn't kill myself to try at our love story again.

His face swam in my vision: his beard, the slits of his closed eyelids, and the midnight hair that'd grown loose and wild. I blinked the blur of tears away, but they filled the well of my eyes again immediately. I was vaguely aware of footsteps approaching from somewhere in the distance. Maybe Freya had found a way to Midgard too and had come to cut me down.

Though that wasn't possible now, was it? Not with Yggdrasil turning to ash alongside Odin. Everything was cut away from me now: my powers as a witch, and the abilities granted me when I became a chosen huntress.

But Drak was the only piece of this that I could focus on for more than a breath. All else that I'd lost fell away as quickly as Odin's body became ash and floated into the ether. Only my husband remained, a blur in my eyesight, a blade to my heart.

We didn't even get one night together. Not one single night where we both remembered and *knew* who we were. Rune and Myrah, Drak and Lux, vampire and huntress, warrior and shield-maiden, Skald and farmer.

Husband and wife.

The claws of Odin's ravens seemed to close around my heart as their squawks echoed from above, and my chest tightened. Somehow, tears still spilled out of me, a flood of my sorrow turned tangible. Hot and stinging, they rolled over my cheeks and slipped between my lips, tasting of salt and bitterness.

"I'm sorry," I whispered. "I'm sorry it took me so long." Hel, I'd wasted so much time. These past months hiding in Mara's Keep, preparing to leave for the wasteland, the trek to Yggdrasil. All of it could have been spent with us *together*, not just side by side. Not pretending to be married, but truly and fully wedded in love the way we had in the little temple nestled in the center of Old Skaldir. If only I'd listened to him sooner, we'd have become a true team the way we were at the Battle of Sundered Sky. But even then, he hadn't survived, and I was powerless to stop the Valkyrie from taking him. Even then, I lost him, just not forever.

A shadow stretched over me, providing a weak relief from the heat of the fire ravaging the center of the nine realms. My mind was empty now, devoid of any other presence, of anything else except this moment.

Despite what I knew, I made a hollow promise to Drak anyway. As stupid as it was, I couldn't stop myself from saying it. My lips stung, swollen and cracked as they parted. "I'll follow you, Drak. Into the next life. Every life." Feeling the solid bone of his skull against my forehead grounded me in the present.

"There won't be a next life," a voice said from overhead.

Craning my neck, I dragged my eyes up over brown boots, a simple black skirt, and then up to the tight bodice attached.

My sister stared down at me. Tendrils of auburn and umber hair framed her face, while the rest of the loose hair fell down her back. Though we were nearly reflections of one another, white scars circled small punctures around her lips, remnants of where someone had once sewn her mouth shut. My scars were more ragged and less uniform, torn by the fang of a vampire and a rose bush. Where my face was thicker and rounder, hers was longer with sharper, fiercely beautiful edges, but it was her eyes that were the most different. Hers was a warm dark brown while mine were all black. Or at least they had been… Drak said they'd changed.

Fire cracked behind her head—her doing, of course, aided by Ylva and Darius who stalked at her side. Ylva, the wisp of a vampire woman, stared at me with large, hollow eyes, like two moons balanced on a skeletal frame. Darius was significantly plumper and paler, his skin nearly glowing white against the bright flames engulfing the gods' tree.

I didn't know if I cared anymore that Yggdrasil burned. What did any of this matter? I didn't know if my mother or Stasia, or anyone in Skaldir, was still alive. Ragna had become one of the monsters I was supposed to kill.

And Drak was gone.

Silver cocked her head with a watery smile lingering on her lips. "There won't be a next life," she said again. Her brown eyes fell to the pieces of Drak that were left in this realm. The withering body that I clung to, but was steadily deteriorating from my hold. "Not for him."

Not for a vampire whose soul had been ripped away by… me.

My heart stuttered. *Fuck.* I'd been so messed up, so selfish and desperate, and I didn't care. I didn't care that I'd made this wretched mistake because I'd done it for him.

The worst mistake wasn't making vampires, and it wasn't my attempts to bring him back to me. My worst mistake was denying what I knew about myself. I had been selfish. No amount of hunting monsters would change that, and I didn't even want to anymore. I had been selfish *for my husband.* That was the real me. Just selfish enough, and willing to throw this entire world into chaos just to find a way to him.

All of my actions in this life and the past had led to the burning of the center of the nine realms, and though I cared for the witches, for my friends and family, I'd risked it all to hold him one last time. The darkness in me had called to the monster in him. We'd both become devoid of our morals in pursuit of one another; he'd forced his own father to sacrifice his son and give up his only chance to be together in Valhalla. I'd done so much worse.

Right and wrong blurred into gray, and I felt no shame. Perhaps he'd ruined me a lifetime ago when I vowed myself to him in marriage. He'd ruined whatever sense of justice I had, and we killed recklessly alongside each other, defending our farm, our home. Alongside him, I was just myself, and now, I claimed no identity.

I was simply ruined.

The solid feel of his body swept away, like water falling through my fingers. I couldn't cling to him as I grieved. Even his clothes withered to ash from the acidic black blood, leaving the only two things behind that were his—the sword discarded on the ground several paces away, and the ring he'd taken from Sten. I snagged the bronze chain that'd fallen into the moss when his neck turned to ash. Picking it up, a fresh wave of pain rose in my chest, crowding my heart and throat with unbearable pressure.

"He's gone," I whispered, barely aware that my sister still loomed over me.

"Well," she said, sucking in a breath. "If you want to give up that easily, then yes, he's gone."

Narrowing my eyes, I twisted my neck to squint up into the orange glow that gave her silhouette a hellish halo. I formed a fist around the chain and ring, pushing it hard against my palm. Likely resembling Odin's ravens, I stared at her with gleaming black eyes, full of grief and a dash of hatred for toying with me. "You're taunting me."

"Nope," she said nothing more, turning her attention to a loose thread on her undershirt sleeve beneath the bodice. Silent and patient, she did not flinch as the heat edged nearer.

I seethed, and the fingers of my free hand grabbed at nothing, tightening into an empty fist now that I could no longer touch Drak. "What are you saying?" My voice cracked, though not with the same vicious whip as the flames. Where I was weak, the fire ebbed stronger. Having reached the lower branches now, the fire zipped out to the tips of the branches, creating a ceiling of embers above us. Ash rained down, leaving flecks of black and grey in her loose hair. "You won, Silver. It's over."

She rolled onto the tips of her toes and then back to her

heels with her hands now clasped in front of her, just the way she used to do as a child. Seeing my sister made Skaldir feel like a world I was only just remembering. Despite her cruelty and hunger for power, she was still the girl I once shared a bed with.

That mischievous curl of her lips told me she had something I wanted. I remembered the last time she wore that grin: she'd swiped the final meat pie from my plate, leaving me to stare at the empty dish with my stomach gnawing. Then she'd made her offer—my own pie in exchange for doing her chores—and I'd learned, even then, that mischief always came with a price.

Though it was decades ago, my memory was sharp after recalling an entire lifetime before this one, and my childhood in Skaldir felt like it was just yesterday.

I pulled my dry, bloodied lips apart, wincing. "I have nothing left." I opened my arms, showing that they were empty of a stake, of any weapons, and of Drak. My heart squeezed. "I know you want something, but what can *I* possibly give you?"

Her wicked smile spread further, crinkling the edges of her unblinking eyes. Crouching beside me, she tapped her skull. "Think about it, *Silver*." She used her own name, likely to remind me of my lies, and of how I'd let her get taken by the executioners and suffer half a life buried beneath Mara's Keep.

"I'm sorry," I said, unsure if she wanted another apology. I couldn't change what I'd done as a child. Seeing the former leaders of the Blood Council at her side made something within me both recoil from Silver and pity her at the same time. She wanted to make them proud, just as she had with our father when he let her sit in his Vyl's chair. She was still that same desperate child, needing love. Though I accepted my selfishness when it came to my decisions around Drak, I'd never forgive myself for ripping my sister away from our home.

Shaking her head, she hummed. At first, the sound was almost beautiful, like a song, but it grew haunting as it stretched out and vibrated at a high pitch. The melody cut off quickly, and her eyes flashed with that same taunting mischief. What could she possibly want from me now? She could simply march out of here with her army and take the throne she'd had her sights set on.

"Where's our mother?" I asked.

"She's safe." I didn't know why I believed her. Perhaps I had well and truly lost my mind.

"And my friend, Stasia?"

"Well, Stasia is friends with a witch, so right about now…" She tapped her chin and then shrugged. "I suppose she's probably nearing the end of her journey to Einnland's shore."

My brow furrowed. "The shore?"

"The Blood Council had plans before you and your husband wrecked them. I'm simply restoring what was meant to be so that I can feed my army."

"Mother is the friend," I said, finally understanding. "Stasia stayed with her."

Of course she did. Stasia was loyal, caring, and the man she loved was an executioner. If Silver aimed to continue the Blood Council's plans, he would send all the witches and defected executioners to sea to explore beyond Vylheim. The witches would be used for any remnants of magic they might hold as Yggdrasil turned to ash, guiding the way with glimpses of the future. If they still had such abilities now that the center of the nine realms was burning to the ground.

"Now you're thinking," she said.

Cool relief spread over my chest, temporarily lifting the grief that twisted beneath my ribs. They were alive. My mother and Stasia still lived, and though the sea was treacherous, they'd survived so much already. Could they survive the storms at sea?

Would the storms be so bad now that Thor couldn't throw his thunder into Vylheim to punish us? His power over the weather ceased. Yggdrasil's complete destruction would weaken his reach, possibly to the point of non-existence.

It gave me a brief slice of peace, just enough to feel my body again. My limbs were heavy, but no longer completely numb.

Silver's tongue clucked, snapping me back to the present. "Where's your crown?" I blinked and then glared at her. What the Hel did that mean? Before I could ask, she tapped the top of my head hard with two fingers. "You're the queen, sister, so where's your crown?"

I shook my head. "I don't understand what you want."

"You," she said. "To bow. Before the new queen." With that, she straightened, rising again to her full height. A branch behind her snapped and tumbled to the ground, flaming bright like a torch, and she didn't so much as flinch.

"You don't need me," I said, looking away. "I was barely their queen."

She popped right back down to a crouch again, nimble as a child. With a cocked head, her wide brown eyes gaped. Then, she grabbed my jaw and lurched my chin back as if I were the childlike one incapable of focusing my attention. "Are you going to let yourself burn alive here like the witch that you are—"

"Stop!" I cried.

"Or," she went on, entirely unbothered by my anger. "Are you going to keep your promise?" Nodding toward my vacant hands, her peculiar smile expanded.

My eyes narrowed to two slits. "I have no idea what you're talking about."

She let out an exaggerated sigh and swept past me, kicking at the ash littering the moss. "This is why Father so easily persuaded you to lie for so long." Her footsteps froze behind me. "You don't think for yourself. What do the sagas say about souls? What happened to the soul when Myrah turned humans into vampires? I know you haven't forgotten what it is Odin did to give humans life. You're a god now, sister."

I was a godkiller, and yes, a type of god with Odin's powers. But I didn't ask for this immortality. Fuck. All this meant was that I'd exist forever, which was a goal I'd had when my husband was in Valhalla, but now he didn't exist at all.

"Since I'm a god now, I could kill you and I don't think you'd be able to stop me." Odin's perfect reaction came to mind. Gods always had glimpses of the future, though I had no idea how to harness that or if it would simply come upon me during a fight. The sagas said that times of distress sparked the gods' abilities.

She shared an amused glance with Ylva and Darius, and an odd chuckle escaped her. They said nothing, but Silver's need to get their approval was unmistakable as Ylva offered her a meager nod. Silver shrugged. "You wouldn't kill me if it was the only way to survive."

"Why not?"

"Because I know something you need. To restore a soul, you need to know what happened to it in the first place." She hummed briefly, then brushed past me.

With that, Silver and the Blood Council marched away, their footsteps growing quieter as the crackle of the fire overwhelmed them. Alone now, I let my head fall forward, and my arms go limp at my sides. I succumbed to defeat.

What could Silver possibly know about Myrah's powers that I didn't? Nothing. There was nothing I could do to protect my mother or the other witches. Even the gods had limits, which was exactly why they needed a huntress to do their bidding. A god has influence and authority over creation. Not control of that life, not until the afterlife.

Nothing remained of Drak, only ash.

Overwhelmed by the fire's blistering heat, I shut my eyes tightly and slowly succumbed to the ground. The flames licked at my skin, and it felt as if I might melt here, pooling over Drak's ashes, utterly wasted, just as I had over the last few weeks we had shared.

Folding into myself, I lay where he'd died, unable to cry. No tears came. Only numbness returned, slithering through my limbs and settling over me like a bitter fog. I tried to will it away, but it clung, heavy and relentless. For a long moment, there was nothing but the echo of absence and the hollow beat of my own chest.

At least I could no longer feel the heat of the fire.

Chapter Thirty-Nine
Lux

Where is your fire?

A voice echoed in my head, though it didn't belong to Loki or Freya, and it certainly didn't sound like Odin. *Show me your fury.*

"Drak?" I whispered before opening my eyes. When I did, I was only met with the sting of smoke. Of course he wasn't here. The words were only echoes of my own memories, pieces of this lifetime that'd been stolen away from us. *Are you not angry at the injustice of it all?*

Which injustice? The gods taking my mind captive? That Drak and I had spent so long apart, unable to remember that we had returned to this realm for each other? Or that Silver had won and would finally take the one throne of Vylheim?

What about Kayn's final betrayal? I almost pitied him for what his desperation pushed him to do. We shared a connection, however small, and though his choices were terrible, his death added a feather to the weight pushing me into the ash-covered ground.

Perhaps the injustice was that I'd fought this hard and this long to stop my mother from being sent to certain death at sea, and even if it wasn't as dangerous without Thor's storms, I had failed.

Despite failing Drak as well, his voice continued to trouble me, breaking through my numbness and stopping me from giving up.

Curling tighter within myself, my instinct was to block the words. But this wasn't from the gods, and Drak wasn't here to infiltrate my mind. These were *my* thoughts, coming from a buried memory of the moment he'd stopped my execution. He'd stepped in because he saw something in me that led me all the way here, scrunched into a pathetic ball beneath a burning tree.

He'd saved my life, and yet here I was, wanting to throw it away.

Rage welled up inside me, scorching my throat. My sister, the gods, and my own desperation took everything I had fought for.

I was alone again, but not unchanged. Drak gave me the truth until the end, and he gave another chance at life—again. The memory of his voice was clear and firm in my mind. My memory was all I had left, and it would not quiet.

You're the only part of this world I'm connected to, Lux. He'd been right. My desperation to find him again created vampires, and in this lifetime, he became one whose soul was stripped away. But he was still connected to me because it was from my own power that vampires existed at all.

And a Valkyrie's power was tied to Odin's power, the power of creation. Could I really restore a soul? The answer felt just out of reach, like it lingered at the edge of my mind. And what had Silver said about a vampire's soul according to Brynhild's interpretation?

The words suddenly came to my lips as if I were reading them. "Shattered," I said. "Scattered across Midgard." Like the remnants of bodies, both human and undead, after they were destroyed. And like ash dispersed on the ground, their fragmentation prevented them from ever mending as a vampire's body once could.

An ember landed on my shoulder, and my eyes flew open. I scrambled to brush it off me as I jumped to my feet.

Walls of fire surrounded me. Branches broke and rained down, clattering and splintering into pieces as they hit the ground. I seethed, the heat too much now that I was more aware of the world around me.

In the haze, I could barely make out Silver as she walked away, flanked by Ylva and Darius. Others were likely nearby, dozens of them. It was either burn alive or die at the hands of a vampire, and my sister hadn't ordered them to kill me yet.

I hung my head, taking one last look at the flecks trapped in the moss. Whether they were pieces of Odin or Drak or ash from the tree, I didn't know. This wasn't him. Drak was gone.

But his soul… Was it scattered out there somewhere? A curious thrill sent my heart beating faster.

Where did the aspects go?

Step by agonizing step, I dragged myself out from under Yggdrasil and into the shadowy night. I raised the necklace and bowed my head through the chain. The weight of the gaudy ring fell heavy between my breasts. Though it had originally belonged to Sten, the ring had become a symbol of Drak's protection of me.

In the end, he gave me everything. I would push forward, gradually learning to harness the powers that would come with time—powers to see the future, to command Odin's ravens, and so much more.

Hope was within reach, but for now, I still relied on what Silver knew. Hel, I didn't trust my sister for one second, but desperation had an energy of its own. She knew Drak at the time his soul had shattered. If I wanted any chance of bringing him back, I had to deal with whatever she was going to throw at me.

I dragged myself forward, gasping for air, forcing my focus

on the world ahead. Yggdrasil, the witch and huntress, was behind me. Now I was at my sister's mercy.

Silver and her army were already several paces away, but two vampires awaited me. They grabbed me before I could take another step.

"Silver!" I shouted.

She flashed me a wide, painted smile. "Right on time."

I scraped my molars together. Even after all this time apart, she'd accurately predicted how I'd behave. "I don't trust you, but you know something."

"I know something," she echoed, dipping her head in confirmation. "If you want to know it too, I'd be *happy* to tell you." How she managed not to blink against the brightness of the fire, I didn't know. I wasn't sure I wanted to know what pleased her…

A chill shot through me, crisp and severe, even with the fire burning behind me. It was far worse to think about what Vylheim would become under Silver and the vampires' reign. Would they reinstate the Blood Council or the bloodshed law? Could it get worse?

But I couldn't stop an entire vampire army on my own.

They dragged me forward, their grip unyielding when Silver's grin met me like a blade. "Bow before me and declare me queen in front of all of Vylheim, and I'll tell you where to find him."

"What does that mean?" I asked.

That peculiar laugh seeped out of her again. For someone who hungered for authority and vengeance, she was oddly gleeful. A bit like Loki.

She leaned into me, her breath warm on my ear as she yanked me back to the present. "I know where the first fragment of his soul is." When she pulled away, she shrugged. "It'll be up to you to find the rest."

"Find the rest of…his soul?"

"All of him, yes. Hel, Lux, did you lie about loving the

sagas too? I thought you'd read everyone there is to find, especially after Drakkar built you that damn library."

I shook my head. "This is a trick. I'll bow to you and then you'll throw me in the dungeons."

She spun around, half-shrugging again as she strode away from me. "Throw a god into the dungeons? Maybe you don't care for them anymore, but I'll not risk angering Thor and Freya and Loki by keeping one of their kind captive beneath my castle."

"They don't care for me."

"No, but they care about their image, and about how those who still worship them perceive them." She halted and turned again with her neck bent and her eyes glistening with a type of delusion I did not recognize. "I'm going to restore Vylheim to honor them."

Now I was the one who couldn't stop a laugh from bursting out of me. "You just set fire to Yggdrasil."

"Cleansing of the old ways," she said. Holding up a fist, she uncurled her fingers. At the center of her palm sat a tiny seed. "To bring anew." Snapping her fist shut, she smirked. "On my terms, of course. You gods will make bargains with me this time."

I frowned. Nothing about that sounded…okay.

"And what stops me from killing you after you tell me where this…"

"Fragment," she said.

"Where this *fragment* is."

That disconcerting smile spread before her lips shaped around a barely audible word. "Time." She spun on her heel and kept walking.

I tugged against the vampire's grip, but they didn't loosen. Instead, they thrust me forward. "What does that mean?" I asked. Silver was as cryptic as the gods themselves, but I was done with riddles. I was so depleted that my soul felt like it hung heavy in my throat.

"You won't have time to kill me. I have an entire army protecting me, and the longer you take to weave the fragments, the more impossible it becomes to complete. His ashes were just scattered. The most difficult part is to knit his body back together, and without the body, his soul will only have one place to go..." Her pale lips stretched.

"Valhalla?" I guessed, speaking in a crackling whisper. This couldn't be possible. My rational mind grappled with the idea of restoring a shattered soul. A vampire's lost soul.

But the less rational side of me, well...my heart sped up, pounding faster and faster at the thought of keeping my promise. Drak had kept his vow to follow me. He'd come back from Valhalla and found me, and as soon as he knew the truth, he'd tried to tell me. He'd been the only person in my life to tell me the truth every single time.

Hel, I missed him. The way he'd warm my hands when they turned blue. How he looked at me, care swimming in both his scarred eye and his clear eye. That he knew every horrible choice I'd made and, still, he chose me. Even though I was the witch who'd damned this entire realm to the scourge of vampires in the first place. Now, he was lost in the ether with no soul, no afterlife, and no way to keep the vow he'd made during our first wedding.

And our second wedding.

I'll follow you. An unseen grasp tightened around my heart and throat.

Silver's smile was enough to confirm my suspicions about Valhalla. I would lose Drak again if I didn't restore his body to his soul in time. "If you want to save Drakkar, you'll do what I say and then you'll leave me the fuck alone."

Was I this selfish? Did it matter if I bowed before her? She'd already won; she'd take the throne. Even Drak's loyal guards couldn't stop an onslaught of vampires—especially many of whom were courtiers and on the Blood Council. They were well aware of Mara's Keep and its weak points, and without Drak and the huntress, very little stood in their way.

I licked my lips, eyes narrowing on my sister. "Is this a trick?"

"I know you've lived a life of lies, Lux, but even you feel the truth. Deep down." Reaching out, she poked the base of my rib cage. Somehow, she found a bruised rib, and the pain of her touch sucked the breath out of me. "Sure, you're not as well-read as a girl who grew up in Mara's Keep, but you know pieces of the sagas."

Frowning, I wriggled under the grip of the vampires. Though sagas and the history of our people were my obsession, she was right; I didn't have access to the complete records that the Blood Council had buried in the castle. If only I'd hung from Yggdrasil and gained Odin's knowledge, this slow fucking process of fully developing into a god would kick forward and my life would be a Hel of a lot easier right now. But it was coming. I just had to bide my time and deal with Silver a little longer…

"You were in the dungeons," I said. "The records were kept in a hidden library nowhere near you."

"And Drakkar knew exactly where they were. We were friends once, you know? Me and your precious Drak. We grew up together. He brought me material to read and food, and in exchange, I kept him company. And then, when he grew up, I gave him the greatest gift of all." Pausing, she let the full effect of her words sink in.

My frown deepened. "You broke his soul when you turned him."

Shrugging, her smile shifted to one of pride. "He wanted it." Of course, I knew that was the truth. I squirmed from the sting of the vampires' fingernails digging into my arms.

Losing interest, Silver's smirk vanished. Her lashes flickered as she looked away and continued down the cliff. Neither of us spoke, and the two vampires holding me simply marched on with me under their grip.

Over and over, my mind returned to only one thing: Drak's words. *I wish we had never left Old Skaldir.* If we'd never marched into the Battle of Sundered Sky, we'd have lived a quiet life as a farmer and skald. I'd still be his skald, and we might be together in the afterlife. Life on the farm was stolen from us. A simple, happy life together had been torn away. Both by our own choices, and the choices of the gods.

Now I was the only one of us left. My choice could change everything and bring us back to the life he wished for.

Drawing a biting breath, I raised my chin. "I'll do it."

She didn't stop walking as she snorted. "Do what?"

"I'll bow before you while you take your seat on Vylheim's throne."

"Hmm."

"Where is the first fragment?"

Hair tumbled down her back as she threw her head back and laughed. She didn't answer, and I didn't prod her. Somehow I knew my sister would make good on this deal. Once I touched my forehead to the ground in front of her, and once all of Mara and Vylheim watched me relinquish the throne to her, she'd give me the location of Drak's soul.

Or a piece, at least.

With a last look at the gods' domain, I followed the path back into the haze of the wasteland.

"I'm coming back for you." *After I've practiced and harnessed Odin's powers, I'm coming back. Thank you for giving me this.* A rush of energy surged through my veins, a reminder that I was a god and could shape my own fate. *Our fate, Drak, to be together.* I formed the words around my tongue but didn't give enough voice to them. Drak couldn't hear me anyway.

Not yet.

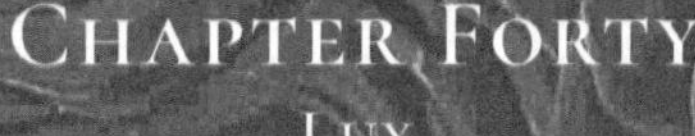

Chapter Forty

Lux

Mara's Keep

Thirteen days.

Thirteen days ago Drak was taken from me, again, and thirteen days later, a new leader would sit on his throne. Something told me this would probably be my last time sitting in the library my husband had built for me.

Tonight, Silver would make her ultimate and official claim to Vylheim's crown. I would kneel before her as all of Mara witnessed her lift Drak's crown onto her head.

After traveling through the wasteland with her, I began to understand how my sister's mind functioned. It was easy to identify, since she shared every bit of her excitement with me as if we were children in New Skaldir again, anticipating the autumnal twilight celebrations. She didn't care how much I knew, because she was fully aware of the power she held over me.

And I had to believe her, even if I didn't trust her. I had to believe she knew the truth about Drak's soul, or I too might fade.

A forceful sigh pulled me from my thoughts. I blinked and

turned toward the door. Silver floated into the library, her footsteps feather-light, always barefoot and walking on the pads of her feet like a tiptoeing child. Why she moved this way, I could not say. Silver had too many strange habits for me to ever understand, and I didn't even try, because I couldn't imagine what she endured growing up under this castle.

"Still don't believe me about Drak's soul?" she asked.

Her tongue flicked over the tiny holes scarring her upper lip as she peered down at me. I craned my neck and granted her a grim smile. "If I didn't believe you, I would have found a way to stop you from taking Vylheim. How can you choose the law of bloodshed again after seeing what it did to people like us?"

She shrugged. "I saw nothing but the gray walls of the dungeon, sister. The bloodshed law is the only way to keep my army, and the only way to keep my throne is with an army."

"Why do you want it? The throne?" I didn't understand this greed.

Her unnerving joy wavered for a second, and something sinister dimmed her brown eyes. "The only way to keep the vampires is with blood." Her voice came out monotone, and she didn't blink. "The only way to take and keep the throne is with them. The only way to ensure that everyone who ever hurt me suffers is to sit on that throne. Of course."

"Revenge," I said. The same goal that Drak had. In the end, it only killed him. Vylheim could only be so lucky if the same happened to Silver. But the thought of her dying, after everything, pinched my heart. My sister stood before me, broken and raw and desperate, and I couldn't blame her for wanting revenge. I locked eyes with her. "So even if I restore Drak, you'll just make him suffer?"

"I made Drakkar, sister."

"He existed as a human before you."

Leaning back slightly, her eyes glimmered with mischief. "He was nothing without me."

"That doesn't answer my question. If I bring him back, will you take him from me again?"

She clucked her tongue and shook her head as if she were a parent scolding a child. "Oh, sister, don't you see? Drak's path taught me how to claim power and become the monster who controls everyone." Suddenly, she turned her attention to the books and drifted to the shelves. She ran her fingers along the spine of a journal that looked ready to crumble under her touch. "Without him, I'd know nothing." Breath stilled in my throat as I absorbed her words. Was this an answer? She drew a sharp breath and yanked the journal from the shelf. Skipping to me, she dropped it in my lap, and all the air I held within me released. "You'll want to read this one. This is Brynhild's vision from Freya."

"Brynhild was a witch?" My fingers traced the journal's smooth leather.

"Of course Brynhild was a witch!" After a taunting laugh, she wiped her eyes with the heel of her palm. "What follows is an eyewitness account of restoring a vampire's soul. All Freya's idea, of course."

"Of course," I repeated what seemed to be my sister's new favorite phrase, though I had no clue why Freya would restore a soul to someone who had already become a vampire. "But Freya and Odin just wanted vampires erased."

Silver snapped her fingers and pointed at me. "Now you're getting it." My brow furrowed. She clearly caught on to my confusion because she sighed exaggeratedly, as if I was that stupid little child again and she was the adult who had to teach me something obvious. "How much more erased can they become if you unmake the monster by restoring their soul? Then giving the gods access to humans again for the afterlife. It's all about being erased. Gone. Forgotten. Vampires are proof that gods are not all-powerful, but still, when you have a lot of power, you only want more of it. People knowing they're not all-powerful reduces them even more. Vampires will always be a reminder that you gods are not as strong as you believe you are. Another reason I keep them around. The gods want what they want."

"So you always knew they were selfish?" I said.

"Not always. Our mother ingrained a lot, but after years of reading these—" she waved toward the shelves, "my mind expanded."

"Brynhild says they're selfish?"

She snorted. "She doesn't have to. The sagas speak for themselves. Brynhild was a skilled seer and recorded her visions precisely so she could aid the gods in eradicating vampires."

"Does that mean she actually put a soul back together?"

Silver nodded, and pride beamed across her angular face. "Well, she tried to restore a soul, but she wasn't a god, so the last step is all just conjecture based on how Odin gave us life."

I racked my brain, recalling one of the first sagas our mother had ever shared with us. Silver and I sat at her side, curled into her arms as she told us about the creation of humans. About how Odin blew the breath of life into the two tree trunks that he'd formed into the first man and woman.

"The final step," I repeated as I clutched the journal's spine. "It's all in here?"

"Sort of," she said, and then she tapped her temple. "And the rest is in here." Reaching out a hand, she offered to help me up. "You'll have to read later. It's time to come with me." I stared at her long, pointed fingernails. "Time for you to declare me the new queen."

I didn't take her hand, but I followed her into the throne room, moving silently behind her. Once inside, she insisted I stay at the back of the room as she stepped up to the throne.

Hundreds of courtiers and commoners alike stared on, eyes afraid, anticipatory, maybe even a little curious for the fresh change. News of their king's death and Silver's arrival left Vylheim on edge after they heard what she'd done to

Skaldir, but the people of Vylheim were nearly numb to change now, each new development became a fragile hope that light was at the end of these long winters. Winters that at least would no longer suffer from the gods' wrath.

Until Silver planted that seed.

Still, most of the men and women did not stare at their new queen in terror. They instead fixed their eyes on the vampires surrounding her.

Once she took her seat on the throne, I was to offer Drak's crown. The cold bronze felt like dead weight in my hands. Drak rarely wore it, and I had never looked at it closely until now. The crown gleamed in the candlelight. A serpent coiled among the spiky roses that decorated it, sharp and taunting.

The vampires prodded me forward, and time slowed as I moved through the thick air of the throne room. Whispers fell to the background, and I only heard my breath and the tense thump of my pulse. Echoes of my footfall mingled with my erratic heartbeat until I stopped before the throne. It felt another lifetime ago that I'd bowed here before Drak, the first time he presented me with the idea of marriage.

And then another lifetime when we finally spoke our marriage vows, however fake, here. He'd wanted them to be real. If only I'd known then…

I shook it off, my muscles compressing under the weight of a marriage we had never experienced. Forcing myself to Silver, I held out the crown, and then my body moved on its own. I followed the instructions she had given me earlier, the same ones her vampires repeated as we entered the throne room.

Sinking to my knees and tucking my chin to my chest, I bowed in front of Silver with Ylva and Darius as her right and left-hand advisors, declaring her the one and true queen of Vylheim in front of hundreds of frightened witnesses. My chest constricted as if the serpent on the crown encircled it, closing its muscular body tighter around my heart and lungs.

Just as our mother had predicted, Silver sat on the throne. Her vision had come true because, like Brynhild, Mother's powers as a seer were strong. Silver's success wasn't solely because of fate; my decisions played a role too. I let this happen because I couldn't bear the thought of giving up on Drak that easily. Not after the gift he'd given me, freeing me from the gods.

Perhaps this was what it meant to truly become a god, stepping into my pure selfish will, unburdened by the woes of others, and willing to let the entire world crumble just to get back to the man I loved. This should sicken me, but a smile curved onto my face instead.

I fixed my eyes on Silver as I rose to my feet. Having fulfilled my obligation, the next step was hers.

"Where is the first fragment?" I asked.

Rather than respond, Silver raised her chin and scanned the crowd behind me. She clutched the throne's arms so tightly her knuckles turned white. "Subjects of Vylheim, now that you have a true queen, and the council is restored..." She glanced at Ylva, who patted the queen's shoulder as if she were a child. Drak was right about their influence over my sister. The need swimming in Silver's gaze was that of a daughter beaming at her protective mother, and her chest swelled with pride as she continued. "I am pleased to announce the return of a hope that will bring us new lands, new foods, and new life."

My stomach lurched. What the fuck was she talking about? Why wouldn't she look at me?

"Silver," I growled.

She acted as if she hadn't heard me and pitched her voice higher. "We will enact the Age of Exploration immediately."

"No," I breathed.

Ylva took over to finish Silver's announcement. "All surviving witches will accompany executioners across Drukna to expand our home and our communities with a larger population."

The vampires' food source. This was the purpose of the exploration. The Blood Council had created it for that reason alone, and yet a hum of excitement suddenly rippled through the throne room. People whispered in low tones, eager at the thought of new land to till, and more food for us too.

Finally, Silver looked at me, and her eyes sparkled with the same menace as when she first declared that she was going to kill me and take the throne. "All surviving witches…"

A bitter taste stained the back of my tongue, and my heart dropped to my gut. "Silver, the fragment—"

"Queen Silver," she said. Next to her, Ylva's angular face cut into a predatory grin. "And you should know that I always mean what I say. All surviving witches will be on those boats at first light, including you."

There it was: Silver's next betrayal, made possible by the restored Blood Council. I suspected as much.

Once again, Drak was taken from me because my own desperation drove me straight into foolishness. Fresh grief rose in my chest, clawing at me not just with the pain of loss but with a feral anger that felt like a god's wrath.

Because even though I expected Silver's betrayal, I could not contain the wrath it stirred.

Chapter Forty-One

Lux

As a god, I felt different. Not because my ailments had vanished; I still suffered from a weakness of the heart. The distinction was in the flashes I saw before they occurred.

Standing before my sister's betrayal, I seethed, but I also saw myself bolting forward, my hand wrapping around her throat and choking her. I saw her fighting back until the light in her eyes faded, not because I had impossible strength—I wasn't Odin—but because I had a tenuous grip on the fate of humans.

And Silver was only human.

So what if she was a queen? She was a mere human queen, and I wanted to fucking kill her.

But all I did was blink. I'd never actually moved at all. My fists loosened, and I let the wrath melt away because time marched forward, and when I saw another glimpse of the minutes to come, I didn't need to murder my sister. Killing her would solve nothing now that the Blood Council was back in power.

"Sister, Drakkar's fate is at sea," she said, as if I should have simply known that. Like I was stupid for not realizing it.

Her words made no sense, and the fragments of the future crowded my mind, impossible to piece together. "Did you hear me? The first fragment, his fate. You'll see when you read the journal."

I gaped at her as I echoed her words. "Drak's fate is at sea..." Of course it was, because nearly succumbing to Drukna's waters was the point he became a vampire. His fate had been to drown beneath the surface until she changed it and shattered his soul. My ribs grew tight with the dread building in my body. "How am I to find a fragment of light across the entire sea?"

"If I thought you could find a piece of his soul, you didn't think I'd actually tell you, did you?"

My pulse stammered, even though I expected every betrayal from her. My sister was cruel—truly cruel—but also a genius in her own way. Either divinely inspired or because the reasoning was logical, I realized she was right. Drak's fate was at sea, which made finding him essentially impossible.

But not *entirely* impossible.

Silver rose and loomed over me. "Let The Age of Exploration begin."

Before I could open my mouth again, two vampires seized me. The room filled with cries as more vampires grabbed other women in the same fashion. Witches taken into custody by Silver's army with fragments of visions, and seers who might guide the way during the exploration.

The curve of Silver's smirk tilted me sideways, turning my world upside down once again. Delicate chains made of silver and gold clinked against one another at her wrist. She was well and truly in control of all vampires and all humans.

Raising her arm, she presented her palm to me, where a winged-shaped seed sat at the center. A promise for Yggdrasil to return. Or was it an omen?

"This seed will take root when you're out at sea," she said. "Visions will come to the other witches again. Odin is gone, thanks to you, which means you'll no longer have the strength to fight my army. But the visions from Freya and the others will come back. Even they cannot deny witches. There are many beings; they do not have control over what they do with simple humans. Elves, dwarves…" she rambled until I cut her off.

"But the gods will destroy you for burning Yggdrasil."

"And yet they could not destroy me when they had access to Midgard."

I frowned. "Why would you want to give them access to us again? You can't trust them."

She bent forward, bringing her lips to my ear. "You see, sister, when our mother taught us to worship the gods, you listened. But when she taught us to work with them, I listened. They are not my enemies. They are my tools, no different from a sharpened scythe to till the fields." I shivered. But Silver had kept her promise, and for that, she was more trustworthy than them. Than me, even.

"Do you remember I'm a god now too?" I said. "I can kill you—"

"Not when I'm surrounded by an army, you can't. Glimpses of the future and the ability to breathe life into a soul? Those won't help you now, Lux."

"People kill people just fine. You're only human."

"And you're only a commoner plotting to assassinate a queen. If you want me to spare your life, you will embark. Gods can still bleed. We learned that at Yggdrasil, didn't we?" Gritting my teeth, I held back my tongue. Fighting with her now yielded nothing useful, and she had already told me everything she knew. When I didn't bite back, she continued. "If you die now, you will ensure Drakkar is lost forever. Nobody else is going to go through all the trouble of putting a forsaken king's soul back together. And wasn't he nothing but a farmer before that?"

I refused to take her bait, but it took everything in me not to correct her and call him a warrior, a husband. *My* husband. And fuck her for looking down on farmers. Without those who grew the food, entire kingdoms would shrivel.

Since I hadn't satisfied her need to argue, she glowered. "Let's not keep our ships waiting on the witches any longer." Rising, she cast one last, long look at me. "Say hello to our mother for me."

Firsthand account of weaving the spirit of one who died as Draugr.

- *Brynhild. Seer and Skald.*

The light of a spirit is as bright as the star in Sunna's chariot.

Freya has revealed the three fragments of human essence in the order with which they must be woven to create the whole of the soul.

Fate.

Mind.

Memory.

And with the spirit sewn together, the ashes of the soul's living space resume the shape of the human's body. The final fragment, though not a fragment at all, but nearly a whole, if not for the hole of the missing spirit.

Each fragment requires the creation of a new rune to be revealed. The rune carved into the blood of he who receives the light. The rune directed by the individual soul.

The individual soul's fate.

The individual soul's mind.

The individual soul's memory.

At the location of the fragment's purpose, the light can be found. Working backward in time, the fragments are ordered. The fate of the Draugr upon making. The mind of the Draugr upon their most significant moment as a flesh and blood human. The memory of the Draugr's human self most treasured. Working forward, each reveal becomes significantly trickier, demanding more time and more effort.

Upon revealing, the fragment materializes into a shard of light at each location, like a crystal sharp enough to pierce through the chest of the body. But even with the restored soul bound as a shard and buried into the chest, absorbed and reformed, the body, though appearing whole and healthy, does not respond. The body needs the breath of life.

Unless the Gods risk coming to Midgard and beckoning Ragnarok to breathe into the body, ashes, the Draugr will remain. In the hope of all Gods and witches and humans, forgotten. Though none of us, Gods and witches and human will ever forget who we have lost.

For the loss of a soul, a spirit, is far greater than death.

Ashes they remain.

Chapter Forty-Two

Lux

Longships bobbed on the shore in the distance. I clutched Brynhild's journal to my chest, my gaze fixed only on the water. The sea stretched it's long fingers over the ruddy sand, foamy and bubbling as it receded. Each time it pulled back, I felt Drak slipping away, tangled with grief, reckless hope, and rage. So much fury swelled within me as the sea flowed, and when it ebbed, grief muted it for the briefest of moments.

I glanced at Ingrid on the horse beside me, another witch bound for Drukna despite the care she had shown Silver all those years ago in the dungeons. Of course, if my sister would send our own mother to her death at sea, why not throw away Drak's mother too? My heart sank as I watched her frail frame hunch forward, her eyes darting through a confused haze. She looked ready to slip from the saddle at any moment, but the executioner leading her neither noticed nor cared as he yanked the reins and barked for the horse to gallop faster.

"Ingrid," I said, my voice hoarse and quieter than I intended. Her head lolled, but she did not look up. "I don't know if you can hear me, but I want you to know that your son isn't gone forever. Drak will return." I had faith because there was no other choice. If I didn't, I knew I would not survive the journey across Drukna.

For the entire horseback journey to Einnland's shore, I pressed the journal harder and harder against my chest, as if I could absorb it the way Brynhild described the Draugr's body absorbing the crystalized light of the soul. I embodied her account, thinking of nothing else, drawing each breath as if I could blow it into Drak's mouth and give him life. It felt within reach, and yet impossible at the same time.

The only distraction from this account was the reminder brought on by the horse's steady gait. The last time I rode on horseback was when Drak had brought me from Skaldir to Mara. He'd sat behind me, his firm chest pressed against my spine, and his warm hands wrapped around my rigid fingers.

Now the tips of my fingers faded to a pale blue, the same color as the dress I left behind in Mara's Keep, trading soft skirts for the beige single-layer fabric of a commoner's dress so that I could move with ease. I'd be lying if I didn't admit that I also chose it because the simple clothing comforted me. As if I were Myrah, tilling fields and chasing after lost sheep when I wasn't studying the sagas and recording the history of Old Skaldir by Rune's side.

Memories of our marriage—our true marriage—surfaced more often now, clearer and full of detail that tugged at my heavy heart. A heart that still skipped painfully, not only when I thought of what we could have had but also when I hadn't slept well or when I pushed my body too hard.

Now, though, I didn't push it. I didn't run myself ragged in hopes of a vision. Freya had cursed me long ago with blood made of tears, and the curse stretched into this lifetime, into this body, wearing down my heart until it was so weak I could hardly breathe.

But I had enough breath. When the rage swelled again and I drew a long intake of sea air, the salt stinging my tongue, sharp and awakening, I knew that my breath, however weak, would be enough to push into Drak's lungs if I could restore his body and soul.

"Huntress," a voice hissed. The hair at the back of my neck stood on end, and my hands shot to my temples. Panic tightened my throat, even though I knew the gods were no longer in my head. "Daughter," the voice spoke again.

My head whipped toward Ingrid. Her spine was straight, her neck tall, and her eyes shone brighter than I had ever seen, as crystalline as Drak's icy blue eyes had once been.

"Daughter?" I echoed without even thinking.

"Are you not Drakkar's wife?"

An unexpected warmth spread across my chest, matching the blush heating my cheeks. "Yes," I said, my eyes suddenly brimming. We had never actually sealed our marriage in this lifetime, but I could not think of that now.

"You should be queen," she said. I didn't know how to respond, because despite Drak's plans to improve Vylheim, we would have been better off returning to a farm. Keeping our weapons sharp and our skills honed to protect the kingdom on the ground. Ingrid blinked slowly, one eye at a time. "You must sit on the one throne, Moljnir's cousin."

"What?" It sounded like nonsense, but Ingrid's eyes were crystal clear.

"Do whatever it takes to take the seat on Vylheim's one throne. Swear it!" Her voice grew shrill, and I resisted the urge to clamp my hands over my ears. Swears and demands like this sounded too much like what I had endured from Odin and the gods these past months. I couldn't take any more.

And I didn't have to wait long. The executioner guiding her mount moved ahead of us and took the lead in the procession. Ingrid must have wanted me to become queen because she understood the horrors Silver was capable of. That was the only explanation for her words about me on the throne.

Loose hair caught against my wet cheeks where my tears had yet to dry. Brackish wind threaded through the tendrils that I'd left loose on one side, while I wore the other half of my hair pulled into three tight braids that followed the arch of my skull from my temple to the back of my head.

I wiped the tears with the back of my knuckles, my other hand still clutching the journal. This grief over the chance Drak and I had lost had to end. I needed to leave the pain behind on this shore and embrace the rage burning beneath my ribs.

A shriek ripped me from the thoughts simmering and spilling through every crack in my mind. I blinked, trailing my gaze across the shore.

Hundreds of men and women dotted the landscape; masked executioners now served as guards, traveling with the witches and the others who had to search and conquer land beyond Vylheim. Sand the color of my dress sank deep beneath the horse's hooves.

We'd finally arrived at Einnland's shore. Like the other witches and those captured in Vylheim and chosen for this venture, heavy cuffs encircled my ankles, preventing any attempt to run. The weight made it difficult to lift a leg, let alone swing both over the side of the horse. But the executioner, disguised as a boar, paid no mind to my struggle.

He grabbed me by the back of my head, my braids and loose hair pulling taut at my skull. "Get off and get moving," he snarled, his breath stinking of sour mead and dried cow meat. This suddenly felt all too familiar, like the time the executioners dragged me from Skaldir to King Drakkar. Long before either of us realized it, he had always felt a strange pull toward me.

I would never forget the way he looked at me the first time, across the path of the footrace at the edge of my tiny village. Like he wanted to devour me, take me, and bind me to him, though even he didn't know why. The call of the past took me so much longer to recognize and answer, and I'd never forgive the gods for that. Not only for stripping my memories of the man I'd come back to Midgard to find, but for taking control of my thoughts and wrecking my very identity.

"Fuck you all." It slipped out with my breath, and the boar-faced executioner whipped his head in my direction. Without warning, he smashed the heel of his other hand against the base of my skull. He released his grip on my braids and let me fall. My hands flew out, catching me before I ate sand.

Some of these damn executioners loved their job way too much. These were the wretched men and women who followed Silver and her vampires. Only people obsessed with these fleeting moments of apparent power would choose the side of blood and death.

But this bastard had no clue that if I quieted my mind, I could see his next move. He was about to step left, so I swiftly extended my ankle into his path, causing him to stumble. Because the mask's shape obscured his vision and his muscles were thick and slow, his reflexes were not as fast as mine.

The boar fell face-first into the sand. I scrambled to my feet and moved away before he could grab me. Tripping him had been a foolish choice, offering only a fleeting thrill, but I felt deliciously reckless. Reckless, ruined, and ready for something drastic. Being around Silver had that effect. Being manipulated by Silver doubled that effect.

A familiar voice yelled my name from across the beach. "Lux!"

I spun, scanning the sea of faces for my mother, squinting against the glow of the full moon shimmering across the foamy waves. Before I could spot her, the boar was on his feet, yanking at my hair again. My back arched and my neck was forced into an awkward angle. He thrust me forward and marched into deeper sand, and even in that uncomfortable position, I saw the one who had called out for me.

Among the masks, the frightened witches, the men taken

and mandated to explore and conquer, was the angelic, heart-shaped face of a loyal friend. Unlike many of the others, she'd already boarded one of the longships and stood at the back.

"Stasia," I said. That same warmth spread over my chest at the sight of her, and I almost smiled. The small-boned woman was dwarfed by a mane of white-blond hair that tumbled over her shoulders. Though she looked thinner than she used to, an unusual sense of hope, or perhaps peace, softened her slim features in a way that none of the other panic-stricken faces around her could match. Her pink lips flashed into a quick smile when we locked eyes.

A man of wiry muscle with short-cropped black hair, clad in a wolf's mask, stood like a statue beside her. The Wolf, she'd called him. He was the childhood friend she swore to help break free from his life as an executioner. The man she followed here.

The boar yanked my head back further, cutting off my view of Stasia. I could resist, trip him again, perhaps even fight and kill him if I focused, but none of it would make this sea voyage any easier, and the boar was already steering me toward the same ship Stasia was on. Fighting would only put a target on my back for the executioners accompanying us. At least for those who derived pleasure from their perverse power.

Stasia claimed the executioner she loved was different, and Drak had said his mother never wanted to be an executioner, so they couldn't all enjoy this brutality. Maybe I had just gotten unlucky with the boar-faced man, and those on the same ship as mine might be like Ingrid and Finan. It was a tenuous hope to cling to as he kicked at my heels to make me move faster.

Waves rolled over my boots, soaking the hem of my skirt. The deeper we waded into the sea, the more piercing the cold became. I held my breath as another wave splashed over me, soaking my trousers and making them cling to my frozen legs.

They quickly went numb, but with the executioner's prodding, I kept moving, boarding the ship already wet and miserable.

Since it was Stasia's ship, I didn't resist when a masked man pulled me aboard.

Once my boots hit solid wood, the boar let go and trudged back up the shore. Free at last, I stretched my neck and pushed through the other travelers. Stasia was on me before I could take two steps. Her bony arms wrapped around my neck as she pulled me into a tight embrace. I buried my face in her warm, honey-blond hair, enjoying the softness of wheat and the warmth of sunlight.

"I can't believe you're here," I heard myself say. "I'm so glad you're okay. I'm so sorry… for everything."

She immediately yanked back, leveling me with as serious a gaze as her persistently joyful face could make. "Sorry?"

"For Silver. It's my fault you were taken captive." My voice dropped, matching the chill of the sea and the tremor rushing through me.

"It's Silver's fault I was taken captive. Not yours."

A sudden well of tears stung my eyes. "And then Kayn abandoned you and my mother—"

She scoffed but kept her voice hushed and our conversation private from the surrounding ears. "I've been dying to tell you not to trust that bastard. All he talked about was making you work harder and faster at hunting. Like you weren't a woman, but a…a…I don't know." Her hands flew about. "A weapon, or something! I'm sorry, but I hate him."

Tears streamed over the edges of my eyelids as a laugh stirred from deep inside me. "You don't have to be sorry. I know. I…" I blinked the tears away. "He was using me."

"I knew it. I told Finan—"

"Finan." I cut her off. "The Wolf. How did you find him?" My gaze hovered over the man standing at the back of the ship.

Executioners grabbed our shoulders and forced us to sit.

The open ship let the ocean wind whip our hair and sting our eyes, but the sides of the vessel afforded some shelter from the worst of it. I huddled closer to Stasia, careful to stay away from the edge of the hardwood where the waves would eventually splash over and soak us.

Turning to me, she finally answered. "I stayed with your mother as long as I could. Lux, I'm sorry, I lost track of her when we arrived at the shore, and Finan, he wouldn't let me go search for her."

"He denied you?"

She looked away. "I know you don't understand, but he's not a bad person. I know he's not."

I nodded, trusting her. Stasia's first instinct with Kayn had been dislike and distrust. If I had listened to her, maybe I wouldn't have trusted him either. I never would have thought of him as someone who truly cared for me, and never—a shudder rippled through me—would I have slept with him. If Stasia knew Finan wasn't cruel, who was I to argue? The gods had blinded me for so long that I was too muddled to tell right from wrong and good from bad. Too desperate to trust anybody at the time that Kayn found me, and yet too afraid to trust the man who'd actually told me the truth.

My heart pinched as Drak's words echoed in my mind. *I love you. And that's enough for me.*

I clutched the journal closer and stared at Stasia. "I believe you," I said finally. "You're going to have to believe me too." I offered a watery smile and grasped her fingers with my free hand, partly for warmth, partly because I needed her to understand. I needed her to see, to hear, to help me make sense of Brynhild's account and pinpoint where this fragment could be.

"What do you mean?" she asked.

"I'm Myrah, the witch who created vampires."

Her eyes widened, but it was not at me or my confession. She stared past me, at the last witches boarding the ship. I craned my neck to follow her gaze, and my heart skipped a beat.

My mother.

She was frail and looking sicker again, but she was conscious, alive, and on the same ship as me. I floated to my feet, my eyes never leaving her face. Sensing my gaze, she looked up at me with faded eyes. I wanted nothing more than to fall into her slight arms and cry. If anyone could help me interpret Brynhild's account and the attempt to restore a soul, it was my mother.

The child-like hope blossoming in my chest spread to a small smile on my face. She mirrored it until I glimpsed the moments to come. Her smile fading away as they pushed her away from me and to the opposite end. The executioners forcing her to sit at the front of the ship and guide the way as an experienced seer. The fox-faced woman nearly breaking my mother's fragile forearm as she yanked her to her appointed seat.

My smile was swept away by a gust of wind that cut across my cold cheeks and dry lips, but the hope remained, warm and light within me.

It grew stronger when the executioners declared our destination.

West Anglor.

Drak and I had visited this kingdom long ago for our first battle, me a shield-maiden and him a warrior. Finding a shard at sea might be impossible, but perhaps I could find one in West Anglor. Even if I couldn't have all of him, I could still carry a piece of him with me.

Chapter Forty-Three

Lux

7 DAYS AT SEA

Memories haunted my sleep, and my waking hours churned with sickness. The dull dread of the infinite blue and the ocean's monotonous sway pressed down on us, eased only when Stasia asked to hear stories of Rune, or when my mother whispered for me to tell her more about the gods' betrayal.

Though her understanding came slowly after a lifetime of worshipping Odin and Freya, she believed me. Just as when I was a child, she was one of the few people who truly listened. As much as it went against her instincts and beliefs, she trusted me and let her knowledge of the gods grow.

Unfortunately, hours had passed since any of these minor distractions because Finan had finally spoken to Stasia for the first time, and she had stayed by his side ever since. My mother was busy too, sleeping whenever she could. Only to be shaken awake by the boar-clad executioner who screamed at her for visions of what the kingdom across the sea looked like. Or how far we were from our shores. Or how many more sunrises we'd see before the ships hit land.

At least I could sit beside her, even if sitting too long was begrudged. Executioners often encouraged us to stand and move about the ship to keep our legs from growing useless because they expected us to conquer and fight once we hit land.

Another hour passed before my mother woke, refreshed enough to look at the journal. She quietly studied the brief passage of Brynhild's account, her eyes flitting over the lines quickly as she read and reread every word. After I had told her everything, down to the fake marriage and the former life, she had become almost as transfixed by the idea of restoring Drak's soul as I was.

"I'm a seer, Lux," she'd said when I'd expected her not to believe me. "I had dreams of your past life and Silver's future. But I was never lucky enough to see your future, and I thought these images of your past life were simply confusing dreams, not visions. Now I know the truth."

Now I know the truth.

How many times had that same thought brushed the edges of my consciousness since I finally emerged from the haze of the gods' control? How often had my muscles tightened with furious frustration at my past self, the blind witch who thought she was a seer but whom nearly everyone around her and the very gods she worshiped had tricked?

And yet my mother simply accepted it. That was what a true seer was: not merely trusting the gods but understanding that their visions could aid her when used carefully.

She hummed, yanking me out of my thoughts. Looking up from the pages, she frowned. "I think I understand."

My pulse stopped and beat twice as fast once it started again. The effect left me dizzy and my already-upside down stomach queasier. "Which part?"

"What you need to do to find the fragment." With a sigh, she looked out over the water. "Sacrifice. Blood. Just like at the altar."

The last time I'd cut myself open and bled for answers, it was while entrusting that the gods would help me. I didn't know if I could do it again. For this, the outcome was entirely different, still brought on by blood and sacrifice but not in pursuit of an answer from Odin or Freya. This was magic, spiritual, yes, but from within.

My mother's glazed eyes met mine. A sad smile creased her face as she took my wrist in her hand and gently opened my fist. Tracing the lines of my palm, she murmured. "You are to create an original rune meant just for the fate of his soul. Then you will carve it into your skin and bleed over the location of his fate."

"The sea?" I shook my head. "It can't be that simple, right?" Brynhild herself recorded the difficulty, saying that revealing each shard became harder and harder. Perhaps his fate was as simple as bleeding into the water.

"You won't know unless you try. The tricky part is knowing what words to combine into a single, new rune that will reveal *his* spirit."

His spirit. Drak's soul. What had been his fate upon his making as a Draugr?

Silver's interpretation was that his fate lay at sea. No, it wasn't an interpretation. She'd made him, created him, and shattered his very soul to shape him into the undead monster he became. She *knew* where that first fragment went, which meant the first rune was Laguz. Water. The shape of this rune was a simple upward line and a straight arm reaching down to the right.

Water and what else?

Another word was required to form a new shape into a full rune. What else was Drak's purpose when he sacrificed his soul?

A single word formed in my mind. *Vengeance*. He'd become a vampire for revenge. I stared down at the journal in my mother's lap, fixating on the line about the runes. The answer seemed so simple. Combine the shape of an arrow representing vengeance with the rune for water.

Etching it into my arm would have to wait until night, when most of the executioners slept. Privacy on a longship was virtually impossible, even if the deafening wind and waves granted secluded conversations.

So I waited, biding my time with the sharp Y Tree in my pocket, where it always remained. I ran my thumb against the cold silver as my courage built.

Once the moon rose and darkness stretched across the water, I pulled it from inside my skirt and scooted to the edge. Grateful for the shallow sides of the longship, I reached out over the calm water and pressed the bottom tip of the Y-shaped object against the soft flesh of my palm. I swallowed a grunt as the metal bit into my skin. Blood beaded at the surface, and I seethed at the sting of the cut, but I kept dragging the sharp edge to carve a new rune, one that combined water and vengeance, Drak's fate, and the goal he had at the time of its making.

Blood pooled at the center of my palm until I curled my fingers inward and squeezed. It spilled out around my tight fist, as if I were trying to hold on to it.

Red dripped into the water, glinting in the moonlight, and I craned my neck to watch it sink into the darkness below. It spread across the surface, then vanished almost as quickly as it appeared. As minutes passed, my chest tightened, and my heart sank. The sea remained the same. Nothing happened.

I didn't know what I had expected. I was no longer a witch who could mingle with magic. Drawing a slow breath, I watched the moonlight dance across the water as the ships bobbed at the ocean's will, the same way the gods had controlled me. I was no longer a huntress either.

And I never got the chance to be Drak's wife, not in this life.

I was nothing. That thought filled me as I let myself

become mesmerized by the gentle waves guiding our ship onward. I didn't know who I was anymore, except ruined.

Drak had called me a survivor because I saw the value in my life. No matter how low I had fallen, I fought to keep going. Even ruined, I had to fight, and I could use the fire inside me to push forward.

The anger simmered, as if the rage itself could keep me warm. My mind and heart reached for it. My hand still hovered over the water, blood dripping into the black sea, but my soul was reaching for the fire within.

The wrath of a ruined woman.

Though it burned to tighten my grip on the rune, I clenched my fist as if I were holding the fire itself. Blood poured freely, hot and sharp, as I let the anger fill me, feeling the same fury Drak must have felt when he swore revenge on everyone who had wronged him. I closed my eyes and allowed his rage to mingle with mine, letting it course through me raw and unstoppable, and quietly, I swore the same.

Everyone who had hurt Drak would feel my wrath, from the other vampires to the gods themselves. No matter the sacrifices it demanded, I would endure. I had sacrificed plenty before and still lived.

I'd always been a survivor, a simple girl with a broken heart who defied the odds. I would find Drak, and together we would seize our lives, our fates, and the throne of Vylheim. We would take it from Silver and free his mother, my mother, and everyone who had suffered under the Blood Council.

I'd survive for them. For *him.*

Peeling my eyes open, I no longer saw only black water. Something shimmered beneath the surface, clearly not a reflection of the moon because it grew brighter as it rose from the depths. A shocking white, the light bobbed above the waterline.

A breath hitched in my throat, and I shot to my feet. Reaching into the water as if reaching for the wrath within me, I grabbed at the light. My fingers closed around a solid, icy object barely larger than the silver pendant in my other hand.

Pulling it out of the water, I opened my fist to reveal a long, narrow, and triangular crystal bearing light so bright it forced my eyes to narrow.

"The fragment," I whispered. It worked. It had fucking worked. The glistening, pure crystal was streaked with my blood, but it was the most beautiful thing I'd ever laid eyes on. A piece of Drak's soul in my own hands.

Clutching it close to my heart, a sob rose in my throat.

In the dead of night and lost among the waves, I made a vow to my husband, and at the moment the crystal shifted from frigid to warm, I knew that this piece of him had heard me.

"Into every lifetime."

Thank you for reading.

To keep reading about the king and the huntress, dive into book 3 of ***The Boodrune Saga: Home of the Fallen.***

Please consider leaving a review at your favorite place to purchase books! Also, a share with your friends who love badass FMCs and their possessive MMCs would be greatly appreciated.

For bonus chapters and Updates: Join the Frostborn Baddies Facebook Group or join my newsletter at Elsa Frey Romantasy Books.

To stay up to date on new releases and connect with me, join the Frostborn Baddies Facebook Group or follow me on social media under Elsa Frey Romantasy. I love to hear from readers, so please slide into my DMs and chat about books! If you'd like to learn about my cozy fantasy books and follow me there, look for Author Emily Fluke on Tiktok, Instagram, Threads, and more.

About the Author

Anemic and sarcastic, much like her favorite female protagonists in vampire novels, Elsa writes about what she's obsessed with—possessive paranormal guys and badass FMCs. As much as she loves reading and writing about them, she'd never survive as a vampire in sunny California. After all, with the personality of a golden retriever, she craves her daily walks in the sunshine.

Join the Frostborn Baddies Facebook Group or follow me on social media under Elsa Frey Romantasy. If you'd like to learn about my cozy fantasy books and follow me there, look for Author Emily Fluke on Tiktok, Instagram, Threads, and more.

www.ingramcontent.com/pod-product-compliance
Lightning Source LLC
LaVergne TN
LVHW100506110826
845146LV00002B/529

* 9 7 9 8 9 9 0 1 6 0 1 6 3 *